DARK WINE
AT
MIDNIGHT

A Hill Vampire Novel
Book 1

Jenna Barwin

Hidden Depths Publishing

Dark Wine at Midnight by Jenna Barwin
Copyright © 2017 Jenna Barwin. All rights reserved.

Printed in the United States of America
First printing & ebook edition, 2017

Hidden Depths Publishing
Orange County, California
www.hiddendepthspublishing.com

Cover design by Momir Borocki
Images used under license from Shutterstock.com

Interior Design by Author E.M.S.

Editing team: Katrina Diaz; Katie McCoach, KM Editorial; Arran McNicol; and
It's Your Story Content Editing

Library of Congress Control Number: 2017934603

ISBN 978-0-9986549-1-1

1) Urban Fantasy 2) Paranormal Romance 3) Science Fiction & Fantasy 4) Romance

JOIN JENNA BARWIN'S VIP READERS

Want to know about new releases, and receive special announcements, exclusive excerpts, and other FREE fun stuff? Join Jenna's VIP Readers and receive Jenna Barwin's newsletter by subscribing online at: https://jennabarwin.com/jenna-barwins-newsletter

You can also find Jenna Barwin at:

Facebook: https://www.facebook.com/jennabarwin/

Twitter: @JennaBarwin https://twitter.com/JennaBarwin

Instagram: JennaBarwin https://www.instagram.com/jennabarwin/

Email: https://jennabarwin.com/contact

DARK WINE
AT
MIDNIGHT

CHAPTER 1

Orders from the Lux couldn't be ignored—a fact Dr. Cerissa Patel knew too well. Since her birth, they had controlled her, drumming a simple message into her head: her wants and needs had to yield to the greater good.

As if anyone truly knew *the greater good.*

But the Lux thought they did. So here she was, packing for her next assignment. She slammed her makeup bag into the suitcase, stuffing it into the corner, pressing it down until it fit into the last remaining space, grumbling to herself.

She didn't want to go to New York. She didn't want to be a Lux pawn. And she especially didn't want to become a vampire's envoy.

No, she'd rather stay in her laboratory, researching the human genome, and looking for ways to truly help the world, but her mother's family had spoken; they'd insisted she take this assignment.

I'm a good little soldier, aren't I?

She looked around her bedroom. Had she forgotten anything? If she had, she could buy it in New York. Sighing, she flipped the lid of the suitcase closed.

"Hey, Ciss, why the gloomy face?"

She looked up at the sound of her cousin's voice. "Do you really need to ask?" she replied, not bothering to hide her displeasure.

Ari stepped through the doorway into her bedroom and brushed back his wavy hair from where it'd fallen over his eyes. It immediately flopped down again, mimicking Superman's famous curl. With his darkened complexion and hair the color of brown mink, they could almost pass as siblings.

"Don't grouse at me," he said, raising his hands in surrender. "I just work here."

"Work here? It's your fault I have this assignment."

"Look, kid, show a little respect for your mission supervisor. Yeah, I convinced them to put you in my unit, but only after they decided to send you. Who else could I trust to look out for my little cousin on her first big assignment?"

He grinned at her, a smirk that reminded her of their time together as children. When she'd first arrived at the Enclave, he'd taken her under his wing when no one else had, but it came with a price: he loved teasing her.

"Speaking of your assignment," he continued, "I've got your final orders."

He held out a computer tablet for her to take, the screen already open to a communiqué detailing her mission. She accepted it and touched the screen to scroll through it, shaking her head. "I still think this is a bad idea. I'm a scientist, not a spy. With my medical training, my first undercover assignment was supposed to be at a government research facility."

"Yeah, but we don't have anyone else to infiltrate the undead. You saw the same intelligence reports I did—something's brewing in the vampire communities, something that could threaten all humankind."

"You're exaggerating the risk," she said, scowling at him. "The treaty communities have a zero population growth rule, remember?"

"It's not just a numbers game. Sure, their population is stable now, but each community needs almost five hundred pints of blood a week, the equivalent of what six trauma hospitals use for the same time period—and they're having trouble getting enough blood bank discards to meet their needs."

"They still have another option. If supplies get scarce they can supplement with live feeding—so long as no one is killed."

Ari shook his head. "The numbers are still too close for our comfort. And let's not even consider what would happen if they started drinking animal blood again."

Yeah, vampires could live off animal blood, but not for long—the results gave a whole new meaning to "mad cow disease."

She tossed the tablet into her suitcase. "Tell me something I don't already know."

"How about something you've conveniently forgotten? We need eyes and ears on the ground now if the rumors about a vampire revolt are true—especially with humans on the losing end of that revolution."

She frowned. "Evidence of a vampire dominance movement is weak. A few intercepted emails and a little phone chatter—nothing to prove there's a real plan to enslave mortals."

"We can't take a chance. If it catches fire, we'll have a harder time stopping it. You know what we had to do to stop their last war." He held up his thumb and index finger, pinched together. "It was this close."

Yeah, the butterfly effect. The Lux rarely got directly involved in a conflict, but when they did, they nudged events ever so slightly to change the outcome. But sometimes a larger nudge was required...and the results weren't always predictable.

Ari plopped down on her bed next to her suitcase and lay back, tucking his hands behind his head for support. "Besides," he continued, looking up at her, "you made first contact with Leopold. You're the only one they could send in."

"Another operative could have tried—someone with more covert experience."

"You saved his life. Leopold owes you. These vampire communities, they pay their debts. We couldn't have staged it any better."

"You mean they were too afraid to try."

"We couldn't let the vampires learn about us, at least, not any more than what you told Leopold, for the same reason vampires hide what they are from humans. Once the cat is out of the bag, we're toast."

"I know..." she said, twisting a lock of her long hair around her finger.

"And don't forget the enticement the bigwigs dangled in front of you. Your cover assignment comes with a pretty large bonus. If you pull this off, you'll have your own research lab to run, independent of the Lux Enclave."

Yeah, the lab was a huge incentive. She may not like working undercover, but Ari was right. Someone had to do it, and a twist of fate had put her in the best position to do the job.

Besides, it was a done deal. Leopold had already agreed to sponsor her. Six months of training in New York, and then she would be his daytime envoy, getting investors from among the treaty vampires for a large biotech research facility she had designed and would run. But Leopold's support came with its own consequences: to be his envoy, she'd have to live among vampires...for years.

Though it was better than living in the Enclave. The place was a cave. Literally.

"Just remember," Ari continued, "your job is observation only—watch and report. Don't try to investigate; don't ask questions. You'll only make them paranoid."

"Don't you think I know that better than you do?" She crossed her arms and glared at him. "Like you said, *I* made first contact."

He bounced up off the bed and gave her a brotherly hug, trapping her arms between their bodies. "You're going to be fine," he said, patting her back. "You're just feeling opening night jitters. You'll knock 'em dead, kiddo."

Yeah, right. Knock 'em dead. That's the problem: they're already dead.

As soon as Ari left, dread pulsed through her. She didn't want to live in a vampire community for several reasons, but one pained her more than the others. She would always be an outsider; she could never let them know her true self.

It just wasn't safe.

She reached for the charcoal drawing hanging on the wall, a picture of her *pita*—her father—and, seeing her reflection in the glass, stopped herself. *Not a good idea to bring it with me.* She ran her fingers over the glass as painful memories entwined with her dread, pulling open the scar around her heart, the pain of past loss flowing out, leaving an empty well behind.

She took a deep breath and slapped the wall.

It didn't help.

The hole in her chest wanted to be filled with something—and it wasn't her mother's love. Her *amma* had abandoned her when she was a toddler. When her father died seven years later, the Lux family hijacked her childhood. She squeezed her eyes shut and held her breath, hoping the pain would die down. She understood the reasons she never felt loved, never fit in anywhere, never seemed comfortable in her own skin, but it didn't pay to regurgitate the whole mess again. Not when—

"Dr. Cerissa Patel. Report to Conference Room A," the loudspeaker announced.

Duty called.

She kissed her *pita*'s picture goodbye, stuffed her feelings down, and grabbed her suitcase. She was going to New York, whether she liked it or not.

CHAPTER 2

Cerissa ran her finger along the line on the map that represented Sierra Escondida's infamous wall. The wall formed the third leg of a triangle of protection, with two mountain ranges forming the other two legs, creating a private valley of rolling hills where vineyards flourished and vampires lived in secret with their mortal mates.

It reminded her of where she'd been born: the walled city of Surat in India. Why did people think a wall would keep them safe? It never worked out that way.

Her basic training as an envoy had wrapped up last night when she passed her oral exams with flying colors. Being grilled by three vampires on the nuances of their law and etiquette had left her wrung out, but Leopold refused to give her time off. The next phase of her training started tonight, with the town of Sierra Escondida first up on the agenda.

Leopold wanted their research lab built in the small California town, in the business district located on the public side of the town's wall, where wineries and other vampire-run businesses were open to unsuspecting mortals. If Sierra Escondida's council approved her project, she'd have to live in the private valley behind their wall.

She'd have to live where *they* lived.

Sure, after six months she was accustomed to being around Leopold and his friends, but her trust didn't extend to these strangers. They had founded their town over a century ago, and through a clever use of zoning laws combined with a series of land trusts and a homeowners' association, they controlled who could live there—much like the Collective controlled the New York high-rise in which she currently sat.

The clink of glass told her Leopold was in the kitchen, preparing for her next lesson. She looked around his tastefully modern living room, her focus stopping on the balcony, visible through a large sliding glass door. Gentle flakes of a spring snow fell, piling high on the balcony rail to form a steep slope, like an alpine roof, the ice crystals sparkling in the moonlight.

As CEO of the New York Collective, Leopold had the entire forty-first floor of the apartment building to himself. She'd been staying in his guest suite, and now that her basic training was complete, Leopold insisted on conducting the next phase of her training—teaching her how to persuade the residents of Sierra Escondida to invest in their biotech research lab.

Leopold joined her carrying a wooden tray laden with three wine bottles and four glasses. One of the glasses was filled with a murky red liquid that didn't look like wine—most likely donor blood for him. A large envelope was clutched under his arm.

She stood up out of respect for her sponsor and waited for him to deposit the tray on the large coffee table and sit down. Standing, he was a little shorter than her and painfully skinny. His brown hair was cut short and plastered straight back with some kind of pomade, an attempt to defeat the natural wave of his hair. It didn't work. A thin, angular mustache grew from his cupid's-bow indentation to the corners of his upper lip—a style favored by the seventeenth century residents of Amsterdam, the city he lived in when he was turned vampire over three hundred years ago.

"You've had dinner?" he asked, his clipped Dutch accent faint but still there. "I wouldn't want you to get tipsy on an empty stomach."

"No need to worry about that—I ate shortly before you woke up."

"Good." He sat down in the brocade winged chair across from her and handed her the envelope he carried. "These are dossiers on the vampires you'll meet."

She read what was written on the envelope. "The Hill?"

"Their nickname for Sierra Escondida. Read through the dossiers and let me know if you have questions." He poured an inch of red wine into one of the glasses. "Now, these are three wines produced by the Hill."

She perched on the sofa, accepted the wineglass he offered her, and started to raise it to her lips.

"No, no," he said, waving his hand to stop her. "Never just drink." He picked up the wineglass filled with blood and held it below eye level. "First, look straight down into the glass and roll it." He did that with his glass. "You're looking for color. Color tells you a lot about the wine, and we'll go over those details later. For now, I want you to know the steps until they're so ingrained you do it without thinking."

He held his glass straight out, and she mimicked what he did. "Next, look for clarity. Is the wine clear or murky?" He then swirled his glass, and she followed suit. "See those tears forming down the inside? Those are the wine's legs."

"What's their significance?" she asked.

"I said we'll get to that. For now, just get used to the order of things."

She gritted her teeth and tried not to let her irritation show. Leopold often acted like little time had passed since she had been a young student and he her tutor. He fell back into his role seamlessly. She didn't.

"Fourth, tip the glass, angling it over a white tablecloth if you have one. Focus on the area where the wine thins." He then placed the glass below his nose. "Next, the sniff. Give the glass another swirl, then hover above it like a hummingbird hovers over a flower, and take a quick, *silent* sniff."

She did, and a lovely scent of ripe berries and oak suffused her nose. But all these steps seemed like overkill. Would the Hill's vampire vintners really care if she viewed the wine at three angles?

Finished with his sniff, he raised the glass to his lips and, with a nod, said, "Now you may sip."

He took a drink from his glass—more than a sip—while she took a small one from hers and rolled the wine around on her tongue. *Not bad.* She picked up the bottle and examined the label—a Cabernet from a boutique winery named Vasquez Müller Wineries.

"If the Hill's main economy is wine, why do you want our lab built there?" she asked, returning the bottle to its tray.

He reached for the map she'd left on the coffee table and pointed to a section highlighted in orange, a part of the town's business district. "This area is undeveloped and still within the boundaries of Sierra Escondida, a prime spot."

"The scientists who'll work for us can't live in—"

"They'll live in the neighboring city of Mordida."

She took a breath. Why build in the western foothills of Central California, an area without infrastructure or resources to support the kind of research facility she planned to build? Of all the treaty communities to choose from, Leopold had insisted their project must be located near Sierra Escondida.

"Okay," she said, "so there's space to build, but that doesn't explain why you want it there. There are better locations near other established medical tech businesses—South San Francisco, for one. Many biotech firms have established there. We'll have no problem luring top scientific talent to the area."

"Too far from the San Francisco Lodge."

"Then what about Austin, Texas?"

"Too crowded. The millennials have taken it over."

"Eau Claire? Plenty of room to expand, and they're offering investment incentives to new businesses."

"Have you ever spent a winter in Wisconsin? Besides, it's not even close to an existing treaty community. We've been through all this before, Cerissa. The lab needs to be near the Hill."

Yes, she had heard it all before. And hearing it again for the umpteenth time, his explanation still sounded fishy to her. She suspected his reasons had more to do with New York losing the war forty-five years ago, not that he'd ever admit it.

As part of her envoy training, she'd learned that the war between North American vampires started with embargoes and travel restrictions in the 1950s. Then the Malibu Incident in the late sixties enflamed matters—a few East Coast residents ignored the travel restrictions because they wanted to night surf; the West Coast communities sent their remains back in boxes.

The vampire communities couldn't conduct their war in public—not if they wanted to remain hidden—and their numbers had never been large. Plus, no one wanted to turn and then sacrifice a mate to the war. And if they hired mercenaries, they'd have to feed and house them later—after the war ended.

In a game of chess with no pawns to sacrifice, the leader of each community became the target, and assassination the goal. When the head of the New York Collective was killed, Leopold became their CEO and signed the North American Treaty.

He blamed Sierra Escondida for coercing him into doing so.

A momentary shudder went through Cerissa. What would Leopold think if he knew the Lux had engineered the events that led to his predecessor's death?

She pushed the thought aside and took another sip of wine, returning to the key question: why did he really want her lab in Sierra Escondida? It put their project in his enemies' backyard.

Leopold poured out the second trial wine and handed her the glass. She went through the same motions before taking a sip. As she did, Ari's caution echoed in her mind: *observe and report.*

Leopold's insistence on the location of the lab was a red flag if she'd ever seen one, one she'd report to Ari, but what to do about it? She had to go along with it to gain entry into their secret world. If she questioned his motives any further, he might get suspicious and cancel their project. She couldn't risk it.

During the six months she was in training, she'd seen no real evidence that the vampire dominance movement existed, but she had heard a lot of grumbling about the treaty and the quality of banked blood.

The Lux had an old adage: *With time, truth is revealed.* She just hoped they had enough time to learn the truth.

CHAPTER 3

SIERRA ESCONDIDA POLICE DEPARTMENT—THE NEXT NIGHT

For close to seventy years, Tig Anderson had served as chief of police for Sierra Escondida.

Some nights, she wondered if it was worth it. Tonight looked like one of those nights.

On the corner of her desk sat a tall stack of binders. She reached for the next one and plopped it down, flipping to the Executive Summary. Another consultant who just didn't get it. Town hall, including her office, would never be moved outside the walls of their gated community.

Yes, she'd read the legal arguments before—a government facility didn't belong behind a wall, in a privately owned area. Yes, they should move town hall to the business district and merge it with the small annex of government offices currently there, so the general public would have free access to all town departments.

It will never *happen.* Not while Sierra Escondida hid a community of forty-two vampires and their mortal mates.

So why was she wasting her time reading another longwinded report on the subject, the page count clearly an attempt to justify the consultant's fancy fee?

She let out a long exhale. Maybe it was time to move on. Even though she had the honor of being the first black police chief in California, anything seemed better than the administrative cesspool her job had become.

Yeah, first black *female* police chief, and the only vampire to hold the job. Of course, mortal police agencies didn't know that last part. It took some occasional fast talking, but she'd become an expert at giving believable reasons for being absent during the day. Besides, no outside police agency ever questioned the old standby: "She's in a meeting."

She reached for the insulated tumbler on her desk and took a sip. The blood was so stale, it was hardly worth drinking. How could they call *this* "dark wine"? The name was an insult to the fine wines produced by Sierra Escondida's vineyards. She returned the tumbler to its coaster and refocused on the consultant's report—ruminating wouldn't get it read.

Her cell phone rang. Yacov's name popped up on the screen—one of the vampires who served on the homeowners' board and had direct access to her private line. She gladly swiped "accept call."

"Tig, I have a problem."

Yeah, probably some touchy political situation—that, or someone's cow had wandered into his yard again. She shoved her phone into the crook of her neck.

"What is it, Yacov?" she asked, trying not to sound bored. Out of habit, she glanced at the digital clock on her office wall: 8:01 p.m.

"Two shooters. I'm trapped in my car on Main Street, a mile past the gate."

That got her attention. Before he finished speaking, she keyed the portable radio on her desk and called for backup. Rushing past the coat rack, she snagged her gun belt.

"Are you armed?" she asked him, still holding the phone to her ear.

"Of course."

"Leave the phone on. I'm on my way."

She hit the door at full run and sprinted out into the dark night, reaching her police cruiser just as gunfire exploded over the phone. She clipped the phone to her belt, the car's Bluetooth capturing the call, and then slapped the car's siren switch on. The noise might scare off the shooters before they hurt Yacov.

"Do I have backup?" she yelled into the radio. She put the car in gear and sped down the two-lane road, the homes and vineyards along the road nothing but a blur.

"Four on the way," the dispatcher responded.

"Jayden with them?" She could only hire mortals who knew about vampires, and Captain Jayden Johnson was the most qualified among them.

"Roger that, chief. Jayden and three reservists."

In radio-speak, that meant three vampires.

The car's insulation muffled the siren, but out of habit, she leaned toward the hands-free microphone. "Yacov, are you still there?"

No answer. Not good.

What was Yacov doing in the town's business district tonight? He ran his diamond import company from home. So what was he doing outside the wall and in the public area?

Tig swerved. A car had pulled over to let her by. The gate stood open—the guards must have heard the siren. She raced into the business district.

The dashboard clock read 8:05 when she slammed on her brakes, stopping at an angle behind Yacov's disabled Mercedes. His two flat tires faced her, the sidewalls chewed up, probably from gunfire. *Shit.* Fear for Yacov's safety crawled through her belly. She killed the siren and cautiously inched out of the car, using the door as a shield to get the lay of the land.

She scanned wide, taking in the storefronts—all dark. The wineries and other tourist-oriented businesses were closed for the night. No sign of anyone moving, but plenty of places to hide.

One man lay sprawled on the sidewalk, shot through the forehead with his face pointing at the sky. She didn't recognize him. No heartbeat audible, so probably dead. Another man hung halfway out the driver's side of Yacov's car. Most of the car's side windows were shot out, the remaining glass held together like a fragile spider's web. She approached with caution, trying to watch both Yacov and the nearby storefronts, her hands wrapped firmly around her Sig Sauer pistol. The smell of fresh blood tickled her nose. Her fangs extended reflexively, and she forced them back in. Now was not the time to lose focus.

Yacov sat in the driver's seat, leaning back against the leather upholstery, his eyes closed. The man hanging halfway out of the open door lay across Yacov's lap. Yacov's arms wrapped around him in a loverlike embrace, and the man's head lolled to one side. Multiple rows of fang marks gouged the man's neck—he must have struggled against Yacov's bite.

She detected the sound of one beating heart. No blood flowed from the man's mangled throat, so the heartbeat must belong to Yacov. Some of the tension eased from her body, and she scanned the street again. Nobody on foot, but she caught the sound of cars fast approaching, and spun around. Two police SUVs skidded to a halt and blocked the street at an angle, forming a defensive perimeter.

With reinforcements guarding her back, she holstered her gun, reached in, and pulled out the dead body, depositing it on the pavement—another stranger. She bet the body would stay dead where she dropped it. Yacov would never have given the attacker his blood, and it took both vampire blood and the venom in a vampire's fangs to turn a mortal vampire.

She offered her hand to Yacov and helped him stand. He seemed all right, aside from some cuts inflicted by the broken glass, but those would heal quickly. *Good.* She didn't want to consider the consequences if he'd been killed.

Yacov still gripped his gun. She pulled a plastic evidence bag from her back pocket, where she always kept one or two, and threaded it over the barrel. She held the bag with one hand and gently pried the gun loose from Yacov's fingers with the other. From the look in his eyes, he wasn't ready to talk—still too dazed from gorging on a body's worth of blood.

Turning to the arriving officers, she barked out instructions. "There may be others. Liza, Zeke—take the north side. Rolf—take the south. Go."

Give her just one live perp and she would have the truth by sunrise.

She searched the dead bodies. No form of identification. "No car keys," she called out. "Be careful. They hid the keys or someone drove them here. That someone may be nearby."

Jayden arrived in the crime scene van and she signaled for him to join her. He placed his kit on the ground next to Yacov's car.

"ID first," she said. He took out an electronic fingerprint scanner, printed the two dead men, and then handed the scanner to her. Seconds later, a *ding* told her they had a match. The names of two known felons appeared on the screen. She returned the scanner to him, pulled on gloves, and picked up the gun near a dead shooter.

Yacov still leaned against his car. A small amount of blood clung to his unruly brown beard and his olive-toned skin looked rosy. At the sound of her approach, he opened his eyes. "Tig, my friend, I had no choice. They tried to kill me, I swear." He inclined his head toward the nearest dead man. "I don't know why. I've never met them before."

"Do you recognize their names—Anthony Luzzari and Rocco Giordano?"

He shook his head, rubbing his eyes with the palms of his hands.

She unclipped her phone and started the built-in audio recorder, letting Yacov see what she was doing. He nodded his consent, and she slipped the phone into her shirt pocket so she wouldn't have to hold it. "Tell me what happened."

"I was on my way to Los Angeles. A new shipment of diamonds to cut."

"Were you carrying any?"

"Not this time. The raw diamonds are at the wholesalers."

So he did carry diamonds sometimes. She'd heard rumors, but never confirmed them. "Continue," she said.

"What's to tell? A loud bang and my car dropped in the back. I thought I'd blown a tire." He shrugged, looking sheepish. "The second bang—I realized it was gunfire. With two tires gone, I stopped the car and ducked down."

Lucky for him he drove an older-model Mercedes with bench-style seats—no tall center console, so he could get below the window line.

"I grabbed my gun from the glove box and called you. Bluetooth," he said, tapping his old-fashioned earpiece. He paused, looking down. "They may have wanted me alive."

"What makes you say that?"

"Well, either that, or they were stupid." He tugged at the end of his long beard, twining and untwining his finger in the ragged ends. "They approached from behind, one on each side, shooting out the windows. Then they stopped."

She saw Yacov's point. Why stop shooting? They had him cornered.

"I heard footsteps," Yacov continued, "and the sound of a heart beating louder as it came closer. I took the chance. I sat up and shot him."

"The man on the sidewalk?"

"That's right. Then the other man opened my door. No one told him how fast we can move." He chuckled and released his beard. "I grabbed his gun and pulled him in. You know the rest."

His story matched what Tig's eyes told her. The council would probably clear him of any wrongdoing for draining his attacker. Self-defense and heat of the moment—even an older vampire like Yacov, amped up on adrenaline from the attack, couldn't stop a feeding frenzy.

"Has anyone threatened you?" she asked.

"No. No one. And it makes no sense. Why attack me while I'm driving? Why not wait until I'm alone and not in public?" He gestured while he spoke, his whole body taking on the appearance of a question mark.

She ejected the clip from the gun the assailant used. "Silver," she said, running her finger along the half-full cartridge and feeling the telltale burning sensation through her glove. "How did they know to use it?"

"I have no idea, my friend."

She shoved the clip back into the gun and dropped it into another plastic bag. "A business dispute?"

"I'm on good terms with the diamond merchants I cut for. Besides, they wouldn't know to use silver. They don't know what I am."

"What about ex-lovers?"

"None who want me dead. Besides, I've been with my wife for ten years. I'm a faithful husband, Tig."

She kept her eyes locked on his. "You have no idea why they attacked you?"

"Believe me, I wish I knew."

"Anyone know your travel plans?"

"Only about half our community, as well as the community in the Fairfax District—I was going to stay with them."

That didn't narrow it down much. "I'll need their names and contact information."

"Of course, of course. I'll email it to you later."

She clasped his shoulder. "I'm glad you're unharmed," she said, releasing him. "One of my officers will drive you home." She motioned to Zeke.

Yacov waved him off. "I'd rather walk."

She got it—he wanted to walk off the effects of the kill before his wife saw him. It wouldn't do for him to arrive home with blood in his beard, mortals didn't always understand that sort of thing, and she touched the corner of her own mouth before pointing to his. He caught the message and wiped his beard clean.

"When we're done with your car, we'll have it delivered to your house," she told him.

He nodded, and she watched him hike back to the guard gate. One of their own kind was behind this, or word of their existence had finally escaped to the world beyond their walls. To date, none had figured out the true nature of Sierra Escondida, although other vampire communities had been attacked by self-proclaimed hunters of her people.

"Fucking bigots," she mumbled. She said nothing of her suspicions when her officers returned empty-handed. Better to keep her mouth shut until she had an idea of who or what was behind this.

CHAPTER 4

R

lines, particularly cross-country d have chosen different means, ly traceable, and business class the large, muscular man in the he scrunched away as far as her

adrest flap and closed her eyes After a two-day frenzy of last-a Escondida, she needed sleep,

r. Five minutes later, the crying

" a male yelled from behind her. se me," she said to the muscled e and let her slide past him. The sat two rows from the back in an ed and opening its mouth to let another one rip.

A curly-haired man sat in the row behind the mother. "Get that brat outta here," he said. It was the same voice that made the earlier threat.

Cerissa stopped in the aisle. "I'm a doctor. Can I help?"

The mother, who looked young and scared, clutched tighter to her baby. Another bloodcurdling yell ensued.

Cerissa touched the mother's shoulder. "It'll be all right. Just let me check him out."

"Her," the mother said, a look of hope invading her stressed-out eyes. She lifted the baby, offering the squirming bundle to Cerissa.

She cuddled the child in her arms. The baby stopped crying, her eyes checking out the change in who held her, before screwing up her face again for another round.

The curly-haired man stood up, hunched over to avoid the overhead compartment. "Screw this. Let me out."

With her free hand, Cerissa stepped forward and reached for Curly's shoulder, directing her aura into him. "Please sit down."

Curly sat down, and the baby let out another yell. Curly glanced up at Cerissa, his face relaxing, the anger leaving his eyes. "Hey, beautiful, you want to join the mile-high club?"

Ah-oh. Too much aura. Ten years into adulthood, she still hadn't mastered the art of subtle influence, especially when faced with an angry person. Direct touch only made it worse. Another reason not to use her aura once her mission on the Hill began.

She ignored Curly and whispered to the baby a soft "Shhh." To the mother, she said, "Do you have a burp rag?"

The woman handed her a cloth, which Cerissa draped over her silk blouse, and gently rolled the baby to her shoulder, humming a lullaby. The baby stopped mid-screech to listen to her song. A few gentle taps later, the baby burped, sending a small stream of spit-up onto the rag.

Cuddled close to her face, the baby smelled of warm baby powder and sour milk. "When was the last time she fed?"

The mother held up a small bottle. "I was trying to feed her, but she's not used to the bottle yet."

"Breast-feeding?"

The mother looked embarrassed. "Yes."

At Cerissa's direction, the flight attendant found a blanket and draped it around the mother, while Cerissa rocked the infant. What a sweet face—she wished she had one of her own. Reluctantly, she laid the baby back in the mother's arms. "She'll be fine—she's just hungry."

The baby disappeared under the blanket, and the light sound of suckling followed. The mother looked relieved. "Thank you."

"My pleasure." Cerissa started to return to her seat.

"Hey, lady," Curly called out. "You sure don't wanna—"

"I'm sure."

She settled into her seat as the flight attendant's "prepare for landing" announcement echoed over the speakers. The man in the window seat next to her eased up the closed shade, and she watched the plane's descent through an orange-brown layer of smog with rows of cookie-cutter homes barely visible through the late afternoon haze—neither reassured her.

Her stomach growled at her, and not from lack of food. Did she really want to call this home? If her project was successful, she'd be here for a long time. Frowning to herself, she decided to withhold judgment until she saw the Hill in person. She still had a long drive before she reached her final destination.

She took out a compact mirror and ran a brush through her long, dark hair, the thick waves fighting back. Her makeup had survived the six-hour flight mostly intact, but she sponged on a bit of base to even out her skin tone. Whatever possessed her to buy this brand? Each time she flipped the bottle over to pour some out, the label read "nutmeg." The same word the other children taunted her with for being dark brown like her *pita*. She shook off the ages-old memory.

A short time later, she collected her luggage, signed for a rental car, and drove west to Sierra Escondida. The sun had set by the time she arrived, and a canopy of stars blanketed the night sky, a spattering of white pinpoints across an expanse of black. Sometimes, she wished she could pick one star and follow it to wherever it might lead, instead of going where she was ordered to go.

The guard at the gated entrance examined her credentials before directing her to the country club where she'd find the mayor of Sierra Escondida. She drove up the main road through low, rolling foothills, which were dotted with floodlights illuminating the vampires' homesteads. Large, sprawling vineyards, the woody grapevines showing no sign of awakening from their winter slumber, created dark patches between them. She rolled down the car window and took a deep breath of the clean night air, perfumed with the smell of freshly turned dirt and wild sage.

No smog. Much better.

Maybe this will be a good place to live after all. If only she didn't have to live among vampires. Then it might just be perfect.

CHAPTER 5

The country club's parking lot was well lit. Cerissa stepped out of the car, straightened her suit jacket, brushed the wrinkles out of her skirt, and then threw back her shoulders—time to take center stage and wow them. She'd spent her whole life pretending to be something she wasn't. How was this any different?

A man quickly appeared at her side. He removed his black cowboy hat, his fingers sweeping his honey-blonde hair to the right, smoothing it out. His intense cerulean-blue eyes pinned her, sending an uneasy shiver across her skin, the hair on her arms standing at attention. She steeled herself to ignore the predator vibe he gave off. She *wasn't* prey.

"Are you lost, miss?" he asked with a friendly smile, flashing a little fang, his eyes turning solid black.

His reaction could signal aggression, hunger, or sexual interest, and with vampires, she had a hard time telling the difference. Even before he smiled, she had pegged him as one of *them*. Easy to spot the visual differences: a certain shining intensity in the eyes, the paler skin, the enlargement of pupils when aroused or angry. But deep ridges in the fingernails were the confirming feature. The ridges grew more pronounced the longer a vampire lived, like rings on a tree. She quickly glanced at Zeke's nails—he was well over a hundred years old.

"I'm here to see your mayor," she said, showing him the parchment envelope, sealed with red wax. "My name is Cerissa Patel."

"And I'm Hezekiah Cannon. Zeke to my friends."

She didn't recognize him. His picture wasn't in the dossiers of politically important vampires she'd studied.

"The mayor's at the dance," Zeke added, holding open one of the large doors to the country club's entrance.

She stepped into a carpeted hallway, where people in evening gowns and tuxedoes milled around. The slightly muffled sound of a dance band bled through the wood-paneled wall.

The sudden touch of Zeke's hand on her arm startled her. She jumped slightly and glanced up at him, and he smiled, pointing the way with a tilt of his head.

Relax. He only wants to guide you through the crowded ballroom.

Yet the way he held her arm carried a "she's with me" message, as if daring others to challenge him for the privilege. Many of the male vampires, and some of the females, were tracking her every move.

The dance band wrapped up a song and announced a break. The momentary silence was replaced with the white noise of voices. She spotted the mayor's table before Zeke directed her to it. The town's council members were seated with the mayor or hovering nearby. All going according to Leopold's plan—not that she agreed with his plan.

All right, here I go. First impressions can never be redone.

"This little lady's here to see you," Zeke told the mayor. She kept her mouth shut, even though Zeke's "little lady" comment rubbed her the wrong way—some of the older vampires clung to their sexist lingo. Not her battle—at least, not tonight.

She bowed to the mayor in the old-fashioned "make a leg" style she'd been taught. With her left leg extended forward, right leg bent at the knee taking her weight, the bow was a customary sign of respect when greeting a vampire of his rank, and also kept the bower off balance, unable to attack. In her outstretched hand, she offered Leopold's letter to him.

Even with her eyes lowered, she could still see the mayor. He looked just like his dossier photo—Old England was written all over his face. She waited for permission to rise, but he was slow in giving it. He took the envelope and broke the seal. Only then did he nod at her. Well, scratch him off the list as a potential investor in their project. His little show of power told her all she needed to know about him.

While he read the letter, she looked for other high-ranking officials who matched her dossiers. To the mayor's right, in the seat of honor, sat the Hill's vice mayor, Rolf Müller, a thin, square-jawed vampire. Except for the modern tuxedo he wore, he could have stepped out of a Nazi recruitment poster. His light blonde hair sported a style popular in the early 1940s: long on top, combed over to one side, with a buzz cut on the sides and back.

The mayor *harrumphed* and tossed Leopold's letter on the table, his expression turning sour. No surprise. She'd warned Leopold that closed societies didn't like strangers, and with the recent attack on one of their founders, her presence would be doubly unwelcomed.

"Let me text Leopold to confirm it," Rolf said, his fingers flying over the phone's screen.

The rest of the vampires at the table stared at her silently. A tall, striking woman of African ancestry strode toward them, moving with the muscular grace of a warrior—the town's chief of police, another important vampire from her dossiers. The chief's afro wasn't more than an inch long, but the severe haircut looked good on her, letting the angular beauty of her face dominate. She arrived just as Rolf's phone faintly buzzed.

"The letter is legitimate," he announced, tilting the phone in the mayor's direction. The chief leaned over to read it too.

The mayor returned his stern gaze to Cerissa. "In spite of Leopold's seal, we had to confirm he sent you. Our community doesn't use envoys—it's not part of our tradition."

She nodded. She wanted to seem agreeable. Her project needed his vote of approval, along with the rest of the town councils', to succeed here.

"Won't you have a seat..." the mayor said, glancing down at the invitation again, "Dr. Patel, is it?"

"Yes, Dr. Cerissa Patel."

"Mayor," the chief interrupted, stopping Cerissa from taking the offered chair. "She should be searched first."

"Of course, you're right." The mayor gestured toward the chief, inviting her to go ahead. "I hope you don't mind," he added, glancing back in Cerissa's direction. "We can't be too careful. I'm sure you understand."

"I do," Cerissa said. If she carried a bomb, they would have smelled it. Same with a gun—gun oil usually gave it away. But a silver stake? Even a vampire couldn't smell silver.

Without a word, the chief tapped Rolf's shoulder and positioned her body between the mayor and Cerissa, acting like the mayor's bodyguard.

Rolf got up and started his search with her small purse, yanking it off her arm. Had the chief picked Rolf because he was the highest-ranking vampire on her small police force? From what Cerissa had observed so far, rank mattered more among vampires than gender sensitivities.

He dumped her purse onto the linen-draped table and pawed through the contents. At least she didn't have anything embarrassing in it. All he found were her keys, wallet, phone, and a tube of lipstick. He opened the tube of lipstick, brought it up to his nose, and sniffed it.

Eww. Note to self: replace lipstick.

He dropped her purse onto the table to join its contents and moved behind her, roughly patting her down. "You don't belong here," he angrily whispered in her ear.

After checking her sides and back, he ran his hands up her legs above her hemline. His fingers came within a millimeter of touching an area he had no business touching. She ignored him, keeping a pleasant smile plastered on her face despite Rolf's inquisitive fingers.

"She's clean," Rolf announced to the group, removing his hands from her body and returning to his place at the table.

Her shoulders relaxed slightly. She swept up the contents of her purse, returning them to her small bag.

"Won't you have a seat?" the mayor asked, his voice becoming solicitous. "And what Leopold writes is true? You're here to represent him on a business proposal?"

"We're investigating possible locations for our biotech research facility."

The mayor tapped his fingers on the introduction letter. "I wish Leopold had picked a different date for your arrival. Inconsiderate. He should have known the dance was scheduled for tonight."

"Leopold thought the dance would provide an excellent opportunity to network and find investors for our project. We hope to convince all of you," she said, making eye contact one by one with each power holder at the table, "that our research lab will offer an investment opportunity with explosive profit potential."

"Who's going to run this lab?" the mayor asked, squinting at her with suspicion. "I don't see Leopold moving here."

"You're right; he's quite settled in New York. I'll be in charge."

He interlaced his fingers over his substantial paunch. "Envoy or not, no mortal who isn't mated to a vampire is permitted to live on the Hill."

"I understand. My immediate plans are to take up residence in a nearby city, not on the Hill, if your town proves to be a good location for our lab." She'd prefer that over living on the Hill, but didn't hold out much hope. Leopold had warned her how they would react.

The mayor *harrumphed*. "Well, it's not that simple, Dr. Patel. You'd still need the council's permission to do so, but first things first. We'll have to figure out who you can stay with tonight."

"I'm happy to find a hotel."

"That just won't do."

"Well then, Leopold mentioned Ms. Greenleaf—perhaps I could stay with her until we decide whether Sierra Escondida is the right location for our project."

"He did, did he? But he couldn't be bothered to call Gaea in advance and make the arrangements with her."

The mayor stared at her, like he was waiting for her to defend Leopold's bad decision. She kept her mouth shut. Leopold hadn't wanted to risk being told no. While the treaty required them to give her access to the Hill, if the mayor cited security reasons, he could have delayed her arrival. By showing up unannounced at a public event, it would catch the mayor off guard.

Zeke cleared his throat, and the mayor glanced his way. "Sorry to leave you standing there, Zeke. Why don't you pull up a chair?"

"Don't mind if I do, but if the little lady would like to dance, I'd be just as happy to escort her to the dance floor."

There he went with the "little lady" stuff again. Oh well, this wasn't the place to say anything.

"Go ahead," the mayor said. "I'll take care of the arrangements with Gaea in the meantime."

The band had returned from their break, kicking off the set with a stale dance tune from the 1990s. Cerissa didn't like mixing business with pleasure, but Zeke and the mayor had decided the matter without consulting her. Zeke tossed his hat on the table and offered his hand.

Once on the dance floor, she mirrored his moves to the music's upbeat rhythm. He had a languid style, like a tiger moving across the hot savannah. "If you're not Leopold's mate, do you have a boyfriend?" he asked. Then he seemed to catch himself. "Or girlfriend?"

"Neither."

"You're awfully pretty—too pretty to be single."

She smiled, tilting her head and dipping her eyes in a self-deprecating way, a look she'd seen other young women assume.

He returned her smile. It rounded his cheeks into two little balls and lifted the corners of his eyes, giving him an innocent look. She didn't buy it.

"A fellow would be pretty lucky to have you for his girl."

She smiled again, a little less than before. She didn't want to encourage this—Zeke was cute, but she was here on business and couldn't afford any distractions. It was better to keep him at arm's length.

Hell, it was better to keep them all at arm's length. The treaty may afford her certain protections, but they were *vampires*, after all.

"If you're going to be on the Hill for a while," he said, "maybe we could go out sometime."

"Thank you for asking, Zeke, but I don't think I'll have any free time."

He looked disappointed. Still, it couldn't be helped.

They danced through another song before she asked him to return her to the mayor's table. He took her hand and walked her back through the maze of partygoers. The glances following them didn't look friendly.

Damn. I should have worked harder—there must have been a diplomatic way to decline Zeke's offer to dance.

Just as that thought crossed her mind, she locked eyes with a dangerous-looking vampire who'd glanced her way. His eyes beckoned to her while his lips played the straight man. She felt a jolt of attraction deep in her solar plexus, the electric buzz traveling south to tickle her root chakra.

Whoa, who is that? She didn't recognize him—another missing dossier. Her vision narrowed until all she saw was him. He sported a long black ponytail and had skin the color of dark caramel. Did he come from Latino origins? He looked terribly handsome in the tuxedo he wore.

His eyes started to blacken, drawing her in like iron ore to a magnet. She pulled hers away and then glanced back as she passed closer to him.

Oh yeah, those eyes. Fully black now, his eyes dared her to dance for him, dared her to strip for him, dared her to trip him and fall to the floor with him.

Not good.

Ari had warned her years ago: *If you spot a guy and feel that jolt of lust, run the other way. Nothing good could come of it.*

She walked right past the ponytailed vampire and shook her head to clear it. *Remember what you told Zeke. You're here on business.*

When they reached the mayor's table, Zeke pulled out a chair for her and asked, "Would you like some wine?"

"A glass of Cabernet would be nice. Thank you." The Hill was known for its Cabs; she couldn't go wrong ordering it. She snuck a quick look in the direction of the ponytailed vampire, but his back was toward her now. *Nice shoulders.* The tuxedo jacket nipped in at his waist, fitting him perfectly.

Zeke walked off to the bar, and a full-figured woman with a determined stride brushed past him. "Winston, what's so important you've dragged me off the dance floor?"

Oh well, back to business.

Gaea Greenleaf stopped in front of the mayor, her hands firmly planted on her broad hips. Leopold had described her as Rubenesque. Her pale white skin—quite abundantly visible thanks to a strapless dress— looked like it had never seen the kiss of sunlight, not even in life.

"We have a guest," the mayor replied. "Dr. Cerissa Patel will be joining our community for a while. She's Leopold's envoy. I thought she might lodge with you."

He continued his explanation while Gaea's eyes skewered Cerissa. Now she knew what a specimen under her own microscope felt like.

"Hmm," Gaea said, one finger poised on her chin. "She's welcome to stay the night at my place. If I decide I don't want to be bothered with her, you can make other arrangements."

Cerissa exhaled, but stayed silent. Her envoy training had taught her to wait until directly addressed.

"Tell me, dear, are you tired?" Gaea asked. "Would you like to leave now? If you've just come from the East Coast, you must be jet-lagged. We can leave any time you want."

Cerissa gestured toward the other partygoers. "It would seem strange to retire now, with the dance just getting underway. Besides, I'm eager to start meeting members of your community."

Eager? Anxious was more the word—crashing the party might end up dooming her project. *I was right and Leopold was wrong. We should have delayed this.*

"Well then," Gaea said, "you're sure you won't mind waiting here for me?"

"Not at all."

Gaea pulled the mayor out of his chair and stepped a few yards away, lowering her voice. The remaining council members—except Rolf— started vying for Cerissa's attention, telling her about themselves. The way they flirted so aggressively made her skin crawl. She briefly glanced over at the ponytailed vampire. Why did his attention generate a different feeling?

Not the time to think about that. She refocused on the vampires in front of her and cocked her head in Gaea's direction, splitting her awareness. She kept her face from revealing she heard every word Gaea said to the mayor.

"Well, Winston, do you think she is what she says she is?" Gaea asked.

"Rolf verified it with Leopold."

"How long will she be staying?"

"She didn't say yet."

"Hmm. I don't want her as a long-term guest."

"We can work it out later," the mayor replied. "For now, have her luggage and car searched for weapons." He pointed a finger at Gaea. "And you can't let her go roaming about the Hill until we know more about her. Make sure she has an escort wherever she goes."

"You needn't remind your elders how to protect the community." The edge of Gaea's voice was sharp enough to cut bone.

The mayor flinched and looked away. "I didn't mean to give offense."

"You may be mayor, but remember who you're speaking to in the future."

The mayor nodded and looked at his feet.

"For now," Gaea said, tapping her chin, "I'm going to treat her with the respect due an envoy. If we find nothing suspicious, we'll wait for her to play her hand."

"I don't mean to sound intrusive," he said, his face still pointed at his dress shoes, "but you should take extra precautions to protect yourself during the day."

"I appreciate your concern for my welfare, Winston, but you needn't. I haven't lived this long without learning a thing or two."

"Do you want me to tell Leopold to direct payment to you?"

"That will be fine. And there's no need for you to return to the table." With a dismissive flip of her hand, Gaea left him standing there alone.

Cerissa suppressed her smile. *Good. At least this part is going as planned.* When the mayor didn't return but proceeded across the room, Rolf strode off following him, an auburn-haired woman in tow.

The chief of police took a seat at the table. Cerissa smiled at the nice-looking mortal who joined the chief. He wasn't introduced, and he wasn't in her dossiers either. His lapel pin read "Captain Jayden Johnson." He was of African descent, but she suspected his ancestors and the chief's had originated from different tribes. He was shorter than the chief—his muscular shoulders made him look more like a boulder to the chief's stick, and his coloring more like a latte to her espresso.

Before she could greet Captain Johnson, Zeke appeared at her elbow with a glass of wine. "Thank you," she said, accepting the glass.

She took a sip, skipping all the other winetasting steps. In spite of Leopold's instructions, swirling and sniffing at a social event like this seemed gauche.

Zeke started to sit down, but Gaea stepped in, grabbing his arm and pulling him back up. "She's staying at my place. You'll get another opportunity to talk with her." She waggled her fingers at him. "Now shoo."

"But Gaea, I thought I'd show her around—"

"Don't you have responsibilities at the door?" the chief interrupted him.

"I reckon I do, chief. Cerissa, it certainly was a pleasure meeting you." He picked up his hat from the table and tipped it in her direction. "I hope to see you again real soon."

Zeke sauntered off. Still standing, Gaea leaned over, her abundant bosom almost popping out of her dress. "You'll have to be careful. He's one of our biggest players."

"That's good information to have."

"So, my dear," Gaea said, taking the mayor's vacant chair with a graceful swoop, "are you going to wait here for them to line up, or shall I take you around the room and let your purpose be known?"

"I suspect they already know—nothing travels faster than gossip." As if to prove her point, Rolf had left the mayor and headed straight to the ponytailed vampire. They were now deep in conversation. From the glances headed her way, her arrival was the topic. "What do you suggest?" she asked Gaea.

"I think we're better off getting you out of here and making you seem more mysterious. Vampires are used to being the hunters, not the hunted." Gaea stood up and motioned to the door. Abandoning her wineglass, Cerissa grabbed her purse off the table and joined her.

"You know," Gaea continued as they walked through the crowd, "it may take a while for them to accept an envoy. You're not bound by the loyalty bond—that will be a problem for them, let me tell you. We're very protective of the Hill. The loyalty bond must first seal the mortal's lips from speaking of us before they're brought here."

"I understand. While I'm not bound by blood, I have signed an envoy contract, and I understand the penalty for violating it."

Gaea paused near the doorway and turned to look at her. "What's your project going to do?"

"Biologics. I've perfected a cloning technique—it uses biological processes to produce medicinal products."

"I'm not sure I understood even half of what you said."

"Let's put it this way. You can create medicines such as aspirin by combining chemical compounds. Or you can use live tissues to produce a medicinal product—insulin for diabetics can be made that way."

"And what you do—you use human tissue to create something?"

"Exactly. I'm going to need a sizeable parcel for the lab, one that can accommodate our expansion as the business grows."

Gaea looked thoughtful for a moment. "And if you decide our little community doesn't work for you?"

Leopold had prepared her for this question. Even though he wanted her project in Sierra Escondida, this would be a business negotiation. It meant they couldn't seem too eager. "I have letters of introduction to the other treaty communities. I'd prefer a rural setting, but I'm not absolutely tied to it. So I'd probably try the rural communities first."

"And the mayor would lose face with Leopold if we didn't make you feel welcomed here," Gaea said. Cerissa started to protest, but Gaea cut her off. "That isn't your problem, although we'll have to proceed carefully. I don't want the mayor becoming territorial about you, deciding who you can meet and who you can't. He can be a real jerk when he wants to be. I guess I should know—I'm the one who made him what he is today."

"You're the power behind the throne?"

"No, you misunderstand. I'm the one who turned him. Wait here while I gather up my latest boy toy, and we'll leave."

CHAPTER 6

Enrique Bautista Vasquez—or Henry Bautista, as his current driver's license read—was deep in conversation with a fellow founder when he heard someone approach from behind him. He looked over his shoulder to see Rolf, his business partner, come to an abrupt stop. He felt a few stray hairs brush his jaw when he turned his head, and he swept them behind his ear. The rest of his shoulder-length hair was tied back in a ponytail, the same way he had worn it when he died at twenty-four years of age.

"I'm not happy Leopold has imposed her on us," Rolf said, almost shouting to be heard over the band's rendition of "We Are the Champions."

What was bothering Rolf now? Rolf's girlfriend Karen, in stilettos and an evening gown hugging every curve, was walking toward them, trying hard to catch up with Rolf while also maintaining a semblance of grace. Did Rolf resent being shorter than his mortal mate when she donned high heels? Rolf had never said anything, but then, he wouldn't.

"Leopold?" Henry repeated.

"Dr. Patel is here on his behalf."

He glanced over at the young woman in question, sitting at the mayor's table. So that explained her unorthodox entrance. He had noticed the arrival of fresh blood and the familiar way Zeke had touched her arm, but she wasn't Zeke's mate. He would have heard if Zeke had gotten lucky.

When Zeke escorted her from the dance floor, Henry had stared at her because an unmated mortal didn't belong here. He had also stared because her figure rocked the business suit she wore. The closer she walked toward him, the more he reacted to her enticing scent. At the time, he couldn't stop his eyes from challenging her—but at least his fangs had stayed sheathed.

"Just a moment, Rolf," he said, and turned back to the tall blonde he had been talking with. "I will email you the proposal. The hedge fund takes a contrarian view—I think their approach will pay off if this country keeps fighting senseless wars designed to make rich those who are in the business of war."

He'd seen history repeat itself time and time again. Though disappointing, betting on mortals to act against their own self-interest had made him very wealthy.

"Thank you, Henry," his fellow founder purred at him. She laid her pale white hand on his jacket sleeve. "It's difficult planning for the future when mortals can spin this country into such deep debt. There are times I wonder whether we were smart to avoid national politics and limit ourselves to the Hill. Can you imagine what it would be like if one of us ran things? On a global scale, I mean."

"Indeed," he replied, with a slight nod. "I am sure if you were in charge, Mistress Abigail, you would whip them into shape in no time." One corner of his mouth turned up at their inside joke. Then he grew serious again. "Short-term thinking by mortals is a burden we will continue to bear, but it's still possible to make a profit in spite of it."

"With your advice, I'm sure I will," she said. "Have you spoken with Yacov since he was attacked?"

"I hoped to see him here tonight. I returned yesterday and only then learned about the attempted carjacking."

She leaned in close, and he almost felt her lips on his ear. "I must say I'm jealous," she whispered. "It's been more than a hundred years since I drained a mortal. I hope someone tries to attack me." Rolf took that moment to clear his throat. Her lips left a quick imprint on Henry's cheek before she backed up and looked down her nose at Rolf. "Well, your business partner sounds like he's about to wet his pants. Ta."

The tall blonde strolled off, and he reluctantly turned his attention to Rolf. "I noticed Dr. Patel's arrival," Henry said, "but you'll have to fill me in on the details."

"Leopold sent us his so-called envoy. She wants community members to invest in Leopold's business, so she can live here and run it."

"Is she Leopold's mate?"

"*Nein.*" Rolf made the word a short staccato sound. "She's unmated and doesn't belong here. Her presence will trigger a return to the old days when we fought over mortals, ignoring the property rights of the vampire who'd laid first claim."

Henry raised an eyebrow at Rolf's brazen attempt to lecture him. "You don't have to recount the history to me—I lived through it."

"Mark my word, there will be battles over her," Rolf said with a disdainful snort.

"Oh pooh," Karen chimed in. "You're being ridiculous."

Rolf narrowed his eyes at her. "Don't you have someplace else to be?"

"Not if we're going to dance," she said.

"Does it look like we're about to dance?"

"No, it looks like you've forgotten your promise."

Rolf glared at her. "Go get something to eat. I'll find you when I'm done here."

"Fine," she said lightly. "I know when I'm not wanted. Besides, I saw Haley over at the buffet. She always likes to hear the latest gossip."

"Be careful what you tell her," Rolf said, just short of a snarl. "She's part of that uppity group of mortals who want voting rights. As if we'd ever let Hill mortals vote for *our* council."

Karen picked a piece of lint off Rolf's lapel. "Don't worry. I won't encourage her. I just thought she'd like to hear about the envoy's arrival."

She leaned over and kissed Rolf, who sneered back at her over the public display of affection. Henry suppressed a grin. He'd seen this scenario played out many times. Rolf still carried old-fashioned attitudes about such things, but Rolf's reaction never seemed to bother Karen. She took off in the direction of the buffet.

Rolf gave a low growl of disapproval. "The mayor is a fool to let Leopold's envoy stay here."

Henry brought his eyes back to Rolf and kept his opinion to himself. Under the treaty, it would be a diplomatic *faux pas* for the mayor to turn away a visiting envoy. "What kind of business is it? Leopold has never been interested in winemaking before this."

"Medical research. I don't like it. Her presence will invite lawlessness."

Rolf's doom-and-gloom scenario seemed unlikely. The community had too many safeguards built in for one woman to set them back, but her presence raised another concern. "If she is not mated in blood, then how are we safe with her among us? She has no loyalty bond."

Rolf curled his upper lip. "The *mayor* seems satisfied, since Leopold vouched for her."

"This makes no sense," Henry said, rubbing his gold crucifix, his tuxedo shirt between his fingers and the sacred object. "If she is not already mated, why would she seek to live among us? She cannot want a vampire mate. We are unable to give her children, and we stay young while she grows old. Unless her work really is all she cares for."

"Who knows what her real reasons are. She *said* she wants to be part of the community so she can manage Leopold's research lab. She was quite clear on the subject."

Why the Hill? Henry rubbed the crucifix one last time and released it. "Nothing in the treaty requires us to let Leopold build his project here."

"Don't you think I know that? The town council will vote with me," Rolf said, turning toward the mayor's table, motioning in the envoy's direction. "Her project will never be approved. It's the next few weeks I don't like. She shouldn't be allowed to roam unfettered among us. How could we sign such a treaty?"

Henry had been on the negotiating committee that drafted the final agreement and refused to argue about it one more time. "Could she be a spy for Leopold?" he asked instead. "Leopold wasn't happy with the treaty either, but I can't believe he's preparing for war again."

"I'm glad you said it. I would be accused of paranoia if I had."

He glanced over at the mayor's table again, but the envoy was gone. "Perhaps I should arrange to meet the young lady, so I may evaluate the truth of her intentions."

Rolf's eyes lit up. "An excellent idea. You won't be taken in by a pretty face and a short skirt. The rest of them seem blinded by her. Zeke practically fell over his dick when he met her."

"Rolf, your language—"

"Is accurate. Everyone at the mayor's table was flirting with her."

"Everyone but you, I presume." He sighed, scanning the crowd to find her again. *There*—walking out the door with Gaea. She was a pretty young woman, the rear view as good as the front view.

"Everyone but me," Rolf growled. "It was obscene. How could they forget what such competition could lead to?"

Henry felt the shadow of his past wash over him. "I do not know. But it's something I will never forget. You may trust in that."

CHAPTER 7

GAEA'S HOUSE—THE NEXT MORNING

A bright light penetrated Cerissa's closed eyelids. Why was someone pointing an LED flashlight at her face? She opened her eyes and found the real source—a blinding strip of light where the black-out curtains hung slightly opened. Squinting, she looked away, and red spots danced before her eyes in the dark room. *Where am I?* She reached for a bedside lamp and switched it on, glancing around the room.

That's right—I'm in a guest room at Gaea's mansion. Last night, the matronly vampire had called it "her little house," but from its tiled roof to its intricate balcony grilles, Gaea's home looked like it had been transported from an Italian countryside and dropped onto the Hill.

The digital clock on the bedstand read 7:30 a.m., and she plopped back onto the pillow. Way too early to be awake—she hadn't said goodnight to Gaea until three in the morning. Yawning, she sucked it up and rolled out of bed. She needed the bathroom more than she needed sleep.

The whole room felt alien, like she had awakened in someone's idea of a hip Victorian boudoir. A crystal chandelier hung over her bed, its curving, branchlike wire supported only a few crystals dangling here and there, reminding her of a dried-out Christmas tree, most of its needles lost. The rest of the room wasn't any better. Overstuffed chairs. Whitewashed dresser. Fringed lamps. Heavy drapes. All drenched in feminine floral prints with plenty of frills.

A private bathroom connected to her room. She stepped into the shower, the warm water making her forget the strangeness she felt. Once clean and dry, she rummaged through her suitcase. Whoever searched her luggage had done a lousy job covering it up. They had rearranged stuff, but it didn't matter—everything she needed was hidden on her body. Rolf just hadn't known what to look for when he patted her down.

Contact lenses. No choice; she had to wear them. She put one back in—and resisted the urge to fish it out, hating the slight shock as the lens sent out small, tentacle-like threads, which slid around her eyeball to connect to the optic nerve on the other side.

A complete microprocessor, etched on each contact lens, allowed her to retrieve data and view it privately. A pinpoint video camera recorded everything she looked at while wearing them, which had come in quite handy last night. Between the camera and face-recognition software, Leopold's dossiers on politically important vampires came into view each time she neared her subject.

Once her contacts were in, she slipped on earrings, each hiding a small microphone with a micro-amplifier. Ah, the advantage of secret technology—technology more advanced than what the general public used. As much as she wanted her freedom, being part of the Lux had its perks.

She held her hands in front of her, and a virtual keyboard appeared. She typed in a summary of what she had learned last night about the current power structure, her fingers tapping at the projection only her mind could see. The information she typed wouldn't go to Leopold. Her reports and videos were meant for her people—not that she'd made any real progress on her mission. It would take time before Hill residents relaxed around her enough to slip up and reveal anything useful.

A two-beat buzz from her phone signaled a calendar appointment. Her first meeting with a real estate broker was in thirty minutes. She finished dressing, grabbed her purse, and drove down the Hill to Mordida.

Tig stepped close to the wall of her home office. Tonight's early moonrise meant she was up before sunset, and to avoid the sunlight streaming in, she snaked her arm past the window sill to pull the blinds shut.

She sat down at her desk, flattening her bare feet on the polished hardwood floor beneath it. The smooth, cool wood felt good. Her husband, when she was still mortal, thought she had the biggest feet of his five wives. *You'll never tip over in a strong wind*, he had said, laughing. His words were like a spear through her chest. The scar on her self-esteem still felt tender four hundred years later.

She clenched her teeth, suppressing the memory, and turned on the computer. First priority: the background check she ordered last night. Cerissa Patel had been on the Hill all day—if the report warned of problems, they had to get her off the Hill now.

An email from Gaea was first in the queue. The update summarized what the envoy told Gaea after they left the dance. Tig fired off a quick reply: *Thanks, Gaea. Please keep Dr. Patel away from anyone of political importance.*

Attached to the next email was the background check. For someone in her twenties, Cerissa had a high FICO score, but nothing else of note. Tig switched screen views and brought up V-Trak, the custom database of all known vampires, their mates, and business associates. She scrolled through the information V-Trak had on the young woman—born in India, educated in the States, nothing unusual.

According to the gate logs, Cerissa left the Hill midmorning. So Cerissa wasn't snooping here—at least not yet. Should she have Cerissa followed during the day? She noted it. She would see if the mayor wanted to authorize the funds. *Unlikely*, she thought with a snort. He was so cheap he refused to replace her clerk, so why would he pay to have Cerissa followed?

Her mortal records clerk was on sick leave, recovering from back surgery. Maggie had left the station on a rainy evening, walked outside, and, as Jayden put it, went "ass over teakettle." Tig had found her sprawled on the sidewalk and in pain. Turned out Maggie had a ruptured disk—something even vampire blood couldn't fix, not without turning the person.

After Maggie was taken to the hospital, Jayden had investigated. The sidewalk was slick with more than water—a thin layer of clear oil covered it. They still had no clue where the oil came from.

They couldn't hire a records clerk from outside the community. Only a mortal who lived on the Hill could be trusted with the job, which wasn't the problem. There were qualified mates to choose from, but instead of hiring one of them, the council nixed the idea, since Maggie was still drawing sick pay. *Cheap bastards.*

Thinking about the council reminded her—they wanted a status report on her only unsolved case, the attack on Yacov. She clicked on a web link to the police department's multi-user investigation program, and scrolled through the notes and evidence related to the attack. No getaway car was found—it meant a third person was involved. Neither assailant lived locally. Both shooters had criminal histories.

Hmm, what's this? Jayden had added a new email message from the state's Department of Corrections—it must have come in during the day. According to the parole officer responsible for both perps, the shooters served time in the same San Diego prison, and their sentence dates overlapped. In reply, she asked for a copy of their prison history.

Mordida's crime lab had examined the guns and other evidence, since that was more efficient than wasting Jayden's time to do it in the Hill's way-too-small forensics workshop. Other than those of the assailants, the lab reported no fingerprints. The lab technician had looked askance at her when she dropped off the unspent silver bullets for analysis.

"Nut jobs," she'd said, in answer to his unasked question. He seemed to accept her two-word summary. Not many people in his position would consider a supernatural explanation—such speculation would be a career killer in police work. The lab reported the unspent bullets were pure silver and custom made. No identifying marks.

The assailants had used stolen guns, with the registration numbers still visible. The online gun registry traced them to two cold-case burglaries in Oceanside, just north of San Diego.

Other leads turned into dead ends. Too many people knew about Yacov's travel plans, and no evidence pointed her in any one direction. She'd made a few discreet inquiries with the Fairfax community, but Yacov was on good terms with everyone there.

Leopold's envoy, arriving so soon after the shooting…Tig didn't like coincidences. It was worth a phone call to Yacov. After a few pleasantries, she asked him, "Have you had any recent business dealings with Leopold?"

"Not since I left New York when the Draft Act was passed," he said. "The Civil War, you know. I decided it was best to move out west."

Good reason. He wouldn't be able to hide his vampire nature fighting side by side with mortals—and they'd notice he wasn't available during the day.

"But you were in business with Leopold before you left New York?" she asked.

"I was part of the group who invested in Henry's first restaurant— Enrique's. So was Leopold."

"Really?" She had heard the tales about Henry's restaurant, but not Yacov's involvement.

"There was a small group of us who backed Henry's experiment with, well, passing himself off as mortal. In those days, most of us kept to ourselves. We didn't run businesses, at least, not ones that required daily contact with our prey. Henry broke that taboo."

"Was there any animosity between you and Leopold when the venture closed?"

There was no answer from the other end of the line. Tig quickly lifted the phone from her ear, checking her cell signal. "Yacov, are you there?" she asked.

"Yes, Tig, I'm here. Why do you ask about Leopold?"

"The arrival of his envoy—any reason Leopold might be behind the attack?"

"None I can think of."

She said goodbye and noted the conversation in the file. *Dead end.*

She frowned to herself. Nights like this she wished she was back doing mercenary work for Phat—much less frustrating than police work. Phat had run a unit of vampire assassins in the Middle East during the height of European imperialism. The Egyptian vampire never revealed to mortals the nature of his forces—he just delivered what they wanted, for a price.

She became part of his special forces through a misunderstanding. Her tribe in Kenya had been known for being fierce warriors. Only later did Phat learn Maasai women weren't warriors, and the elders thought he was looking for a wife. A widow who had seen thirty-five winters—they were glad to get rid of her for the bride price he paid: five head of cattle.

After turning her vampire, Phat was shocked to learn she had no fighting skills—but she did have a flair for languages, quickly adopting local accents. It made her a valuable asset. Besides, Phat saw to her martial arts training. He later commented that, unlike his other students, she didn't have any bad habits to unlearn.

A few centuries later, she and Phat parted ways. She was freelancing in 1951 when she received Sierra Escondida's offer to lead their military forces at the start of the North American Conflict. Too bad it took a war to convince some that zero population growth was the only way for vampires to survive.

Idiots. Science didn't care what people believed. While the statistical calculus was beyond her, she didn't need higher math to understand the conclusion. Left unchecked, vampires would outnumber their prey in less than fifty years, and then all hell would break loose. Wholesale slaughter, vampire against vampire, as they fought over a limited food supply— something she never wanted to witness. Thank the ancestors that war was averted without too much bloodshed and the treaty was signed.

Wait, was that it? With zero population growth now the law, Yacov's death would create an opening on the Hill. Did someone put out the hit, wanting to turn a mate? She made a note in the investigation plan: *Ask the town clerk for any pending petitions.*

Since the treaty was signed, no mortal had been turned in Sierra Escondida, and she should know—she'd been chief of police the entire time. The vampire ability to gradually age and then reverse the process made it possible for her to stay chief for thirty years before she had to change her name and start over. She'd shorten Tigisi—her birth name—to Tig, and picked "Anderson" for a last name because it sounded American to her. The neighboring cities never questioned why the Hill had two successive black female chiefs. Go figure.

She got up and went downstairs to the kitchen. Fresh blood had been delivered during the day, and she began the steps to warm it gently, heating a pot of water to 102 degrees Fahrenheit, using a candy thermometer to get the temperature just right, and then turned off the flame, gently adding the bag to the water. The heat transfer would bring it up to body temperature. She had tried using a microwave once—what a clumpy mess that made.

Jayden would be reporting in soon after he wrapped up his daytime duties. He was her second in command, her daytime eyes. She counted on him to keep the peace while she slept. But he was more than a colleague— he was her mortal mate. The kitchen timer *dinged*, and she poured the heated blood into a tall insulated tumbler, smiling to herself. She wanted to feed before he returned, so she'd be ready for him.

CHAPTER 8

The small glass table in Gaea's guest bedroom, covered by a floral cloth trimmed with eyelet lace, provided an adequate work area. Cerissa typed a quick email to Leopold the old-fashioned way, using her computer tablet. It included a short summary listing the parcels she'd seen today.

She then turned her attention to a large bound document labeled "Covenants, Conditions, and Restrictions (the 'Covenant')" that had been waiting for her when she returned to her room. *Oh yeah, some light reading.* She skimmed through it, the rules and regulations for living on the Hill. Somehow they'd managed to write it without using the V-word. "Permanent residents" must mean vampires. This was more than "don't paint your house purple and no parking on the lawn." They had a rule for just about everything, most of it regulating interactions between "permanent residents" and "guest residents."

Hmm. What Zeke attempted last night violated the Covenant. Vampires were forbidden from dating an unmated mortal within the Hill's walls. Now she had an easy way out to deal with any untoward advances from him.

But that meant she couldn't date the ponytailed vampire with the magnetic eyes either. *Probably for the best.* What she felt for him was just lust, and she never trusted lust, especially lust for a vampire. She'd heard too many stories of love affairs gone wrong while in New York.

She skimmed through a few more provisions of the Covenant. Dueling wasn't permitted either; the winner risked banishment if they started it. *Wow.* Did they really solve disputes through violence? That seemed so last century. And hunting mortals within a hundred-mile radius of the Hill was forbidden. She closed the book and dumped it onto the nightstand. She'd pass the Covenant on to Ari when she turned in her next report. It was certainly different from the rules the Collective used—less progressive, to say the least.

The sound of someone at her door caught her attention, and she turned to see who'd entered the room.

"You're in luck," Gaea said, sailing through the open door. "A group of younger vampires are headed out to gamble at the local Yokumash casino. You and Blanche can drive together."

"Blanche?"

"I mentioned her last night. She's staying here while she applies for Hill residency. Her sitting room is just down the hall from your bedroom, remember? And Seaton's staying here as my guest for the time being, but he doesn't get out much, so he won't be joining you."

"Why not?"

"Oh, Seaton's, well, how should I put it...his maker had only been a vampire for twenty-five years. Much too young. Everyone knows you should *at least* wait until you're two hundred before becoming a maker, but that didn't stop Jane." Gaea shook her head, a look of disapproval in her eyes. "Anyway, it left Seaton, well, a little bit off. He doesn't connect well with mortals, and the council doesn't want him wandering around on his own now that Jane has moved on."

So Jane wasn't a resident. Cerissa would get the scoop from Leopold later.

Gaea started to leave. "Wait," Cerissa said. "I thought we were going to set up meetings so I could introduce Leopold's project to potential investors."

Gaea smiled indulgently over her shoulder, continuing toward the door. "You'll have plenty of time to meet with investors on another night."

Should she go to the casino? *Watch and observe* was her mandate. Well, this would give her an opportunity to do some of that while meeting other Hill vampires. And she wasn't concerned for her own safety. As an envoy, they wouldn't try to hurt her—the penalties were severe if they did.

"Ah, one more question," she said.

The vampire matron gave a small huff of annoyance and turned around. "Yes, dear?"

"What should I wear?"

"Oh, blue jeans are fine. Nothing fancy," she added, flipping her fingers in that dismissive way she had, "though you may want to touch up your makeup. And don't take too long. You should leave in fifteen minutes if you're going to be on time."

Cerissa didn't wear much makeup, but she could take a hint. She got ready quickly and hurried downstairs. Blanche—well, she assumed it was Blanche—waited in the foyer, wearing a classy pencil skirt with a silk jacket, tapping her high-heeled foot impatiently. *Shit.* It was too late to go back upstairs and change out of her jeans into something nicer. She'd have to suck it up.

A short time later, they arrived at a brightly lit casino located on the outskirts of Mordida. "Been here before," Blanche said with a slight Midwestern twang, leading the way inside.

From the back, her pageboy haircut needed a serious update. The fine strands of her blonde hair brushed her collar whenever she turned her head, like fringe on a surrey.

"Don't get me wrong," Blanche added, stopping near the roulette wheel. Cerissa caught up with her and Blanche leaned in conspiratorially. "I like gambling, but I don't gamble all that much here. These Hill residents, they got no respect for a girl who loses money at the tables, ya know? And I gotta impress 'em if I'm gonna get investors for my project."

"Investors?" Cerissa repeated, her throat going dry.

"Startup capital. Can't work a day job, ya know. I refuse to be a hooker, and they won't let you steal, cuz they're too afraid it'll lead back to them. So I gotta find investors and start a business I can run at night. Gotta earn my buy-in fee." Blanche started walking again toward the back of the Casino.

I'm in competition with Blanche for investors? Why hadn't Leopold included her in his dossiers? Sure, Blanche didn't live on the Hill, but this was important information.

Cerissa swallowed hard and walked fast to catch up with Blanche. "What kind of business?"

"I'm still working on my plan. I got this idea—I just need the right partner." Blanche shrugged, her hair doing the fringe thing again. "If I don't hook up with a community soon, they might brand me a renegade."

Cerissa opened her eyes wide with disbelief. "But when the treaty was signed, all unaffiliated vam—" She stopped before saying the forbidden word in public. "Ah, you were given fifty years to join a treaty community. What happened?"

"Things didn't go as planned, ya know?"

"So you have—"

"Four years, seven months, and three days left to join," Blanche said with a laugh. "Yeah, I know, I'm cuttin' it kind of tight, which is why I gotta make some serious money soon. I'm not the only one out there looking for a community. The deadline drives up the buy-in price each year." Blanche stopped in front of a closed door. "Hey, here we are."

Blanche opened the door and, still holding Cerissa's arm, gave her a gentle shove into a small private room and let go. The room was partitioned from the rest of the casino by a floor-to-ceiling glass window, draped with satin curtains, which were closed, blocking out the view. In the middle stood a blackjack table, covered in green felt, with five player seats filled. Cerissa's contact lenses identified the lower body temperature of the five players—all vampires.

Zeke bounced out of his chair and covertly showed a little fang when he greeted her. Geez, couldn't he keep it under control?

"Hey, Cerissa, you wanna sit by me?" he asked. He grabbed her hand and tucked it into the crook of his arm. "Blanche can have the other seat."

She dislodged her arm from his and slid onto the red leather stool next to Zeke's. Blanche took the empty one on her other side.

"Glad you could make it," said a pale woman with brunette hair. "We talked last night. I'm Liza," she added, reaching around Blanche to shake Cerissa's hand.

"Thanks," Cerissa said, gripping Liza's hand firmly. Liza had been at the mayor's table last night with the rest of the council members. "Maybe we'll have an opportunity to talk about Leopold's project."

"No work talk," Blanche said, giving her arm a squeeze.

The dealer tapped the table, getting Cerissa's attention. "Place your bets. I'm on the clock here."

Her eyes widened—a vampire working at a casino? She hadn't focused on the dealer when she first walked into the room.

"Slick," Zeke said, hooking a thumb in the dealer's direction, "works the night shift."

"And since I want to keep my job, would y'all place your bets?"

Cerissa slipped three hundred dollars out of her purse, the remainder of her traveling money until payday, and laid it on the table.

"Minimum bet is fifty dollars," Slick said, pushing colored chips at her, each imprinted with a dollar amount.

Her fingers squared up the stack of chips while she glanced around the table. Some pretty high rollers—bets from fifty to two hundred dollars sat in front of the others. Blanche's warning threaded through her thoughts. She didn't want to appear frivolous by losing too much too fast. Besides, she couldn't afford to, so the table minimum seemed the only choice. She picked up a fifty-dollar chip and set it in the betting circle.

Liza eyed her bet. "Have you played blackjack before, Cerissa?"

"Some."

"Don't let Liza pester you." Zeke laid down three black chips—three hundred dollars. "Most of us are used to higher stakes."

Slick dealt first cards to the players face up, placing his own card face down. Liza introduced the other three vampires at the table during the deal, one woman and two men. Cerissa didn't recognize them—none were on her dossier list.

Liza leaned around Blanche. "You're working for Leopold, but you aren't his mate, right? When you do take a mate, which will it be, a man or woman?"

"Couldn't it be both?" one of the men asked. He looked brightly interested, like a cat left alone in a tuna factory.

"Hey," Slick said. "Are you here to gamble or duke it out over the new blood? Blanche, the deal's to you. Are you taking a card or standing?"

New blood? Cerissa had learned the term in New York—not exactly a polite way to refer to a mortal. When Slick turned to her, her eyes must have communicated her displeasure.

"Sorry, miss," Slick said. "No offense intended."

"That's all right," she said, and accepted another card, standing on eighteen.

After a few hands, she was up by a hundred dollars. Zeke lost three hands in a row, Blanche and Liza seemed to be about even, and the chip stacks in front of the others had dwindled significantly.

"Play by the book," Ari had taught her. *"If you follow basic blackjack strategy, your odds of winning improve, and you won't piss off other players who use the same strategy to increase their odds."*

Zeke leaned in close, his hand sneaking under the table to squeeze her knee.

Why was he so grabby? The Covenant forbade dating on the Hill— *Wait*, they weren't on the Hill. *Is that why he's making his play here and now?*

He squeezed her knee again. "When you're ahead," he whispered near her ear, "you ought to increase your bet. Play with the house's money."

She brushed his hand away. "Really?"

"Come on." He grabbed her knee again, shaking it a little, but let go before she could react. "Loosen up."

She had kept her bets at fifty dollars, trying not to stand out. Maybe Zeke was right. If she upped her bet, they might take her more seriously. She picked up her fifty-dollar bet, replacing it with two black hundred-dollar chips.

Liza gave a light whistle. "You go, girl!"

"All right, place your bets," Slick said. "The rest of you—get in the game or call it quits."

Some of the vampires exchanged cash for more chips. Once bets were placed, Slick started pulling cards from the two-deck shoe. He laid down a ten in front of her. Her contact lenses had tracked the previously dealt cards—her ten was the last ten-point card in the shoe. Her next card was a two. Twelve. She had to beat Slick's hand without going over twenty-one. His up card was a six. Assuming his down card was a ten, he had sixteen.

The basic strategy said to stay. Don't take a card, don't do anything. The dealer had to draw more cards until he reached seventeen, so the odds were he'd bust—except there wasn't anything left in the deck higher than a nine, and only one of those, so his down card couldn't be a ten. Odds were Slick would draw a series of low cards and beat her twelve.

Blanche took one card and stopped at seventeen.

Now what do I do? Go for the big score to impress them? I'll break every rule in the book if I do it. What would Ari do? Her cousin always knew the right move. She'd rather be in the lab than a social situation, but put Ari in a room with people and everyone fell in love with him.

The dealer raised one eyebrow at her—a look of *don't just sit there, it's your turn.*

"Cerissa stays," Zeke said.

She clenched her teeth at his speaking for her, sucking it up one more time. She didn't want to upset any potential investors, and "investor" was the only role Zeke had a chance at.

"Wait a minute," Liza said, stopping Slick from moving on. "Cerissa gets to choose. It's her money. What do you say, girlfriend?"

She didn't look in Zeke's direction. She took a deep breath and pushed her last two black chips into the betting circle. "Double down," she told the dealer.

The table became very still.

"Four hundred dollars riding on one card." Slick snapped a card out of the shoe with a flourish and set it face down across her other cards. "Good luck."

"Wait. Don't I get to see it?" she asked. She had to know whether she'd just lost all her travel money.

"Local rule," Slick said. "We deal it face down. Adds to the fun. You'll see it soon enough."

Zeke's first two cards totaled eleven. "I'm gonna follow Cerissa's good example," he said, pushing three black chips into his betting circle. "I'll double too."

Slick dealt Zeke's card face down and added, "Good luck." No one else took a card, and all heads turned to Slick. He revealed his downturned card—an eight. Fourteen. He had to hit. Raising one eyebrow, Slick slowly pulled the card from the shoe and turned it over: a four, giving him eighteen.

A few growls of displeasure—some of the players weren't happy.

Slick tapped the table in front of Liza, who also had eighteen, breaking even. He swept up Blanche's chips and cards. Her seventeen had turned into a losing hand.

"Fuck," Blanche spat out.

Cerissa held her breath, a lump in her throat, her pulse beating a cha-cha. Why had she risked it all on one hand? She didn't have four hundred dollars to lose.

Slick slowly reached for Cerissa's downturned card, flipping it with a one-finger flourish: the last nine, added to her twelve, gave her twenty-one. He winked at her and paid her winnings—four black chips. She exhaled sharply.

"You go, girl!" Liza extended her hand for a high five.

Cerissa met Liza's hand with a slap, a warm flush spreading through her.

Slick then flipped over Zeke's downturned card. An eight. His nineteen beat Slick's eighteen.

Zeke grinned at her, a grin that would have made the Cheshire Cat proud. Slick pushed six black chips to him.

Cerissa breathed another sigh of relief. She wasn't the only big winner. Now they had to respect her.

"Didn't anyone teach ya the rules?" Blanche asked snidely. "You screwed it for the rest of the table. Zeke would have got your nine and stood on twenty." She tapped Cerissa's card, then pointed at Zeke's. "Zeke's eight would have busted the dealer. Then all of us would have won."

Her stomach lurched. "I'm sorry, I didn't mean to—"

"Hey, it's okay," Liza said. "I'm impressed. You played a good hand."

Blanche grabbed Cerissa's shoulder. "Stupid new blood."

"Lay off," Liza warned.

"Fuck you. I don't have to put up with bad playing from a *new blood*."

"I said, leave her alone." Liza grabbed Blanche's arm, pulling her off Cerissa. "You don't like how the table's going, you can walk away."

From behind her, a cold hand suddenly gripped Cerissa's shoulder. *What the hell?* The hand belonged to Zeke, who turned her to face him. *Just because we aren't on the Hill doesn't give him the right to manhandle—*

He yanked her closer and kissed her. Disgust radiated through her and she pushed back against his chest, leaning in the direction of Blanche, who snarled and pressed her fangs against Cerissa's bare neck.

"Public place!" Liza shouted.

Cerissa pulled away, almost falling off her stool, her heart going into overdrive.

Liza jerked Blanche back by her hair. "Shut your damn mouth before the surveillance video catches you. You out us here and the council will skin you alive. Literally."

Blanche clamped her lips shut over her fangs, and Liza let go with a push.

Cerissa quickly glanced over Zeke's shoulder. Her contacts had flashed a warning, telling her someone else had entered the room. A lone vampire stood at the door—the same good-looking guy from the dance last night.

He zeroed in on her, a look of contempt on his face. *Damn.* Using her lenses, she tried to identify him, but the readout still gave a null report.

She kept her eyes on the ponytailed stranger and whispered to Zeke, "Who's that guy?"

By the time Zeke turned his head, the ponytailed stranger had spun on his heels and left. Zeke sniffed the air, and an expression flashed across his face, almost imperceptible because he hid it so well—he didn't like what he smelled.

Zeke shrugged. "Don't know. Didn't see him."

Why had Zeke just lied?

A security guard quickly replaced the stranger at the door. "Need assistance?" the guard asked, his question directed to the dealer.

Slick waved him off. "It's all good, thanks."

The guard left, and Cerissa whispered to Zeke, "I, ah, I think I should leave."

"Now? Don't let Blanche get to you."

"You know what they say, 'quit while you're ahead.'" She clutched her purse, grabbed her chips, and slid off the stool. Last night, Rolf had spoken to the ponytailed stranger for a good twenty minutes, with frequent glances in her direction. Not good.

Zeke was in front of her in a flash, blocking her exit. "Don't go," he pleaded, looking at her with puppy dog eyes.

"It's okay, really," Liza added, grabbing Zeke's arm and moving him aside. "Cerissa isn't leaving, right, girlfriend? She just needs a moment to go to the women's room."

"Sure," Cerissa agreed, anything to get out of there. She had to find out who the stranger was and undo the damage. "I'll be back, okay, Zeke?"

"I'll walk ya there." He reached for her arm.

Liza hissed at him. "Zeke, give the lady some space. Go on, Cerissa."

Zeke stepped aside, and Cerissa scurried to the front of the casino. She ducked into the alcove where the restroom sign pointed. Hidden by the alcove's wall, she peeked around the corner.

The stranger stood near the front entrance, talking to a mortal man. The two shook hands, then the stranger walked outside and the mortal turned in her direction. The mortal's name badge read "Beverage Manager."

She quickly scooted toward the main door and out into the brisk night air. It didn't take her long to catch up with the stranger. She started to say hello, but he spun around so fast that she plowed right into him and stumbled, the impact zapping though her. He grabbed both her arms, holding her firmly. He had looked thin, but felt very muscular. Plowing into him was like running into a punching bag.

"Excuse me," she said, regaining her balance and taking a deep breath. The spicy scent of his cologne and masculine musk tickled her nose.

He continued holding her arms. A pleasant tingle began at the base of her neck, running down her arms to where he touched her. She gave a quick shake of her head to clear it and pointedly looked down at his hands. Based on his fingernail ridges, he'd been vampire around two hundred years, and based on the perfect shape of his nail tips, he had an on-call manicurist.

From the way she stared at his hands, he got the message and released her. She looked up into his dark brown eyes, feeling the same pull she'd felt last night. But nothing had changed—he was still a dangerous predator, still off-limits under the rules, and still waiting for her to say something.

"I'm sorry," she said, trying to sound friendly. "I was just coming out to ask if you'd like to join us inside."

"Why? So I can watch you debase yourself?"

She stepped back. "I beg your pardon?"

"You heard me. The way you flirt with them and flaunt your blood, your very presence incites their lawlessness."

This was far from the conversation she'd expected to have. "I didn't mean to cause a problem between Blanche and Zeke."

He crossed his arms. "Then why did you do it?"

"I didn't *do* anything."

"One mortal among a group of us? What did you think would happen?"

"All I did was play cards."

"Rolf is right. You don't belong here." His Spanish accent thickened the angrier he got. "Leopold should never have sent such an inexperienced envoy, one lacking knowledge—such basic knowledge—of our ways."

Heat rose to her cheeks. *Inexperienced?* "Look, I received the same training all envoys receive. My only mistake was trying to impress them with a high-stakes hand."

"And what would you call that kiss?"

She poked his chest with her finger. "*Zeke* kissed *me* without asking—not that it's any of your damn business."

Something flickered in his eyes at her touch, and his posture relaxed, the tension draining from his face. *Oops.* She'd promised herself she wouldn't use her aura.

"Hey, Cerissa!" Zeke called out from behind her. "We need ya back inside—the table's been stone cold since you left. No one's winnin'."

She turned to look at Zeke. His voice was friendly, but his pupils had turned solid black. He stared at the ponytailed vampire and curled his lip in a snarl, the same way Blanche had. Another territorial display—she really wished he'd stop doing that.

"I'll be right there," she told Zeke. She looked into the deep brown eyes of the ponytailed vampire and tried one more time to be charming. "Gaea is going to hold events so I can meet other Hill residents. I hope to see you at one of those."

"I'm sure you will," he replied, looking puzzled. His tone wasn't exactly warm, but at least it had lost its disdain.

Zeke grabbed her hand and pulled her back into the casino. The sliding door *whooshed* closed behind her. "Slow down," she said, barely keeping on her feet. "Zeke, stop."

"You shouldn't go outside alone." He came to a halt and glanced over her shoulder toward the ponytailed vampire. "It ain't safe. Ya never know what's lurking out there."

"Can I have my hand back?"

He looked down at the vise grip he had her in.

"Ah, sure," he said, letting her go. The wild look began to fade from his eyes.

They stood in the aisle between slot machines, halfway to the private room. She rubbed the red mark on her hand. "Who was that?"

"Him? Ah, his name's Henry. He's business partners with Rolf, the vice mayor. They own the Vasquez Müller Winery." Zeke looked down at her hand again. "Hey, sorry 'bout hurting ya. Sometimes I don't know my own strength."

The dossier for Enrique Bautista Vasquez popped up in her lenses. Born in Veracruz, Mexico, he was a founder—one of the five vampires who formed Sierra Escondida in the late 1800s. The only photo she had of Henry was blurry and taken at an odd angle, with his hand held up in front of his face, like he didn't want his picture taken. Not surprising—older vampires avoided social media and rarely allowed themselves to be photographed.

Damn. The face-recognition software in her lenses was good, but it couldn't overcome bad data.

Anger started in her throat, crawled down her windpipe, and lodged in her stomach like a burning ember. Because of Blanche, a founder now hated her.

But how could I have handled things better?

The answer shot through her mind before the question finished forming: she should never have tried to impress them. Dread quashed her anger, putting out the fire and replacing it with a lump of singed wood. She needed the founders' support as well as the council's.

I'm an incompetent idiot. First I screw up at the card table, and now an important Hill vampire hates me. What am I doing here?

She clenched her fists. Giving up wasn't an option. Not only would Leopold be pissed, but her mission for the Lux was too important to abandon it now. Not to mention she'd lose her chance at gaining some freedom, some independence from her family's interference with her daily life. She had to find a way to turn this around.

Zeke rambled on with his apology, attempting to reach out for her again, but she carefully avoided his touch by walking ahead of him to the table. Liza had switched places with Blanche, taking the chair next to Cerissa's. When she sat down, Zeke kissed her on the cheek before her lenses could even warn her. His smooch felt like a dog marking his territory. She wanted to swipe at her cheek to remove it, but instead increased the sensitivity on her lenses to warn her sooner. No one would own her. Ever.

CHAPTER 9

Henry slid behind the wheel of his Dodge Viper and sped out of the casino's parking lot, irritated by his conversation with Dr. Patel. What he saw at the blackjack table suggested Rolf was right: she wasn't a good influence and she didn't belong on the Hill.

But something else was bothering him. He rarely felt this riled up by one person—or by much of anything anymore. Why had she gotten under his skin? *Why her?*

Tapping the button on his steering wheel, he phoned Yacov. "Are you free?" he asked. "I could stop by. I would like to hear what happened."

"I can only give you a few minutes. Shayna is asleep and I have diamonds to cut. My client shipped them to me." Yacov chuckled lightly. "I have a wife who has threatened to chain my coffin shut if I so much as step a foot off the Hill until Tig solves this."

He laughed politely at Yacov's joke. Lucky for Yacov they didn't sleep in coffins, because Henry had no doubt Shayna would do it.

Yacov's ranch-style home sat at the valley's base on one acre of land, near smaller homesteads leased by other vampires who weren't in the wine business. Yacov was outside, waiting for him on the back porch swing, wearing a fedora.

"Why have you begun wearing a hat?" Henry asked, walking up the porch steps and taking a seat next to Yacov on the porch swing. It bounced, swaying a little.

"Keeps the sun off my head," Yacov replied with a mock grin. He cocked his head to one side, posing in the moonlight. "Makes me look distinguished, don't you agree?"

Between the beard and the hat, Yacov looked like an advertising image from an old bottle of patent medicine. "The real reason?" Henry asked.

Yacov rolled his eyes toward the night sky. "Shayna. She feels my kippah makes me too recognizable."

"And a fedora does not?"

"I've learned not to argue over the small things, and being right is a small thing."

Henry shook his head—he prided himself on being right. "Has Tig figured out why you were attacked?"

"Not yet, my friend."

"Could it be Zeke?"

"I know where you're going. Tig already asked."

Henry crossed one ankle over his knee and turned to face Yacov. The motion started the swing moving again. The whole contraption felt like a threat to his dignity. He uncrossed his legs and planted his feet firmly on the ground to stop it.

"And what did you tell her?" he asked.

"That Zeke smuggles in jewels occasionally, but I no longer help him dispose of them. I gave that up shortly after Shayna married me. She is devout and believes if we are going to live the righteous life, we need to abide by the laws of the land in which we live, unless those laws are themselves unethical." Yacov fell silent for a moment. "I was very fortunate to find Shayna. A good woman is a good influence on the likes of us."

Henry had heard it all before. Yacov had been married many times over his long life and believed in "until death do us part"—he never abandoned a wife simply because she grew old. In spite of Yacov's prodding, Henry had never married. His conscience wouldn't let him.

Yacov rolled his eyes skyward. "Tig asked me about Leopold."

"Leopold? Why?"

"I think the envoy's arrival sparked her concern. I told her we ended our business on good terms with Leopold. She doesn't need the whole history."

"Everyone profited when I sold the restaurant." Henry started to play with his crucifix, and then stopped himself. "Leopold wanted to keep it going longer. I told him what I told everyone else—I was tired of New York, and with the Civil War just starting…."

"The very reasons I voted with you on the sale," Yacov said. "But I wasn't the only one who supported selling out. We made a sizeable return on our investment—it was time to move on."

"Leopold still carries a grudge over it," Henry said. The last time he visited the New York Collective, Leopold had made a point of snubbing him. "And don't forget, you were the driving force behind the prohibitions against creating new vampires—a second reason for Leopold to be angry with you."

Yacov frowned. "But it's been over forty-five years since the treaty was signed. Why wait until now if that's his reason?"

"Still…" Henry said, and let the thought remain unspoken. At the time, Leopold had railed against them both, claiming they were doing it on purpose to stop *him* from siring any new vampires. "Tell me, how do you feel about having Leopold's envoy on the Hill?"

Yacov shrugged. "Doesn't bother me. I'm sure Tig has checked out her background, or she wouldn't still be here."

"Background check or no, she doesn't belong on the Hill." Henry clenched his jaw, and then added, "I saw her at the casino, gambling with Liza's group. She was the only mortal in the room."

"So? No harm in that."

"No harm?" Henry said, his voice rising. "Zeke kissed her and Blanche challenged him—an open challenge in a crowded casino."

"Are you sure they were fighting over Dr. Patel?" Yacov asked. "I've heard Blanche is more than a little hotheaded. Perhaps Zeke insulted her."

Of course he was sure. His own eyes had witnessed the challenge. "What if mortals had seen her bare her fangs? I can well imagine the trouble it would cause us."

"I don't know, it sounds harmless enough." Yacov waved his hand airily. "All these mortals running around, pretending to be us with their fake teeth—easily explained away."

"I'm supposed to meet with Blanche tomorrow evening, to hear her pitch. After what I saw tonight, I may cancel."

"Don't do that." Yacov patted Henry's leg. "The young ones need our help. Try to keep an open mind."

Keep an open mind? Not likely. He didn't need to be in business with someone who had no self-control. But Blanche wasn't what really bothered him—Leopold's envoy was the bigger concern.

"While I was speaking with Dr. Patel, something happened," Henry said. "Something I can't explain."

"Wait a moment, my friend. You spoke to her?"

"She came looking for me after Blanche's challenge." Should he admit what he suspected? It seemed strange at the time. Now, it sounded silly, but he'd opened the door and Yacov was waiting for him to explain. "Have you ever seen a lightning rod work?"

"Of course. Attracts the bolt and takes it to ground."

"I was furious at her when I saw her sitting there, alone, the only mortal at the table. The temptation—"

"Henry—"

"Let me finish. She approached me and we exchanged words. By the time Zeke pulled her away, all my anger had drained out of me like electricity through a lightning rod, and I felt this overwhelming sense of peace replace it. A short while later, my anger returned."

Yacov pursed his lips and then asked, "You believe Dr. Patel somehow absorbed your anger? Isn't she mortal?"

"She certainly smells mortal." Henry looked down at the palms of his hands. He'd grabbed her arms to keep her from falling—the delicate scent of her human musk still lingered.

"Perhaps there's another reason," Yacov said, smiling impishly. "I hear she's quite pretty. Maybe she charmed you with her beauty."

"I doubt that," Henry said, scowling. "I'm not like Zeke."

Yacov chuckled. "Indeed you are not."

He should have kept his mouth shut about Dr. Patel. His imagination was running wild—he was stupid to raise it. A change of topic would put an end to Yacov's smirk. "Does the chief have any leads on your attackers?"

"No, and she raised the same questions you did. I had just as few answers. Why would anyone want to hurt a harmless old vampire like me?"

"I wish I could help you."

Yacov patted Henry's shoulder. "Enough about me and my problems. How are you faring these days?"

"Business is good."

"Business is never enough to make life satisfying."

Why couldn't Yacov leave it alone? He didn't need to be reminded he was mate-less.

"The Mordida Bugles are playing a night game in a few weeks," Henry said. The local baseball team had lost their last four games; they were due for a win. "I'll get us tickets."

"You know what I meant, and it wasn't baseball." Yacov shook a finger at him. "Is life itself holding your interest?"

"For the most part." Henry looked at his hands. Dr. Patel's scent wafted off them, distracting him. "I have my moments."

"You and I both know boredom is dangerous for the likes of us."

"I am far from bored."

"You're approaching a dangerous age. You've been vampire more than twice the human life span. It's easy to miss the signs until the malaise hits with full force."

Henry pushed the idea away with a sweep of his hand. "Do not fear, Yacov. I will breeze past two hundred with no problem."

Yacov pursed his lips again, a grim look forming. "Let's hope you are right."

CHAPTER 10

Cerissa stayed for a few more hands of blackjack, but her thoughts were on her encounter with the ponytailed vampire. Both Rolf and Henry were disagreeable types, yet the gnawing feeling it was her fault kept growing. She'd never been good in social situations, and she'd clearly blown this one. Give her a problem to solve in the lab, and she was on it. But wooing investors? Not her area of expertise. She decided to cut it short and leave before anything else happened.

She wasn't sure what to do about Blanche, especially since they'd driven to the casino together in Cerissa's car. Liza solved the problem for her. "I'll take Blanche by Gaea's," Lisa said. "Zeke, you walk our young friend to her car, make sure nothing happens to her, got me?"

"I got ya," Zeke said, standing up.

Cerissa swept her chips off the table—six hundred dollars more than she started with. Not a bad night for her pocketbook, but a lousy night when it came to finding prospective investors. She tipped the dealer generously and exchanged her chips at the cashier's cage. Zeke followed close behind her.

In the parking lot, she pressed the unlock button and her car lights flashed. Zeke picked up the pace, reaching the car ahead of her. She stood back, assuming he meant to open the door for her by his sudden rush.

He didn't. Instead, he stepped closer and reached for her.

Her lenses flashed a warning: attack imminent. She pushed at him with both hands, using the force to propel herself away from the car, preventing him from caging her in.

"How did ya do that?" he asked, looking startled.

Time to lie. "Most people pause before acting. I've learned from working around vampires that when they move, I shouldn't pause." She took a couple of deep breaths, trying to calm her racing heart. "Back away so I can leave."

"Wait." He raised both palms in surrender. "Did I get things wrong?"

"Yes." She looked straight into his eyes. He wouldn't risk the death penalty—any attempt to mesmerize an envoy violated the treaty, even if they weren't on the Hill. That rule applied *everywhere.*

Zeke scratched his head, looking puzzled. "I don't rightly understand. I heard on the grapevine you were lookin' for a mate. I thought we got along fine tonight."

"Is that what they're saying about me? I'm here to find a mate?"

"Yeah. You wanna live on the Hill, you need a vampire mate."

She glared at him. "I'm here to make sure the Hill is the right place for Leopold's project. I'm not looking for a boyfriend."

"You're serious?"

"Yes."

The arrogance fell from his face. "Ah, Cerissa, I'm sorry if I got the cues wrong. Here," he said, swinging the car door wide open and standing by it. "I'll hold the door, and you can get in the car."

She bit her lip. She could defend herself, but she didn't want to reveal too much. She glanced around—there were other people in the well-lit parking lot. He wouldn't do anything here, not with all the rules the Hill lived under.

"It's okay, no harm done." She cautiously walked by Zeke to get in the car.

He held his hat in his hand, rolling the brim. "Ah, you're not...you ain't gonna tell Gaea, are you?"

"I won't say anything if you won't." The last thing she wanted was more gossip.

"Deal," he agreed, then leaned over and kissed her cheek. "But if you ever change your mind, call me. You smell delicious," he said, licking his lips.

CHAPTER 11

VASQUEZ MÜLLER WINERY—THE NEXT NIGHT

Henry unlocked the door to the private room at his winery and left it open for Blanche. After her display at the casino, listening to her pitch seemed like a waste of time, but he'd made the commitment, so here he was to meet with her.

He inspected the room to make sure building maintenance had cleaned it after the last party. He and Rolf frequently entertained wine distributors here. A long oak bar occupied one wall, used for pouring samples. The remainder of the space looked like an oversized living room, which allowed their guests to mingle. A fireplace was centered on the wall opposite the bar.

He opened his briefcase and dropped Blanche's application folder on the coffee table by the large couch.

The *tik tik tik* of high heels on stone announced Blanche's arrival. He stepped to the door. "Please come in."

"Thanks, Mr. Bautista."

He offered his hand to shake. "Please, call me Henry."

She curled her fingers around his the way women did eighty years ago when men still kissed hands. He didn't accept the invitation.

"Okay, Henry it is," she said brightly. "And I'm Blanche."

She had the grace and eyes of a 1930s movie star, enhanced by a generous application of eyeliner and smoky eye shadow. She smiled at him, the smile making her blue eyes shine. He gestured to a chair across from the couch. She smoothed out her short skirt as she sat down, sexily crossing her ankles.

"Thank you for meeting with me," she said.

He took a seat on the couch across from her and motioned to the file folder on the coffee table. "I've read your application. You've been vampire, what, almost eighty years?"

"I was turned in 1937."

"What I don't understand is why you haven't accumulated more capital." Or why she wasted what little she had on clothing. He hadn't missed the designer suit, red-soled shoes, or the purse—the outfit had set her back at least three grand. "According to your balance sheet, you only have $100,000 in savings."

"Well, it's like this. I got bad investment advice and followed it. Now that's on me; I own up to my mistakes. My real mistake was trusting those suits in New York."

"You were living at the Collective?"

"No, I had permission from them to have my own place in the Financial District. I was working my way through various private equity firms—"

"What positions did you hold?"

"Ah, I meant, I was, like, hookin' up with guys, gettin' insider info…"

"I see."

She tensed abruptly. "If you're gonna to judge me for my methods, I'll just leave."

He waved for her to sit. "I don't care about your sex life. I am concerned about your use of insider information. We don't want the Securities and Exchange Commission investigating anyone on the Hill."

"Oh, that. You don't have to worry—I learned my lesson. I got too greedy when I thought I had the inside track. You know what they say about something being too good to be true. I had everything I owned invested in real estate derivatives. Borrowed every cent I could against my other holdings. I was overleveraged, and when the derivatives market crashed in 2008, well, I lost it all."

Hmm. Blanche wasn't the forgiving type. What did she do to the guy who sold her the derivatives? Probably nothing criminal, or the New York

Collective would have locked her up. They wouldn't risk an unsolved murder leading back to them.

He glanced down at her application. "At that point, you had fifteen years to join a community, yet you risked everything." Her recklessness didn't speak well for her. "And now you're feeling the pressure because of the treaty deadline."

"I'm willing to buckle down and do what it takes to earn my buy-in fee. I won't let them brand me a renegade."

"Tell me why you're interested in Sierra Escondida." She was dressed for Fifth Avenue rather than the Hill. "If you're accustomed to a New York lifestyle, why come here?"

"It's time I got back to my roots. I grew up on a pecan farm in Oklahoma."

"This was during the Great Depression?"

"Yeah, and the Dust Bowl—I was seventeen when one of the worst black blizzards hit our area. I'll never forget the dark dust cloud when it came at us. The dust overtook everything until the sun was wiped outta the sky."

"How did it affect your family's farm?"

"Oh, by then, Daddy had lost the farm. When the drought first started, well, it just about killed all the trees. He had to borrow against the next crop. You've been around long enough to know how that turned out."

Henry crossed his arms. "I am surprised with your background you were willing to risk so much in the derivatives market."

"In hindsight, you'd be right. But I was so close to having my buy-in amount—if I risked just a little bit more, I woulda had everything I needed to join the right community. Besides, Daddy never invested in the stock market. The 1929 market crash wasn't the reason we were poor."

"And in spite of your father's experience, you still want to return to agriculture?"

"Sure, it's what I like best."

"Well, tell me about your business plan."

She took a colorful portfolio out of her oversized designer purse. A photo of a vineyard was on the cover, with the words "Dystopian Wineries" printed on the cover.

"Here's my idea'r," she said, her voice rising a bit with her excitement, her Midwestern accent thickening.

She stood up and, in two steps, gracefully sat next to him on the couch. His eyes couldn't help but follow her lovely legs when she moved. She handed him one side of the notebook so it was balanced between their laps, her knee touching his. He moved away, and she scooted closer until they touched knees again. If he kept sliding over, she'd soon pin him against the armrest.

"Blanche," he said, moving the notebook so it no longer covered their knees, "this is a business meeting."

"Oh, sorry about that." She smiled and slid away a half-inch. Taking the notebook from him, she turned to a chart. "Women are the biggest buyers of low-priced wines—wine for everyday drinking. So we market to them using fiction as a tie-in. Right now, dystopian novels are hot. I figure our slogan is something like this: Dystopian Wines—for when you have that end-of-the-world feeling."

He cringed inside.

"When dystopian novels tank," she continued, "we phase out Dystopian Wines, and then it becomes Incubus Wines or Mysterium Wines or whatever. It doesn't matter what we put in the bottle, 'cause they'll buy it for the feeling the name gives them."

How could she sit there and say quality didn't matter? He hadn't made his winery famous by deceiving people into buying cheap wine. Why would he start now?

She finished the rest of her presentation and closed the binder so it was now in his lap, her fingers lingering on his. Her sultry eyes held his for a second. "Now you," she said, "you pride yourself on making high-quality wines. I'll be after an entirely different market."

He may not like the idea, but she'd put some thought into it. He wouldn't be competing with himself if he invested in her project. "This is what you want capital for?"

Her fingers stroked his again. "I'm looking for a partner. Someone I can work *closely* with."

"If you're granted membership in our community, will you bring a mortal with you?"

She gave him a coy look. "I don't got a boyfriend."

"I saw you last night at the casino—the fight over Dr. Patel."

"Oh, that. You thought I wanted her as a mate? Nah, I'm into guys. Not that I'm a picky eater, though—male, female, doesn't matter—blood is blood."

He raised one eyebrow. "That's why you challenged Zeke? To feed?"

A good thing for her she didn't have membership in a treaty community yet—the fine for public feeding would have been sizeable.

"I wasn't gonna bite her," she said, averting her eyes sheepishly. "Look, I lost my temper at the casino. I'm sorry, but Leopold's envoy broke the first rule of blackjack—don't screw it for the rest of the table. It pissed me off. I know, I can be such a drama queen sometimes, but believe me, for the right community, I can behave myself."

Henry stood, tucking the notebook under his arm. She couldn't behave herself for two weeks while the community considered her application. Why did she think her promise made a difference to him? "Let me consider it," he said. "I'll discuss your proposal with Rolf and get back to you."

Still seated, she raised her hand to take his. "I hope you'll say yes." She fluttered her eyelashes at him. "I think we'd make great partners."

After she left, he tossed the notebook into his briefcase, shaking his head. Her proposal belonged in the trash can.

And the envoy—should he believe Blanche's explanation? Not a challenge for possession, just Blanche blowing off steam over gambling losses? He closed his briefcase and locked the tabs. It didn't matter why. Neither of them belonged on the Hill.

CHAPTER 12

THE MAYOR'S OFFICE—THE NEXT NIGHT

Tig watched the mayor punch in Gaea's phone number, preferring to watch him rather than look around. She was already too familiar with every little pitiful thing in his office, right down to the most recent scratch on his credenza, which had resulted when the mayor's ex-girlfriend threw a heavy vase at him in a jealous fit. He'd ducked, and the hardwood suffered.

Jealousy was a frequent motive for violence—particularly in this town. *So strange.* Maasai women could have sex with any warrior in her husband's class—a five-year age range. If a warrior drove his spear into the ground by her hut, her husband had to wait outside until the warrior removed his spear. A husband's jealousy might rear its head if a warrior spent too much time with one of his wives, but the possessiveness she saw on the Hill was rare among the Maasai. Then again, she had loved her sister-wives more than her husband or any of the other warriors. When Phat took her away from her tribe, she'd missed her children and her sister-wives the most. The warriors were way down on her list.

Now the Hill was her tribe, and she was their warrior. Not that she'd plant her spear in front of someone else's hut—not with Jayden in her life.

She tapped her fingers on the chair arm. The mayor sat behind his ornately carved desk in an overstuffed, ergonomically correct recliner on wheels, and she sat on a hard, narrow guest chair. If she had her way, this would be the shortest conference call on record. She had more important work to do.

Five nights since the attempt on Yacov's life, and she had no solid leads. According to the town clerk, no applications were pending to turn a mate vampire. She expected as much. The culprit wouldn't be stupid enough to file the application before trying to kill Yacov.

But the attempted carjacking wasn't the reason for their conference call. Dr. Patel was the reason she sat in a chair designed to deter visitors.

"Hello, Winston," Gaea answered, her voice coming from the speakerphone on the mayor's desk.

"I'm going to let the chief take the lead," the mayor said.

Tig understood why. The uneasy relationship between Winston and his maker was legendary. She had to include him on the call or she'd risk offending him. While Gaea was the oldest vampire on the Hill—and that brought with it a truckload of authority—she wasn't on the council, nor was she part of the small group who originally founded the town. *Politics!*

"Hi, Gaea," Tig said, scooting her chair closer to the phone so Gaea could hear her. "We wanted to find out what you've learned about Dr. Patel."

"Well, I haven't noticed any concerns. I've tried to keep Cerissa busy and out of trouble. A few nights ago she went with Blanche to the casino, and last night I held a small soirée here to introduce her to some of the less important members of our community. No real problems, although I heard there was a small, shall we say, *squabble* at the casino."

Tig rolled her eyes, which brought a smile to the mayor's frequently dour face. Everyone in town had heard about Zeke and Blanche's little turf battle.

"Could she be a danger to us?" Tig asked.

"If I thought she was, I would have told you already." A huffing sound emanated from the phone's speaker. "Cerissa's behavior is consistent with her story. She's anxious to meet investors, but clears everything she does through me."

The mayor pursed his lips, as if considering something. "Perhaps I should ask her out to see how she reacts. There was something appealing about the fragrance of her blood—"

"She's not looking for a mate right now," Gaea said. "The dear child said so on more than one occasion. She even raised the possibility of bringing someone from another community to live here."

Now there was a motive—killing Yacov would create an opening on the Hill for another vampire to buy in.

"Who is she interested in?" Tig asked.

"She didn't seem to have anyone in mind—it was more of a general question for the future than a specific one for the present."

Tig tapped her fingers on the chair arm again. Still, as a motive, it was something to consider.

Wait. Blanche was looking for a community. Could that be it? But it didn't make sense. Blanche didn't have the money to buy in right now. If she killed Yacov, the Hill would fill the vacancy long before she could earn the buy-in fee.

"Well, you'll have to disabuse Dr. Patel of the notion of bringing someone here," the mayor said, punctuating his statement with a sniff. "We're very selective."

"I wasn't inclined to say anything to her. We may want to learn more about her plans, unless the council has decided to reject her project and ask her to move on?"

"We haven't discussed it." The mayor glanced from the phone to Tig. "I want more information about her before I put it on a council agenda."

"I'll get you what I have," Tig said. "I'm still digging into her background."

The mayor nodded. "For now, we don't want anyone to invest in her project. It would only make it more difficult if we have to oust her from the Hill."

Gaea *tsked.* "I don't know if we can keep investors away. She's quite insistent on meeting other Hill residents."

"Find a way," Tig said, adding "please" at the end, hoping her direct approach hadn't offended Gaea.

"One more thing," the mayor said. "We have a small problem I wanted to bounce off both of you. I'm getting pressure to allow mortals to vote."

"But it's just a small group of discontents." Gaea's voice carried a sense of disbelief. "Tell me you're not taking them seriously?"

The mayor's face looked pinched. "I appointed Yacov to meet with their representatives. A small exploratory committee."

"You did what?" Tig demanded. "When did you appoint him? Yacov didn't mention it to me."

"I appointed him shortly before he was carjacked. I've tried to keep it on the down-low. Most mortals are afraid to say anything. They think we'll kick them off the Hill if they complain openly. But Father Matt has heard from them in private. Many are unhappy because they don't have a mortal representative on the council." The mayor rubbed his bottom lip, looking pensive. "Yacov's good at diplomacy. He should be able to fix things."

Tig gripped the chair arm, restraining her urge to throttle someone. She couldn't protect the Hill if everyone hid things from her.

"Who knew Yacov was in charge of your committee?" she asked.

The mayor raised his bushy eyebrows. "You think Yacov may have been attacked because he's on the committee?"

"Mayor, there are vampires on the Hill who have no intention of sharing power with mortals. So yes, it's a possibility."

"Well, I reported it to the council in my weekly newsletter. It wasn't a confidential matter, but I didn't expect them to start blabbing about it—"

The musical tones of a distant door chime emanated from the speakerphone. "I better go see who is at my door," Gaea said. "Winston, I'll call you later to discuss your problem."

Tig rose, her back stiff from the poorly designed chair. She needed to consider this new information. "I'll be at the police station if either of you need me."

Cerissa lingered at the kitchen table after dinner, reading the latest issue of *Science* magazine. She looked up when Blanche and Seaton walked out from the utility room—she hadn't noticed another door leading to the basement, but there must be one. Gaea's house was a labyrinth, with the below-ground sleeping rooms off-limits to mortals.

Why didn't I leave the kitchen at dusk? The sun had set almost an hour ago; she should have gone to her room to read. Her irritation sat like sour wine on the back of her throat. She couldn't risk another confrontation with Blanche. She stood to go, and almost cleared the door when Blanche called out, "Don't be in such a hurry."

"Ah," Cerissa said, stopping in the doorway.

"Sit yourself back down. This will only take a minute."

She really didn't want to talk to Blanche. So why were her feet carrying her back to the table? Blanche plopped two bags of blood into heated water and, an awkward ninety seconds later, fished out a bag, snipped the corner, and poured blood into a glass. Only then did Seaton take his bag out of the water. She felt a little sorry for the maker-less vampire. She'd learned the whole sordid story from Leopold last night. Jane had been staked for turning Seaton without permission. When Gaea had told her Jane "moved on," she thought it meant Texas, not the afterlife.

"Gosh, thanks for waiting." Blanche plopped into a chair across from her and took a long sip of her drink. "I'm sorry about the casino. I so overreacted. Forgive me?"

"Ah, sure," Cerissa replied, not feeling it. "I should have stuck with the basic strategy. Then everyone would have won."

"Now that's where you're wrong. It's every girl for herself. I learned that early on. No one will watch out for you; you gotta make sure number one gets paid first."

Yeah, right. Except for Ari, no one had watched out for her. But she never put herself first. No matter how much she wanted to, it just wasn't done among the Lux. "I guess—" she began.

"Ya need to do more than guess. Ya need to remember the golden rule—'he who has the gold makes the rules.' And last night, you made the gold." Blanche tilted up her glass again. "Yeck, stale. Why can't we get any fresh blood around here?"

Cerissa furrowed her brow. One of the Hill residents ran a business collecting hospital discards. What did Blanche expect? Expired blood was thrown out for a reason.

The front door chime sounded. Everyone glanced in the direction of the hallway.

"I better go answer that." She stood quickly—anything to get out of this conversation. "I haven't seen Gaea yet."

She hurried to the foyer and opened the front door. Zeke stood there. What was he doing here? He had promised to back off.

"Evenin', Cerissa," he said, with a tip of his cowboy hat. The sound of footsteps came up behind her before she could answer. "Evenin', Gaea," he added. "Just thought I'd stop by and see if Cerissa wanted to attend the square dance tonight."

Shocked speechless, she stared at him. What part of "not interested" didn't he understand?

"What do you say?" he added. "We'll have a good time."

"I told you at the casino," Cerissa began sternly, and stopped. Making a scene in front of Gaea wasn't a good idea—better to offer a friendly-sounding excuse. She took a deep, calming breath and let it out. "I told you I don't know how to square-dance. Thanks, but I think I'll pass."

"There's a beginner's lesson at the start," Zeke replied. "It'll be real easy, you'll see."

So much for being subtle. Now what do I say?

Gaea gave one of her habitual clucks. "You should go. It'll give you an opportunity to meet others on the Hill."

Damn. Gaea was right. As much as she didn't want to go with Zeke, social events were a good way to fulfill both her missions.

"Take Blanche with you, too," Gaea added.

"Blanche?" Cerissa repeated. She definitely didn't want to attend another event with Blanche and Zeke.

Gaea gave her shoulder a little squeeze. "Don't worry. Blanche will behave herself. We had a little talk."

Zeke's smile got broader. "I'd be mighty happy to escort both you gals."

Oh well, no choice now. Maybe Zeke could act as an ally and introduce her to others at the dance. She could even pitch him on her project. After all, she'd made her position on dating perfectly clear.

"Sure, Zeke," she finally said. "Just let me change clothes."

CHAPTER 13

THE HILL CHAPEL—THE SAME NIGHT

Henry stared at the closed office door. Turning around and going home sounded good to him. His monthly tithe paid for the time, so it didn't matter whether he showed up or not. Yet here he was, because his *papá* taught him a man honors his commitments. Almost two centuries since he last saw him and the old man's angry voice still rattled in his head. He squared his shoulders, raised his fist, and knocked.

"Come in, Henry," Father Matt called out.

Henry opened the door and stepped into the priest's office. The familiar smell of old books greeted him, emanating from the shelves filling one wall. An intricate mandala, drawn with vivid inks, held the place of honor over the couch. Its concentric circles of reds, oranges, and yellows reminded him of the sunrise he would never see again.

"Good evening, Father," he said, sitting down on the couch. Father Matt was still at his desk, his pen poised to jot down some last-minute note. Henry eased back into the soft cushions and crossed one leg over his knee. The familiar surroundings of Matt's office calmed his edginess.

"I'll be right with you," Matt said, before returning to whatever he was writing.

Henry glanced at his watch. He was on time, even if Matt wasn't. He prided himself on being punctual. Prided himself on not making others wait. Prided himself on doing what was right. Prided himself— *¡Híjole!* Now he had another sin to confess tonight, a sin he'd confessed to all too often over the years.

As a young vampire, constantly moving from town to town, he had sought out the local Catholic priest to hear his sins. Not now. Matt wasn't Catholic, but Henry had no option—going to a Catholic priest in nearby

Mordida was unthinkable. Not if he was going to be honest in his confession.

The Episcopal priest stood up from his desk. With his neatly trimmed beard, he looked like a young John Lennon. "How are you feeling?" Matt asked, taking the chair opposite Henry.

"I'm fine," he said. "I saw Yacov last night."

"How's he doing?"

"He seems well. We are both concerned about the attack."

"Is that why you called me?"

"No."

Father Matt paused, looking thoughtful. "Shall we begin?"

Henry didn't like face-to-face confession. He'd spent too many years hiding in the dim light of the confessional booth, where he revealed his soul in the comfort of anonymity. But Father Matt insisted on a more modern approach.

With no choice in the matter, he crossed himself and began the ritual. "Bless me, Father, for I have sinned. It has been twenty-two nights since my last confession."

Matt sat quietly while Henry confessed his litany of sins. When he finished, Matt spoke up. "Is that all? Or did something else prompt your call?"

Henry grew quiet for a moment. "I—I have been tortured," he finally admitted, "by dreams of lust."

"What kind of lust?" Matt asked.

Henry looked away, his vision tunneling, the room fading out. His mind's eye saw past events he desperately tried to forget. Yacov's comments had resurrected them.

"Henry?" Matt asked softly.

"Bloodlust," he finally said, his quiet voice betraying his reluctance to admit it.

"Have you acted on these feelings?"

"Not yet," he said, lifting his crucifix from underneath his sports shirt. He began twirling it between his thumb and forefinger.

"What do you think is triggering your feelings?"

Feelings? He frowned and focused on Matt's 1968 doctorate diploma in psychology. He was here for confession—he wasn't some weakling who needed counseling.

"Henry? Please tell me what's on your mind."

He released the crucifix and looked down at his shoes. If he remained silent, maybe Matt would let it go.

"Henry?"

He kept staring at his shoes. They needed shining. How could he allow himself to go out with shoes so scuffed? Disgraceful.

"Henry, what's wrong?"

He took a deep breath. The good father wasn't going to let it go. "I keep having this dream."

"Describe it to me."

He still stared at his shoes. He had told Yacov he would breeze past two hundred years with no problem.

He had lied.

"It's early morning; the air is cold and still, the time when creatures of the night begin to look for shelter and the creatures of daylight begin to rouse. In the dream I'm chasing a woman. I can only see her from behind; her long, dark hair is flying behind her as she runs." He reached out, his long fingers sweeping the air in front of him, like he could touch her hair if he tried. "We are in a rural area, but it is not like our vineyards. I'm chasing her across a dry, grassy field. The homes are spread out, and she's seeking shelter, she's trying to get away from me. I know she is beautiful even though I cannot see her face. I want her. Try as I might, I cannot catch up with her."

He held perfectly still for a moment, his anxiety fading away. He watched the woman run and felt his legs move beneath him, the wind whipping past him, bringing with it her scent. The feeling of bliss brought on by the chase cradled him. He took a deep breath, enjoying the feeling of being happy again.

"And then?"

Father Matt's voice brought him back to the dream. "Dawn is fast approaching. She is running toward a house. It looks nothing like my real home, yet in the dream, I know it's mine. There is a large, shady pine tree in front, its branches hanging low, close to the ivy covering the ground. The ivy runs up the front of the house, covering it, and the house looks abandoned, smothered as it is by the ivy. I think in the dream, why would she choose my house to run to when others were clearly lived in? But I know the house calls to her. I cannot explain how I know it attracts her, but it does. She runs under the tree and I lose sight of her for a moment. It's starting to become light out, but the sun's rays don't touch me, and I reach the safety of the tree's shade unharmed. I almost catch her. She wants me to catch her; I can feel it. She's excited I'm near. I'm certain she wants me to make her mine. I don't understand how she could want to be my mate. Before I reach her, the dream ends."

"What would happen if you caught her?"

The question caught him off guard. His vision resumed its sharpness and he focused on the priest. "I don't know. I woke up before I could capture her."

His tone wasn't convincing, not even to himself.

"I think you do know," Matt replied.

Henry looked at his shoes again. They definitely needed polishing.

"Henry, what are you afraid of?"

A cold chill washed over him, hardening into a thick crust of ice. He stopped seeing his scuffed shoes. Instead, he saw the look on Nathaniel's face when he killed him, the look that would never leave him.

"What might happen?" the priest asked him.

"You want to know what would happen? It is simple, Father. I would kill again—so she could never leave me."

The horror he expected to see in Matt's face wasn't there. All he saw was the acceptance Matt had always shown him.

"We both know that's no guarantee," Matt said.

"I can assure you it is."

"Making the person you love into a vampire doesn't guarantee they'll love you forever."

"I am not talking about turning the woman."

"Then what are you talking about?"

Henry sat there, the burning jealous rage resurfacing with the century-old memory. Nathaniel had stolen what was his. He had no choice: he challenged the thief, the duel accepted, the lines drawn. And what happened after—

The crust of ice around his heart melted under the remembered blowtorch of jealousy's fire, flooding him with pain. A mortal sin, his soul damned forever. He buried his face in his hands. He had never explained his past to Matt or the guilt he carried; he could never explain, not without losing Matt's respect. Only a few of the original residents who had been present to witness the worst moment of his life still lived. And those few knew how to use lip glue.

Matt leaned forward and lightly touched Henry's knee. "You don't have to kill to hold on to love. You're a good man. You deserve to be loved for who you are."

"I am evil," Henry said, his face still buried in his hands.

"Tell me why you believe that," Father Matt said softly.

"You wouldn't understand."

"Henry, I've heard it all in this room. You can talk to me."

He lowered his hands and kept his eyes focused on them. He began saying the Act of Contrition, the prayer signaling his confession was finished. As much as he appreciated Matt's intentions, Matt had missed the point. He had missed the point entirely.

I can never overcome my past. No one can save me from it, not even God.

Henry put the car in gear and started driving to Mordida, where his mortal friend-with-benefits lived. Not that he wanted to see her—going to her place was more like an old habit, but he'd made the date a week ago.

Perhaps the next time I see Father Matt I should confess my compulsive inability to cancel appointments.

When his phone rang, he punched the "accept" button on the steering wheel.

"I just heard a rumor," his business partner said when he answered. "The envoy's looking for a mate and Zeke Cannon is following her around like a puppy dog. Word on the street is Zeke will challenge anyone who makes a play for the envoy."

"And this affects me how?"

"Mark my words," Rolf said, "it will be like the old days. There will be battles fought over her; there will be bloodshed."

Henry scrubbed at his face. His guilt sat too close to the surface for this conversation. Besides, Rolf knew nothing of those battles. *He wasn't there when I killed Nathaniel, or for the aftermath.*

The aftermath. In an attempt to pay penance for his unforgivable acts, he had forced the other founders to rewrite the Covenant, abandoning the more barbaric practices. Those rules should have been good enough. But Rolf had run for vice mayor on a platform advocating rigid restrictions— restrictions limiting how mortals and vampires could interact on the Hill.

If Rolf had his way, each mortal mate would never be left alone with another vampire not their own. While Henry disagreed, he understood why. Younger vampires tended to see every mortal as a temptation, and given Rolf's own little problem, Rolf's desire for strict rules was even more understandable.

"Henry, are you listening?"

"I heard you. I don't like having the envoy here either, but the treaty allows it, at least for a short time."

"She may be a spy, if not for Leopold, then for another community. We need to conduct our own investigation. Find out why she's really here."

"And how do you propose to do that?"

"Well I can't pretend to be interested in her, because of Karen..."

Henry was beginning to see where this was going. "I will not pretend to court her. There is something wild about her. I saw her at the casino with the younger vampires, and I didn't like what I saw."

"You don't have to be *serious* about dating her. Gaea told me Zeke is taking Dr. Patel to the square dance tonight. Just go and see who she talks to, see whether she's pumping people for information about the community, that sort of thing."

"I have plans tonight."

"The safety of the community is more important than you getting laid."

Henry scowled at the phone. "Easy for you to say. You have Karen."

"Look, call what's-her-name and move your date an hour later, and go to the square dance first."

"Hmm," Henry said. His friend-with-benefits probably wouldn't mind, and he didn't really feel like seeing her anyway. "I suppose I could stay in the background and listen."

"Precisely. Just be the dark, brooding vampire everyone knows you are."

"I do not brood."

"Henry, I've known you for seventy years. You brood."

"I do not. I just think about things."

"Very well, you don't. But however you do it, then, keep your distance. And be careful. I've also heard through the grapevine she's immune from being mesmerized. What was Leopold thinking, sending her to us?"

CHAPTER 14

Cerissa wore a knee-length denim skirt and soft white shirt to the square dance. When she arrived at the country club with Zeke and Blanche, a small crowd was already there. She purchased a glass of wine on the way in. According to Zeke, the room would fill up after the beginners' lesson. The three of them grabbed a table at the edge of the dance floor.

"How's the wine?" Zeke asked, sitting down next to her.

Since he asked for her opinion, she went through the steps Leopold taught her before taking a sip. "It's good for a Pinot Noir."

"You a wine connoisseur?"

Cerissa laughed. "Not really, but I did learn a little about them before Leopold sent me here, since the Hill's economy is based on wine."

"Not true." Blanche grinned knowingly from where she sat on the other side of Zeke. "Wine's just a cover-up—it's not how Zeke makes his money."

"You know I ain't in the wine business, Blanche," he replied smoothly. Turning to Cerissa, he added, "I thought of having my own cattle ranch, a large operation, but I reckoned there was too much day work involved. So I cut it back to a small herd, all organic and raised free range. More money in it. I'm also a part-time deputy on the police force."

Blanche continued to smirk at him. "You should tell her about your freelance work."

Zeke's eyes lit up, and not in a friendly way. "Don't you have someplace else to be?"

"Oh come on, we could be partners," Blanche said, smiling at him in a way that wasn't friendly either. "What you do pays way better than the wine business. Maybe I can do both."

"I don't need a partner," he replied, his eyes going solid black.

"Have you spoken with the founders?" Cerissa asked, directing her question to Blanche. Being in the middle of another public battle between Zeke and Blanche was the last thing she needed. "What about the founder who's a diamond cutter...Yacov, right? No interest in the diamond industry?"

Blanche turned up her nose. "He's nothing more than a hired hand, working for *mortals*. Vampires shouldn't denigrate themselves that way."

Cerissa frowned. Another reason not to like Blanche—*she thinks she's better than mortals.* Some New York vampires had made similar comments, but different didn't mean better.

"What about you?" Blanche asked her. "Got any investors for your mad scientist project?"

"I'm still working on it."

"Then ya should get out there and ask." Blanche stood and added, "Ciao, lovebirds."

Blanche was right. She should work the room instead of sitting here next to Zeke. She started to scoot her chair back to get up, and Zeke reached out, placing a hand on her forearm. "Hey, don't listen to her. We're here to have fun, not work."

She removed his hand and covered it up by taking a sip of her wine. Would it be rude to leave him by himself? Maybe she should wait until a little later, after the beginners' lesson.

"Do you always come to the square dances?" she asked.

"When I'm on the Hill, I try to. Even if you don't have a mate, you can dance at a square dance. There's always someone who needs a partner, even if it's another vampire."

"Really? Leopold told me vampires prefer dating mortals rather than each other."

"You learned right. It's not that we can't date each other, or that there might not be an attraction there on occasion—it's more a case of mortals having something to offer other vampires don't." She understood what Zeke was alluding to—human blood. "Besides," he continued, "it helps to have someone who can do your day work, ya know?"

While Zeke was speaking, she caught sight of Henry Bautista. He entered the room looking just as dangerously handsome as the first time she saw him. He took a seat two tables away, joining a group of vampires and humans. *So other humans can mix with vampires, but it's wrong if I do?*

"Do ya know how special you are?" Zeke said.

"I'm sorry?"

"We don't often get friendly with mortals who know what we are. I mean, before we bite them."

Oh no. This was beginning to feel more like a date than a networking opportunity. "Zeke, we're on the Hill. We can't date."

He winked at her, a conspiratorial sort of wink. "Not a date, missy. Just being hospitable, showing you around. Nothin' to worry about; no one's gonna get in any trouble."

Trouble? He was the one who was going to be in trouble if he didn't back off. "Ah, you said you freelance. You aren't on the Hill all the time. What do you do when you're gone?"

"I get things done for people. Government work, you might say."

"How do you keep what you are secret?"

"Well, it's not all that hard. The work I do takes me out of the country, so it's not like I'm reportin' to an office or something like that."

"And what exactly do you do?"

"Whatever they need."

Something about his glib answer felt off. Before she could respond, he asked, "What about you? What's your research lab gonna produce?"

"We have a number of projects underway. It's like I told Gaea—biologics."

She sounded too vague, even to herself. Leopold didn't want her giving out details. He thought a general description would entice them, and she thought Leopold was nuts. Why would anyone on the Hill invest in the lab until they knew the benefits? But orders were orders.

"I could give you a prospectus if you're interested," she added.

"Sure, I'd like to see that."

She used her phone to email it to him. "Once you've read it, let me know if you have any questions."

"Will do."

She glanced back over at Henry. He was staring at her stonily. *What? What does he think I did now?*

She smiled at him with a polite nod. If she acted like nothing was wrong, maybe he'd lighten up.

He turned away, looking peeved.

Oh well, so much for that theory.

The band started playing and the caller took the microphone, inviting the dancers to line up for the beginners' lesson. Zeke stood and offered her his arm. A quick glance in Henry's direction—he was watching her again.

She smoothed her skirt along her hips just to make sure it wasn't caught in her underwear and joined Zeke on the dance floor.

Henry's paramour had agreed to a later rendezvous, so here he sat, listening to Dr. Patel and Zeke. He found nothing suspicious about their conversation. It was just the usual inanities of small talk.

The way she glanced at him and smiled—did she think flirting would change his mind? He had turned away to avoid her eyes.

When she began dancing, he studied her again. She had dark brown skin and almond-shaped eyes, but her eye color was deep green, a bit unusual for someone from India.

Whatever he felt at the casino didn't return. She may have nice legs and a pert behind, but watching her didn't flood him with a strange sense of peace.

Lust, maybe, but not peace.

His fingers thrummed the table. When her gaze hit his again, ever so briefly, a *zing* of blood coursed through his body, the buzz of desire growing. He disliked feeling anything for her—even lust. And Rolf's scheme was ridiculous. If she was spying for Leopold, she wouldn't tip her hand here.

"Henry."

"Good evening, Winston."

The mayor strutted over and sat down. "We don't usually see you at the square dances. What brings you here?"

"I had a free night."

"Sure you aren't here because of Dr. Patel? I saw you watching her."

"Not at all, Winston." Henry crossed his arms. *Why did I listen to Rolf?* Being caught watching her was the last thing he needed. He forced the knots in his neck to relax. "I was watching all the dancers," he continued. "Square dancing isn't as elegant as the traditional dances of Mexico, but I may try it sometime."

"If you say so, Henry, if you say so. Still, I would have sworn your eyes were on her."

"Then you would be mistaken."

"Of course, Henry, of course. But if you should change your mind, it would be good if Dr. Patel found a mate here." The mayor nudged him and raised a conspiratorial eyebrow. "Strengthen our alliance with the New York Collective, if you get my meaning."

Seriously? A mate? Never in a million years. "If you think it's a good idea, then why are you not courting her?"

The mayor sniggered. "I plan on attending some of Gaea's mixers, but I don't want to seem too eager. Give her a chance to reject some of the other bachelors first, like Zeke—might make me look better."

As if anything could make this pompous fool of a mayor look good. "How long will she be on the Hill?" Henry asked.

"Marcus said we have to let her stay at least three weeks, maybe as long as four. The council can extend it, of course."

Henry shook his head. He should have said something to the town attorney before this. Marcus had given his legal opinion and now they were stuck with her for a month—no point in arguing the wisdom of it. "Well, I wish you all the best in your pursuits."

"Thank you, Henry. I'm glad to know you aren't interested. It's always difficult competing with one of the founders."

He hesitated. Should he continue with the plan to spy on Dr. Patel? If she was going to be here for a month, someone had to keep an eye on her. "I would not say I'm not interested. I may go to one of Gaea's functions myself."

"Well, may the best vampire win," the mayor said, rising and walking off.

This was why he didn't care much for the current mayor. For all of Rolf's complaints, Rolf was right. The Hill was designed to prevent competition over mates.

He watched Cerissa until the dancers took a break. He'd always thought of himself as a breast man, and hers were lovely, but the swing of her hips as she danced truly caught his attention. He could imagine holding those hips and... *Enough.* He walked outside to the adjacent gardens and phoned Rolf.

"I've learned nothing new and I'm leaving."

"Couldn't you stay—"

"No. I doubt my presence here is helpful to our cause, and indeed, it has been embarrassing for me."

"Embarrassing?"

"The mayor caught me watching her and thought I was interested. The last thing I need is to be tied to gossip about her."

"Wait a minute, Henry. Remember what's at stake. She's a threat to our community. It may be worth a little embarrassment to find out the nature of the threat."

"Rolf, there's nothing to be done about it tonight."

"Look—Gaea cornered me after the council meeting. I've agreed to host an outing for Dr. Patel tomorrow night. Horseback riding. You should come along."

"And just what use would my presence be? You'll be there; you talk with her."

"I'm the host. I won't have a chance. I'll get Zeke to help me with the horses—leaving her free so *you* can talk with her. Get a sense of her real motives."

"Perhaps she wants what she says she wants."

"In which case, you've spent a pleasant evening riding a horse."

The thought of seeing her again, the image of his hands on her swaying hips, sent an unwelcomed surge of longing through him.

He pushed the feelings away. "It's against my better judgment, but I'll be there."

He returned his phone to his pocket and glanced up at the bright array of stars overhead. Tig was charged with protecting the community, not him. He'd speak to Tig about her plans for the envoy. Why should he waste a month of *his* time spying on Dr. Patel? Not when the envoy sparked such unwanted feelings in him.

"She's not for you," he grumbled, and rolled his shoulders, trying to release the anger he felt.

He walked to his car and thought of phoning his friend-with-benefits to cancel. When he was in this kind of mood, it was best to be alone. He put the car into gear and sped to the main road. Maybe he should do more than cancel their date. It was time to end the relationship. Yacov was right, but for the wrong reason.

His phone call to her didn't take two minutes. Breaking off the relationship was easier than he envisioned. His friend-with-benefits sounded unsurprised, like she had been waiting for him to end their arrangement before this.

Sadness settled on his shoulders, the weight of his past sins causing him to slump in his seat. He didn't deserve pleasure and he certainly didn't deserve happiness. Given his past, he deserved the torture of being alone forever.

CHAPTER 15

The scent of fresh horse manure hung heavy in the cool night air. Cerissa walked toward the corral where Rolf and Zeke were saddling the horses. She didn't need the floodlights to see them, not with a full moon illuminating the darkness. She glanced up and found the Big Dipper, tracked the edge of its cup to the North Star. The guiding light twinkled brightly in the clear sky. What would it be like to follow it?

Her boot snagged on a rock and she stumbled. *Earth to Cerissa. Eyes forward.*

She looked around to see if anyone noticed her klutziness. The corral surrounded the front half of Rolf's property where the main road and a dirt trail intersected. Chief Anderson and Captain Johnson stood on the other side of the corral, heads turned away from her, along with Blanche, who was talking nonstop to Council Member Frédéric. His long mustache twisted out at the ends, reminding Cerissa of Salvador Dali at his craziest. Karen was nearest, but facing away.

She stepped up onto the split-rail fence next to Karen. Schmoozing Rolf's girlfriend could be her ticket to winning Rolf's support. The auburn-haired woman looked to be around twenty-eight years old, but looks weren't reliable in Sierra Escondida, since ingesting vampire blood slowed the aging process. And the dossiers Leopold gave her didn't include information about any mortal mate.

If mortals weren't part of the Hill's power structure, did she really want to live here and be a second-class citizen? She would enjoy more freedom here than at home, but was it worth it?

"Hey, Cerissa," Karen said. "I like your emerald shirt. Good choice."

"Thanks." The early spring night was warm enough, so she hadn't worn a jacket. Karen was similarly dressed in blue jeans and a long-sleeve shirt, except she wore a gun holster on her hip. "Why the gun?"

"Betsy? She's just a precaution. It's too cold now for rattlesnakes, but mountain lions and coyotes live up here. We sometimes run into them on rides."

Cerissa tucked her long braid under her arm so she wouldn't accidentally sit on it, and pushed herself up onto the top rail of the fence, turning to face Karen. Mid-turn she spotted Henry park a Dodge Viper at the curb and get out. She wasn't surprised he drove a fast muscle car. It went with his personality.

Then it occurred to her—he owned a vehicle named after a fanged reptile. Was it an inside joke?

No, he didn't strike her as the type who had a sense of humor over the car he owned.

He walked toward the corral, his obsidian-black ponytail pulled back tight, revealing a slight widow's peak. Where his straight nose might have hooked, it instead narrowed, widening at the tip. Not hawkish like Aztec or Mayan noses. She suspected ancestors from Spain and a good childhood diet—bought by Spanish wealth—accounted for his height, but indigenous genes from Mexico gave him his facial features and dark skin.

I hope he's in a better mood tonight.

He strode to the other side of the corral where the police chief stood. He moved with a sense of confidence and authority, like he knew what he wanted and knew how to get it. She cocked her head and watched him. His confidence intrigued her.

She nudged Karen and motioned in his direction.

"Oh shit," Karen said quietly.

"What's wrong?" Cerissa whispered back. Vampire hearing could detect the movement of a field mouse at fifty feet. If she wanted to speak privately, she had to lower her voice.

"I try to avoid Henry," Karen said. "It's his fault I lost my BFF."

"I don't understand."

"Erin was his girlfriend. She caught him cheating on her with another vampire."

"How did she find out?"

"Fang marks on his neck." Karen pointed to her own unmarred neck. Cerissa didn't want to imagine where Rolf had left his mark. "She woke up early one morning while he was sneaking back into the house. His collar was unbuttoned. Two red pinpoints were staring her in the face."

"Couldn't it have been, ah, a medical need?"

"You kidding? There's a protocol for everything on the Hill. Wrists are used when a vampire donates blood. A neck bite always involves sex."

"So what happened?"

"Erin stuck around for a month afterwards, but she couldn't let it go. He wouldn't tell her who it was, and she felt like everyone knew but her. She'd go to a Hill event, see a vampire, and think, *Is she the one?*"

"How did she know it wasn't a guy?"

"Henry? Some on the Hill swing both ways, but conventional wisdom says Henry isn't one of them." Karen ran her hand through her hair, pushing it away from her eyes. "Son of a bitch let her walk out and didn't try to stop her."

"I'm missing something here. I can understand taking your friend's side, but you sound, well, bitter."

Karen glanced down, her fingers twisting the moonstone ring she wore. All the Hill mates wore at least one piece of jewelry made of moonstone—the community's stone, a symbol of the mortal's tie to a Hill vampire.

"They won't let an unmated mortal stay on the Hill." Karen's fingers twisted the ring again. "Once they stop taking our blood, they're petrified the loyalty bond will wear off and we'll tell someone what they are." Karen's face looked hard in the harsh floodlights. "They made her leave."

"So what? Can't you still go visit her?"

"She doesn't remember me. It's one of the powers they retain from the old days when they used to hunt. Boom. Just like that, they wiped her mind of them, and Erin no longer knew who I was. Her memory of me was too entwined with Henry and Rolf and what they are. So they took her away from me."

But why? Sure, if he'd wiped Erin's memory of seeing the bite, he wouldn't be able to wipe her mind later if she left him. The trick only worked once. *So why doesn't Henry just tell her who bit him? What is he hiding?*

Karen sighed. "You'd think after a year I'd be over it, but I really liked her."

"Could it have been his maker?"

"Anne-Louise?" Karen said with a laugh, looking completely incredulous. "Nah, it would keep him under her thumb, and he's too old; he'd never allow that. Besides, she lives in New York."

"Does Leopold know her?"

"He must. She lives in the Collective's building."

Maybe Leopold could enlist Anne-Louise's support. Anne-Louise might be able to persuade Henry to back her project. "Is Henry on good terms with her?" Cerissa asked, mentally crossing her fingers.

"Not from what I heard," Karen said, smirking. "Their relationship is pretty messed up. Rolf told me anytime Henry and the countess get together they fight like cats and dogs. Besides, Anne-Louise prefers mortals; she doesn't want Henry around." Karen reached into her pocket and took out a hair scrunchy, then gathered up her hair, which was just long enough to pull into a ponytail. "Besides, he still resents it that she turned him."

"What gave you that idea?" Cerissa asked, watching Henry. He had left the side of the corral Rolf was on and was walking in their direction.

"It's how she did it. She was pretending to work as a prostitute—he expected a one-night stand and ended up with a lifetime commitment." Karen snickered. "Ask me later. He's almost in earshot."

Damn. Why can't I catch a break? She'd have to figure out another way to persuade him. Her gaze traveled from his shiny boots, up along his straight-legged jeans, and stopped at his belt buckle. *No, not that way.*

She swung off the rail and brushed her hands against her jeans to remove the gritty residue of splintered wood. In a few short steps, he joined them.

"Good evening, Karen," he said, with a slight incline of his head.

"Good evening, Henry," Karen replied, a formal chill in her voice.

Henry turned to Cerissa. "We were not properly introduced before Zeke pulled you away. I am Enrique Bautista Vasquez. My friends call me by the English version of my name, Henry."

"I'm Dr. Cerissa Patel," she said, offering her hand to shake. "I'm sorry about what happened at the casino. I hope we'll have an opportunity to discuss Leopold's project this time."

Instead of shaking her hand, he bent over and kissed it. A pleasant shiver went up her arm at the touch of his lips, and her root chakra woke up.

Stop that, she told her body.

He looked up at her, his lips still hovering above her knuckles.

Confidence—I can do this. She gave a nod in his direction. "I'm pleased to meet you, *Señor* Bautista," she responded in Spanish.

He rose up, his eyes meeting hers again, releasing her hand. "I'm impressed," he said in Spanish. "You are familiar with the naming traditions of Mexico?"

She rubbed the spot he'd kissed, forcing her mind to focus and translate his question. His dialect was different from the way Spanish was spoken in Mexico today. He pronounced the words closer to the way the original Spaniards spoke, substituting a J sound for the double L, probably the way he'd learned to speak the language as a child.

"Not that impressive," she answered in Spanish, trying to match his dialect. "For a gentleman from Veracruz, his surname always follows his first name. And your mother's family was Vasquez?"

"Indeed, but you have the advantage on me. Where are you from?"

She tilted her head and smiled. "An enchanting place, far from here."

"You make it sound so mysterious," he said, smiling back at her—a smile telling her if she wanted to play mouse, he'd play cat.

She had no intention of being chased by him. "I was born in Surat, which is on the Tapi river in India, near the Arabian Sea, but I spent most of my childhood in Europe and South America. My family traveled a lot."

He raised an eyebrow. "Surat? Another walled city."

"Now it's my turn to be impressed."

"Not really. As a child, I enjoyed reading stories about faraway places. Walling a city was not uncommon in the era I was born, a way to protect against invaders."

"I'm still impressed you know about Surat. My home was between the city's original inner wall and the later-built outer wall. Of course, neither protected my city from the British invaders."

Oops. She should have omitted that last part. It was never good to mix politics with business.

"What brought you to the United States?" he asked smoothly.

"Medical school."

He raised one eyebrow. "It was in South America you learned Spanish?"

"Yes, initially."

"That's strange." He sounded puzzled, his eyebrows knitted together. "By your accent, I would swear you were from my home village."

"Just a coincidence." From the look on his face, he didn't believe her.

"We should resume speaking in English," he said. "Karen doesn't speak Spanish."

"Agreed," Cerissa said, switching to English.

Henry turned to Karen. "When I first spoke with Dr. Patel, it was under strained circumstances." He nodded in Cerissa's direction. "I would suggest a fresh start, if you are willing."

"Of course, Señor Bautista, but please, call me Cerissa."

"And you may call me Henry."

She motioned toward the horses. "Are you riding with us tonight, Henry?"

"Indeed. It's been a while since I rode our properties' perimeter. It will be a good opportunity to ensure all is well."

Interesting. He was being much nicer than the first time, but he could be acting. Vampires turned on the charm when it served their purposes. Well, two could play at that game. She refused to flirt with Zeke; it would only encourage him. But Henry—he'd shown no interest in her before. Being charming in her own way wouldn't hurt.

Before she could say anything further, Rolf walked up, leading two horses. Henry accepted the reins to the palomino and then walked the horse a short distance away. The short-sleeve shirt he wore showed off his well-built chest and trim waist as he adjusted the saddle strap. Judging from his nicely developed arm muscles, he wasn't a stranger to hard work when he died—few people in the early 1800s worked out lifting weights.

"Cerissa, this one is for you." Rolf handed her reins to a beautiful chestnut mare with a white blaze on her forehead. "You have ridden before, yes?"

"I have."

"Good. She is generally a well-behaved horse, but sometimes spirited. Handle the reins firmly and you should be fine."

"What's her name?"

"I don't name my horses."

"I call her Candy," Karen piped up defiantly, "because she's so sweet."

Cerissa tensed, expecting Rolf to bristle at the comment. He didn't. He ignored Karen and went back to the corral, with Henry following him, riding the palomino.

She spent a moment greeting Candy, running her hand across the mare's forehead and sensing a basically happy animal. *Eager to run, not liking the corral, not liking Rolf.* She hoped there would be an opportunity to let Candy run. The horse nickered and nuzzled into her shoulder, as if reading her mind.

"Howdy, Cerissa," Zeke said, leading two more horses out of the corral. Turning to Karen, he asked, "You riding this filly?"

Karen took the reins from him. "Yes, Ginny's my horse. Thanks."

"Then this one must be for Frédéric. Hey, Frédéric," he called out. "Got yer horse here."

The council member joined them and accepted the reins from Zeke. "Dr. Patel? I'm Frédéric Bonhomme," he said, speaking to her from across the back of his horse. "How are you doing with your search for investors?"

"We're still early in the process. I'd be happy to send you a prospectus."

"I can't invest in it." He smoothed his long, thin mustache with two fingers, almost twirling the ends. "Leopold's project will have to come before the town council for approval—wouldn't be prudent to vote on a project I invested in."

"I understand," she said, forcing a smile. "Perhaps you'd like to see a prospectus, just to have additional background before you vote on it."

"Not necessary. Rolf has told me all about it. I'm not sure it's a good idea, having an unmated mortal on the Hill. We'll have to see." He mounted his horse and started it trotting in the direction of the dirt road.

Her stomach clenched. *Let him go. Can't press too hard, not yet, it'll just cement his opposition.* She preferred a unanimous vote of the council, but she'd settle for a majority. Liza liked her. That left the mayor and Carolyn, the fifth council member. *And the founders. Can't forget the founders.* She took a deep breath. She could do this—she had the entire ride to get Henry on her side.

She slid her small purse into a saddlebag, and then grabbed the horn of the western-style saddle, stepping into the stirrup and swinging up onto Candy's back.

Karen pulled up next to her on Ginny, and leaned over to whisper, "Don't let Frédéric get to you. He and Rolf have some odd ideas, but you're going to like the Hill. Give them time; you'll find investors."

Karen took off in the same direction Frédéric rode. Guessing Candy had been western trained, she held the reins lightly in one hand, and applied right leg pressure to turn left. It worked. She followed Karen's horse, directing Candy to the dirt trail, which ran along the edge of Rolf's vineyard.

The North Star was now at her back. Why did it feel like she was going the wrong way? She glanced over her shoulder to see it, wanting to turn around and follow the star instead. Henry rode out of the corral next to Rolf, talking about something. Was she the topic of conversation? She tried to ignore the strange feeling that gave her. *No need to be paranoid.*

She turned back to the trail. Floodlights from the vineyard lit the way.

She faced a low mountain range, its rounded peaks forming the shape of a potbellied giant asleep on his back underneath the night sky, with the taller, jagged mountains hovering over it. Off to her right, clusters of scrub brush and oak trees studded the buffer zone between Rolf's property and the next vineyard to the west. The floodlights didn't penetrate the dense oak forest, which remained masked by dark shadows.

Cicadas and tree toads clicked and chirped, their song stopping when her horse walked near their hiding places. She took a deep breath of the night air and was rewarded with the vineyard's musty-sweet scent.

Rolf passed her and joined up with Karen. The two urged their horses on to take the lead, with Frédéric near them, followed by the chief and Captain Johnson. Henry's horse trotted up, and he slowed it to keep pace with hers, riding between her and the vineyard. *Good.* Now she'd have a chance to bring him over to her side.

"I'm impressed by your knowledge of Spanish," he said.

"I learned Spanish as a child. It makes speaking it like a native much easier."

"You speak it excellently. Do you know other languages?"

"A few," she said, and glanced around at the sound of another horse approaching.

Zeke caught up with them, sandwiching her between the two vampires. He tipped his cowboy hat at her in greeting, and she nodded in return. He exuded a boyish charm, his smile showing off his cheek dimples. She glanced back over at Henry. Where Zeke was boyish, Henry was handsome in a more masculine way. Why was that more attractive? His dark eyes looked at her intensely, even when he smiled, and his strong brow line gave his deep-set eyes more power. His lips were full, enough to be kissable, with a perfect bow in the upper lip.

What would it be like to be in bed with him?

She gave herself a mental shake. *Time to get my mind out of the gutter.* She didn't want to be emotionally close to anyone, let alone a vampire. She kept too many secrets to let anyone past her shields. *So what's ramping up my reaction to Henry?* It didn't matter in the end. The Hill's rules allowed no casual fun, not while she was there on business. She had to stay focused. Although a little flirting wouldn't hurt...

"Do you ever go back to Veracruz?" she asked Henry, trying to get the conversation started again.

"How do you know I'm from Veracruz and not Spain or South America?"

"Karen told me about you."

"Not all bad, I hope."

"She tells me you make excellent wines from the grapes you and Rolf grow."

"I try," he said, with a formal nod of acknowledgement, sitting straight in the saddle. "It turns out being a vampire has given me an excellent nose for winemaking."

"In that case, I'll have to try one of your wines myself."

"I'll send a bottle to Gaea's for you."

"Thank you, you're very kind." She smiled at him, trying to hold his gaze. "And it was kind of Rolf to loan us his horses for the ride."

"Four of the horses are jointly owned by Rolf and me. It is easier to keep them in one place, so we built the stable and corral on Rolf's land. Zeke brought the other horses from his ranch."

"Then I should also thank—"

"Oh Henry," Blanche called out from behind them. "I'm glad to see ya here."

Blanche rode up on the other side of Henry's horse, crowding them on the trail, her stirrup almost touching his. She had a bright smile on her face.

Grrr. Not Blanche again. Cerissa wanted to rip the smile off her rival's face. *I was just making progress with Henry.* Why did the blonde vampire keep creating problems for her?

"Maybe we can hang out after the ride," Blanche said, her hand brushing Henry's arm. "I could answer any questions you have about my proposal."

"That's not necessary. After the ride, Rolf and I plan to discuss your idea."

"Well, if you or Rolf have any questions, just call. I can come to your place and we can talk." She fluttered her eyelashes.

"I will keep that in mind."

"I hope to hear from you soon." She wet her lips and smiled before urging her horse forward to join Frédéric.

Cerissa stuffed down her irritation. The way Blanche flirted with Henry made her look desperate. *Hmm. Maybe my idea of flirting with him is a bad one.*

Henry turned back to her. "And your project for Leopold, tell me about it."

"Once we have sufficient investors," she said, trying for a more businesslike tone, "we plan on buying a large property for a research lab.

We're considering Mordida, but would prefer Sierra Escondida. We'd have to apply to the town council for a zone change to permit manufacturing in the business district."

"You'll need Rolf's support for your project."

"And the rest of the town council, too. It'll mean increased income for the town from the lab's business tax."

Zeke touched her shoulder. "Not every vampire is going to want a mate who works."

She looked over at him, frowning. When was he going to get the message she wasn't interested?

"You presume I'm looking for a vampire mate," she replied, perhaps a little too briskly.

"Can't live on the Hill without it," Zeke said. "Now me, I don't see nothin' wrong with what you're proposing, having a business in town, but not everyone on the Hill is as understanding."

Zeke gave Henry a significant look. What did that mean? Had Henry already decided against her project?

"It's gonna take you a while to set up a new lab," Zeke added.

"That's true."

"You gonna stay with Gaea the whole time?"

"We haven't discussed it yet. But I could always get a place in one of the nearby—"

Zeke suddenly reined back on his horse. "None of that," he said to the horse.

She brought Candy to a halt and turned to see what had happened. Zeke's horse was trying to nibble on a wildflower growing near the trail— purple trumpetlike blossoms jutted out from the greenish-gray stalk.

"Darn thing has a taste for locoweed." He held the reins taut to keep the horse from dipping down again. She gently nudged Candy with her heels to catch up with Henry, who was a few paces ahead of them.

"Sorry to interrupt ya," Zeke said, riding up beside her and Henry. "But you know, Cerissa, I've been thinking about what you told me at the dance. If you don't mind me saying so, it seems kind of strange to pick our backwoods community—not to mention, a lot of effort on your part. Wouldn't New York be better?"

She couldn't tell him Leopold had insisted on the Hill. "I prefer living in the country over city living. There's a lot more freedom. For one, it's not easy to keep a horse in Manhattan."

All true, and she patted Candy's neck to emphasize her point.

Zeke shook his head. "Well, I just don't think the council will let you live in Mordida. They're mighty particular about that sort of thing. It'd be much easier if you had a mate on the Hill."

"Love is the only reason to mate," Henry said sternly. "And not to gain residency here."

She turned to him and widened her eyes. *Henry's a romantic? Really?*

They were in a low-lit area between floodlights, the moon having disappeared behind a wispy cloud. A flash of something caught her eye. A red light danced in the darkness on Henry's chest—a laser light.

She urged Candy forward and turned toward the laser's source to block it. Sewn into her sleeveless undershirt was a thin, Kevlar-like material, which would stop any projectile—the problem would be explaining it later. Her lenses found the source—an armed man lay in the distance between a couple of scrub oak trees, the nose of his rifle supported by a short bipod stand.

His bullet had to be made of silver. It would kill Henry.

She softly said "whoa" and pushed down on the stirrups as she stood up. The horse stopped. Now the red light centered on her stomach. She braced for the bullet—the impact would leave quite a bruise.

Then Candy took one more step.

The sound of rifle fire and hot pain pierced her arm. The impact twisted her backward, and she kicked free of the stirrups, free-falling a moment, then a heavy thud as she landed on the hard dirt road. *Can't black out. Can't.* She rolled onto her back, closing her eyes, agony racking through her from the fall, the nerves in her arm screaming from where the bullet tore into her flesh. In the next second she heard more gunfire, multiple shots from different guns. Then silence.

CHAPTER 16

Henry reined his horse around to avoid trampling Cerissa. He swung off before completing the turn, and Zeke's horse started to bolt, spooked by the gunfire. The cowboy got the horse under control enough to slide out of the saddle to land near Henry.

Feet on the ground, Henry ran to her side and almost collided with Candy. The horse had calmly stepped across Cerissa's body, blocking him. *What is wrong with this caballo loco?* He grabbed for the bridle but missed. The horse reared back, and he lunged for the bridle again, catching it. With a good grip on the leather straps, he tried to move the horse away from Cerissa. Candy struggled against him, striking him with her muzzle and breaking his grip. She pawed the ground, eyeing him as if to say, "Just try it."

"Zeke, help me get the horse back." He grabbed for Candy's bridle again and latched on. He had to get to Cerissa. A bloodstain bloomed on her sleeve, growing fast.

From underneath the horse, Cerissa murmured something incomprehensible. Candy whinnied and tried to lower her head, straining against his grip. "Go," she gasped, her lips barely parting to say the word. Candy stopped struggling and stepped away, her hooves gracefully avoiding Cerissa.

He quickly knelt next to Cerissa. For a moment, her image seemed to waver and then firm up again. He dismissed it—the smell of blood must have affected his vision. He steeled his willpower to ignore the liquid's allure and brushed the fabric away from her arm, checking for damage. Blood pumped rapidly from the gunshot wound. He pulled off his belt and looped it around her arm above the wound, tightening it to act as a tourniquet. He then ripped off his shirt and wrapped it around her arm, pressing down to stanch the flow.

Her eyes sprang wide open. "Fuck," she moaned.

"I'm sorry," he said, keeping pressure on the wound. "I know this hurts, but we must stop the bleeding."

"Hold fire," Tig yelled. Four guns had fired at the sniper, including her own. She galloped in the direction of his sprawled body. Additional hoofbeats told her the others followed.

"Spread out," she ordered, jumping from her horse. "He may not be alone."

The shooter lay flipped on his side, a tarp underneath him, his face partially covered by his arm. Multiple shots from her team had hit him, and the impact must have rolled him over.

His semiautomatic rifle lay near him: a Smith & Wesson M&P 15-22, a military training weapon. The kind of gun designed for rapid-fire center-body shots, using small-caliber ammo. Probably silver. She kicked the gun out of his reach. Not that he was ever shooting again—her bullet had shredded his trigger hand.

She quickly assessed the rest of the wounds to his head and chest. Not her shots; she wanted him alive. Using her foot, she pushed him over to see his face. Mortal. No one she knew. Where were they coming from?

Karen rode up and swept her flashlight along the edge of the clearing. Tig tracked the light, her gun drawn, searching for other snipers. Rolf and Jayden rode toward an opening in the dense brush.

"He came through here," Rolf called out, and reined his horse back to ride between broken branches. Jayden followed him.

Tig looked over her shoulder to the trail where Frédéric and Blanche had stayed.

"Keep lookout," she shouted to them, and knelt down. The rifle was fitted with an infrared laser sight, which produced a beam invisible to the naked eye. It explained why his eyes were covered by infrared goggles.

"Tell me who you work for," she demanded, leaning over him. Her shadow crossed over his face, her head blocking Karen's flashlight.

The shooter gurgled. Tig stripped the night-vision goggles off his face, taking bits of brain and hair with it. He let out a choking, strangled breath.

"Who are you working for?" she yelled. She pried his eyelids open. His pupils were fixed, staring off into space. She bit her wrist and forced his mouth open. "Drink."

"Your blood won't be enough to fix that head wound," Karen said, "not without turning him first."

She didn't need Karen to tell her that. "I want to bring him back, just enough so he'll talk."

The sound of the shooter's breath rattled in his throat. Tig squeezed her wrist to force more blood into his mouth, but with a final *whoosh*, his breathing stopped completely.

"Damn," she said, standing up. "What the fuck is going on here!" She threw the night-vision googles on the ground. "Go help with Cerissa," she told Karen.

"Cerissa? Something happened to Cerissa?"

Tig looked at her like she was crazy, and pointed in Cerissa's direction. "She was shot."

Swinging up onto her horse, Tig clicked her tongue, and reined her horse around to follow Rolf and Jayden. Behind her, she heard Karen's startled cry: "Oh my God!"

Henry glanced up when Karen rode over and dismounted. "What can I do?" she asked.

He ignored her. "Zeke, ride to Dr. Clarke's and bring him to my house. I'll take Cerissa there."

Zeke hesitated, and then grabbed his phone from his belt. "I'm calling the doc," he said.

The phone emitted a beep, telling Henry the call didn't go through. They were in a dead zone—he and Rolf could never use their phones from here.

"You're the fastest rider, Zeke." He leaned over Cerissa, keeping pressure on her arm. "The dirt road is a shortcut. You'll be at Dr. Clarke's in less than ten minutes if you ride quickly."

Zeke swung up onto Candy. His horse had taken off. "Don't worry, Cerissa. I'll have the doctor to you in no time."

He left at a gallop, a trail of dust following him.

Henry started to pick up Cerissa. "Don't do that," Karen said. "You shouldn't move her after a fall."

"She might bleed out if we stay here." He unwrapped his shirt from her arm to see how it was doing. "An arterial bleed—see how it still pumps rhythmically." His belt was too wide, her arm too small, for it to act as an effective tourniquet. "I have medicines at my house that should stop the bleeding. If Zeke can't find the doctor, I can call an ambulance from there."

Besides, there was always the healing power of his blood, even though he didn't want a blood connection to her.

He tied the shirt around her arm again, tighter this time, and gently lifted her. She cringed with the movement. Karen picked up Cerissa's braid and wrapped it over his arm. He took off, running down the dirt road, moving as smoothly as he could, leaving Karen behind.

His Viper was parked by the corral. A fleeting thought—should he carry her the rest of the way? If he drove Cerissa to his house, the leather seat might be damaged by bloodstains. He dismissed it—Cerissa's wellbeing was more important than his car.

He worked the door handle without putting her down and gently slid her onto the passenger seat. She stopped him from closing the door, motioning for him to come closer.

She's asking for my blood. He started to bite his own wrist. She reached across and grabbed his arm, stopping him.

"I can't," she said between gritted teeth. "Allergic."

He had never heard of an allergy to vampire blood, but this wasn't the time to argue it.

"In my front pants pocket," she said, "an injection kit. Get it out."

He reached in and pulled out a short, cylindrical object. Near the tapered ends were the manufacturer's letters, AB.

"It's cutting edge," she said, panting. "A hypodermic loaded with different medicines. You dial in the one you want." She gasped and held her breath, her back arching. When she finally let out her breath, she added, "I can't use my right arm. I need you to dial it for me—1-2-3-4. Simple."

He tried to do what she said—he saw the numbers 0-0-0-0—but it wasn't working.

"Imagine there's a wheel encircling each number," she said, growing paler. "Feel for where the ring should be and turn it. Picture it there in your mind and it will be."

With those instructions, he dialed in the first number and soon had the hang of it. When he finished, she grabbed it with her left hand and jabbed it into the bare skin of her neck. Moments later, she sighed with relief and stuffed the device back into her pocket.

He watched her wounded arm—nothing happened; blood continued to seep through the fabric tied around it. "Keep pressure on it," he commanded, taking her free hand and pressing it against her arm.

"Drive," she mouthed, no sound coming from her throat. He closed the door gently and got in on the driver's side. Soon they were on the main road, where he gunned the engine.

"What was the medicine you took?" he asked, shifting into second.

"Can't talk right now." She leaned back into the seat, her eyes closed. Her head lolled to the side.

At his house, he parked in the circular driveway and jumped out, moving quickly to the passenger side. Dr. Clarke drove up behind him, and Zeke bounded out of the car before it stopped.

"How is she?" Zeke demanded.

Henry tossed his house key to Zeke. "Open the front door. I think she passed out."

He scooped up Cerissa and carried her inside his house. Not sure where to take her, he stopped in the tiled entryway. Dr. Clarke spared him further quandary. "I need her on a firm surface so I can examine and treat the wound."

CHAPTER 17

Cerissa heard every word. She hadn't spoken because she needed all her focus to maintain control. The stabilization fluid did its job, freezing her current form and keeping her from taking the easy way out to escape the pain. But it wasn't enough—she had to use all her energy to stop the transformation.

She cracked her eyes slightly to see where Henry carried her—a dining room. He held her while the doctor whisked away a large floral centerpiece, and then he laid her on the table. She bent her knees, the hard surface of the table digging into her back, her braid trapped under her shoulder pulling her head at an odd angle. Henry lifted her and freed her hair, draping it to the side.

"Cerissa, can you open your eyes?" the doctor asked, disturbing her focus.

I can, but I don't want to. The stabilization fluid and blood loss were making it harder for her to weave the micro-changes needed to stop the bleeding. The doctor's knuckles dug into her good shoulder. *How am I going to repair the artery if he keeps bothering me?*

"Cerissa, look at me," the doctor insisted. "Cerissa!"

Damn it, he isn't giving up. She opened her eyes and saw a vampire peering into her face. *Dr. Clarke is a vampire?* He shined a light into her eyes, and then flicked it away. *No, I don't have a concussion. I've been shot, you stupid ass.*

"Has she had any medication?" he asked.

"No," she replied in a parched whisper and slipped her fingers over Henry's wrist, squeezing it. Henry looked back at her, puzzled.

"Did you give her your blood?" Dr. Clarke asked.

"She refused."

"Stupid mortal." The doctor lifted Henry's shirt from around her arm. The material tugged at her wound, igniting more pain. The sound of scissors cutting fabric followed, the cold air hitting her bare arm and shoulder when he peeled back the fabric of her blouse. "She's lost a lot of blood."

It doesn't take a doctor to know that.

He removed Henry's belt from around her arm and replaced it with a rubber-tube tourniquet tied loosely above the wound. He reached across her and, with Henry's help, fitted an automatic blood-pressure cuff on her other arm.

The machine *dinged.* "Eighty over fifty-five," Henry said.

"Not good. What's your blood type?"

"O negative," she replied weakly.

Dr. Clarke looked up at Henry. "Do you have any in your refrigerator?"

"I doubt it."

"Not surprised. It's a rare enough blood type. Hey, chief," the doctor called out.

Tig poked her head through the doorway. "Yes?"

"Check Henry's refrigerator for O negative. If he doesn't have any, can you call around and see if anyone has some? She may need a transfusion."

"Will do," Tig said, and left.

The doctor continued to inspect the damage to Cerissa's arm. "Did the bullet go all the way through?" he asked.

"I don't know," Henry replied.

"Help me roll her on her side."

The movement caused agony to shoot through her. Henry held her braced against his bare chest. His thick chest hair was already matted with her blood; a little more wouldn't matter.

The doctor peeled away her sleeve. She groaned when he traced his fingers over the back of her arm.

"What are you doing?" Henry asked.

"The bullet's still in there." The doctor ran his fingers over her arm again. "Close to the surface. Silver. I can feel a burning sensation as I pass by it, like someone dragged a lit match across my fingers."

She groaned again. *If that idiot doesn't stop touching me…*

"Probably a small-caliber, low-velocity bullet," the doctor continued. "Designed to penetrate tissue and stop. Lucky for her they didn't use a hollow point." He laid out blue sterile sheeting over her arm and tucked it between her and Henry.

"How can you tell the bullet type?" Henry asked.

The doctor's featherlight touch traced across her skin again and sent another wave of pain through her. "It traveled a short, clean path. Straight. A hollow point would have caused more damage, and a high-velocity bullet would have gone all the way through her soft muscle tissue. Lucky for you it hit her. Silver bullet hits vampire flesh, it instantly kills what it touches."

"Isn't it expelled?" Henry asked.

"I can see you haven't had much experience with silver bullets. Wish I could say the same, but trust me, your body wouldn't be able to push it out." She heard the doctor reach into his medical kit for something, relieved he was no longer touching her. "Do you have any allergies?" he asked her.

"No," she replied, pushing out the word between clenched teeth. He didn't need to know about her allergy to vampire blood—the fewer people who knew about it, the better.

The doctor pinned her arm tightly to her side and pushed her against Henry's chest. As Henry held her close, the doctor spread a cold solution over her arm, and the antiseptic smell of Betadine invaded her nose. The sound of tearing paper followed.

"What are you doing?" she asked.

"I have to stop the bleeding."

"Yes, but how—"

The bite of a sharp scalpel sliced into her arm.

"You fucking asshole!" She jerked from the pain, her control slipping away in spite of the stabilization fluid. She struggled to break Henry's grasp. "Haven't you heard of painkillers?"

The doctor swabbed her arm with gauze. "We don't have time for a painkiller to work. I have to find the bleeding artery and stop it. You're losing too much blood too quickly."

"We have time, damn it," she yelled at him. She was fighting the pain and something bad would happen if they didn't quit screwing with her. Twisting in Henry's arms, she finally broke free and found herself looking at the scalpel the doctor held. She freed her left hand and grabbed his wrist.

"Now!" she demanded.

The doctor looked at Henry. *What, does Dr. Asshole think I'm Henry's property? If he waits one second longer, I'm going to take the scalpel and use it on him.*

"Do what she asks," Henry said.

"It's her arm," the doctor said snidely, retying the rubber-tube tourniquet more tightly. "I'll need the portable ultrasound. It's in the bag over there."

Henry released her, and she rolled onto her back and closed her eyes, trying to block the burning, stinging pain radiating down her arm and the nausea welling in her stomach. Then she shivered. *Uh-oh.* She touched her face with her left hand, her fingers detecting a layer of cold moisture. She was going into shock. Dr. Asshole should have given her a painkiller and started an intravenous infusion of saline solution to compensate for the blood loss.

Idiot! When did he last see the inside of a medical school? Before Oliver Wendell Holmes coined the term anesthesia?

She opened her eyes again and saw Henry rummaging through one of the bags. He pulled out a couple of pouches before he held up one. "This is labeled 'US Scan.'"

"That's the one." The doctor looked into another bag and pulled out a hypodermic syringe and a bottle of a local anesthetic. "I only have lidocaine; it will work for about two hours."

He loaded the syringe and injected the nerves around the wound.

Using the portable ultrasound, he located the peripheral nerve in her shoulder and injected the anesthetic directly into it.

It made no sense to her. If he knew how to perform a nerve block—an advanced technique—why did he slice into her without a painkiller? What was he, some kind of sadist or something?

Five minutes later, her whole arm went numb. The doctor kept pressure on the wound, frowning at her the entire time, clearly not happy taking orders from a patient. When the throbbing pain stopped, she signaled with a nod for him to begin.

Henry rolled her onto her side. She couldn't see what the doctor was doing—but, thank God, she couldn't feel it anymore, either.

"Got it." Dr. Asshole held the bullet with surgical tweezers, waving it in front of Henry, who pulled back quickly, almost rolling her onto her stomach. The doctor dropped the silver bullet into a dish or bowl or something—the clink of metal on china. He grumbled as he continued to explore the back of her arm for a few moments then gave up. "The bleeder's not on this side. I'll close the incision once we find it. There— I've got it packed—help me turn her onto her back."

She could watch now as he worked. What good it would do, she didn't know—maybe she could stop him from making any big mistakes. There was no reason for him to do this kind of surgery in Henry's dining room. They should have taken her to a hospital.

The doctor started exploring the entry wound. "The source of the arterial bleed has to be the front of the arm," he said. "The tourniquet is holding it back for the moment, but we can't keep the blood supply blocked much longer."

"You're sure you can repair it?" Henry asked.

"Of course I can. The bullet missed the bone completely and didn't fragment. Straight, clean path. Ah, here's the bleeder. Let's see." She felt pressure but no pain. "Good news: it's only slightly nicked."

Using a cauterizing tool, he sealed it off. The acrid smell of burning flesh—her own—accosted her nose, and she sneezed in the direction of Henry's blood-smeared chest. "Excuse me," she mumbled.

"Bless you," he replied, grabbing gauze squares from the pile by the doctor and wiping her nose for her.

The wound oozed a bit, but the rhythmic gushing stopped. The doctor released the tourniquet, and it held. He cleaned the wound and applied a chemical hemostat. The wound clotted and stopped bleeding. *Finally, he did something right.*

But it still didn't make sense. If he wasn't completely incompetent, why did he perform field surgery? There was time to take her to a hospital. Or did someone order him to cover up the shooting?

Dr. Asshole added a topical antibiotic and stitched up the torn muscle, then closed the entry site and the incision in the back of her arm with a series of short stitches. Finished, he wrapped the wound in gauze and pulled a vial from his bag. He loaded another syringe. After asking whether she was allergic to any antibiotics, to which she curtly replied, "No," he unbuttoned her jeans, pulled back the waistband of her underwear, and gave her a shot in the meaty part of her hip.

She still gripped Henry's wrist tightly. Realizing it, she let go and, seeing the mark on his arm, mumbled, "Sorry."

"It is nothing," Henry replied.

Dr. Asshole rechecked her bandages. "She's in no condition to be driven back to Gaea's. Can she stay here with you?"

Henry hesitated. "Shouldn't we take her to a hospital?"

Tig answered from the doorway before the doctor could. "The hospital will report it to Mordida PD. I don't want them interfering."

She tried to sit up to see Tig better. So the doctor *was* under orders to fix her here. She didn't care why—she was in strong agreement with Tig.

"Don't move." Dr. Asshole grabbed her shoulder above the wound, holding her down. "You'll tear the stitches."

Henry furrowed his brow. "Are you sure, Tig? The hospital staff will be better equipped to care for her."

Tig shook her head. "No hospital."

Cerissa crooked her neck to meet Tig's eyes and nodded back at her in agreement.

"Any luck finding O negative?" the doctor asked Tig.

"No, but we have a couple of mortals on the Hill who are O negative."

Dr. Asshole rechecked Cerissa's blood pressure. "Ninety over sixty. Let's hold off for now on the transfusion. She may not need it."

"They would have O negative at the hospital," Henry suggested.

"No hospital!" Tig and Cerissa said in unison, Cerissa's voice a dry croak. They all gave her a surprised look.

Dr. Asshole reached into his bag to pull out another vial of injectable medication. He loaded the syringe. "In that case, she should stay here."

"Here?" Henry repeated. "We should move her to Gaea's house at least—Dylan can care for her during the day."

I take a bullet for him and he doesn't want me in his house?

"Her body is in shock," Dr. Asshole replied, giving her a second shot. "The less movement, the better. Just find a mortal to stay with her during the day."

She grasped Henry's wrist again, letting her eyes do the begging. He had to say yes. He'd seen the injector. She needed time to convince him to keep his mouth shut.

"All right," he said. "I guess she can stay here."

CHAPTER 18

Guilt hung heavy in Henry's chest. Foisting responsibility for the injured woman onto someone else was selfish. She deserved better hospitality from him than that.

"You'll be all right," he said softly to her. "I'll be right back."

With those words, she let go. He walked to the door and glanced over his shoulder at her, meeting her eyes. His guilt seemed to drain from his body, his chest relaxing. A sense of tranquility burrowed inside him and the warmth spread out to his fingertips.

He was making the right decision, letting her stay.

He left the dining room and stopped in the entryway, rubbing his eyes with the fingers of one hand. That peaceful feeling—the same thing happened at the casino. How did she do it?

"Henry?" Tig said.

"Coming." There would be time later to figure out what just happened. He followed Tig, his riding boots clacking on the burnt-orange tiles, the sound echoing off the smooth plaster walls.

Zeke leaned against the doorway of the drawing room. "How's she doing?" he asked.

Henry swept past Zeke without answering him, the sound of his boots deepening when he stepped onto the hardwood floor. Rolf and the other riders, with the exception of Jayden, were gathered in his drawing room. All heads turned toward him. He stood there in front of them shirtless and covered in dried blood—he felt like the star of a bad slasher movie.

Karen sat on the edge of his leather couch, biting a fingernail. "Will she be okay?"

"Dr. Clarke thinks she will be," he replied, crossing his arms to cover his bare chest. "But she can't be moved back to Gaea's."

Zeke stepped closer to Henry. "No offense to Doc, but I'd feel a mite better if we got her to a hospital. They'd be able to tend to her there."

"I'm with Zeke on this," Karen said.

Make that three of us, Henry thought. He didn't want Cerissa here, but it wasn't his choice to make.

"Dr. Clarke believes she'll be all right if someone stays with her during the day," Tig said.

Zeke gestured toward the dining room with his cowboy hat. "I know Dr. Clarke's a smart fella and all, but this just don't seem right."

Henry shrugged. "The doctor and Cerissa have agreed she will remain here. Karen, would you stay with her tomorrow?"

"Of course I will," she replied. "But if she gets worse, I'm calling the paramedics, and I don't want any noise about it."

"Understood. We will trust your judgment." He wouldn't have much choice in the matter—he'd be asleep and unable to protest. "I'll carry her upstairs to Erin's old room, but I'm sure she would prefer your help getting into bed."

He gestured for Karen to go ahead of him. Before she could, Rolf grabbed her arm, pulling her back. "I don't agree. Karen is my mate and I won't have it."

"This is not the time," Henry said.

"She doesn't belong in your home."

"Rolf, you have nothing to fear. Karen is safe—"

"I'm talking about Cerissa! *Cerissa* doesn't belong in your home. She's Leopold's agent. Now we have a chance to get her off the Hill. Send her to a hospital."

"Rolf, she's staying here," Tig said.

Karen extracted her arm from Rolf's grasp. "If she isn't going to the hospital, then I'll take care of her tomorrow."

"You are my mate, *Fraulein*, and you will do what I say."

Tig stepped between Rolf and Karen. "Rolf, this is for the good of the community. We don't want Mordida police butting in. Karen will stay here with Cerissa."

"*Ach! Pfui!*" Rolf scoffed in German, and stormed off, pushing past Henry.

Henry started to follow him. "Rolf, there is no need—"

The sound of the front door slamming reverberated to where he was, making further comments futile. He'd talk to Rolf later. Even if he didn't want Cerissa in his home, his sense of honor demanded he let her stay.

He escorted Karen to the entryway, the rest of them following. Karen climbed the stairs to the guest room on the second floor alone. The last time she'd climbed those stairs was to help Erin move out over a year ago.

He pushed those memories away. They didn't lead anywhere good.

Tig withdrew a plastic evidence bag from her pocket. It contained a piece of paper, the edges torn. "Before I go back to the police station, I wanted to show you this."

He accepted the small bag, flipping it over to see both sides. "Where did you find it?"

"In the shooter's pocket. It looks like part of an email, but the sender's name was torn off."

Zeke, Blanche, and Frédéric leaned in close to read it over his shoulder, so he read it out loud. "'Male Hispanic. Tall, thin. Long black hair, ponytail.'" He stared at it, reading it a second time. "The shooter was targeting me, not Zeke."

"That's my guess."

"And the envoy was shot because of me." He scrubbed his hand across his face. Why had she ever come here in the first place? Now he owed her a debt he'd never agreed to and didn't want. "The shooter was an idiot to try. Rolf's floodlights along the trail aren't strong. No wonder he missed me and hit Cerissa."

"Actually, his rifle was fitted with an infrared laser sight," Tig replied. "The targeting beam it projects isn't visible to the naked eye—infrared light is invisible; even the vampire eye can't see it, not without infrared goggles. He shouldn't have missed you with that setup."

"Invisible? In the movies, isn't it visible light?" He'd seen those scenes before, where the red light danced on the chest of the bad guy just before the trigger was pulled.

Tig rolled her eyes. "Sometimes police will use visible light lasers so the perp knows he's been targeted, as a means of intimidation, to get him to surrender, just like in the movies. But the sniper had military-grade equipment. The laser projected a tightly focused infrared dot. The dot can only be seen with special goggles, which is why no one saw it. How he got his hands on equipment restricted for military use is a good question."

A good question indeed—why would someone with access to military technology come after him? He took one last look at the email and handed the evidence bag back to Tig. "Did the sniper say anything before he died?"

"He never regained consciousness. Jayden took the body back to the station. I'm going there to help him process it."

"I would like to hear if you learn anything else."

"Certainly, Founder." Tig returned the plastic bag to her pocket. "If you had to guess, who wants you dead?"

Now he understood how Yacov must have felt. "I have no idea."

"Who knew you'd be part of the group tonight?"

"Rolf posted our route on the community's website, with a list of invitees. Anyone on the Hill who looked at the posting would have seen it."

"Why would he post the list?"

"Off-road bikers frequently use our trails. We allow it, subject to our permission. When Rolf or I want the trails to ourselves, we post it."

"The horses," Tig said. "You do it so the horses aren't spooked by the bikes."

"Precisely." He had other reasons for wanting complete privacy, none worth mentioning to Tig. When he was still with Erin, she had indulged him in an occasional game of chase to appease his desire to hunt. No one need know about that.

"What about Yacov's committee?" Tig asked. "Are you working with him on it?"

"Committee?"

"Yeah, the voting rights committee—for mortals."

A hot rush of anger shot through him. "He's doing *what*?"

"I guess you aren't." Tig gave a wry grin. "The mayor appointed a small committee to meet with some of the mates to discuss their concerns."

Were they insane? He looked toward the front door. Why hadn't Rolf told him about this? Why hadn't Yacov? He was a founder. They couldn't change the rules. *Damn. They could.* He was no longer on the council, part of the deal struck when the treaty was signed—stupid of him to give up so much power in exchange for peace.

"Rolf told me there was some mild discontent among the mates," he said, keeping his anger in check. "But I was unaware a committee had been formed."

"Okay, that helps." Tig's phone beeped, and she glanced at it. "Once I'm done with the body, I'll come back to take your statement."

"Please email me first. I should be available, once Cerissa is settled into the guest room."

Frédéric twisted the ends of his long mustache. "If you don't need me, I'll head home."

"I want to question you first—and Blanche, too," Tig said. "Are you coming with us, Blanche?"

Blanche gently grasped Henry's arm. "If you need my help, I can stay."

"That isn't necessary."

She gave him the sultry look she was so good at. "I hope you'll call. You smell so yummy." She ran a finger down his blood-smeared chest. "I could just lick you all over."

Repulsed, he jerked away from her. He needed to shower, and soon. "Go with Tig. I will call you when things are settled down."

Blanche pouted at him, but followed Tig out, along with Frédéric.

Zeke pointed at the staircase. "If ya don't mind, I'll wait upstairs for Cerissa. I'd like to see her once Karen gets her settled into bed."

Henry nodded his reply. "I'll carry her up once the doctor says she may be moved."

He returned to the dining room and took a tentative breath. The savory smell of blood still permeated the room.

To avoid temptation, he had held his breath during surgery. How could Dr. Clarke work around so much fresh blood without succumbing and taking a small taste? No wonder Blanche acted out.

The doctor reached into his bag. "The local anesthetic will wear off shortly. I've given her a shot of morphine." He pulled out a container of pills and handed it to Henry. "She can have one of these every four hours for the pain. I'll check on her once she's upstairs—I want to make sure the bleeding doesn't start after you move her."

Dr. Clarke picked up his bags, and when he cleared the door, Cerissa mumbled, "Butcher."

Henry stuffed the pill container into his pocket. "I am going to pick you up now and carry you upstairs," he told her. "You'll spend the night here and Karen will watch over you tomorrow."

Her arm was in a sling, immobilized. He carefully lifted her, leaning her uninjured side against his chest.

"Thank you," she said weakly, "for not telling the doctor."

"We can discuss this tomorrow night. Right now, save your strength."

CHAPTER 19

Cerissa felt strangely protected by the way Henry held her when he carried her upstairs. She rested her head on his bare shoulder, the light scent of his cologne mixing with the odors of Betadine antiseptic and dried blood—a memorable olfactory combination.

When they reached the landing, Zeke stood there. "She looks so pale. Is she gonna be okay?"

"She'll be fine," Henry replied, and took another few steps. "Karen, please turn down the bed."

"Just lay her on the bedspread. Once I have her cleaned up, she can get under the covers."

Cerissa's blurry gaze took in random details. Blue and yellow flowers covered the wallpaper, the furniture was maple, and a couple of chairs sat in one corner. The room felt empty, devoid of any personal touches.

Henry gently laid her on the bed and slid his arms away, walking off without saying anything. He seemed in a hurry to turn her over to Karen's care. Was the smell of blood bothering him, or was it something else? She closed her eyes and sank back into the soft pillows, too drugged and exhausted to care.

"Can you bring me something for Cerissa to wear?" Karen called after him.

"I will see what I can find."

The door latch clicked shut and Karen began peeling away the rest of

Cerissa's shirt. The cloth stuck to her skin, then broke free. At least the painkiller was still working.

A knock at the door and Karen cracked it open, accepting something. "Thanks, Henry," she said, and closed the door again. "This should work." She held up a man's tank top from a jazz festival, a green bathrobe draped over her arm. "The tank top armhole should be big enough to allow the bandages to pass through."

"Uh-huh," Cerissa agreed, growing drowsier from the painkiller.

Karen unhooked the sling and helped her undress. Her shirt was ruined; her beige bra and undershirt were now splotched a rusty red. Using a wet cloth from the adjoining bathroom, Karen washed the sticky blood from Cerissa's skin and then worked the tank top over her head, refastening the sling. With help, Cerissa slipped under the covers.

"The robe is here," Karen said, hanging it on a hook by the closet. "Do you need anything?"

"Water," Cerissa croaked.

Karen returned with a glass of water. Cerissa drained it. "What happened...to the shooter?" she asked.

"Dead."

Cerissa closed her eyes for a moment, gathering strength to continue, and then looked up at Karen. "Can you...can you please bring me something to eat?"

"You're hungry?"

"Uh-huh. Please."

"Let me check with Dr. Clarke." Karen opened the bedroom door and Zeke pushed past her before the door was half open. "Wait a minute, bub," Karen said, grabbing his arm.

"It's okay...he can come in."

Karen gave Zeke a warning look. "All right, but I'll be right back," she said, leaving the door wide open as she left.

"Howdy, Cerissa," Zeke said. He stopped at the foot of her bed, his hat in his hands, rolling the brim back and forth. "How are you feeling?"

"Sleepy. Hungry." She slowly let her eyes shut.

"The doc thinks you'll be laid up for a week." The mattress moved, and she peeked at him from under heavy lids. He sat on the bed next to her. "Are you in much pain?" he asked.

"Gave me a shot," she said, slightly slurring her speech.

"That's good."

She raised her arm, trying to find a comfortable position. With her arm lower than her shoulder, the stitches tugged, stretching her skin. It wasn't painful yet, just an icky feeling.

"Do you need somethin', Cerissa?"

"Ah, a pillow."

He dropped his hat on the end of the bed, retrieved a decorative pillow from the corner chair, and gently slid it under her bandaged arm. "I'm so sorry this happened," he said.

"It's okay."

The mattress moved again when he sat down next to her. He looked shaken, his hair mussed from the ride. What did her hair look like? Her braid had come partly undone when she fell, and Karen had finished unwinding.

He took her good hand in his and wrapped his other hand around it. She closed her eyes and drifted off for a moment, too tired to object.

"Ah, I wanted to talk with you," he said, and she opened her eyes again. "'Cause I have to leave right away. Ya see, my work's takin' me away for a few weeks."

"Okay."

"Yeah, it's unexpected, but that happens in my line of work."

"What work?"

"I'll tell you all 'bout it when I get back."

"Okay." She started to drift away again.

"If you need anything, call my cell phone. Even if you just wanna talk."

"Uh-huh."

He leaned over and kissed her softly, too fast for her to stop him. His kiss felt different from the time at the casino. With no one else watching, she supposed he was doing it because he wanted to, not to mark her as his. Still, he needed to learn to ask first.

"I wish I didn't have to leave," he said, grabbing his hat off the bed and backing away toward the door. "Truly I do. I'll be back just as soon as I can. I promise."

Chapter 20

Henry recognized Rolf's impatient knock and opened the front door without checking the security cameras. His business partner's moods could be volatile, but over the years, he had learned to live with it.

Why didn't I insist everyone leave and not come back? He still hadn't showered, and disliked being half-naked when everyone else was clothed. He'd been talking to Dr. Clarke in the entryway, discussing Cerissa's care. Rolf joined them without comment.

At the sound of Karen walking downstairs, Henry looked up. Seeing her there, it seemed so natural, as if Erin would follow her down any minute. He shook off the feeling.

"How is Cerissa doing?" he asked.

"Zeke's with her now. She's out of it, but she doesn't seem in much pain."

Dr. Clarke picked up his medical bag from a nearby chair. "That will change when the morphine wears off in a few hours. I should go up and check on her."

Karen stopped him. "She's asking for food."

"I don't recommend it. The shock and blood loss might upset her stomach."

"Are you sure? She seems insistent."

"Hmm. A good sign—I gave her an anti-nausea drug with the morphine. It must be working. Start with something light. Soup or broth. If she can keep that down, she can have something more substantial."

Henry gave a slight nod to acknowledge Dr. Clarke's directions and walked down the short hallway to the kitchen. He wasn't sure what he had—he hadn't restocked after Erin left. Rummaging through the pantry, he found a can of chicken broth. He opened the can and heated the soup.

Karen joined him and set out a bowl, spoon, and napkin. She popped the lid on the cracker tin, took out one, and broke it in half. The snap told him it wasn't too stale. She shoved the cracker into her mouth and nodded it was okay. He poured the soup, and she placed crackers on a small plate.

Karen removed an antique enameled tray from the lower cabinet and unfolded the legs. It was the same tray he had used to bring Erin dinner in bed when she was ill once. A small thing, but it marked a phase in their relationship when he still held hope for them.

Erin had had every right to leave him. He wasn't honest with her. But his hurt over Erin had become a thing of the past, just like all the other wounds he'd suffered since becoming vampire. Now it was back. *Enough.*

He pulled a small bottle of chilled sparkling water out of the refrigerator, added it to the tray, and left without a word, leaving Karen to take the food to Cerissa. He didn't want to deal with these feelings again. All he wanted was to shower and wash away both the past and the present. Everyone else could just see themselves out.

Propped up by pillows, Cerissa floated on a very pleasant cloud. Zeke had left and the doctor had checked on her, leaving a vial of antibiotics with orders to start taking them tomorrow. She closed her eyes and let the painkiller do its work, but roused when Karen entered the room; the aroma of broth enticed her into opening her eyes.

"Here you go," Karen said, setting the tray across her lap.

The spoon shook when Cerissa raised it to her mouth, some of the broth slopping back into the bowl. She tried not to slurp it, but she was so hungry that she rapidly shoveled the salty broth into her mouth.

"Slow down," Karen said. "The doctor doesn't want you upsetting your stomach."

Cerissa slowed down, hard as it was to do. She couldn't explain to Karen why she desperately needed food to replenish her energy. She bit into a cracker, and crumbs rained down onto the front of her tank top. She leaned forward so the flakes would fall into the soup.

When she finished eating, she lay back, wanting more. Karen picked up the tray. "I'll be back."

"Would you pl-please send up Henry?" The food had begun to revive her, clearing away some of the drowsiness.

"Shouldn't you rest?"

"I will. I need to… I want to…thank him."

Karen agreed, and left the room.

Cerissa closed her eyes. The pins and needles in her arm meant the local anesthetic had begun to wear off—an unwelcome warning of things to come. The morphine kept the pain distant, like it waited across the room from her, a caged wolf looking for its opportunity to escape. The bandages showed signs of bleeding. Not profuse, but still oozing. Dr. Asshole thought it looked all right. *Charlatan.* What she needed was food. *Real food.*

A tap at her door—she slowly opened her eyes and beckoned Henry to enter. He wore a clean shirt, soft black with a gold thread woven through the fabric. His slightly damp hair hung straight to his shoulders, and a light, warm scent followed him into the room.

In spite of her exhaustion, she still felt his magnetic pull—just enough of a tingle in key places to tell her surgery hadn't dulled her attraction to him. *Looking good. Definitely.*

Or was it the morphine talking?

Nah, he just looks damned fine in those tight jeans, a magnificent hunk of man candy.

Okay, maybe the morphine was talking a little bit.

He picked up one of the chairs and brought it to her bedside. Concern showed in his deep brown eyes. She liked the way he looked at her.

"Karen tells me"—she paused briefly—"the shooter is dead."

"True. He will not hurt you again."

"Was there any-anyone else?"

"No one was with him."

"Who…?"

"He's a criminal. Chief Anderson thinks someone hired him. Rolf has placed some calls, and we will see if any of our sources can provide information on the vampire behind this."

It was too soon for this conversation—the broth and crackers hadn't been enough. Her mind felt fuzzy and her ears were slow. Half of what he said didn't make sense. She was fading again. *Doesn't matter.* Hearing him speak was enough, his melodic accent a pleasant distraction. And his hair—he looked so darkly handsome, the way his black hair hung straight to his shoulders, framing his face.

Oops. She was staring at him, and he was patiently waiting for her to say something.

"Why do you think…a vampire?" she asked.

"Because we don't exist for mortals, unless they become part of a vampire community. They are too easy to mesmerize, to be made to forget what they saw and heard about us. So a vampire must be behind it."

"Oh," she said, gathering up her strength to continue. She had to get her errant mind off his sexy mouth and deep-set eyes. He swept his hair behind one ear with his fingers—very long fingers. What he could do with those fingers....

Okay, the drugs were talking again. *Focus. How can I convince him to keep his mouth shut about the injector?* She couldn't afford having the Lux pissed off at her if word of their secret technology leaked out. Letting Henry see her use it had been stupid.

"Ah...thank you," she said, "for not telling Dr. Clarke."

"Pardon?"

"The injector. Thank you...for keeping my secret."

"Why not tell him what medicine you took?"

Tell Dr. Asshole? Not going to happen. She closed her eyes. "It's new technology. No one can know...not while the patent's pending," she added, throwing in a little white lie.

He had to understand—after all, he was a businessman. Didn't wineries have trade secrets to protect? She crossed her fingers and opened her eyes.

"I see." He twisted the chain of the crucifix he wore. "I am sorry you were hurt on my account. The gunman was targeting me."

"I know...I saw the red light on your shirt."

He frowned. "You saw the red light?"

"Yes."

"But that's not possible."

"Why?"

"Because the shooter used an infrared laser."

She froze. Why did she volunteer anything? *Oh shit. The morphine strikes again.*

"Look at me," he demanded. He was out of his chair, his angry face looming over hers. "You couldn't have seen the light, but you looked for him. How?" His hand wrapped around her uninjured arm, lifting her off the bed. "Are you part of the conspiracy with the shooter?"

"No—no."

"It's the only way—"

She tried to twist away from him. "Henry, you're hurting me."

He let her go. "You will tell me the truth."

"I have."

"You want me to believe you saw infrared light, something impossible for a mortal to do?"

"Yes."

"I don't believe you."

She closed her eyes, shutting out his anger and reaching for sleep. "I don't care."

"You will when I call Chief Anderson and tell her what you told me."

A frisson shot down her spine. Her whole body started to tremble, and suddenly she was wide-awake. "You would—you would tell her after I saved your life?"

"I would do it because you're in league with the shooter."

"No, I'm not. I'm just an idiot."

She tried to stand. Her head spun, and he gently pushed her back onto the bed, hovering over her.

"You will go nowhere until you answer my question."

The dizziness made it hard to focus on his words. "You won't—you won't believe me," she said, and ran her fingers down her wrist. *Time to leave.* Feeling for her watch, she traced her fingers back and forth. *It has to be here somewhere.* Her breathing quickened and her heart thudded in her chest as she frantically searched for the missing timepiece.

Shit! Karen must have removed it.

"Where's my watch?" she asked, not thinking to mask the desperation in her voice. Then she saw it across the room on a chair, sitting atop her blue jeans, next to her cell phone.

She made one more attempt to stand. If she could just get to it—

In a flash, Henry was in front of her. "I don't want to hurt you. Sit back down."

She tried to step around him, but her head spun, there was a loud buzzing in her ears, and gravity sucked her to the floor. He caught her in his arms, holding her body pressed against his, her legs shaking. She looked up into his eyes. For a moment, they went all black, and she felt her desire stir in answer to them. Then his pupils slowly retreated, the dark brown returning.

Had her weak aura affected him through touch? Or was it just the closeness of her body? He lifted her back onto the bed. The tank top rode up her legs, and he gave a careful tug to the hem so it covered her thighs.

The rushing sound of blood in her head slowly died off. She ran her tongue across her lips. "Water, please?"

He handed her the glass Karen had refilled and left on the bedside table. She took a few sips and handed it back to him, sinking once more against the pillows. She didn't bother pulling up the sheet to cover her legs again. If she got the chance and the strength, she'd be up and gone.

He returned the glass to the table. "You will not be allowed to leave here until I have answers."

"I saved your life. Isn't that good enough?"

"You have thirty seconds to tell me the truth, or I'll call Chief Anderson. You can answer her questions. She isn't known for being gentle with mortals who are a threat to us."

"I'm no threat to you."

He crossed his arms, twisting his wrist to pointedly glance at his watch. "Your thirty seconds are almost gone."

She set her jaw. "Are you...an honorable man?"

"I am vampire."

"Yeah, I know...a big, bad vampire," she said, rolling her eyes. "What I mean...are you an honorable vampire?"

"My honor is not in question. Your trustworthiness, however, is."

How did she wind up here? Oh yeah, she was stupid enough to save his life. *Options, quickly, options.* Bluff her way with the chief? *And if that doesn't work? Disappear?* Her phone and watch were across the room. Her lenses didn't transmit—they only stored and retrieved data. She had no energy left to influence him with her aura. *Damn that fucking painkiller.* She had to think her way out, but her mind was moving at the speed of an Edsel when she needed to be a Ferrari.

He glanced down at his watch again. "You have two seconds left to answer my question."

What would Ari do? "Play by the book," Ari had taught her, a truism in the spy business as well as in blackjack. Okay then. First rule: when all else fails, buy time. But how? The book said—

That was it! The Scheherazade gambit. She could tell Henry the truth—well, at least some of the truth. Straight out of the playbook. Her great-grandmother had done it, so why couldn't she? *He won't believe me, but if I can hook his curiosity with the story, he might hold off calling Tig.*

She took a deep breath. "What I just told you...I can prove it. But you...you must promise me...you'll say nothing to anyone. Not Tig. Not even Rolf."

He didn't respond. His eyes held only his cold resolve.

"Go downstairs...tell the others to leave and send Karen up here. Once they're all gone...I'll prove it."

"How do I know this isn't a trick?"

"Do I look like I'm any threat…in the condition I'm in? I don't want them overhearing. Get them out of the house…and I'll prove what I say."

Henry eyed her suspiciously. She tried her best to look helpless, which wasn't hard to do. He stood and kicked the chair aside. "I will take these with me," he said, grabbing her phone and watch.

Damn. Double damn. How could I be so stupid to tip him off? She closed her eyes and focused on clearing the human painkiller from her body. What little energy the broth provided was consumed in the purification process—hunger gnawed at her body and pain radiated through her arm. At least she was clearheaded by the time Karen returned.

"How are you doing?" Karen asked. She stopped at the foot of the bed. "You're not looking good."

"I'm all right," Cerissa replied curtly, feeling edgy from the pain. At least she wasn't stuttering anymore. "I need something to eat, something more substantial than broth. You're going home to pack an overnight bag, right? Bring food with you."

"I'll check with the doctor and find out what you can have."

"Damn the doctor," she shot back, her arm on fire. "I need high-quality calories—chicken or fish. Even soybeans would do."

"Okay, don't worry. I have to eat too, so I'll pack a cooler."

Karen left, and Cerissa closed her eyes. *Now what can I tell Henry to get him off my back?* She was still mapping out her strategy when a strong knock at the bedroom door interrupted her.

Okay, here we go, ready or not.

CHAPTER 21

Henry opened the door when she called out, "Come in." He still carried her phone and watch, and slid both devices into his shirt pocket. Lines of pain surrounded her eyes—lying there, she looked beautifully fragile.

Sympathy should be one of the seven deadly sins. He couldn't let her pain sway him. He sat on the chair by her bed, crossing his legs. "They have gone. Now prove your innocence."

She took a deep breath. "First, do I have your word of honor you'll tell no one?"

Experience had taught him to be careful with what he promised. After all, she was the one who'd deceived him. Why should he make an absolute vow?

"Yes," he finally agreed. "But only if I decide you aren't a threat to our community."

"I'm not. A threat. I am...." She stopped. "May I have more water, please?"

He narrowed his eyes. "You are trying my patience," he said, and handed her the glass.

She took a sip and then held the glass, her eyes directed toward the water. "I was able to see the infrared light, well, because I'm not human."

He had already figured that out. "So what are you?"

"I'm part of the Alatus Lux."

"Winged light?"

"Or winged enlightenment," she said, her eyes widening. "You know Latin? I guess I shouldn't be surprised."

"I know many things. Before we're through, I'll know more." She kept staring into the water. He was tempted to yank the glass out her hand and force her to look at him. "A name is not enough. No more stalling—tell me what you really are."

"Ah, well, we're not entirely sure."

"Do you take me for a *tonto del culo*?" he demanded, his anger rising.

"No, I don't think you're a fool. We can appear to be human, even though we aren't."

He raised one eyebrow. "How? Are you fairy or werewolf? There are legends, but I have never met one."

"You believe all that supernatural stuff, don't you?"

He looked at her sternly. "I have no choice, given what I am."

"Well, *you* may be supernatural, but I'm not, not in the way you mean it." She took another sip of water and set the glass on the bedstand nearest her. "I'm not a fairy—I can't do magic or any of the stuff fairies are supposed to do—and I'm not werewolf either. The moon doesn't compel me to change back to my native form. Pain and stress do; they interfere with my control. The medication in the injector stops me from morphing. It's a stabilizer."

Now we're getting somewhere. She grimaced, her mouth twisting with pain. He hated seeing her pretty mouth so distressed, but he had to know the truth.

"If you are able to change shape, why have you not healed the wound?" he asked.

"The stabilizer keeps me locked in human form. Without food to fuel the process, I can't overcome it to heal the internal wound. Besides, if I healed it completely, the doctor would guess something was wrong."

"Prove what you say."

"I'll need the injector again." She pointed to her jeans, draped over the other chair.

"Why?"

"To reverse the effect of the stabilizer."

He removed the injector from her jeans pocket and handed it to her. She dialed in a number. "A reduced dose of the antidote," she said, and pressed the injector against her left hand. Finished, she held out her hand to him. "Take it in yours."

He accepted her hand, trying to be gentle. With her touch, he began to relax, a light feeling of peace invading him, a hint of sexual desire rising. He ignored it.

"Watch the fingers and the back of the hand," she said.

Slowly her fingers elongated and her hand became slenderer than a normal human hand. The color changed ever so gradually, until her skin was almost translucent, with a bluish radiance. Five fingers were replaced with six. Four were delicate, the two opposable thumbs sturdy. The change stopped at her wrist. She sighed.

He ran his finger across the back of her hand, which had the feel of fine silk. Her skin lightened where he touched it, the blue shimmering slightly from the pressure. He turned her hand over and gently touched the pad of a delicate fingertip. "You are not human."

"Told you so." She raised her hand to his face. "Prove it to yourself."

He sniffed her palm. "The scent of your blood is not right."

"It wouldn't taste right to you, either. I assume it won't hurt you, but I don't suggest drinking it—it's nothing like human blood." She looked distressed again. "I need to change back, or let the transformation continue. I can't stay this way for long."

She took her hand back and closed her eyes while her hand slowly transformed. Her blue skin gave way to brown, the sixth finger reabsorbed, and her fingers shortened. He picked up her hand and sniffed it again.

Human blood—tasty, pungent, seductive human blood. His fangs extended, his control gone. The stress of resisting her blood since the shooting had zapped his restraint. Bloodlust roared through him. He dropped her hand like it was made of silver, and fled the room.

So the self-righteous Henry was capable of succumbing to bloodlust just like any other vampire? A small smile crossed Cerissa's lips. Watching him run off was the most fun she'd had since being shot.

She closed her eyes and focused on the delicate process of repairing the damage caused by the bullet and the clumsy surgery of Dr. Asshole. The muscle fibers began weaving together, only to come undone the moment she stopped. When Henry returned, his color was better. He must have gone downstairs to feed. If only she could eat some real food.

He folded his lean body onto the bedside chair and looked at her suspiciously. "If your blood is not human, how can you be sure a vampire will be able to feed on your human form?"

That's his first question? Really?

"Do you concede I'm not human?" she asked.

"All you've proven is you can change shape." He picked up her hand and tentatively sniffed it, like he was sampling a wine whose pedigree was uncertain. "You could just as easily be a cursed mortal."

What, he wants a taste to prove it? She yanked her hand back. *Not going there. No we are not.* "Do you believe I have abilities a normal human doesn't?"

He paused. "Yes."

"One of those abilities is enhanced sight." She stared at the ceiling while she spoke, the pain wearing her down. "I may look like my human father—"

"You said you weren't human," he snapped at her.

"We, ah," she said, and stopped. She never considered herself human until he questioned it. "We need humans to procreate. My father, he was from India, his genes set my human form, but our Lux genes dominate, so we're Lux and not human." She looked down at her human hands. "Thanks to my Lux genes, I see a broader spectrum of light, even when human. When I saw the red light on your chest, I figured a silver bullet would follow. Silver wouldn't harm me the way it would you."

She didn't mention the Kevlar-like undershirt. He didn't need every little detail.

"Why are you here?" he asked, his voice dark and demanding again.

"Right now? To study your community, much like humans study indigenous cultures."

"Mortals have not always been kind to native populations."

"You expect us to be just as aggressive? We've lived here four thousand years and haven't done anything to harm humankind. We have a strong ethic against interfering with their free will."

"Four thousand years?" he repeated, not hiding his disbelief.

"My family—my people—our history goes back four thousand years, and then we hit a brick wall," she said with a shrug, the bandages restricting her to a lopsided movement. "From our records, well, it appears we were stranded here. The first humans we came in contact with called us 'those who fell from the sky.' Later we were called the Alatus Lux. The name stuck. But it doesn't tell us where—what place—we came from. Our origin seems to have been lost."

"How is it we've never heard of your people?"

"There aren't many of us, and after our first contact, we worked to keep our presence secret, just as you have," she said, telling only part of the truth. He knew about her people—hell, *everyone* had heard the story— he just hadn't put all the pieces together. "Originally, there were two hundred of us. By breeding with humans, we've increased our number to around a thousand."

"If you've been here that long, why so few? Did a great illness decrease your numbers?"

"We—we live for a long time, much longer than humans, but our ability to procreate, well, it's limited."

"Why?"

"We can't morph back to our native forms while pregnant. If you knew what it felt like to stay human for nine whole months, you wouldn't ask that question. The stabilizer—the medicine in the injector—it's based on a hormone. The hormone keeps us locked in human form when we're pregnant."

She didn't volunteer how they kept the baby from killing the mother when the mother was human. Some things just weren't meant to be shared.

He crossed his arms. "If your DNA is so different, how can a mortal man impregnate you?"

"Do you want the deep science or the big picture?"

"An overview will do."

"Well, each human parent normally contributes one strand of DNA—one from the mother, and one from the father. With us, there's a third strand, sort of an overlay morphing around the double-stranded human DNA, completely changing the double strand."

He looked thoughtful for a moment. "Where do your people live?"

"Once adults, we are free to move through your world so long as we don't interfere." She moved a pillow under her arm. The longer she stayed in one position, the more it hurt.

"You avoided my question."

"We have a base—the Enclave—and we can return to it."

"Where is it located?"

"Some things I just can't tell you. That's one—" She stopped abruptly, grimacing at the pain shooting through her arm. "Sorry," she said, closing her eyes and holding her breath, waiting for the wave of pain to subside.

Why couldn't he just let it go for now? Until Karen returned with food, only meditation would help her control the pain. And as much as she liked hearing his voice, all this talk wasn't helping.

He took a vial of pills out of his pocket—the painkiller the doctor gave him. "You may have one of these if you need it, but you will not postpone this conversation."

She pushed his hand away. "I don't want one."

"If you change your mind, they are here."

He placed the brown plastic vial on the bedstand, next to the one containing the antibiotic, and settled back into his chair, his brows knitted together. She pinched the arm nerve in her shoulder. The pressure relieved some of the pain, but not much. She closed her eyes and tried really hard to focus on peaceful thoughts.

"I don't know what to believe." His voice interrupted her meditation, and she opened her eyes again. "All this could be a lie." He made a sweeping gesture toward her. "You could be in league with the assassin. Perhaps your plan was to get shot and gain entrance to my home."

How dare he? I've told him far more than I ever should, yet he has the gall to call me a liar? Her nostrils flared and she held her chin up. "If I wanted to enter your home, I would simply enter it and you'd never know I had. I don't need anyone's help."

The corner of his mouth twitched. "Such pride. You do know what the priests say about pride."

"I should never have demonstrated my abilities so openly. Others might guess what I am." She stopped rubbing her shoulder. It wasn't helping. "I should have let you die," she grumbled.

"You don't mean that."

"If you keep acting like I'm the enemy, I will." She moved the pillow again, pounding it flat with her good hand. When would Karen be back with food? Much longer, and she'd morph into an oversized termite and start gnawing on the furniture.

"Why are you working for Leopold?" he asked.

She looked up at him. "Uh, it's a little complicated."

"Then simplify it."

"I let him feed on me to save his life. Is that simple enough?"

"And Leopold has not claimed you?"

She narrowed her eyes at him. *Neanderthal.* "You vampires may believe the world revolves around your fangs, but he can't 'claim' me without my consent, and I haven't given it. Besides," she continued testily, "Leopold was one of my teachers, it would seem wrong to be with him now. I can't get beyond it and neither can he—he will always see me as a child."

"A child?"

"I was much younger when it happened."

Her arm spasmed and began shaking violently. The injector lay on the bed next to her, and she scooped it up, dialing in a different number and pressing it to her naked thigh, just below the hem of her tank top.

"What is that?" he asked, his eyes following her actions but lingering on her legs.

"I increased the dosage of the stabilizer. It'll help me deal with the pain, but I need to eat to fuel the healing process." Her arm stopped shaking. She no longer risked morphing spontaneously, but the pain still bit with the teeth of a tiger.

Henry's eyes took on a faraway look. He sat there silently, and then something brought him back to the present. "I would like to verify with Leopold how you met him."

"Give me my cell phone."

Henry hesitated.

"It's not a weapon. I have to contact Leopold or he won't tell you the truth about when he met me."

He handed it to her. Using her good hand, she texted Leopold: *Henry Bautista will call. Answer his questions truthfully.*

She showed him the text message before she sent it. "Do you need Leopold's phone number?"

"I have it. We go back many years."

"Do you trust him?"

"As much as I do any vampire."

"Good. I hope—" She was cut off by the ring of her phone. "Hello?" she answered.

"Cerissa, my child, this is Leopold."

"You received my message."

"So. Henry Bautista wants to invest in our project?" He sounded almost gleeful.

"No," she replied, taken aback. "Something happened—I was shot."

"Are you all right?"

"I'll be fine, but he thinks I'm in league with the shooter."

"Why would you help someone who shot you?"

"I'll let Henry explain his reasoning. He'll call you shortly—please tell him whatever he wants to know."

"Anything he asks?"

"Even how, and when, we first met." She glanced over at Henry when she spoke those words—his eyes were watching her intently.

"I'll expect his call."

"Thanks."

There was a pause. "You're sure you're all right? You don't need me to send help?"

"I'm fine, truly I am." She ended the call and looked at Henry. "Leopold doesn't know what I am. Please don't tell him."

He looked at her with those cold, dark eyes. She saw no sympathy in them.

"I will take this with me for now." He grabbed the phone from her hand and slid it back into the pocket holding her watch.

After he was gone, she tried to stand again. He may have her phone and watch, but he didn't have everything. When he removed her injector from the pocket of her jeans, he picked them up, revealing her purse. *What luck!* Zeke had been smart enough to retrieve her purse out of the saddlebag, and there it was, hidden under her jeans.

She took a step away from the bed, but her knees buckled, and her body met the floor. A few breaths later, she began crawling on two knees and one hand. When she got to her purse, she popped open the flap and pulled out a power bar. *Manna from heaven.* Ripping the wrapper with her teeth, she stuffed the whole bar into her mouth, chewing and waiting for the room to stop spinning, and her energy to return.

Chapter 22

Henry placed the call to Leopold from the desk of his home office. Four rooms separated his office from where Cerissa lay in the guest room. It was unlikely she would hear him from there.

Upon answering, Leopold immediately demanded, "How did you let this happen to my envoy?"

Henry ignored the accusation and explained the night's events, including Dr. Clarke's surgery. "I shouldn't tell you this, but there was an attempt on Yacov's life a few days before Cerissa arrived. I'm sure you can see my concern. Could she have been in league with tonight's shooter and gotten cold feet at the last moment?"

"I would never use an envoy that way. Unlike you, I honor my agreements."

Henry suppressed a growl. It was fortunate for Leopold they were on the phone, or the New York CEO would be wearing Henry's silver knife through his spleen. The knife sat securely in his gun safe, but for Leopold, he'd take it out of retirement. "She told me you met her when she was a child."

A long pause—when Leopold spoke, he sounded guarded. "What *exactly* did she tell you?"

"The same thing she told you—you would confirm the truth of how you met her."

Another pause. "In the 1820s, before I came to New York, I was advisor to Count Gustaferro in Italy—a minor count, but one with designs on gaining power in the region."

"You've mentioned him before."

"It was the last time I would try meddling in mortal politics, as it almost cost me my life. Mortal politicians are not to be trusted."

Nothing new there—Leopold had been outspoken against the formation of Sierra Escondida for just that reason. "What does Gustaferro have to do with Cerissa?"

"I'm getting there. I'd been the count's advisor for over a year when Cerissa was sent to his court to be fostered. I assumed her people placed her there to find a husband. She was fourteen, or so I was told, just beginning to bud into womanhood—"

"You're telling me she is over two hundred years old?"

"Precisely."

"Two hundred," Henry repeated. He reached for his cross. "Her appearance—didn't it raise questions back then?"

"I had assumed she was the bastard child of a wealthy European military officer who had served in India or Egypt. At the count's request, I tutored her in politics and history. We worked together for many months, until I fell out of favor with the count.

"The count didn't know what I was," Leopold continued. "He locked me in his estate basement, a windowless granite hole, having lured me there under false pretenses. He was very religious, and a large silver cross covered the only door into the basement, woven into an ornate silver grille running floor to ceiling. With the cell door closed, I was trapped by the silver barrier it created. During the day, a food tray was shoved through a slot under the door. I would dump the food down the dung hole to make it look like I was eating, so they wouldn't grow suspicious. I slept during the day and paced at night, wondering when I would have the opportunity to mesmerize a guard. Of course, I grew hungry."

When Henry first heard the story, he figured Leopold had gnawed on a few rats to survive. So there was more to the tale.

"Somehow Cerissa convinced the count to allow her tutoring to continue. The guards brought her to me and left her with me unguarded."

"They left her alone with a prisoner?" Henry asked, his voice rising with disbelief.

"What can I say? She can be persuasive when she wants to be. She brought with her the books and papers from our previous lessons and placed them on the small table. A table, bed, and chair were all the furniture in that dank cell. She sat down on the chair, used a small knife to open a vein in her wrist, and held it out to me. At first I refused, fearful I might harm her, but the blood began to pool and drip. I took her wrist and licked the blood from it before wrapping my lips over the wound."

"So what? She fed you. Is there a point here?"

"When I finished, she seemed fine. Before my eyes, I watched as her wrist healed. She told me not to fear. My secret was safe with her. She explained she came from a family of people who were long-lived and had remarkable regenerative powers. She understood the need for secrecy and returned each night with the knife to feed me. Eventually, the count decided to release me, having realized I was not behind whatever paranoid delusion had gripped him. I suspect Cerissa had a part in changing his mind."

"And you offered her your blood?"

"She told you that? Did she also tell you it made her violently ill?"

"She mentioned she was allergic to vampire blood."

"I guess you could call it an allergic reaction, though the symptoms were closer to food poisoning. I stayed with her all night, giving what comfort I could. By the next evening she was well. Not long afterwards, she left the court. I didn't hear from her again until a few years ago."

Henry rubbed his hand across the tight muscles in his forehead. "You still haven't answered my question. Could she be responsible for the attacks?"

"The odds are so unlikely I would bet my entire fortune against it. She had no trouble finding me in New York. She knew all about our communities, where they were located, and our treaty. She'd missed a few things, but not much. If she wanted to hurt us, she could have done so without ever exposing herself."

"How did you know it was her, and not some relative posing as her?"

"Aside from the physical resemblance, I recognized her blood, the unique scent of her. Besides, she knew too much, too many details about the time she spent with me as my student. I have no doubt it's her."

"Having found you, what did she want?"

"My sponsorship. I liked the idea she pitched, so I'm backing it. It's going to make me *very* rich."

"What is she researching?"

"It has to do with cloning. I can't say more; we have to protect our trade secrets, you know."

"What do you believe she is?"

"Some form of Dorian Gray? She doesn't sound like she's sold her soul to the devil, but one can never tell," Leopold said with a dark laugh. "Quite frankly, I haven't pushed her on it. I felt she would tell me in her own time."

Henry pressed his lips together to keep his hot anger contained. Leopold had blindly turned her loose on Sierra Escondida? What if her plan was to destroy them all? "Is she a supernatural being?"

"I doubt it—she tastes human—but I can tell you this. I've watched her around both mortals and vampires, and she seems to have an influence, well, call it an aura. Over time, people relax around her, they seem charmed by her, but it's different from our mesmerizing abilities."

"How can you trust her?"

"If she wanted to harm us, she already had enough information to do so easily." Leopold paused. "Why don't you trust her?"

Henry drummed his fingers on his desk. How to answer and keep his promise to Cerissa? He should never have given his word. Still, she'd saved his life—he was honor-bound to protect her for now. He stayed silent.

Leopold chuckled. "Henry, stop being so paranoid. I wouldn't put my reputation on the line unless I believed what she told me. I've tasted her character—she has no intent to harm us."

"I see. Well, if you think of anything to shed light on our situation, please call me."

"I will. But I'm convinced the shootings aren't related to Cerissa."

Henry ended the call, his fingers twirling his crucifix. How could Leopold endanger the Hill by sending this creature to them?

He took Cerissa's watch and phone out of his pocket. He turned the watch over. It looked like any normal timepiece. Why was it so important to her? An emergency signal? Or a communication device? Then why have the cell phone? The watch was wafer thin, much too small to hide anything in, and there was no indication of an opening. He touched the glass cover over the watch. Nothing happened.

The phone looked normal as well. He opened it and scrolled through her contacts. The only numbers listed were for Leopold, Karen, Zeke, and a couple of real estate agents. No emails—the only texts were the ones she'd exchanged with Leopold. He made a note of her phone number.

The true nature of these devices could be hidden behind a layer of ordinary usage. He turned to his computer and scrolled through his email—nothing new from Rolf. Then he saw an email from the chief—Tig wanted to interview him about tonight's shooting. He wrote back asking to postpone the interview until tomorrow night, using Cerissa's care as his excuse. In truth, he had too much to figure out. Was Cerissa lying? Was Leopold lying? Or had Leopold become a doddering old fool?

He needed more information about the New York situation. He picked up his phone and hit speed dial.

"Good evening, Enrique," the Countess Anne-Louise d'Hardancourt Brillon de Jouy said upon answering.

To his annoyance, she insisted on calling him by the name he had when she turned him—a petty reminder of her power over him.

"To what do I owe this call?" she asked. "It's much too soon for you to come to New York."

"True. We have a bit of a problem on the Hill."

"And you want my opinion on it? Has the sun begun circling the earth?"

After what Cerissa told him, it certainly felt like it. Why else would he call the woman who'd condemned him to this existence? "Anne-Louise, you do me an injustice. I have always valued your opinion," he lied.

"I believe the last time I offered my insight, you referred to me as soft-headed."

"If I gave offense, I apologize."

She proceeded to run down her list of grievances against him—at least, the more recent ones. He did his best to appease his maker—he needed to get an insider's view—but after a few minutes of her tirade, he was ready to slam down the phone.

"Anne-Louise, please," he finally interrupted her, "I don't have all night. This is a pressing matter."

"Fine. What is so bloody damn important you actually thought to call me?"

"There have been two shootings on the Hill. The first was an attempt on Yacov's life—the shooters fired silver bullets, but were killed before they could hurt him. The second was tonight. The shooter was aiming at me, but hit a mortal instead, again firing silver bullets."

"*Ah oui?*" she responded nonchalantly.

At least he had her attention, even if she seemed unconcerned he could have met his final death tonight. "Is there anyone in the New York Collective who might carry a grudge against either Yacov or me, or the Hill in general?"

"I would have to ponder it."

That wasn't helpful. "Are you aware of any political maneuvering on Leopold's part?"

"Nothing that would affect *you*," she said condescendingly. "And we all know how the world revolves around you."

"What about the New York board?" he asked levelly, keeping his anger bottled up once more.

"The board of directors were all reelected last month, unopposed. Leopold is still CEO of the Collective. Again, I don't see how this has anything to do with your little problem."

"Might they try for a hostile takeover of Sierra Escondida?"

"If the board were making a play for the Hill, I would have heard."

"Wouldn't they keep it hidden from you because of our connection?"

"Don't flatter yourself. Besides, I have sources the board isn't aware of. I want nothing to happen to your little experiment in democracy—I have no desire to have you on my doorstep, looking for a home."

As if that would *ever* happen. "If you hear of anything, please call me."

"You may rely upon it. I never thought your experiment in mimicking the government of mortals would ever work. I'm surprised it has lasted this long, but I would not want any *external* force to break it apart."

But she'd be happy if it imploded on its own. "*Buenas noches,*" he said, and clicked off. He slammed the phone down on the desk. *¡Puta!* Talking with her was impossible. Why did he even try?

He picked up an index card and began outlining the options:

C is lying—No risk to community
   • Lying for own reasons

C is lying—Risk to community
   • Conspiracy with NY
   • Conspiracy with "X"
   • Threat from "her" people

C is telling the truth
   • Missed opportunity to learn about her people

Anne-Louise's information could probably be trusted. She may be unpleasant at times, but his maker didn't want him dead—at least, not as long as he had what she wanted.

So the Collective's board wasn't behind the attacks. Still, he couldn't rule out Leopold acting on his own. But it made no sense—why would Cerissa put herself in the way of a bullet if she meant to harm his community?

He tapped his pen on the third point: "C is telling the truth." Was it fear or excitement he felt? It was often hard to tell the two feelings apart. The shadow of her shapely body underneath her tank top had awakened feelings better left ignored, and the fragrance of her blood had sent him fleeing the room—both bad signs.

He rubbed his eyelids with the fingers of one hand and looked at the card again, afraid to let his feelings cloud his judgment. Yacov had been right. After almost two hundred years of undead living, the ennui sometimes weighed heavily on him. The thought of being the first to know about the Alatus Lux, to learn their hidden knowledge—well, his desire to believe her threatened to shove his fear aside.

He threw the pen down on his desk. He hadn't become a successful businessman by avoiding risk. His gut told him Cerissa wasn't lying, but his head wasn't buying it. He slid the card into his back pocket and went to check on her, determined this time to ignore how his body reacted to her.

He found her lying on the bedroom floor.

"What are you doing down there?"

"I needed food," she said, pointing to the empty wrapper on the floor.

He scooped up the wrapper, shoved it in his pocket, and then lifted her, an arm wrapped around her back, the other hooked under her bare knees, holding her against his chest to lift her. Her soft skin, her warm body, her alluring feminine musk—the combination threatened to overwhelm him again.

He quickly laid her on the bed and backed away until his legs touched the chair behind him. He sat down and crossed one leg over his knee to hide his reaction from touching her. *Why does she have this effect on me? I have better control than that.*

She reached for the sheet to cover her legs. He couldn't help himself. His eyes followed the movement, the animal part of his brain resenting that her shapely legs were now covered, his arousal becoming a dull ache.

"What did Leopold tell you?" she asked.

"He confirmed your story, and then some," he snapped, his irritation over his body's reaction clouding his response. "To hear him tell it, you should be known as 'Saint Cerissa, feeder of needy vampires.'"

She narrowed her eyes. "I did what I thought was right."

"For a fourteen-year-old child to walk into a room with a hungry vampire, you are either very courageous or very stupid."

"Neither, but at least you seem to believe it happened."

Did he? She wasn't human, but Leopold could still be lying. It cost him nothing to agree with her for now. "I believe you."

"And I wasn't a child," she said softly. "I was over forty at the time. I just didn't have my full body mass yet, so mimicking a teenager was easier."

"You are over two hundred and thirty years old?" She was older than he was. He looked at her closely. Was she paler? Even if she wasn't human, he had no reason to believe she was invincible. "Should I leave and let you sleep?"

"That isn't necessary. I just don't want to spar right now. I don't have the energy."

A loud banging at the front door—he excused himself and went downstairs. Switching on the security camera, he looked at Gaea's image on the video monitor mounted by his door. He saw her arms crossed and her foot tapping. He opened the front door and stepped aside, otherwise she would have run right over him.

"Where are you keeping her?" Gaea demanded.

"Upstairs, first door on the right. The doctor removed the bullet and she's resting."

"Why didn't you call me? I'm responsible for her." Gaea charged up the stairs, threw open the door, and marched to Cerissa's bedside.

"Hi, Gaea," Cerissa said weakly. "Why all the shouting?"

Gaea sniffed the air and looked at him, suspicion in her eyes. He shrugged—he wasn't responsible for the smell of blood in the room. Or was Gaea implying he would take advantage of Cerissa in her helpless state? Gaea should hold a better opinion of him than that.

"Are you all right, dear?" Gaea asked, taking Cerissa's hand carefully and caressing it.

"I'll be fine."

"I was so worried when I heard the news. Leopold will be upset if anything happens to you."

He *harrumphed*. "Cerissa's wellbeing should be your main concern," he said. After his phone call with Leopold, he couldn't care less what New York's CEO thought.

"Vampire," Gaea said, "your presence isn't needed now."

First Leopold's hostility, then Anne-Louise's condescension, and now Gaea addressing him rudely—his pent-up anger finally gave way. "I will not be dismissed in my own house. If you aren't happy, you can leave."

"Why, young man—"

"Please, Gaea," Cerissa said. "I want him to stay."

"Really, dear," Gaea said, sitting down next to the bed, "I just want to talk to you"—the old vampire swiveled her head to glare in his direction— "alone."

A series of loud knocks sounded at the front door.

"Rolf and Karen have returned," he guessed, his eyes focused on Cerissa. She looked tired and vulnerable. He felt guilty for speaking to her the way he had earlier. She had selflessly saved his life and taken a bullet for her trouble, just as she had saved Leopold—without thought to her own safety. Such bravery couldn't be ignored, regardless of how he felt about her deception. He touched her leg, trying to reassure her. "I'll come back up shortly," he said gently.

Walking downstairs, he tried to shake off a feeling he couldn't quite pinpoint. *Is Leopold right? Is she using her aura to influence me?* He froze on the stairs. *The night at the casino—my anger drained away in her presence, and then tonight, when she grabbed my wrist, my guilt was soon replaced with peace—is that what Leopold meant?*

The loud knocking resumed. Now was not the time to figure it out. He hurried down the staircase and then flipped on the security monitor again. Rolf and Karen stood there. He opened the door, and Karen took the bags of food to the kitchen, while Rolf took Karen's overnight bag upstairs. Rolf was still sulking, but it would pass.

Henry followed Karen into the kitchen. "Is she awake?" Karen asked, putting groceries into the refrigerator.

"She is, and she's still asking for food. What did you bring?"

"A couple of salmon filets and a tray of chicken breasts. Why don't we make chicken, since she mentioned it first?"

He set up the grill on the stovetop. Heavy spices might upset her stomach, but he couldn't serve her a naked piece of meat, so he settled for a light brush of olive oil, a sprinkle of dried rosemary, sage and thyme, a little salt and pepper. The chicken sizzled as he laid it on the hot grill. Karen punched the timer on the microwave and placed a potato inside. When it beeped, she microwaved some broccoli. Working together, they had the food ready in no time.

"Do you want to take it up to her?" Karen asked.

"You should. Gaea is there, and she is none too happy with me right now."

He followed Karen upstairs, hanging back at the doorway. Cerissa looked tired, but perked up when she saw what Karen was carrying. "That smells so good."

"Are you sure you should eat so much?" Gaea asked. "You just had surgery."

"Absolutely sure," Cerissa replied. "Karen, would you mind cutting it into bite-size pieces? I can manage a fork with my left hand."

Karen took the utensils and carved up the chicken. "Here you go," she said, handing the fork to Cerissa.

Cerissa took the first bite, and, while chewing it, said "'ongerful," which Henry understood as "wonderful."

He leaned against the doorway, watching Cerissa and mulling over what he had learned tonight. Should he keep her secret? He'd given his word, albeit conditionally. He turned around at the sound of Rolf behind him, who nodded toward the stairs. They silently walked together down to the drawing room.

If he was going to tell Rolf about Cerissa, he could delay no longer. If he waited, how would he justify withholding what he'd learned tonight? It was now or never.

CHAPTER 23

Gaea and Karen kept Cerissa company while she ate. *Blessed sustenance. Fuel.* She quickly converted the food to raw energy, energy needed to restore the blood she'd lost and heal the damaged tissue. When she finished eating, they helped her to the bathroom and left her alone for a few minutes. The room still wobbled, but she could stand without collapsing. She took care of necessities and then washed her hands.

Hanging on to the sink, she peeled back the bandages and examined the red, puckered wound in the mirror. *Stupid, stupid, stupid. How could I be so stupid and get myself shot?*

The stitches were already beginning to itch as the muscle underneath regenerated. *Ah, the price of completing my mission.* She frowned at herself in the mirror. Henry had left with Rolf. Would her mission be over by the time they returned?

No, she couldn't let doubt eat away at faith. What little she knew about Henry, he seemed like a man who would keep his word.

She rebandaged her arm and took a good look at her hair. "Mussed" was too nice a word—her hair was dreadful. She picked out the debris that had become embedded when she landed on the dirt, tossing the leaves and twigs into the wastebasket. Finding a brush in the drawer, she pulled the bristles through her thick hair, the tangles stopping it about halfway through, and gave up.

I might as well keep up the pretense of being wounded for now—I certainly look the part. She opened the door of the bathroom and leaned against the frame, as if unsteady on her feet.

Karen ran to her aid. "Can I get you anything else? I'm going to turn in now, so I'll be up earlier in the day. Henry will be awake until the sun rises, if you need anything."

"I'll try to sleep too." She climbed into bed with Karen's help. "The pain isn't bad right now."

After Karen left, Gaea asked, "Why didn't the good doctor give you some of his blood? It would certainly help you heal faster."

Cerissa averted her eyes. "I, well, I didn't want that kind of connection with him."

"Saving yourself for your intended. How sweet," Gaea said. "But foolish. A little vampire blood would fix you right up. A wound like that can get infected."

"I know you mean well, Gaea. But the doctor gave me an antibiotic and the wound isn't bad. I should be fine with time."

Gaea muttered a few more words of comfort, said goodnight, and stepped out into the hall, where she cautioned Henry to behave himself. By the tone of his reply, Gaea's comment didn't go over too well. Soon after, Rolf must have joined Henry in the hall. He said, "Goodnight," and a short time later the front door closed. So Rolf wouldn't be sleeping here during the day.

Probably likes his own crypt, or whatever.

Henry's footsteps sounded on the stairs, and he returned to her room with a book in his hand. "I thought I would sit with you until I must retire for the day."

She glanced over at the bedside clock. Was it only two in the morning? So much had happened since she was shot.

"I'm going to try to sleep," she said, unsure what to say next.

She wanted badly to know what he'd told Rolf, but asking him would show a lack of trust. She had to keep her mouth shut no matter how much she worried. Besides, if he had said something, Rolf would be in here grilling her himself.

Henry sat down on the bedside chair. From the cover of the book he opened, she guessed it was a science fiction novel.

"Ah, I have a question," she said. He looked up from his book. "When I wake, is it all right for me to leave this room? I mean, I'll probably be up before Karen, but I don't even know where the kitchen is."

"That's a simple matter. If there is a room I don't want you in, I'll close the door. Otherwise, feel free to look around. I do not sleep in the house during the day, if that's what you're asking."

"I just want to respect your privacy. This is an unusual situation. Gaea warned me—vampires are protective of their homes."

"We are."

"I— Are you feeling strange about the situation?"

"Some. I'm still considering it. We have always conjectured there might be other supernatural beings like ourselves, but it's hard to believe that your people would be here all this time and no one suspected a thing."

She remained silent. Sometimes it really was the best policy.

"Or is there another explanation?" he asked, rising from his chair and striding from the room before she could say anything.

Damn. Double damn. She had told him too much—the fall, the number two hundred—he'd put it all together.

When he returned, she recognized the book he carried and let out the breath she'd been holding. His guess had gone in the direction she wanted it to go.

"This was written over forty years ago," he said, holding up the paperback book. "It theorized ancient astronauts had landed on this planet thousands of years ago, but it was harshly criticized by anthropologists who studied the same facts."

Of course it was. Her people had paid the critics who debunked the theory. The Lux couldn't allow even wild speculation to lead back to the Enclave.

He opened the book to look at the photos. Upside down, she could see the geoglyphs created by the ancient Peruvians, the Nazca Lines intended to be seen by the sky gods. "Is it possible to visit your base without revealing its location?" he asked. "You called it 'the Enclave'?"

She held up her hand like a stop sign. "No way. My people aren't going to be happy I told you about it."

"They will punish you?"

She glared at him in reply. No way would she reveal any more about the Lux to him.

He closed the book abruptly. "I would apologize, but if there is any fault, it is yours, for invading my community in the first place."

She turned away, rolling over so her back was to him. Let him be angry. Better him than her superiors. Her superiors—*oh shit.* Her lenses and earrings were still recording. Why didn't she think of it earlier? She turned them off using a series of blink patterns. There was no way she could soften the blow—the Protectors would see it all when she downloaded her videos. *Maybe they won't be too angry....*

Henry's chair creaked when he sat down. The whisper of an occasional page turn told her he was reading. She tried closing her eyes, but couldn't sleep. A heavy anxiety tightened her chest, squeezing her lungs—the same anxiety she had felt when her mother abandoned her. *All alone.* She couldn't turn to her people for comfort, not after she'd revealed so much to Henry. And though she wanted to trust him, could she? At any moment, he might betray her to his people.

She had to do something more, even if it came with risks.

She rolled back, opened her eyes, and looked at him, focusing every ounce of her aura toward him. After a few moments, he glanced up from his book. "Are you all right?" he asked.

"I'm not sure," she said, reaching out, hoping direct contact would make it easier to influence him with her charm.

He took her hand. "Is there something you need?" he asked, concern in his eyes.

"Henry, the lab—it's my only way to gain independence from my people." She held his hand tightly. "I, ah, I don't want to live with mortals," she stammered. "Their life spans are but a blip to me. I'll live at least a thousand years."

He raised an eyebrow. "A thousand years?"

"Give or take. I've seen so many mortals die already, it's almost unbearable."

Her *pita* had died over two centuries ago, and most of the families she'd fostered with were long dead. She rolled her lips under, biting them together, her long-buried grief mixing with her fear of more loss.

He tilted his head, like he was considering her words. "I do understand. It's why we live surrounded by our own kind. Why don't you live with your own people?"

"It isn't possible. We— I have to go out in the world. Our mission is to protect humans. We can't do that from the Enclave."

She glanced away from him, uncertain how to ask what she wanted without saying too much. If she failed this mission, the Protectors weren't known for their mercy, but it wasn't just fear of punishment driving her. Something else had changed. Being around vampires no longer bothered her, but more importantly, she now counted Leopold, Gaea, and Liza as friends. She didn't want to lose them.

She looked up into his eyes and said, "I want to be part of a community that will live as long as I do. Please don't take that away from me by revealing what I am before I'm ready."

She didn't know how badly she wanted it until she said it.

"Everything is all right," he replied. "I won't tell anyone about you."

She blinked back tears. Would he really protect her?

He got up from his chair and sat on the edge of the bed. "You have been through a lot tonight," he said, and stroked her hair. "You are safe here."

Safe. She closed her eyes and a tear rolled down her cheek. He took a tissue from the bedside box and handed it to her.

"I'm sorry," she said, wiping away the tears. "I'm not usually so emotional."

He stroked her hair. "You have been strong all evening, but you don't have to be strong all the time."

She looked up at him again. Maybe he would keep her secret.

He reached into his pocket and pulled out her watch and cell phone. "I almost forgot to return these." He sat frozen for a moment with his eyes fixed on the devices, and then placed them on the bedstand. "You will be here when I rise at sunset? You won't leave?"

"I'm not going anywhere as long as you don't tell anyone what I am."

"Trust me, your secret is safe." He patted her back. "You should try to sleep. Your body needs its rest."

He stood up and softly pressed his lips to the back of her hand. The strange tingle went up her arm, just like the first time he'd kissed her there.

Was he a superb hand kisser, or was it something more?

He moved to his chair and resumed reading. Soon her eyelids felt heavy, sleep finally pulling her under.

With the first glow of sunrise backlighting the curtains, Henry yawned. *Time to retire.* The moon had set earlier, so dawn controlled the start of his slumber. He hated those days when the moon rose before the sun set, when he had to lurk through his own home like a wraith, closing the window curtains to avoid the killing rays of the sun. No one understood why, but exposure to the sun's rays undid the vampire effect, returning the flesh to its dead state—those who survived it described the experience as being slowly cooked from the outside in.

He stood and stretched. Cerissa still slept, her molasses-colored hair in disarray, partially hiding her face. He carefully lifted the errant strands, brushing them softly aside.

She is beautiful.

But her beauty was illusory. It wasn't her real self.

What is reality?

He touched her hand.

Solid matter.

He leaned over and kissed her cheek. She stirred, but didn't wake.

So lovely.

Perhaps he had been too quick to judge her at the casino. There had to be a reason God put her between him and a bullet—maybe he was *meant* to be the first to know her secret.

He hadn't said anything to Rolf. Not yet, at least. He didn't like keeping secrets, but he'd given Cerissa his word, and when the moment came to say something, he couldn't justify breaking his vow.

He went downstairs and into the crypts below his house. He pulled the index card out of his back pocket, the risk matrix. Leopold's comment about her aura, her ability to charm—was he falling under her spell? Would his promise put his people at risk?

He wrote those questions on the card, and then posted the card on an old-fashioned bulletin board he kept in his basement dressing room, which held similar cards, and changed clothes for his day's sleep. When he woke tonight, he would consider the card again to see if it revealed any new truths.

CHAPTER 24

Cerissa sat up abruptly in bed, her heart racing, the room brightly lit with sunlight. Where the hell was she? A tall, dark stranger had leaned over her, kissing her while she slept; the sensation of his lips still echoed on her face. Why hadn't her lenses warned her? She looked at the blue- and yellow-flowered wallpaper, the wallpaper reminding her where she was—at Henry's house. Her lenses hadn't warned her because she'd turned them off.

She glanced around. No kissing bandit in the room, so it must have been a dream—although she'd gladly swap the dream for her current reality.

What am I, a complete amateur? I'll never live this down. She had no idea what the Protectors would do once she reported her mistake. When she saved Leopold's life she'd revealed too much to him; the Protectors were furious at the time. And now this—they wouldn't be happy.

Her stomach growled, loudly. Well, breakfast would cure that problem. She carefully swung her legs out of bed and stood up. Not dizzy—a good sign. She took a step. Legs steady, but her back felt sore from the fall. She took another step and looked around. At least this room wasn't a frilly, frothy mess, like her room at Gaea's house.

The adjoining bathroom was large and luxurious. She found a note Henry had left next to some packaged toiletries—toothbrush, toothpaste—inviting her to use what she needed. A courteous host, even if he had bullied her into revealing herself. She brushed her teeth and washed her face. Her back to the mirror, she lifted the tank top and looked for any bruises. A few scrapes, and one big blue one was already turning purple. Should she morph it back to normal? The doctor's next exam might be more thorough. She let it be, so he wouldn't question her lack of injuries from the fall. But the one on the back of her head, the one hidden by her hair—that bruise she fixed. Dr. Asshole wasn't likely to notice its absence.

She triggered the eject process for her contact lenses, a slight *zzzt* vibration as the tentacles detached from her optic nerve and slid back into each lens, and then she popped them out. Feeling better, she returned to the bedroom and picked up her phone, sliding back the hidden compartment. She dropped in her lenses and adjusted the settings so the video recordings would only be transmitted to her mission supervisor. Ari was smart. Once he saw what happened, he'd know what to do next.

Henry's plush green bathrobe hung on a hook by the closet. The sleeve looked big enough to accommodate her bandages. Slipping off the sling, she donned the robe and took a deep whiff of the clove, cedar, and other spices rising from it—his cologne. Did the dream stranger wear the same scent as Henry? Her dreams must have latched on to last night's trauma and rewritten the ending.

Her stomach growled again. *I need food more than I need dream analysis.*

She went downstairs and found a short hallway leading to the kitchen. She hadn't expected such an impressive kitchen in a vampire's home, right down to the modern appliances. She ran her finger along one of the granite counters.

Preternaturally clean. That, or Henry had maid service.

Karen would probably sleep for another three hours, and she couldn't wait. Taking eggs, bread, and butter out of the refrigerator, she whipped up a simple but filling breakfast.

After she finished eating, her curiosity got the better of her and she went exploring. An antique wrought-iron chandelier hung in the center of his entryway. It may have once held candles—it was now wired for electric lights.

She followed Henry's rule and only entered a room if the door was open. The drawing room was large and spacious, taking up almost half of the first floor and dominated by a large river-stone fireplace with a walnut-stained mantel, the walls painted stark white—very Spanish Colonial Revival.

The room was so perfect, she almost expected a *Classy Homes Magazine* photographer to ring the doorbell any minute. The furniture was all leather, with decorative wooden touches. She could tell a lot about Henry from his decorating—he probably drew comfort from the traditional styles he'd lived with for most of his life. She fitted her fingers into the grooves of one of the armrests, the carved wood shaped like the claw of an animal, and smiled to herself. The chair sat close to the fireplace. From the amount of wear, it must be his favorite chair.

The mantel clock chimed the half-hour. *Enough stalling—time to face up to my mistake.* She steeled herself and went upstairs, switching her phone to a special frequency. She hit the call button. By now, Ari should have viewed last night's video.

"Hey, Ciss!" he exclaimed when a 3-D image of him appeared, floating above the phone. From the surroundings, he sat at a bar in a dance club. "Your reports are getting rave reviews at headquarters."

Her throat tightened. "Then you haven't seen the latest?"

"The gunshot? Marvelous drama. We couldn't have staged it better. Which reminds me—you did stage it, didn't you?"

"No, they were trying to shoot Henry. I got in the way."

"That sourpuss? I can understand why."

"Ari, have you viewed the past twelve hours after the shooting?"

"I scanned it up to the surgery. Gruesome bit of barbarity, wasn't it?"

"You should have been on the receiving end. If I were human, I'd sue Dr. Ass—er, I mean, Dr. Clarke."

"So why the call?" A hand holding a towel wiped the bar in front of him. He swiveled in the direction of the off-camera bartender. "Yeah, I'll take another," he said, before turning back to her. "Looks like things are moving along fine."

"I blew it."

"Come now, my little cousin on her first undercover assignment— there's bound to be a few glitches, but you're fitting in just fine with the natives. The top dogs are happy."

"But the Protectors won't like—"

"You worry too much. You're doing marvelous work, Ciss."

"Ah," she said, raking both hands through her hair. "I got trapped into revealing what I am to Henry."

She started pacing, explaining what happened last night.

"Do you know what the Protectors will do when they find out?" he asked, glowering at her. "They'll cut off your wings—that's what they'll do."

"It isn't fair—I don't have enough experience for this kind of assignment."

"You've had over two hundred years of blending in with humans—"

"As a *karabu*," she insisted, frowning at the image of him hovering above her phone. "It's only been ten years since I made the transition to *principatus* and started 'blending' as an adult mortal."

A hand came into view, and a glass of something clear appeared in front of him. He shot it down. "You better hope the Protectors are in a lenient mood."

She stopped pacing and slumped onto the bedside chair. "Henry's promised not to tell anyone."

"Naïve. The only person who can keep a secret is a dead one. Wait, he is dead. Strike that."

"Maybe we should wait a few years and find a new ruse to infiltrate a different community."

He shoved his glass toward the bartender, pointing at it. "Kid, if he leaks this, we won't be able show up in another treaty community. They'll be on the lookout for our kind."

"He won't leak it. Honor is important to him. He'll keep his promise."

"Honor? Let's get more basic—you have to seduce him. Where his dick goes, so will his loyalty."

"Are you kidding?!"

"Hey, he's not bad looking. If he screws you, he'll feel protective— it's built into their vampire genes."

"But my assignment rules—I can't be, ah, intimate with the subjects I'm observing."

"Geez, Ciss, no operative follows that rule. It's just boilerplate on every assignment. We do what we have to do to get the job done."

She sighed. The thought had momentary appeal. Henry was handsome, in a dark and powerful way. She'd felt a spark of attraction from the first moment she saw him at the dance. And the way he'd taken care of her during surgery showed his compassionate side. *But the other side of his personality—so angry, so suspicious.*

Still, it wasn't right either way. "I'm not going to manipulate him using sex."

"You will if you want to stay in his community."

"That's where you're wrong. If I do seduce him, they'll throw me out for sure. Didn't you read their Covenant? I sent it to you."

"I'm still working my way through that tome. Uptight, aren't they?"

"Then you should know they don't care what happens outside their walls, but they don't approve of casual sex between a mortal and vampire within their walls. They're afraid it will lead to territorial battles."

Ari stopped while the bartender poured more liquid into his glass. "Then the Protectors have only one option: eliminate Henry before he can tell anyone."

"What?" she screeched at Ari's image.

"Really dead men tell no tales. You could always find him now and stake him. Get the job done, and the Protectors need never hear about your little slip."

"You're insane. I can't kill anyone." She buried her face in her hands. Only Avengers could kill another sentient being—Watchers were forbidden from taking a life. Telling Henry the truth was bad enough. But killing him? The Protectors would cook her goose for sure. And even if it wasn't forbidden, all her training, her calling, was to save life. She couldn't bring herself to kill anyone...especially not him.

"Look, kid, you got to lose your compulsion to follow the rules. Besides, he's already dead. Technically, you wouldn't be killing him."

"I'm not mincing words with you."

"Seduction or stake?" Ari said, gesturing as if weighing the options, one in each hand. "Seduction or stake, which will it be?"

"You really believe they'd order his death because of my mistake?"

"Look, Ciss, this is serious—there's no telling what the Protectors will do when they find out."

"They can't. If they kill him, all hell will break loose. He dies, I'm done here. They'll kick me off the Hill and no other community will accept me. They'll be too suspicious." She waved her arms in frustration. "Besides, Henry's not going to say anything. I know he won't."

"Are you sure? Really sure? Hmm." From the look on his face, she could see the wheels spin. "At least try flirting with him. Let him think he has a chance of getting you on your back."

"Flirt?"

"Did you sleep through your human sexuality class?"

"Ari, I'm not some nervous virgin." No, not a virgin, but nervous—that was a definite yes. Pretending to be mortal was easy—until she was alone in bed with a man. Not that she'd ever tell Ari that. "I just don't think flirting will work with Henry. I tried already."

"You got to do something, kiddo. For now, smile at him a lot and flutter your eyelashes," Ari said with a laugh. A woman came into view, slipping an arm over his shoulder and kissing his cheek. "Not now, cute stuff. I'm on the phone." The woman's hand dipped below the bar's counter. "Later," he said, moving the wayward hand back into view. "Go get us a table by the band."

"Sure, Ducky."

"Ducky?" Cerissa repeated.

"Never mind. I'm in London for the night."

So being in a bar at ten in the morning had a logical explanation—the time zone difference.

"Now, where was I?" he asked, his eyes glancing in the direction of the ceiling. "Right. Maybe we shouldn't tell the Protectors about this until we see what Henry does."

"He won't say anything."

"Hmm," he murmured. "Okay, here's what you'll do—go back to charming them, him in particular."

Yeah, right. She had been using her charm judiciously until last night. Unlike Ari, she didn't throw it around indiscriminately. The consequences could be unpredictable. Last night had been the exception—she'd had to do something to turn Henry around.

"Keep sending your videos directly to me," Ari continued. "I'll edit your confession, tag the end to make it look like you clicked off your lenses—it's a good thing you don't wear them all the time. The Protectors will never know about your conversation with Henry."

"Are you sure we should keep it from them?"

"Trust me, it's better that we keep this between us."

"Ah, I have a feeling he's going to have more questions." She couldn't edit her own videos. To keep field operatives from messing with the data, only supervisors could access editing codes.

Ari nodded. "When he starts to talk about us, turn off your lenses. I'll clean up the ends and take care of the rest."

"Thanks Ari," she said, sighing.

"Look, I gotta run." He flashed a roguish grin. "My date is eager."

The 3-D video of him vanished.

She flopped on the bed and scooped up the phone, then tossed it onto the bedside table next to her watch, grateful Henry had returned both items. Getting to and from the Enclave would be near impossible if she didn't have her watch and the flash technology built into it. She had no reason to use it now; she trusted Henry even if Ari didn't.

She slid off the bed, snatched up her injector, and went into the bathroom, turning on the faucet to fill the bathtub. The Protectors could be a real pain in the ass sometimes. A soothing bath wouldn't solve her problems, but it might make her feel better. She unwrapped the gauze—the surface skin, puckered red around the stitches, looked okay. She flexed her arm. The muscle underneath had completely healed.

She looked at herself in the mirror—her shoulders were hunched over, her neck tight, her skin constricted. Was she edgy because of Ari's call, or because she'd stayed human too long? More stabilizer would keep her locked in human form for the day, but it wasn't healthy to use too much of it. She dialed in the antidote and applied the injector to her thigh. Looking closely at her reflection in the mirror, she carefully mapped her wound's appearance so she could reproduce it, and slowly allowed herself to morph back to her Lux form.

In the mirror, her long hair became the color and texture of raw silk, her skin a translucent blue. Turning around, she glanced over her shoulder, seeing the reflection of her long, feathered wings, which ended at the back of her knees, softer than a bird's and more elegant, the same pale color as her hair. She anxiously fluttered the tips. Were her wings really at risk? She'd only had them for ten years. There were rumors of what became of the Lux who were stripped of their wings, dark rumors, rumors she had avoided listening to while still *karabu*.

Karabu—the second stage, the one after childhood. Things were simpler then. During her two hundred years of being *karabu* she was sporadically "fostered" with human families to grow accustomed to being around humans. Mimicking a human teen had been hard work for a mentally mature being. She preferred living in the Enclave, where she could be herself with her friends and use Lux technology to run her science experiments. Of course, her nest mates gossiped about the Protectors in the same way military privates gossiped about generals—quietly but with great relish.

Once she had metamorphosed to *principatus*, she had the body mass to mimic a full-grown mortal, and attended medical school to earn the credentials she needed to pass as a doctor and research scientist—not that she attended many classes. She was so far ahead of human knowledge that the lectures were *borr-ring*. But medical school gave her an opportunity to practice being an adult.

She fluttered her wings again. Did she really want to live on the Hill? Last night, she'd admitted the truth to herself. She didn't want to live with mortals and watch them die so young. Being around vampires bothered her less than it did six months ago; she was even growing accustomed to their creepy, predatory vibe. Given the choice, she wanted her home in a vampire community, where they lived as long as she did. Especially if it meant she could work independently from the Lux in her own lab.

But not if the price for staying here is Henry's death. Ari was right. The easiest way to ensure their secret would be to kill him, but she couldn't do it.

Sighing, she morphed back to human form, right down to the stitches in her arm, and stepped into the bathtub. After turning off the faucet, she slipped into the warm water and relaxed back against the bath pillow. The morning light, filtered through an obscured window, illuminated a collection of bottles next to the tub. She picked up a bronze-colored body wash and opened the cap. Citrus, with a hint of cloves and other spices, similar to Henry's cologne—it probably wouldn't upset his sensitive nose or it wouldn't be here.

She didn't bother washing her hair. Morphing from Lux to human had returned it to its pristine state. After she bathed, she found her overnight bag on the floor near her jeans. Gaea must have brought it with her last night. She slipped into a casual dress with matching sandals and then rebandaged her arm, examining it in the mirror. Not a bad job, considering she had to wrap the bandages one-handed and with only one thumb.

A knock at the door startled her—it couldn't be Henry, not yet. She opened the door and Karen stood there, looking like she just woke up. "How're you feeling?" Karen asked.

"Sore but not intolerable—I just finished bathing and dressing."

"Well, you're a few steps ahead of me," Karen said, followed by a big yawn.

"Let's go downstairs. I'll keep you company while you eat breakfast."

Cerissa perched herself on a high chair at the kitchen island. Karen set out two slices of bread, opened a container of chicken salad, and slathered on a generous layer.

"I'm surprised you're out of bed," Karen said. "You're looking better, but you should rest."

"I still feel weak," Cerissa agreed, feeling guilty over hiding the truth. She liked Karen and hadn't used her charm to influence her. Besides, repetitively using her aura on someone came with too much risk—*the people we charm, charm us.* She couldn't afford to become enamored with anyone, except maybe Candy. She'd used a little of her charm on the horse—it was why Candy had been so protective.

The chicken salad smelled good, so she asked Karen to make a sandwich for her. Karen obliged and suggested they take the plates upstairs to Henry's theater room and watch a movie.

They took a break between movies so Karen could shower and dress.

The second movie was almost over when Cerissa heard Henry coming up the stairs. She glanced at her watch—it was too early. The sun hadn't set yet. Karen answered her unasked question. "Early moonrise tonight."

Cerissa chewed on her lower lip, a sense of unease creeping over her.

Karen laid a reassuring hand on her leg. "It's okay that we're in here," she said, adding, with a mischievous smirk, "Don't worry, he won't bite."

That wasn't what bothered her right now.

Karen grabbed the remote and paused the movie. "We're in here," she called out from the doorway.

Henry joined them, looking classically stylish in casual black slacks with a royal-blue polo shirt. He smiled, but it didn't reach his eyes.

Cerissa sent a wisp of her aura in his direction.

"You're looking better," he said. "Karen must have taken good care of you during the day."

"You bet I did," Karen replied. "Mostly we lounged around up here. A nice, relaxing, easygoing day. Just what the doctor ordered."

His eyes remained directed at Cerissa. "It's good to see you're out of bed, but I hope you're not overdoing it."

"I'm all right."

"That's good to hear. I'm glad you didn't leave." Karen looked at him with a puzzled expression, and he quickly added, "To go to the hospital."

"No reason to," Cerissa replied. "Thank you for letting me stay here."

"My pleasure," he said, inclining his head.

Talk about subtext. She sighed, relieved he was still willing to keep her secret. She stretched out her legs, crossing them at the ankle.

"You look lovely in that dress," he added.

She laughed. "That's nice of you to say. It's the only one Gaea packed."

"It doesn't make it any less true." He smiled at her, and this time the smile reached his deep browns. "Have you two ladies had dinner yet?"

Karen looked surprised to have a question include her. "Ah, no. We forgot about the time. I usually eat before Rolf gets up. He hates being around food."

"That isn't a problem in this house. I would be pleased to cook for the both of you."

Karen's face brightened. "Cerissa, don't turn down his offer. Henry is quite the chef."

She smiled tentatively. "I accept your kind offer of dinner."

"Please finish your movie," he said with bow, "and join me in the kitchen when it's over."

He left the room, and she relaxed back into the couch. His attitude had changed since last night, but then, he had mellowed toward the end. Using her aura on him seemed unfair—still, it was fairer than what the Protectors would do to him if they found out.

Karen cleared her throat. "So what happened after I went to sleep?"

"I don't know what you mean." Cerissa pulled her eyes away from the empty doorway to look at Karen.

"It doesn't take a scorecard to see you two are doing a barnyard dance."

"Beg pardon?"

"You two are flirting with each other. Henry's a courteous host, but all the stuff about your charming dress and cooking for us was not aimed at *me*."

So maybe Ari was right: a little harmless flirting might keep Henry on her side. "Nothing happened," Cerissa replied.

"Yeah, like I believe that."

"He thinks I saved his life. He's just showing his gratitude."

Karen shook her head. "That isn't gratitude showing. But do be careful."

"I appreciate your concern, but I'm not interested in a mate."

"Sure, if you say so." Karen's tone managed to convey her disbelief that any woman would pass up the chance to find a boyfriend. "How's your arm feeling now?"

"It's not too bad, as long as I don't try to use it." Cerissa flexed it. "I haven't taken any painkillers today. I don't like them. They dull my thinking."

Only too true—otherwise she wouldn't have told Henry what she was. What a stupid mistake! But Karen was right—he was being nice. *Will he really keep my secret? Or will I have to seduce him?* She cringed— seducing him to buy his silence didn't feel right.

"Are you okay?" Karen asked.

"What? I mean, yes, just hungry." Wonderful aromas had begun wafting their way. "We should go downstairs soon."

"Let's not rush the chef," Karen said, unpausing the movie. "There's only a little bit left."

It wasn't the movie she wanted, it was Henry's reassurance. *Get over it, kid,* she berated herself, hearing Ari's voice in her head. *You don't need Henry holding your hand, promising to keep your secret safe. You need to hold his hand and lay on the charm.*

She scratched at her bandages, the tightness around the stitches beginning to itch. *Fake it till you make it,* Ari used to tell her. She hated faking it—always hiding her true nature from the people she befriended. Fake everything and don't let anyone in. She didn't want to fake it anymore, and if Henry kept her secret, she wouldn't need to. *I can just be me around him.* The thought sparkled brightly in her mind, like a lovely diamond necklace, one just begging to be worn. She'd never had the chance to be with someone like Henry without having to pretend she was mortal. A long-buried desire rose, tempting her to reach out and slip on those diamonds, ignoring the price tag the necklace came with.

CHAPTER 25

"Wow, this is good," Cerissa said, after biting into the *arroz con pollo*. Henry had done something wonderful with rice and chicken—the rice was fragrant with saffron, and the bite-size pieces of shredded chicken were intermingled with onions, bell peppers, carrots, and peas. How did someone who hadn't eaten food in almost two centuries know how to cook so well?

The kitchen table had been set for two, right down to woven place mats and cloth napkins. He poured a Cabernet Sauvignon from his winery into two gold-rimmed wineglasses and set them in front of her and Karen.

She took a sip of the fragrant wine. "Very nice," she told him.

He bowed graciously at the compliment and returned to his station by the large center island, where he began cleaning up the trimmings from the vegetables he had cooked into the rice.

The front door slammed. She jumped out of her chair, her heart taking the express train to the back of her throat. Who was that?

"Relax," Karen said with a wink. "Nothing's wrong. It's Rolf."

Cerissa sat down and took a long drink from her wineglass, her heart still racing. After last night's shooting, her startle reflex was set too high. Karen patted her arm reassuringly.

Rolf marched into the kitchen and asked with a snarl, "What is Cerissa still doing here?"

"She is my guest." Henry peered close to his partner's face. "Have you fed?"

Rolf directed his eyes at the stove, where the leftover chicken with rice sat in a large cooking pot. "I had *real* work to do," he scoffed. "Then I drove straight over."

Henry removed a bag of blood from the refrigerator and dropped it into a pan of simmering water. He turned off the flame, using tongs to swish the bag back and forth. "Have you heard anything from Tig?" he asked.

"No, but I spoke with the mayor. He wants to reinstitute the Rule of Two."

"That will be inconvenient." Henry fished the bag out of the water, cut off the corner, and poured the warmed blood into an oversized coffee mug.

"'Rule of Two'?" Cerissa asked.

Rolf scowled at her. "Nothing for you to be concerned about. You're leaving."

She sent a wisp of her aura Rolf's way. She hadn't tried using it when they first met at the dance. Maybe a little experiment...

Henry handed the mug to Rolf. "Drink this. It might make your mood less foul."

"My mood isn't the problem—the problem is having Leopold's envoy on the Hill."

Rolf didn't take the offered mug. Henry placed it on the center island's polished granite with a light clink. "Sit down and drink."

"*Du kannst mich mal.*"

"Rolf, there are ladies present."

Rolf grabbed the coffee mug and stomped out of the room.

"Excuse me," Henry said, before following Rolf.

Well, that didn't go well. Next time, she'd up the dose of her aura. She leaned over to Karen. "What Rolf said, 'You can do me sometime'?"

"You speak German? He told me it means 'bite me.'" Karen snickered, and then took a sip of her wine. "Don't let it bother you. He's just cranky from not feeding yet. Those two fight like a pair of old biddies, and it doesn't mean anything. Like Oscar and Felix—the *Odd Couple*, you know?"

"They've been friends for a long time."

"Yeah. Sometimes I feel like the third wheel." Karen glanced hesitantly in the direction the two men had gone. "We should change the subject before Henry comes back."

"What does the 'Rule of Two' mean?"

Karen screwed her face into a look of disgust. "A pain in the ass is what it means. It's an old rule, one they abolished years ago, but if they bring it back, Rolf won't be able to leave the Hill unless he's with another vampire."

Cerissa didn't remember reading anything about it in the Covenant. "Does it apply to mortals too, or just vampires?"

"Shit, I hadn't considered that." Karen drained her wineglass. "From what I heard, the council has never applied it to us before. They originally adopted it to prevent 'unlawful hunting,' as they call it. Everyone's been so well behaved, they dropped the rule."

Hmm. If vampires couldn't easily leave the Hill, she'd have more opportunities to pitch her project and gather intelligence. Maybe this was the break she needed. With Henry protecting her secret, she had to get back on track.

Rolf walked into the kitchen and dropped his empty mug into the sink. He turned to Karen. "If you're done eating, we're leaving. Go pack your bag."

Henry strode up behind him, carrying a binder. He handed it to Rolf. "Here is the proposal I mentioned. It's not worth investing in, but you may as well look at it."

The proposal's cover read "Dystopian Wines by Blanche Larson." Why was he giving it to Rolf if he didn't like it? He hadn't asked to see *her* prospectus. She pursed her lips.

"I'll call you later." Rolf turned back to Karen. "Why are you still sitting there? *Schnell, Fraulein.*"

Karen stood and kissed Rolf. "Keep your pants on, lover boy."

Cerissa followed Karen upstairs. "Why is Rolf in such a hurry to leave?" she asked, sitting down on the bed Karen had slept in.

"He doesn't like it that I stayed here last night." Karen began packing her bag. "He's got some crazy ideas about the Covenant, believes it's *unseemly* I slept in the house of another vampire. Don't take it seriously—he isn't like this normally."

"You certainly have a good attitude about it. I wouldn't be as understanding if my boyfriend was rude to me." If someone treated her like a possession, she'd kick him to the curb, fast. She had enough of that ownership stuff from the Lux—go here, do this, don't do that.

Karen finished putting her makeup into a small bag and zipped it up. "Take my word for it: Rolf can act like a jerk, but when he and I are alone, he turns into a big pussycat. It's strange, but we don't fight." Karen sat down on the bed next to her. "Are you okay being here alone with Henry? Sure you don't need a chaperone?"

"We'll be fine. After the way Gaea scolded him last night, he won't do anything to prove her right."

Karen stood up and grabbed her overnight bag. "Look, I guess I'm still pissed off over the way he treated Erin. But he's one of the writers of the original Covenant—he takes his 'civilized' role seriously—"

"I'm not worried. He's been nothing but a gentleman."

"Then he has you completely fooled. Don't get me wrong—he won't break any rules, but he *is* a vampire, so don't invite something you aren't ready for."

Cerissa smiled. "With this arm wound, I don't feel like inviting anything."

"Sure, but don't forget it smells of fresh blood. That's a bit seductive for a vampire."

"I'll be careful."

Rolf appeared at the door. "Why aren't you ready to leave yet?" he demanded.

She ignored Rolf and walked with Karen into the hallway. They stopped by the door to the room she had slept in. Karen gave her a careful hug goodbye.

"Thanks for everything," Cerissa said, giving Karen a one-armed hug in return.

Tig sank onto the leather couch in Henry's drawing room. He had asked her to come to his house for the interview, and she had agreed. After all, he was a founder; she couldn't insist he come to the police station.

Right now, he was looking off into space, sitting in the leather chair opposite her, considering her theory. From the skeptical look on his face, she hadn't convinced him. She tapped one finger on the couch's armrest and waited for him to finish mulling it over.

When her patience reached its end, she repeated, "The attack on Yacov is connected to last night's shooting."

"It makes no sense," he replied, shaking his head.

"What makes no sense?" Cerissa asked.

Tig whipped around in the direction of Cerissa's voice. Leopold's envoy stood at the open door to the drawing room. Why was she still at Henry's?

"You should be upstairs, resting," Henry scolded.

"I heard voices, but Karen and Rolf had left."

"Let me help you," Henry said, sweeping up beside Cerissa and carefully slipping his arm around her. "Tig is here regarding the investigation. If you aren't feeling up to it, you don't have to be interviewed now."

"It's all right. I might as well get it over with."

"Then we should go upstairs so you may return to bed." Henry turned to face Tig. "You can interview her in the guest room. She is still weak and should lie down."

Tig sniffed the air—Cerissa didn't smell like someone recovering from a serious injury. Her blood smelled strong. How had she healed so quickly? The envoy leaned against Henry as the two of them walked upstairs. Something about it seemed off—like Tig was seeing a tableau acted out for her benefit. She picked up her briefcase and followed them to the guest room. Cerissa crawled onto the bed, and Henry arranged the pillows under her arm. His help seemed unnecessary, since the young woman wasn't favoring her arm.

"What do you want to ask?" Henry said, sitting down on the corner of the bed and gesturing toward the bedside chair.

Tig took the offered seat, removed a file from her briefcase, and handed Henry two photos. "Do you know this man?"

One photo was a mug shot and the other had been taken by Jayden in the Hill's makeshift morgue—the shooter's body wasn't going to Mordida's lab, not without raising too many questions. *Thank the ancestors for Jayden.* Without him, the case would grind to a screeching halt during the day. He was now getting some much-needed shut-eye while she continued the investigation.

Henry's expression didn't change as he studied the photos. "I've never seen him before," he said.

He handed the photos to Cerissa, who seemed equally mystified. "Me neither. He's been in jail before?"

"He served time for armed robbery. Carmine Morietti. Does his name sound familiar?"

"No," Henry said.

"Do you know anyone who did time at San Diego Prison?" Tig asked.

Both answered in the negative. Not what she'd hoped to hear. The prison was the only common denominator.

Henry looked at the photo again before placing it on the bed. "Who is Morietti?" he asked.

"The sniper."

"You believe Morietti and the two men who attacked Yacov are connected?"

Tig picked up the photos, motioning with them. "All three men were incarcerated at the same time. For now, I think the two attacks are related." She put the photos back into the file she held. "I don't think we're facing a vampire hunter."

"I agree with your assessment," he said, "but I would like to hear your reasons."

She frowned. She was here to ask the questions, not answer them. But being chief of police meant she had to coddle civilians, especially the founders, no matter how exasperated they made her.

"None of the shooters erred in the usual ways," she explained. "No religious symbols were used, no holy water. I checked the listserv. No security chief has seen a vampire hunter who didn't make one of those classic mistakes, not to mention they knew silver was deadly." She slipped the file back into her briefcase. "What do you remember seeing or hearing before the shooting?"

"I smelled the blood of a stranger," he said. "I saw nothing unusual."

She pressed her lips together. *Not helpful.*

"What else did you find out?" he asked.

"We searched the woods while you took care of Cerissa, but we found no sign of other accomplices. This was a suicide mission. He couldn't kill all of us before one of us got him. Just another reason why a vampire is behind it—a vampire would view mortals as expendable; a conspiracy of mortal vampire hunters wouldn't." Turning to Cerissa, she asked, "What did you see or hear?"

"I, ah, I didn't see anything."

"Was there any reason you turned in the direction of the shooter? You were facing him when you were shot."

Cerissa seemed suddenly nervous. Could Leopold be involved with the shootings? Henry patted Cerissa's leg, a reassuring look on his face. *Hmm, interesting.* What was going on between the two of them?

He kept a hand on Cerissa's leg, and said, "It's not unusual for a mortal to have amnesia after a trauma such as Cerissa has suffered."

"But it is unusual for one to recover as quickly as she has," Tig said, crossing her arms. "Dr. Clarke told me neither of you gave her blood last night. Did something change after we left?" She wasn't surprised by the blush appearing on Cerissa's cheeks. Cerissa's overnight recovery had a logical explanation.

"It doesn't concern your investigation," he said.

"But it could affect the peace of our community. Zeke is interested in her. I don't want any trouble because of it."

"There will be no trouble."

"I will count on you, Founder, to make sure there isn't any. Now the remaining question—why did the shooter target you? Do you have any enemies who want you dead?"

"None. Nor do I have any major business deals pending that would make anyone richer if I were out of the way."

"Who would inherit if you'd been killed?"

"I have a complex series of trusts," Henry replied. "Rolf is trustee on all of them, and my next identity is the primary beneficiary." He turned in Cerissa's direction. "Tig is familiar with the system, but you may not be. When my current identity is too old to maintain comfortably, a young Enrique Vasquez will inherit."

Cerissa furrowed her brow. "So you age yourself each night? Is this your real appearance?"

"It is. Each day's sleep returns me to how I looked when I died. So I only age myself when I'll be out among mortals who don't know what I am. I have to consume extra blood each time."

"Henry," Tig said, glancing down at the time on her phone. She needed to leave for her next interview appointment. "I don't have all night."

"Sorry," he replied. Turning back to Cerissa, he added, "My next identity has an authentic birth certificate, issued a few years back. I believe his passport shows him living in Costa Rica right now. I'll leave the country as old Henry, and return as young Enrique."

Tig tapped her fingers on her briefcase. Did he think a long story would distract her? He still hadn't told her the name of his current heir. "Who is your secondary beneficiary?" she asked.

"Ah, after Erin and I parted ways, I updated the trust, changing it from Erin to Rolf. Anne-Louise would also receive some of my estate. There are a few other small bequests, but nothing worth killing over."

She had noticed the tension between Henry and Rolf last night. "Does Rolf know he stands to inherit a fortune if you died your final death?"

"Yes, and I don't like where you're going with this. Rolf would do nothing to harm me. He is loyal, if nothing else."

"I understand he's your friend, but I have to go where the evidence leads me."

Henry frowned at her. "Why would Rolf have me killed in his presence?"

"The perfect alibi. Jayden and I were there as witnesses."

"That makes no sense. If you hadn't killed the shooter, he could have identified Rolf. No, Rolf is smarter than that."

Henry had a point, but she didn't have all the facts. Someone had put a bullet through the shooter's brain—was it Rolf who aimed to kill, making sure his accomplice was dead? Time to tread carefully; such speculation could be a career killer, *if* she was wrong. Then it dawned on her—the prohibition on making new vampires could be Rolf's motive—a two-fer: he'd get Karen *plus* he'd get Henry's money.

"Does Rolf want to turn Karen?" she asked.

Henry sat back, clearly startled by the question. "Not that I'm aware of."

"Has he ever mentioned it to you? You're close friends; he must have said something."

"Rolf knows he's too young to turn anyone vampire."

"Then he would if he could?"

Henry's lips spread into a fine line. "I don't believe Rolf is in love with Karen enough to keep her in his life forever."

"I see," Tig replied. She couldn't say Henry's answer surprised her— she'd always seen Rolf as a cold fish. "Please don't mention my suspicions to Rolf. It may turn out to be nothing."

"I will say nothing, if you'll do likewise. I don't want my comments getting back to Karen."

She nodded, and looked at Cerissa. "Do I have your agreement?"

"I won't say anything to him. Or to Karen."

"Thank you for your cooperation." She stood up. There was one other line of inquiry left, and she didn't want to spill Henry's secrets in front of Cerissa. "I have a few more questions for you, Henry. Would you prefer to answer them in private?"

"That isn't necessary. You may ask your questions. I don't mind discussing Erin in front of Cerissa."

"Erin? I wanted to know the name of your bookie."

He raised his eyebrows. "Ah, bookie?"

Did he think his innocent look would fool her? "The men who attacked you and Yacov, they all had mob ties. Are you delinquent on any of your bets?"

"It's not in my best interests to admit to illegal gambling."

Tig rolled her eyes. "You know we don't enforce those laws on the Hill. The council doesn't care if you want to waste your money."

"Still..." Henry hesitated.

"I'll have the town attorney send you an immunity agreement—would that make a difference?"

"Indeed. I'll call you after I receive it."

She started to leave, and then stopped herself. She looked back at Cerissa. "I have one more request. We don't want Leopold aware of the shooting—the council is trying to keep word of it from spreading to other communities."

"Ah—" Cerissa started.

Henry held up his hand. "It's my fault. I insisted on calling Leopold last night to tell him what happened."

The council will not be pleased. Then Tig caught the look in Cerissa's eyes. "Cerissa, if there's something I should know, now is the time to tell me."

The envoy grimaced. "Ah, Leopold already knew about the first shooting, the attack on Yacov."

"How did he find out?"

Cerissa glanced over at Henry before answering. Were they hiding something? Henry nodded, a quick movement, almost imperceptible, but Tig caught it.

"Leopold mentioned it in passing," Cerissa said. "He made it sound like it was over, since both shooters were killed."

"Do you recall what he said?"

"Yes." The envoy got a faraway look in her eyes. "'Give my regards to Yacov. Lucky bastard drained one of the men who attacked him. Not much opportunity for that these days.'"

The way Cerissa parroted it, Tig suspected it was an actual quote.

Henry stood and motioned toward the door. "If you have more questions, Tig, you may speak with Cerissa later. She's been through a lot and we should let her rest."

Tig walked downstairs with Henry. It would take real evidence to crack this case. Vague suspicions about Rolf weren't going to cut it. And how did Leopold learn about the attack on Yacov? She'd have to track down who told him.

She stopped at the front door. "It would help if you made a list of potential enemies," she told him. "We need more to go on than we have right now. Much more."

CHAPTER 26

Cerissa picked up the book Henry had left on the bedstand, but she couldn't concentrate on the words. Tig had assumed Henry gave her a healing boost with his blood. Not good—she didn't want others thinking she now belonged to Henry. It might affect their faith in her project. Even under the guise of a medical emergency, drinking a vampire's blood came with certain implications.

Tig wasn't the only one who'd jumped to a wrong conclusion after observing her and Henry together. *Could Karen be right? Is Henry flirting with me?* He'd been charming and solicitous during Tig's visit. She liked the way he took charge when she was shot, his confidence in making decisions. He'd protected her from Dr. Asshole and then from Tig. When he confronted her about the Lux, his fierce determination to protect his community showed through.

I just do what I'm told, what I've been taught to do. But Henry, he does what he thinks is right. Would she ever have the confidence to make her own decisions?

In retrospect, hiding her mistake from the Protectors seemed like lunacy. She'd gone along with Ari because he was older, more experienced. If only she could be as confident as Henry, though without the anger. *Wait. Is his anger how he responds to fear? He wouldn't be the first guy to mask fear with anger.*

She rolled onto her back, staring at the ceiling instead of looking at the book in her hands. *When will he be back up here?* With everyone gone, what would it be like to be alone with him, to just be herself again?

The scent of his cologne still lingered in the room. She inhaled deeply, and a tingle began in her midriff. An image of him shirtless, dark, and sexy formed in her mind. After she was shot, he had leaned over her like that, pressing on her arm, so intense, so concerned, so enticing. And when he carried her upstairs after surgery, being cradled against his naked chest felt good—really good. He'd been so gentle with her. Even when he forced her back into bed, he'd done so without hurting her.

Wait. Am I feeling truly attracted to him as a person? This isn't just lust?

Oh no—that sounded like a bad idea. *Get a grip, Cerissa.*

She opened her book again and forced herself to read the words. After a while, she stopped dwelling on him and became engrossed in the novel. When Henry knocked at the open bedroom door, she put the book aside.

"How are you feeling?" he asked.

"Really, I'm fine." She raised her bandaged arm and moved it with no effort. After Tig left, she'd taken off the sling.

"Then would you join me downstairs?"

She followed him into the drawing room. He gestured for her to sit in a leather chair identical to his, but less worn. A glass of wine sat on the table next to the chair.

"For you."

"Thank you." She sat down and lifted the glass to her lips.

He took his chair and gripped his crucifix, twisting the chain, his handsome face pensive. She waited, nursing the wine, feeling like a character in a play he'd staged. Earlier, she thought she wanted to be alone with him. Now she wasn't so sure. There was still so much she couldn't tell him about the Lux.

I should have asked Tig to take me back to Gaea's.

He continued staring at his knee. What was bothering him? She sent a wisp of her aura toward him—maybe it would help him relax.

He pursed his lips and then released them. "From what you told Tig, Leopold knew about the attack on Yacov before you arrived on the Hill. When I mentioned it to him last night, he didn't say anything."

At least the Lux weren't making him anxious again. "I could ask Leopold how he found out."

"If you can do so without arousing his suspicions, Tig may find the answer helpful."

"Consider it done," she said. He still clutched his crucifix. "Was there something else?"

"I've been thinking about why you're on the Hill. What reason did Leopold give for wanting his project in Sierra Escondida?"

Her stomach twisted. Did he still think Leopold was behind the shootings? "He wanted it near a treaty community."

"But he specifically wanted it here."

"He was quite insistent. I didn't have any choice in the matter, not if I wanted his help."

"What will your lab produce?"

"Ah, well," she stammered. Leopold didn't want anyone knowing—yet. Should she tell Henry the truth? So far, being honest with him had worked out all right. She ran her finger around the crystal of her watch, its presence calming her. "I've been working on a new cloning technique. It has a number of uses. Take leather, for example."

"Leather?"

"I can grow cowhide from bovine stem cells, without cloning the full animal." She swept her fingers along the side of the leather chair. "Once it's processed, it looks and feels just like this."

"That could be a lucrative project. It still doesn't explain why your project must be in Sierra Escondida."

She took a deep breath. "Using the same techniques to create clones, I've been trying to produce human blood in quantity in a laboratory environment."

His eyes were suddenly bright with interest. "This is artificial blood?"

"No, the real thing. Artificial blood is currently designed as a means of transporting oxygen, as a blood expander. It doesn't have all the component parts of real blood, which is why vampires aren't using it as a source of nutrition. I'm pursuing a different route."

"Why are you doing this research?"

"Isn't it obvious? So we can feed the treaty communities."

He fell silent for a moment, and his dark eyes slowly narrowed. "So the communities would be dependent upon you and your people?"

"Leopold told me banked blood is rather stale and of limited supply. The blood I produce from clones would be fresh. It would make the treaty communities more independent of blood banks, or...other sources of blood."

"In other words, not be tempted to hunt mortals?" he asked harshly.

Shit. He sounded offended. "There would be no need to hunt mortals, if blood from clones was available."

"Even without your blood, we on the Hill do not hunt, so you need not be concerned." He folded his arms and looked away from her.

"I'm sorry. I didn't mean to insult you. I understand the treaty allows live feeding—"

"But not hunting. There is a difference."

"Look, I had no way of knowing whether some vampires still hunt mortals for blood."

"If they do, they don't stay here for long. Hunting within a hundred miles of the Hill is forbidden." He seemed more than a little miffed with her.

Was he truly angry, or was he afraid of something? But what? She increased her aura, envisioning it as a cloud surrounding him. She didn't want him to be afraid of her or her project. "Henry, I'm sorry. Please don't be angry with me."

He crossed and uncrossed his legs. "We have separated our nutritional needs from the hunt. Besides, vampires who are addicted to hunting their victims aren't allowed to stay in the treaty communities. They are tracked down and destroyed."

"But Leopold said there's a difference between feeding and hunting. All treaty communities permit feeding, during, ah...sex," she said, warmth flooding her cheeks.

"We don't need our mates to *feed* us."

She closed her eyes for a moment. The conversation had taken a wrong turn when he asked whether the community would be dependent upon her people. Was that what he was afraid of? She opened her eyes and looked into his. "Henry, the Hill would still have access to banked blood. You wouldn't be dependent on what I produced in the lab."

He remained silent, running both hands across his head, smoothing back stray hairs. He looked like he was fighting some internal struggle. She kept her aura directed toward him.

"The blood you're making..." he said. "You're sure it would be the same as human blood?"

"Of course. It's from a modified human body."

The look on his face moved from confusion to shock. "You did not say 'cloned blood.'"

Ripping the bandage off slowly wasn't going to help. She drained her wineglass first. "I've created a brainless clone of a human body," she said, smiling proudly at her success.

From the look on his face, he didn't agree with her pride. "Brainless?"

"Well, it has to have certain parts of the brain, those controlling lungs, heart, organs like that. It can't think or feel pain; I left those parts out," she said quickly, hoping his face would lose its stony look. She kept her aura flowing toward him. "The clone is like a zombie. It's not human, and it's not truly alive. It's an organic machine that produces human blood."

"Why not just...clone the blood?" he asked, seeming to struggle to find the words.

"Too many component parts—each would have to be synthesized. It would be like making one of your blended wines, but using twenty or more varieties of grapes. To get the right mix would be almost impossible, even for us."

"You have created this clone...this zombie," he said, pausing to rub his eyes with the fingers of one hand, "to feed vampires?"

"That's my goal. I might even supply hospitals with blood. I thought your people would accept the idea. Leopold applauded the concept."

"The Church...would not approve."

Oh no. Would he oppose her project on religious grounds? Her heart went into overdrive as panic swept through her. A burst of her aura shot toward Henry, and his eyes turned solid black.

Oops, too much. He gripped the carved armrests of his chair, his biceps bulging with the effort, and he whipped his head to the side like he was trying to get rid of an annoying gnat. Part of his ponytail had come undone. The tousled black strands framed his face, making him look wild and even more dangerous.

She wanted to untie the string holding back the rest of his hair and see it fall to his shoulders, and then trace his smooth jaw line with her fingers, brush his lips with hers, undo his belt buckle....

Oh damn. The things we charm, charm us. She needed to ease up before her aura backfired on them both.

Why couldn't he concentrate on her words? Something about her distracted him, ebbing and returning, a blissful feeling, one that jacked up his libido. He wanted to wallow in the scent of her, run his hands across her body....

He slouched back in his chair, his hands in his lap, trying to hide his arousal.

He couldn't take his gaze off her lips. They were full, but not too full.

He tried focusing on her entire face—an average nose, nice cheekbones, and clear green eyes—but he kept returning to her beautiful, full lips. Why did they suddenly pull him in, compelling him to press his to hers?

This isn't her real appearance—it's only an illusion. So why am I drawn to her? No, I need to remember...what? What is it I need to remember?

He touched the matrix card in his pocket and removed it. He ran his finger over the words he'd written last night.

That must be it.

He forced himself to sit up straight. "Leopold told me about your aura, your ability to charm."

"I—"

"Don't. If we are to be honest with each other, you cannot use your aura to influence me."

"I didn't mean anything by it." Her hand rose to her lips, hiding them. "I-I was afraid you'd have second thoughts about keeping my secret."

He still felt her pull. "Stop doing it."

"I am—I mean—" She dropped her hand to her lap. "I did stop. I'm not doing anything."

He sprang from his chair, crossing the distance to her in a flash to kneel in front of her, pausing inches from her face. "I said *stop it.*"

Did he see yearning in her eyes? Her scent was a tempting mix of fear and arousal. He leaned closer until his lips briefly brushed hers. The soft, smooth touch ignited a stronger fire in him. Sliding his hands around her, he lifted her up, until they stood facing each other.

He wanted to kiss her. Badly. If it wasn't her ability to charm, then something else about her drew him in. He brushed his lips against her cheek, until they were by her ear. She smelled just like his cologne—the body wash he had left for her to use. Why did the scent of his cologne on her, mingled with the fragrance of her blood, make her even more alluring? *I want...*

"May I kiss you?" he asked.

She tensed. "No—I mean, yes—I mean, I'd like to try."

He held her just a moment longer until her body relaxed in his arms, her arms sliding around him, pressing them closer together. He pulled back enough to see her face turn up to meet his lips and her scent deepen to the salty musk he found so captivating. He brought her close until her warm lips were on his, her breasts lightly brushing against his chest—just this careful and gentle taste of her threatened to drive him mad.

When he opened his lips, she did the same, his desire rising in anticipation, then the touch of her silky tongue on his—when it came, he wanted more. *So much more.*

Her pulse beat faster the longer they kissed, the sound of it urging him to kiss her more deeply. It took all his willpower not to ravish her mouth, to only caress her tongue with restrained need. He pressed against her shoulders, bringing her closer. He wanted to slip his hands lower and cup her shapely bottom, then crush her hips to his and unzip her sexy dress and take her, right here and right now.

But he couldn't move too fast. There was too much he didn't know about her. He eased back from the kiss and brought his hand to her face to stroke her soft cheek.

"So beautiful." He leaned his forehead against hers. "I have to ask. Why are you really here?"

"I-I told you," she stammered.

With their foreheads pressed against each other, his lips were still inches from hers. "I don't mean the clones," he whispered. "Why did your people want you to spy on us?"

"Study, not spy," she said breathlessly. "The Protectors want more information about your people, how your communities are organized. Our whole purpose is to protect mortals…"

She rolled her lips together and bit them. Only he should be allowed to bite those lips. He pulled her closer, until he spoke softly by her ear again.

"And you're here to ensure we aren't a threat," he said, trying to convince himself. "What would they do if they decided we were?"

"But you aren't."

"What would they do?" he asked, his voice still a whisper by her ear. He had to know the truth, what kind of danger her people posed to his community.

"I don't know." She pushed away from him, but he didn't let her go. "They have a strong ethic against interfering, so when they do, it's the least amount necessary to tip the scales in the right direction."

"Tip the scales?"

"During World War II, they stopped a German scientist from creating the atom bomb by substituting a page in his notes—it kept him going in the wrong direction."

"I see."

She pushed at his chest, and this time he released her. She started pacing, circling away from him until the chair was between them. "They aren't a threat to your existence. I wouldn't be here if they were."

She chewed on her lower lip for a second before releasing it. The action made him want to kiss those lips again.

"You," she said, pointing at him. "You should be more interested in finding out why someone was trying to kill you. That threat is real—I mean, I took the bullet meant for you. I can guarantee it was real."

"I feel confident Tig will figure out who is behind the attacks. You, she knows nothing about." He crossed his arms. He'd already made his decision—now it was time to tell her. "As long as I keep your secret, it's up to me to ensure you aren't a threat to my community. You will remain here with me until I decide what to do."

CHAPTER 27

"What?" She tried not to screech her answer, but she hadn't expected this, not after how far they'd come. Not to mention the community wouldn't allow it, not when she wasn't his mate. "I can't stay here. Gaea's already texted me multiple times. She wants to know when you'll drive me to her place. Tig told her I'm out of bed and walking around."

He stood there, looking dark and sexy and barely in control. More strands of his black hair had come loose when they kissed and now hung to his shoulders. She wanted to slide her hands into his hair, wrap her hands around the silky strands, and bring him close to her again. His eyes had turned solid black before their kiss. They were now fading back to normal. She mourned the loss a little. Another kiss wouldn't be out of the question....

No, I have to resist. Her desire for him had to be the result of too much aura. *These feelings can't be real...but that kiss...*

He stepped toward her, but before he reached her, his expression changed, the light of comprehension widening his eyes. "If you're not here to spy on us, then you *do* want us dependent on your blood source. Why? To control us?"

What should she tell him? Technically, she *was* studying the vampire communities; her spy mission focused on a smaller group—those behind the vampire dominance movement.

She couldn't tell him about the conspiracy, the threat to subjugate humans. What if he was involved? *No, that's not possible.* The Covenant, the treaty—he'd created a cloistered world to keep vampires from harming mortals. He didn't want vampires to turn mortals into slaves. *Think, damn it! My instincts can't be this wrong.* Hell, he went to war to protect mortals. *Wait, that's it—*

"Stop making up lies to tell me." He gripped her arm. "I want the truth."

"Ah, the Lux, well, we're a little concerned, if something happened to the treaty. I mean, having an alternative blood source might hold off the Malthusian crisis your war was fought over."

His eyes narrowed, but his grip relaxed. "With an increased blood supply, aren't they afraid we'd lift our restrictions on turning mortals?"

"Clone blood would be expensive to produce, but more potent than blood-bank leftovers. Superior in taste, too—we hope—enough to motivate some vampires to augment their diet with it rather than—and please don't take this the wrong way—rather than hunting. We would tightly regulate the supply, providing some blood, but not enough to justify lifting the ban."

"And if the ban is lifted?"

"We should be able to upscale production to protect mortals. But that's the fallback plan."

"I see," he said, scrunching his eyebrows together. "And the blood comes from human clones?"

"Not real clones—I mean, they aren't really human." He had raised a religious objection before their too-short kiss. She couldn't let it fester. "Do you believe cloning is wrong?"

"I believe it's a complex ethical question." He shrugged. "Stem-cell cloning shows great potential for healing many mortal illnesses. I don't believe a fertilized egg is somehow sacred. It wasn't the belief when I was mortal."

Okay, not the answer she expected. "What do you believe now?" she asked, crossing her fingers behind her back. She had held back on using her charm again. She didn't want to push them into something she wasn't ready for.

"Again, I find it a complex ethical question." He paused, seeming to consider the matter. "But based on your description, I don't think it unethical per se."

"In that case," she said, her voice rising with hope, "I could bring some back for you to sample."

"I would like that, so I may confirm it *is* superior to bagged blood."

"I'll make the arrangements." She took a deep breath and let it out. Maybe everything would all work out okay.

Then Henry looked like a completely different idea had hit him. He smiled, shaking his head.

"What's so funny?" she asked.

He pointed at her, and then himself. "You and I. Dr. Frankenstein meets Dracula."

"Now wait a minute. I wouldn't call my clones Frankenstein's monster—I didn't build them from parts of dead people."

"But you admit there is a similarity."

"Then shouldn't it be Dr. Frankenstein *feeds* Dracula?"

"Touché."

"But if I don't start finding investors here, I'm not feeding anyone." Her cell phone buzzed. She took it out of her pocket—another text from Gaea. "Look, you have to drive me back to Gaea's house or she's going to come over here."

"Hmm. We don't want another visit like last night." He gave a thoughtful frown. "Fine, I will return you to Gaea's. But you must promise you won't leave her house without speaking with me first."

"I have a feeling I'm not going anywhere anytime soon." She held up her bandaged arm. "I still have to pretend I'm recovering from this."

His face took on a determined look. "Then I will count on Gaea to keep a watchful eye on you."

Henry took Cerissa to Gaea's, helping her up to her room and into bed. He resisted the urge to kiss her goodbye. Much as he wanted to, with Gaea hovering over them, it was a very bad idea.

On his way out, Blanche pulled him aside into a sitting room. He didn't take the chair she offered him.

"Would you like some company tonight?" Blanche asked, cocking her head a little coyly and licking her lips.

"I'm sorry. I have business to attend to."

"What did Rolf think of my proposal?"

"I only gave it to him tonight. With the shooting—"

"Oh, don't apologize. You had responsibilities. I'll call you in a few nights, see how it's going."

He excused himself, and instead of catching up with winery business, he returned home and rode his motorcycle up the mountain trail behind his house until the road became too rocky, and then hiked the rest of the way. The mountain overlooked the valley. From it, he could see the gently rolling hills covered by vineyards, each homestead lit up with shaded floodlights. Bud break had occurred and the vines were rapidly greening up. Under the bright full moon, it looked like someone had taken a heavy rake and dragged a sweeping arc across a layer of green paint, allowing the dark brown underneath to show through. He turned his back on the view and faced the mountain's dark forest, sitting down on a bench.

Carved into the gray granite of the bench was a date. He traced the year with his finger. 1889. The year he'd killed Nathaniel over a woman. He had carried the heavy bench up there himself, refusing any help, even though it broke something in his back when he did it, the stone's weight too much even for his vampire strength. A small penance, one of many he'd paid over the years, unable to earn absolution.

He closed his eyes and flattened his hand against the bench, the stone cold and unliving. The bench stood as a reminder of what he truly was and why he could never allow himself to love again.

He opened his eyes again. Instead of seeing the pine trees in front of him, he saw only darkness, the darkness of the abyss. He had enjoyed kissing Cerissa far more than he should have. His desire to see her again chilled his soul with a dark fear. The darkness murmured in his ear: *You will never overcome the evil you are—you will only bring death.*

What was he thinking? He should be doing everything he could to get her away from the Hill. Gone, she would no longer tempt him. Gone, she would no longer threaten the Hill. Gone, he would return to the loneliness he deserved.

He traced the stone-carved year with his finger, feeling sucked in. He couldn't afford to fall in love with her. Whatever he loved, he destroyed. He had chosen Erin because he had never loved her—it was safer for everyone if he didn't love his mate.

He buried his face in his hands. Maybe he should stay here until dawn and let the sun's rays kill him. There was no other way to cleanse the earth of his unforgivable sin.

He shook his head, dislodging the thought. Destroying himself wasn't a solution—it left his community ignorant of the potential threat. He touched the matrix card tucked in his pocket. Why had he agreed to keep secret what she'd told him? Sure, her aura had affected him, but it wasn't what caused him to remain quiet. In spite of his words, he could tell when she stopped using it on him. Yet he had felt drawn to her, compelled to kiss her.

He couldn't tell Rolf about her. Rolf's distrust of the envoy had doubled overnight. Rolf would never keep her secret—he would shout the truth from the rooftops, and the whole council would know.

If I told Rolf, I wouldn't be able to stop the disaster that would follow. And then there were Tig's suspicions about Rolf—another reason to stay silent for now.

I should tell Yacov instead. Yacov can be trusted to keep what she is secret. Then, if something happens to me, the community will know about the Lux. But so far, he hadn't been able to pick up the phone.

Was he so broken that a pretty girl with a sympathetic story could tempt him to sacrifice the safety of the Hill? Yet she was more than just a pretty girl—she was smart and brave and put his welfare above her own.

He had to think. Her scheme to bring a new blood supply to the treaty communities—did it hide a way to poison all of them, to rid the world of vampires for good? Even though he wanted to trust Cerissa, her people may not be so benevolent. It wouldn't be the first time a beautiful female was used to lure the male. Coyotes did it all the time—he'd watched them, watched the calculated way the pack sent a bitch in heat to draw a male dog from the safety of his yard, and right into the jaws of the pack. After all, the pack had to eat.

He slipped the matrix card out of his pocket and looked down at it. Then he looked up at the dark sky, the stars shining with a deepening intensity. He wanted her, wanted her like the male dog he was. He just hoped her pack wasn't waiting to rip apart the community he'd spent his long life building.

CHAPTER 28

"I have a silver bullet pointed at your heart," he said, aiming a gun just above Henry's breastbone.

Henry looked at the gun and then at the shoulders of his opponent. *Always watch the shoulders.* The shoulders told you what would happen next. Moving rapidly, he stepped to the side while pushing the man's gun arm toward the ground, holding it there with his full strength. With his free hand he punched repeatedly in the direction of the man's face and reached down to grab the butt of the gun, twisting it out of his assailant's hand.

"Good job, my friend," Yacov said. "Let's take a break, shall we?"

Henry agreed, grabbing a towel off the pile the Hill gym provided. Yacov made a good sparring partner. Judo, Krav Maga, taekwondo, even boxing—he'd practiced just about every martial art with Yacov. Vampire speed and strength gave him an advantage, but nothing substituted for real skill. He removed his heart shield, a harness with a steel and leather center, which protected his heart from accidental impalement while they sparred.

Yacov's wife had been watching them from the spectator area. She was in her mid-thirties, but reminded Henry of an old soul. A headscarf, which she wore for religious reasons, covered her long brown hair. Yacov offered him a chair, and they joined her, forming a small circle.

"I've been waiting patiently for you two to finish," Shayna said, returning her crochet work to a basket on the floor, carefully folding a half-finished shawl. "Now I want to hear all about the shooting."

Henry used the towel he held to wipe sweat from his forehead before draping it over one knee. "There isn't much to tell. We were horseback riding when a sniper fired at me. Leopold's envoy got in the way."

"Is she all right?" Yacov asked.

"She was doing well when I dropped her off at Gaea's last night. I tried to stop by tonight to check on her, but Gaea turned me away at the door. She didn't think Cerissa was up for visitors yet."

"And the shooter?"

"Dead."

"Any idea who's behind it?" Shayna asked.

"I'm sorry, no."

Yacov patted his wife's hand. "Shayna is still worried over what happened to me."

"It's terrible, that's all."

"I understand," Henry said. "We've always felt safe here, until now." And Cerissa's people upped the threat level—not that he'd tell Yacov that. Last night, he'd made up his mind to stay silent. "Tig asked me to make a list of all persons who might want me dead. Perhaps we begin with our time on the town council?"

"I know, I know," Yacov replied. "I owe her an answer too. She asked me for the same list." Yacov did the math out loud: "We were on the council, what, eighty years?"

"Eighty-four." Henry tied back his ponytail, which had become undone while they sparred. "It's easy to anger people when you're making decisions affecting their lives."

Shayna stared at him in disbelief. "You think it's someone who didn't like a council ruling? You both resigned from the council back in the seventies. That's a long time for someone to carry a grudge."

Not a long time when it came to vampires, but he didn't want to upset Shayna. "Tig also wants a list of those we turned down for residency."

"There is that, isn't there?" Yacov agreed.

He and Yacov still sat on the board of directors for the homeowners' association, which controlled who could live on the Hill. Henry took a piece of paper out of his pocket and unfolded it. "Counting only the requests we've turned down, the number is over twenty-five."

"But you and I didn't always vote the same way on those matters."

"That's why the number is only twenty-five. It would be much higher if I'd included those we differed on." He handed the list to Yacov and pointed to four names on the list, each starred in red. "Those four have made recent requests for residency."

"Tig should be able to work with those names," Yacov said. "Are there any other decisions we should consider, ones that might incite a grudge?"

"Requests to turn a lover are probably a close second."

Yacov frowned. "But requests to make someone a vampire would have gone to the town council. They wouldn't be a board decision."

"True. Denials we were involved with would be much older decisions."

"I see it as a double-edged sword," Yacov said, holding up two fingers. "Some would be angry because their request was turned down and their mate ultimately died, and others would be angry because their request was granted and it didn't turn out well."

"As a group, we can be delusional," Henry agreed. "To imagine it will be different, that a maker and the vampire they sire will remain in love for all eternity, when most evidence points to the contrary."

"Never underestimate the power of the vampire mind to mislead one into folly. Did you make the second list yet?"

"No."

"Then let me," Yacov said. "Is there any other group we should include from our time on the council?"

"We might include those we ordered staked, to see if any relatives are still alive and vengeful."

"I'll take care of that third list too. I have extra time on my hands, since I won't be traveling to Los Angeles anytime soon."

"No you will not," Shayna said, folding her arms across her chest.

"And you wonder why I have never been married," Henry said lightly.

"That's the problem, my friend. You have only known the institution from the outside. Once you have been married, you will know its true value." Yacov took his wife's hand lovingly, unwinding her crossed arms.

"Perhaps you are right," Henry said, mostly to be polite.

"Someday you'll have the courage to find out."

He doubted he would. Even his sudden attraction to Cerissa wouldn't overcome his doubt. "There is another possibility we should discuss. The person behind the attacks may live on the Hill."

"Not something I like to consider," Yacov replied.

"But it is something Tig raised." Henry shifted in his chair, his fingers reaching for his crucifix. "Please don't tell anyone I asked this. Have you ever had any trouble with Rolf?"

"You mean because he was a Nazi and I'm a Jew?"

"I don't like posing the question, but yes, that is the question."

Yacov stroked his beard, intense in his concentration. Finally, he released the wavy end and pointed in Henry's direction. "You see, it's like this. When Rolf first came to the Hill, he became involved in public service, do you remember?"

"Yes, vaguely."

"He worked closely with me on the subcommittee when we designed the new country club. He was always respectful at those meetings, no indication of any problem. But then, why should he have a problem with me? As I got to know him, I learned he was conscripted into the military—he hadn't joined the Nazis voluntarily."

"He told me the same story."

"Over the years, Rolf has remained cordial," Yacov said, looking pensive for a moment, "although at times he seems jealous of our friendship."

"Aside from that, you have detected no prejudice?"

"None," Yacov said. "And once I thought about it, I realized I shouldn't be so surprised. We have managed to do something here on the Hill mortals have not."

"And what is that?"

"Look around you." Yacov swept his hand out like he was surveying the Hill. "Vampires from every continent, of every skin color, live on the Hill. Both men and women. Race, nationality, religion, gender, and sexual orientation—they don't matter here."

"Of course," Henry said. "We have transcended those surface differences. Here, we are all equals."

Shayna shook her head. "You two are missing the point. You haven't created an egalitarian society. You've just changed who's at the top of the patriarchal pyramid."

Henry furrowed his brow. "I don't understand."

"My wife should join the committee on mortal rights, but she refuses," Yacov said.

"I don't like to argue," she said with a shrug. "Haley and Nicholas will do a good job representing all of us."

Will they now? He bit his tongue to stop from saying it out loud. Tig had mentioned the committee two nights ago, but after learning about Cerissa's origins, the conversation he intended to have with Yacov had slipped to the bottom of his mental to-do list.

"You're leaving Henry in a quandary, dear heart. Go ahead, tell him your thoughts."

Shayna motioned with her hand, as if she were pointing at something above her head. "Under a traditional patriarchy, white men are at the top of the pyramid. They make the rules and control the rest of us—we're at a lower rung on the pyramid." She lowered her hand. "You've just changed it so vampires are at the top and in control in this community."

"But we built this community to protect mortals."

Yacov's eyes cautioned him. "You've stepped into it now."

"'Protection' is part of the patriarchal myth," Shayna continued. "'Benevolent protection' isn't possible. It just feeds your belief system: vampires are predators, mortals are prey; vampires are strong, mortals are weak; vampires are smart, mortals are easily fooled; the list goes on and on. And each belief on your list justifies your attempt to retain power and control. As long as you keep thinking that way, you'll never build the egalitarian society you think you have."

"Then why do you stay?" Henry asked.

"I have what I want," she said, looking at Yacov. Her face softened as she smiled at her husband. "Sometimes what you want, and what you think you *should* want, are entirely different things. I was raised in a patriarchal culture, and it's so much a part of me, it's what feels normal—but it doesn't mean I'm blind to the ramifications."

"I never knew you felt this way."

Shayna shrugged. "Why talk about it? Yacov treats me with respect. As do you, for the most part. I've preferred to have peace at home rather than stir things up, but I do see it. Hill vampires are paternalistic when it comes to the mortals you bring here. You see us as something to objectify and master—to serve your needs."

"But mortals are treated well on the Hill," Henry said. This was his community. He'd been a key player in creating it. An attack on it was an attack on him.

"Henry, I don't want to argue with you, but you're making my point," Shayna said. "Vampires see mortals as the 'other' to be taken care of and treated well. It's built into the Covenant—a document written without our involvement."

"But—"

"The person who controls the discourse exercises power—and power on the Hill is exercised by vampires." She sighed. "I've taken us far afield, and I didn't mean to. You were asking Yacov about Rolf. Did you have a reason for asking?"

He shifted in his chair, his stomach uncharacteristically churning. He respected Yacov and his mate. The Hill had been set up to protect the mortals who were brought here, as well as serve vampire needs. How could that be wrong?

"Henry?" Yacov prompted.

"Rolf, yes, well. I don't know how to say this gracefully. Tig asked if Rolf might be behind the shootings."

"Why would Tig think that?"

"Because Rolf is my current heir, he might have something to gain from my death. I've been thinking about it since she suggested it, and I don't know what to believe."

"My friend, what does your gut tell you?" Yacov asked, tapping his stomach.

"Rolf would never do anything to harm me."

"That is your answer," Yacov said. "Trust your gut to know what is right."

CHAPTER 29

CERISSA'S ROOM—THE NEXT MORNING

Cerissa contemplated her breakfast, which Dylan had delivered to her. One week since her arrival on the Hill, and she'd managed to get herself shot, confessed her origins to a founder, and was now stuck in bed, unable to pitch her project or gather intelligence.

She couldn't have screwed up worse if she'd tried.

Last night, Gaea had refused to allow Henry to visit her. Why not? A visit would have hurt nothing. She had to stay in contact with him, to ensure he kept his promise. In spite of his demand that she stop using her aura to persuade him, she couldn't let her enchantment of him fully wear off. A *little* charm wouldn't hurt...or maybe something more?

No, she couldn't seduce him to buy his silence. It wouldn't be fair. *I mean, that is why I want to seduce him...right? To buy his silence?*

With his visit thwarted, the room seemed to close in on her. The heavy drapes, frilly floral comforter, and lace doilies were the trappings of a feminine jail, but a jail nonetheless. And that was after only one day in bed. How would she feel if her confinement went on much longer?

Well, at least she had plenty of food. She dug into her scrambled eggs before they got colder. Dylan's voice suddenly interrupted the silence.

"Hey, Cerissa," he said, standing at her open door. He carried two flower arrangements into her room.

"For me?" she asked, her eyes widening.

"Your name is on the cards."

"Ah, okay. Please put them over there," she said, pointing at the glass table by the window.

Once he was gone, she moved her breakfast tray aside and slid out of bed, reaching for the cards. The first one was from Zeke. He'd sent a dozen pink roses and wrote, "Missing you," on the card. The stunning arrangement of blood-red orchids, intertwined around tall green reeds, had to be from Henry. She opened his card and laughed at his dry sense of humor—the card wished her a speedy recovery.

Shortly after sunset, her phone rang. Could it be Henry? She grabbed for her phone from the nightstand and fumbled it. When she saw the caller ID, she slowed down. Maybe she should leave it unanswered.

She took a deep breath. Better to get it over with; he'd just call back. She punched the accept button. "Hello, Zeke."

"Howdy, Cerissa," Zeke said. "Are you okay?"

"My arm isn't too sore, it seems to be healing quickly. The doctor did a good job." She rolled her eyes, but tried to sound sincere. "And thank you for the get-well roses. They're lovely."

"I'm glad you liked them. I just felt so bad I had to leave, with you injured and all."

"I understand. Business has to come first."

"I'll be back in a few weeks. Can I see you then?"

She hesitated. She wasn't permitted to date him, for crying out loud. Why did he keep pressing it?

"Sure, Zeke," she finally said. "But as friends, okay? Besides, you were going to tell me all about your work, remember?"

"Of course, Cerissa. Whatever you say, little lady."

I'm really starting to hate that pet name. "All right, call me when you're back." Even if she didn't want to date Zeke, she still had her mission for the Lux. Something about Zeke's out-of-town work seemed off—could he be involved in the vampire dominance movement?

"Where are you now?" she asked.

171

"I've made it to Costa Rica. My assignment is taking me to South America, so I have a bit of traveling to do."

Her phone beeped and she glanced at it—a number she didn't recognize. "I have to go now, Zeke. I'll see you when you return."

"You bet."

She clicked over to the new caller.

"Good evening, Cerissa."

Hearing Henry say her name, the way he slightly rolled the R, brought a smile to her face. "Thank you for the flowers. Orchids are my favorite."

"For one as exotic as you, I didn't think any other flower appropriate."

"I appreciate your sense of humor, too," she said.

"Yes, well, I wrote my message in case Gaea saw it. Speaking of your hostess, when does she think you'll be ready for visitors?"

"She's waiting for the doctor to declare I've recovered."

"I see. While we wait for Dr. Clarke's decision, do you need anything?"

She smiled, even though he couldn't see it. "I need someone to let me out of this prison."

"Shall I climb the wall and free you through your window?"

"It would be nice if you did," she said, her smile growing.

"But then I would have to slay the dragon who keeps you there, and I like Gaea too much to harm her."

"Yes, but now I have you at my mercy, or I'll tell Gaea you called her a dragon."

"It's not good to have a vampire at your mercy," he said, his voice taking on a serious tone. "He can be unpredictable."

"Then I take back my threat," she said with a laugh.

"In that case, please call me when Dr. Clarke declares you fit for visitors. I look forward to seeing you again."

"Me too," she said, knowing it was true as soon as she said it.

"Goodnight, Cerissa."

"Good sleep, Henry."

She clicked off the call and stared at the now-quiet phone. Henry sounded like everything was okay. She closed her eyes and sighed, relaxing back into her pillows, reliving his lighthearted banter. Everything was going to be all right.

Henry looked down at the index card. The decision matrix. He had held the card during their phone call, balancing on the precipice, second-guessing his decision not to tell Yacov about her origins. Was his decision wrong? Would it hurt his community? He'd spent his long life learning to unravel the lies mortals spun to serve their own ends, and it made him a formidable negotiator in business. His gut said she wasn't lying. He shoved the matrix card into his pocket. Yacov was right—he would trust his gut.

For now.

CHAPTER 30

THE HILL CHAPEL—FOUR NIGHTS LATER

The rectory office door was open. Henry tapped lightly before peering inside. Matt sat behind his desk. "Father, may I have a moment of your time?"

"Come in, Henry. I have a few minutes before my next appointment."

"This shouldn't take long." He took the guest chair in front of Matt's desk. He hadn't called for an appointment on purpose. This couldn't be a confession, not while he promised to keep Cerissa's secrets. "Shayna said something, and it's bothering me. I wanted to get your opinion."

"Go ahead."

"Do you think the way our community is structured is wrong?"

"In what way?"

"We control everything—the council, the homeowners' association, the police force—and mortals have no say in any of it."

"I see." Matt glanced in the direction of his desk clock. "Your question could take hours to discuss."

"But mortals are protected, they're cherished. All their needs are met. How would it be better for them if they had an equal vote or could be on the council?"

Matt cocked his head, furrowing his brow. "Henry, you lived through the Civil War, the Jim Crow laws, the women's suffrage movement, the civil rights movement, cycles of discrimination against Hispanics like yourself—how can you live through all that and still ask your question?"

"But this is different. We will be part of this community for hundreds of years. Most mortals are here for ten or twenty years. When they start to age, the depression of living among immortal beings becomes too much. They leave. You know they do."

"I know it all too well. Who do you think they turn to when those issues start bothering them?"

Henry's hand sought the cross at his neck. "Then how can you suggest we put our lives in the hands of mortals? They have no idea what it means to be vampire. To live with the temptations we live with. What if they gained political control and voted to change the rules—to allow more vampires to be made so they could become immortal?"

"You're talking as if we're a straight democracy, where the masses can vote bread and circuses. We're not. We're a representative democracy. The Hill residents elect a council, and the council decides, within the limits set by the treaty."

"Still, if enough mortals banded together…"

"They could not control the entire council, not if vampires continue to vote. And you're assuming every mortal on the Hill wants to be vampire. I can tell you from talking with them, your assumption is wrong." Matt looked down at his desk for a moment. "When you asked me to come to the Hill, you recall I was living at the Buddhist monastery in Los Angeles."

Henry nodded. A friend who lived at the monastery had contacted him about Father Matt. His friend had been right. Matt was a good fit for Sierra Escondida. He'd never questioned his decision to invite Matt here until this moment.

"Do you recall how I came to be at the monastery?" Matt asked.

"Your maker abandoned you there."

"I'd been working with runaway teens. I mistook my maker for one of them. When I followed her to her lair to invite her back to the homeless shelter, I must have scared her. She drained me, but I could see it in her eyes. She didn't mean to kill me, and she offered me life. But she didn't want a fledging following her around, so she dumped me at the door of the monastery."

"You'd never told me the details before."

"I was fortunate that the monastery took me in. A small group of six vampires—what they all had in common was this: they were appalled at having to drink human blood to survive. Most had been Buddhists. That small group founded the monastery. One member was an ultra-orthodox Jew who came to live with them, whose religion prohibited drinking human blood. The last resident was an atheist vegetarian."

Henry already understood the dilemma. At some level, whether religious or not, they'd each had to face it and make compromises to live. Yacov kept a separate office refrigerator to hold donor blood, so it wasn't in the kosher kitchen Shayna kept.

"Father, I know you like to use stories to teach, but I don't see how this relates to the Hill."

"Just like you, that small group of Buddhists had to struggle with their own moral issue: did Buddha's prohibitions against eating human flesh mean they should starve to death?"

"I'm assuming they decided it didn't."

"On the contrary. They didn't just 'decide.' One of their members chose to starve to death rather than compromise her beliefs. The rest struggled with what to do, they meditated, and they debated among themselves and within themselves. They still struggle with it. They drink bagged blood, but they do so realizing it's an ethical compromise. They don't do it *blindly*."

"And you think my belief in the righteousness of our community is a blind belief."

"Henry, some of the mortals I've spoken with aren't happy with being disenfranchised, and Rolf isn't helping things by proposing the Rule of Two apply to them. At this moment I'm not saying they are right, or you are right. I'm saying this: until you are willing to question your own beliefs, you won't be open to seeing new ones."

Henry paused. Yacov's suggestion to trust his gut—was it right every time? Matt didn't know the whole story—he didn't know how bad it was in the old days before the Covenant. The community couldn't give mortals free rein; they needed strict rules or the sins of the past would return.

He stood up. "Thank you for your time, Father."

CHAPTER 31

Tig unlocked the police station door and groaned as she pushed it open. *Seven nights since the envoy was shot and I'm still no closer to solving either shooting.* Jayden had grumbled about her going into the office early on a Sunday night, but he understood—she wouldn't rest until she had the culprit in her jail.

At least she had Jayden to help her during the day. Before he joined them, she had no daytime support, just like when she worked for Phat—a lone agent, getting the information Phat needed or making the kill she was paid for. She respected Phat, but she hadn't entirely trusted him.

With Jayden, she had a daytime partner she could trust. But it still felt strange to partner with a man. Before Jayden, men were her targets, a quick lay, or someone she had to obey. She'd missed the partnership she had with her sister-wives. Their emotional closeness had nothing to do with sex or power. She had warned Jayden before he came to the Hill—she had a blank spot in her head when it came to what Americans called romantic love. But Jayden offered both emotional closeness and sex, and having a mortal lover had its advantages. She smiled, picturing the white sheet draped across his naked black ass, her fang marks healing on his neck.

She censored the mental image—time to focus on business. Her community needed her protection. Dr. Clarke, acting as coroner, had completed the autopsy report and left it on her clerk's desk. She dug into the mess of paperwork. Where was it? She thumbed through each stack until she found the official blue paper of the coroner's office. Someone had dumped the daytime logs on top of it.

She took the report to her office and slumped into her chair. She skimmed through it before coming to what interested her most: the ballistics report. Four bullets recovered, three from the body. Karen fired but missed. Jayden's shot lodged in the sniper's chest, entering through the side of his ribcage.

Tig's own bullet had gone through the sniper's trigger hand, a perfect disarming hit—one she had practiced so often it was second nature. Mortal police never tried for that shot; too risky. With the enhanced eyesight and motor control of a vampire, it was easy for her.

The kill shot, though, had entered through his temple, and that bullet belonged to Rolf's gun. Had Rolf done it on purpose so the shooter wouldn't survive? Or was it just the stress of the moment—go for the sure kill? Of Rolf's possible motives—inheriting from Henry or turning Karen—money seemed more likely than love.

But then why try to kill—or kidnap—Yacov? The two men who attacked Yacov had been cellmates in prison, one incarcerated for extortion, the other for knifing a guy while trying to collect an unpaid bet for a small racketeering outfit. The sniper who shot Cerissa had been on the same cell block, serving time for running drugs.

She sat back in her chair, tapping her pen against her lips. A visit to the prison in San Diego was top priority. Information on the three shooters—information that wasn't in the official prison reports—might lead to the real person behind the attacks.

She threw her pen down on her desk. *Damn!* There was no way she could do it herself—how would she explain the interviews had to be at night? She turned to her computer, opened the investigation tracking program, and made a note in the file. Jayden was a good investigator—he could handle it for her.

The sound of a car parking outside her window caught her attention. *Right on time.* The door to the police station buzzed and she went out to greet her visitors.

"I have a few questions for Cerissa," she told Gaea. "Would you mind waiting here?"

Gaea sat down in one of the visitor chairs in the waiting room. "Of course, dear. I brought a magazine with me just in case. Don't mind me."

"Cerissa, if you would come this way?" Tig motioned toward a hallway. She followed Cerissa to the small conference room, which doubled as an interrogation room. She wanted to question Cerissa without Henry running interference this time.

Cerissa still wore a sling to protect her right arm. Henry's blood should have healed the wound by now. Why pretend to be injured? She couldn't shake the feeling Cerissa was hiding something.

After offering the envoy a chair across from her, she laid out mug shots and morgue photos of Yacov's attackers on the conference room table. "Do you know these men?"

"Who are they?" Cerissa asked, picking up each photo and studying it.

"The men who shot at Yacov."

"I'm sorry, I don't."

Not the answer Tig wanted. If Cerissa had seen them around the New York Collective, Leopold would be a viable suspect. "Did you remember how Leopold found out about the attack on Yacov?"

"I did better than that. I asked him."

"You what?" Tig said, her voice rising. The last thing she wanted was Leopold alerted to her suspicions.

Cerissa flinched. "Ah, I asked him. He said Yacov told him."

"Yacov?"

"Yacov called Leopold the night he was attacked."

Tig pressed her lips together. She'd asked Yacov about Leopold. Why hadn't Yacov reported the conversation to her? She could feel her temper flare, and took a deep breath to tamp it down—she didn't want to scare Cerissa into silence. "Why was Yacov talking with Leopold?"

"Leopold said Yacov was very upset."

"Is Yacov an investor in Leopold's project?"

Cerissa looked sad. "No. No one from the Hill has invested in it yet."

Tig placed the photos back in the file. "Do you know anyone at the Camp Pendleton Marine Base?" she asked.

Cerissa tilted her head, a puzzled expression on her face. "No. Why?"

"The sniper scope was stolen from there. The base is near San Diego."

"I don't know anything about it."

Well, it was a long shot. Cerissa didn't smell like a lie, and her facial reaction—the envoy was surprised by the question. "That's all I have for now," Tig said. "I'm sorry to inconvenience you while you're still recovering."

"It's no problem."

"If you think of anything, no matter how small, call me." She started to stand.

Cerissa remained seated. "There was one other thing."

"Go ahead." Tig sat back down. She never knew what might be volunteered. It wouldn't be the first time a conspirator broke the case by saying too much.

Cerissa seemed to hesitate. "Is it possible Henry and Yacov were targeted because they're founders of this community?"

Tig leaned forward. "How is it you're aware who our founders are?" she asked sternly.

Cerissa paled but continued. "Ah, Leopold mentioned them. He briefed me on how the Hill is structured."

"Why would you be interested in that?"

"Well, if we're going to build the lab here, we need their approval. Leopold thought if both the town council and the founders favored the idea...."

"I see," Tig said. "But you haven't explained why you believe our founders are the target. There are five founders. Only two have been attacked."

"It was something Henry said—the most obvious connection between him and Yacov."

"You're right, it is obvious," Tig replied. And Henry should learn when to keep his mouth shut. The Hill couldn't afford loose lips until she ruled out Leopold as a suspect. "We are investigating all angles, and when we catch the vampire behind this, I will personally enjoy putting a stake through their heart, including executing any *mortals* who are involved."

Cerissa stared at her. "Of course."

Tig suddenly wished she hadn't said that. She should be doing everything to protect Cerissa, not threaten her—after all, Cerissa was the victim here. "Do you need help returning to Gaea's car?"

"I can get there myself," Cerissa said, rising hurriedly and moving past her.

Where did that guilt come from? It wasn't like her to feel empathy for a suspect. She shook off the strange feeling and followed Cerissa back to the lobby. Whatever Cerissa and Leopold were up to, it had better not threaten the Hill.

Cerissa returned to her room, and Gaea insisted she go to bed. She didn't fight it. The visit with Tig had unsettled her. She had resorted to using her aura to get Tig to back down, something she didn't want to do, but this was the last thing she needed—Tig suspecting she had something to do with the shootings.

Cerissa threw on lounging pajamas and crawled under the covers, staring at the ceiling, replaying her conversation with Tig over and over again. How could she have handled it differently? When she heard her bedroom door open, she sat up.

"Hey, sunshine," Blanche said. The blonde vampire flounced over onto the slipper chair and put her feet up on the edge of Cerissa's bed. "Gaea says you're still feeling poorly."

"Gunshot wounds take time to heal."

"Come on, everybody knows Henry gave you his blood. Why fake it?"

How did these rumors get started? "I'm tired and want to rest."

"Still milking it, eh? Well, don't shoot the messenger, but there's a rumor going around."

"Zeke already told me, and I'll tell you the same thing. I'm not looking for a vampire mate."

Blanche laughed and leaned back in the slipper chair, balancing it on two legs, her hair doing that fringe thing against her collar as she turned her head. "That was yesterday's news. Now they're saying your lab's a sham. Leopold is using you to spy on us."

Had Henry said something to Rolf? No, she refused to believe it. "Whoever *they* are, *they* don't know what they're talking about."

"Word on the street is no one's gonna to invest in your company. You might as well move on before they throw you out, or worse."

"You'd like me to leave, wouldn't you? No competition for investors that way."

Blanche's eyes flashed black. "Don't make this about me," she said, just short of a snarl. Sitting up, she banged the front legs of her chair on the floor. "I was doin' ya a favor, lettin' you know."

"Next time you feel like doing me a favor, don't. Now please leave."

CHAPTER 32

Alone in his game room, Henry pressed the video controller to capture additional ammunition and reload his AK-47. Now he could resume firing at the military invaders who were headed his way on-screen, laying down cover for his team.

His phone rang. He glanced down at it—a quick moment averting his eyes, and his on-screen alter ego almost bought the farm. He moved the avatar to a safe location in the video game and then glanced down at the caller ID again. Seeing Cerissa's name, a pleasant rush of anticipation flowed through him. He paused the video game and swiped the screen to accept the call. Rolf could carry the team without him.

"Tig suspects something is off about me," she said.

Not exactly what he expected to hear. "Why do you believe that?"

She told him what Tig and Blanche had said. "Maybe I should leave the Hill, at least until things calm down. I can come back and try another time."

Henry's pulse shot up and his mouth went dry. She couldn't leave. Too much was at stake if the Lux were a threat. And the way she kissed him… No, she just couldn't leave now.

"I don't agree with your assessment of the situation," he said, trying to sound confident. "If Tig suspected you were behind the shootings, you would not have been dealt with so lightly. It's a standard technique, to lay out the consequences, hoping to drive the guilty into making a mistake."

"If she suspects me, she might really dig into my background. It won't stand up to close scrutiny."

"Anyone who joins our community is eyed with suspicion for a time. I'm sure Tig has been investigating your background. If she hasn't said anything, then her initial inquiries supported what you told them."

"But what about the rumor Blanche heard?"

Do I tell her Rolf and I were responsible for those rumors? He scrubbed his hand across his face. "There are those who've been opposed to your presence from the beginning," he said. "I don't believe it's as widespread as Blanche makes it out to be, or you wouldn't still be here."

"But—"

"Don't let it worry you. Frankly, I'm unimpressed with Blanche's proposal, and I doubt she'll find sponsors on the Hill. As for Tig, well, she probably became concerned when you discussed my theories with her."

"Is that why Gaea isn't allowing me any visitors? She claims it's the doctor's order, but I doubt Dr. Clarke cares. I mean, he let me go to the police station."

"I'll check with him," he offered.

"Thank you, Henry. Right now, I feel like I'm under house arrest."

"I'll take care of it."

He returned the phone to his belt. She was right about one thing: the doctor didn't care whether she had visitors. Dr. Clarke was acting under Henry's orders. He wanted her confined with no visitors until he could figure out what to do about her people. He hadn't meant the "no visitors" order to include himself, but that was how Gaea had interpreted it.

He pulled the matrix card from this back pocket, recalling the kiss they'd shared. If he wasn't such a cautious person, they might have shared more than a kiss. But he couldn't give in to the feelings she evoked. It wasn't safe for him to fall in love; it would never be safe.

He flicked the matrix card with his finger. *I can't keep her confined at Gaea's forever. She'll disappear if she feels like a prisoner. There has to be another way.*

He turned back to the video game and switched on the headset's microphone, connecting him to the rest of the game players. "Rolf, is Grayson still on? I don't see his character."

"Right here, Henry," Grayson said over the headset, his character poking his head out from behind a wall pocked with bullet holes. "What do you need?"

"Please call me after the game." Henry un-paused his avatar and joined the action in time to save Dr. Grayson Clarke from a sniper. It never hurt to have someone owe you a favor.

"Why, Dr. Clarke, I didn't expect you tonight," Gaea said.

The door to Cerissa's room was open. She was in bed, using her computer tablet to work. Her ears perked up at the mention of Dr. Asshole's name.

Hmm, I better stop calling him that before I slip up.

"Henry suggested I should check on her." The voice of Dr. Clarke grew nearer. "He tells me she's doing well."

"I don't know what he would know about it. He hasn't been here to see her."

"Doesn't matter. I'll see for myself."

Gaea followed the doctor into the room. "Cerissa," Gaea said, "you really should wear your sling. I'm not sure it's good for you to be typing just yet."

Cerissa put her tablet aside, and Dr. Clarke began removing the bandages. "No sign of infection. It appears to be healing just fine. Has she been taking her antibiotics?"

Cerissa handed him the bottle. She'd made a point to remove two pills a day and dispose of them, just in case.

Dr. Clarke counted the pills. "She's been taking them." He returned the pill container to the bedstand. "How are you feeling?" he asked her.

Cerissa's eyes widened. He'd deigned to ask her a direct question. "Uh, fine. I'm doing fine. No pain, but it does itch."

"That's normal." He dabbed on antibiotic cream and replaced the old bandage with a smaller one over each incision. He then went through a series of tests designed to assess her strength and reflexes. Looking satisfied, he turned to Gaea and said, "Well, I see no medical reason to confine her to your house."

"We should talk privately," Gaea suggested.

"No need. I've cleared her, and that settles it." He reached into his bag. "Here."

Cerissa accepted the glass vial he handed her. The clear glass revealed a small quantity of red liquid, the black cap keeping it from leaking out. "I don't understand."

"My blood. Apply it to the stitches a few days in a row and you won't have a scar."

"I'm not sure I can. I'm Leopold's envoy...."

"That didn't stop you from accepting Henry's blood."

She gulped. Too late—now Gaea had heard the theory. "It was an emergency."

"Doesn't matter. Medicinal need trumps Leopold's interest. I checked the treaty."

"Ah, thank you." She accepted the vial, knowing she'd never use it.

Gaea narrowed her eyes with displeasure. "I'll see you out, doctor."

"Keep taking your antibiotic and call me if any sign of infection develops—redness or oozing. Shouldn't happen if you use my blood," he said, pointing at the vial. "I'll stop by in another week to take out the stitches."

Cerissa's smile bloomed as soon as Gaea was gone. Her knight hadn't slain the dragon who guarded her, but he had unlocked the dragon's lair.

The phone rang. Henry looked at the name display and sent it to voicemail. Blanche could wait until he felt like talking to her. She had called a couple of times since the shooting, wanting his answer—would he invest in her idea to market Dystopian Wines? With everything going on, the last thing he needed was another call begging for money.

He laid the phone back on his couch. His fingers had barely released it when it rang again—Gaea calling using Skype. He suspected he knew why.

"Henry Bautista, what do you think you're doing interfering?" Gaea demanded when he answered. She was seated in an office chair, obviously calling from her home computer.

"Interfering?" he asked.

"With Cerissa. Tig wanted her confined to my house and away from anyone of political importance, including you. Instead, you send Dr. Clarke over here to get her released."

Because it was my idea to keep her confined, not Tig's. Or had he and Tig had the same thought? He had instructed Dr. Clarke to keep Cerissa confined. Had Tig told Gaea the same thing? Well, his authority trumped Tig's.

"I just happened to speak with Grayson," he replied. "It had been a few nights since he last examined her, so I suggested he stop by tonight. We would be remiss if we didn't provide Cerissa with the best medical care."

"Poppycock." Gaea planted her fists on her hips. "I saw the orchids you sent. You're smitten with her."

"The least I could do to cheer her up. The shooter was aiming at me."

"All the more reason you should stay away from her."

"Does Tig believe Cerissa had something to do with the shooting?"

"Well, no, not really."

"Then there is nothing to worry about."

"Nothing to worry about, my fat fanny! Someone just tried to kill you."

"That's no reason to hold Cerissa prisoner in your home."

She wagged a finger at him from the phone's screen. "The next time you do an end run around me, Mr. Bautista, you better watch your own backside, understand?"

"Now, Gaea, I just want what's best for Cerissa."

"You aren't taking the shooting seriously."

"I am taking it seriously," he said, "but I do not believe Cerissa was involved."

"You better be damn right."

He raised one eyebrow. "When have you ever known me to be wrong?"

CHAPTER 33

CERISSA'S ROOM—THE NEXT DAY

Cerissa waited for Gaea's front door to close, and then snuck a peek down the stair case.

Good. Dylan's off to his college classes.

She returned to her room, opened the crystal of her watch, tapped the top quadrant of her watch face, and flashed to her private lab at the Enclave.

She wrinkled her nose. A musty smell permeated the mountain caverns in which her ancestors had built their base. In spite of the smell, it felt good to be back, even for a short visit. As much as she wanted her independence, she missed it here. With none of her colleagues around, she shed her clothes and morphed into her native form.

She grabbed the nearest lab coat and, using it like a sarong, wrapped it around her body and under her wings, tying it at her neck. First order of business—check on the experimental clones. She couldn't let their health deteriorate just because the Protectors were impatient. A quick survey of the life-support systems confirmed they were being properly fed and hydrated. She trusted her colleagues, but this was her project. Some responsibilities just couldn't be delegated.

She peeled back the protective cover over one clone and found the embedded catheter. A small tube ran from it—she opened the valve, allowing blood to flow into a special collection bag. She stared at the clone, watching for any sign of discomfort. *Can I be sure they feel no pain?* The brain-wave monitor showed no activity, no change. *Not so much as a twitch, but how can I be certain?*

No time for doubts now. The Protectors weren't going to allow anything to stop the project—too much at risk if vampires didn't have another blood source. It took most of the afternoon to check the clones, collect samples from three separate ones, and meet with the two junior scientists who were tasked with their care. Nothing unusual had occurred during her absence. She examined the incubating eggs, which were developing into the next batch of clones, and gave her assistants instructions to contact her if anything happened.

After she flashed back to her room at Gaea's, she texted Henry: "I have something you'll be interested in."

A short time after dusk, he texted back. "I'll be there at 10. Eat first. Wear jeans and a jacket. Meet me in front of Gaea's."

"This should never have happened." Rolf marched the length of the town hall conference room, pausing to glare at those gathered around the long table.

Tig sneaked a quick peek at her phone. Jayden should be home from San Diego soon, and here she was, stuck in this stupid meeting. She'd sent him there to interview the prison guards. From his earlier report, no solid leads.

She doodled on the pad in front of her, letting her frustration bleed onto the page in the form of ink. Daytime sleep sucked. And so did these ridiculous meetings, fueled by politics—a complete waste of her valuable time.

"Rolf, we understand how you feel," Marcus replied. "Tig's going to report on Dr. Patel's background so we can make an informed recommendation."

Rolf stopped his pacing. From across the table, he fixed his eyes on Marcus. "Her background's irrelevant," Rolf said, his voice a low growl. "She doesn't belong here."

"She's an envoy—"

Rolf pounded the table with his fist. "You're the town attorney—you figure out a way to get her off the Hill. That's what you do for us, right? The town council decides and our lawyer makes it happen."

Marcus shrugged. "The treaty ties our hands. We must let her stay, at least on a temporary basis."

"Then we need to change the treaty!" Rolf shouted, pounding on the table.

Tig smiled and covered it with her hand. *They'll make him pay for the table if he breaks it.* She wasn't the only one seeing the comic possibilities—the mayor looked amused by it all.

The front door of town hall closed. Gaea strode down the corridor toward them, visible through the conference room's glass walls. Tig let her pen fall from her fingers. Now the real meeting could begin.

The mayor rested one hand on his ample belly, a slight smile curling his lips. "Rolf, let's wait until we hear from the chief, see what she's found out about Cerissa."

Gaea sailed into the room. "What's got Rolf so upset?"

"He's convinced the shooting had something to do with Cerissa," Tig replied.

"Why?" Gaea asked, cocking one eyebrow skeptically.

Rolf jumped in before Tig could answer. "Isn't it obvious? Cerissa arrives shortly after Yacov is carjacked, and then Henry is attacked. She must have something to do with it."

"That's all? Don't be silly," Gaea said with a wave of her hand.

"What is wrong with you people? Why am I the only one here who sees the threat she represents?"

"Young man, sit down," Gaea ordered, pointing to a chair. "I want to hear the chief's report before we do anything."

Throwing his hands up in the air, Rolf turned away and resumed his marching.

"Now!" Gaea commanded, pointing once more at the empty chair across from the mayor.

Rolf stopped mid-stride and turned to face her. "Fine," he spat out. He lifted the chair and banged its wheels against the floor before sitting down.

"Let's see," Gaea said, swiveling her chair in Tig's direction. "What information have you unearthed so far?"

Tig dimmed the lights and began her PowerPoint presentation. "Dr. Patel was licensed to practice medicine in New York, where she graduated from Johns Hopkins, completed residency, and went straight into research."

"Ooh, those are impressive credentials," Gaea cooed. "She could be a real help on the Hill. I get so tired of mortals complaining about Dr. Clarke."

"She holds one patent for a process replicating stem cells," the chief said, clicking through the slides. Jayden had put together most of the presentation before he left for San Diego—like she had time to waste on this nonsense. "I've discussed it with Dr. Clarke. Nothing in her prior research threatens us. Perhaps she has some far-fetched notion she might study us or even look for a cure. Not that any of us are interested in being *cured*."

They all laughed with her. Even Rolf gave a short "Ha." None of them would give up the advantages of being vampire. Those advantages far outweighed the drawbacks—including the one she hated most.

"But more likely," Tig continued, using a laser pointer to underscore the words on the slide, "Based on the patent Dr. Patel holds and what she told Gaea when she first arrived, she'll probably continue with her stem-cell research. So further investigation isn't worth the money."

"I couldn't agree more," Gaea said.

She flipped to the next slide—one new point about Cerissa's age. "The most surprising part, according to her birth certificate: she's thirty-two years old."

"But she hardly looks twenty," the mayor said, his bushy eyebrows lifting in unison. "Maybe Leopold has been feeding her his blood. But that's a long time to groom an envoy."

Gaea waved a dismissive finger in the air. "Or there could be another explanation. Cerissa told me her family members are long-lived. She said her great-grandmother is over a hundred and still alive."

Tig frowned. Cerissa's age was irrelevant to her investigation. She pressed the button to bring up the last slide: photos of each of the dead shooters.

"I haven't been able to link her or Leopold to the attacks. We should

DARK WINE AT MIDNIGHT

keep a close eye on her, but there's no evidence she's involved." She hit the console button. It raised the lights and turned off the slide projector.

Gaea sat there tapping her chin for a moment. "There has been one interesting result from the shooting."

"What's that?" Tig asked. So far, Gaea's reports had been benign.

"Henry sent Cerissa flowers. And he persuaded Dr. Clarke to release her. Henry isn't easily fooled—I'll be watching closely to see what he does."

"What about Zeke?" Tig asked.

"I've been concerned about Zeke, too," Gaea admitted. "There is something about the young woman that makes me want to mother her. Strange, I've never thought of myself as the maternal type."

The mayor let out a guffaw that shook the table. Tig sat forward, ready to jump between Winston and his maker in the event Gaea took offense.

Instead, Gaea issued a dismissive sniff in his direction before turning back to Tig. "Chief, you or Winston should talk with the boy, make sure Zeke understands fighting will not be condoned."

The mayor gave a brief nod in Tig's direction. "I'll take care of it when he returns to the Hill," she agreed.

"Are you done discussing Cerissa's background?" Rolf asked coldly.

"There's nothing to connect her with either shooting," Tig concluded.

Rolf stood up. "It still brings us back to the initial problem. An unmated mortal has no business being on the Hill. We should reject her project and tell her to move on."

"And alienate Leopold?" Gaea asked.

"I don't give a damn about Leopold, and neither does Frédéric. Put it to a vote. Frédéric will back me on this."

"Perhaps," Gaea replied, "but if we're counting votes, I doubt Carolyn and Liza will agree with you. Liza likes Cerissa, and Carolyn wants more information about the project."

"Let's stop right there," Marcus said quickly. "Sharing the positions of other council members in a non-public meeting violates state law."

"Fuck state law." Rolf pointed at the mayor. "You're stupid to let her stay."

"Watch your manners, young man," Gaea snapped.

The mayor held up this hand for silence. "From what I understand, Cerissa is shopping for a sizeable property to develop. If she locates the project on our side of the freeway, it'll mean a two percent increase in the town's tax base. I've run the figures. Between property taxes, business license fees, and the like, we'll net a sizeable amount for our town's coffers."

Tig kept her eyes on Rolf—he looked like a cartoon character about to explode. Ramrod straight, he clenched his jaw, the muscles at the joint bulging out. "We—don't—need—the—money," he said, enunciating each word loudly.

The mayor drummed his fingers on the table impatiently. "Easy for you to say, but the town needs certain infrastructure improvements. We've put them off for too long. No one—including you—has wanted to approve a special assessment to fix the old sewer system. Leopold's project could pay for those improvements in development fees. It's a win-win for us."

"Or we get made fools of." Rolf leaned across the table toward the mayor. "There may not be a project. Leopold may have other designs on the Hill. In the meantime, you've given his operative free rein."

"Rolf, you're being paranoid," Gaea said. "The more I'm around Cerissa, the more I'm convinced—she's here to build her biotech business. It's all she talks about."

"Indeed," the mayor said, nodding his agreement with Gaea. "We should be doing everything to make her feel truly welcomed so she locates the project within our town's boundaries and not in Mordida. That way, we get the tax benefit."

Rolf scowled. "Not if it means having an unmated mortal in our backyard. The risk is intolerable—she could let what we are slip out."

"Your fears aren't grounded in reality," the mayor said. "She's an envoy. She knows what would happen to her if she spilled the beans."

Rolf pressed his hands flat on the table, turning his fingers even whiter from the pressure he applied. "We should tell her we're not interested and send her on her way. Now."

"That's not a decision for this subcommittee to make," the mayor said. "It's a decision for the full council."

"Then put it on the agenda!" Rolf shouted.

"In due time, Rolf," the mayor said with a smirk. "In due time."

Tig smiled as well. It was nice to see Rolf get trounced by Winston. Rolf could be so full of himself sometimes. Letting some of the air out of his inflated ego would make it easier to work with him.

"Are we interrupting?" Yacov stood at the conference room door with Father Matt and two mortals behind him—Haley Spears and Nicholas Martin. Yacov pulled out a pocket watch and clicked it open. "I thought we had the room at nine."

"You do," the mayor said, not looking happy about it. "We were just wrapping up."

Rolf narrowed his eyes at them. "And why do you need the room?"

Haley slipped past Yacov. "Committee on Mortal Rights," she replied, crossing her arms.

"You're fucking kidding me," Rolf shouted, his eyes fixed in the mayor's direction. "You appointed a committee? I thought your announcement was bullshit to placate them."

The mayor shrugged. "It's just an exploratory committee."

"Yeah, and we're exploring how to get Rolf's ass off the council," Haley muttered.

Tig heard it. Hell, every vampire in the room heard it, and Haley had done it on purpose. Rumors of Rolf's proposal to apply the Rule of Two to mortals had zipped through the Hill with lightning speed, making the already tense community even tenser. Rolf started to sputter again when Gaea pointed a finger at him. It stopped any further argument. "We're done here," Gaea said. "Let's give these nice people a chance to meet."

Tig's phone buzzed—a text message from Jayden. He was back from San Diego, home and waiting for her. Naked. In bed. She clipped the phone to her belt.

"Is there a problem, my dear?" Gaea asked.

"Nothing serious, but I need to handle it myself," Tig replied, sliding past Yacov and his group to leave the conference room. She smiled to herself, picturing Jayden in the buff. Yes indeed—this matter needed her personal touch.

CHAPTER 34

GAEA'S HOUSE—TEN O'CLOCK THE SAME EVENING

Cerissa waited for Henry by Gaea's driveway, wearing jeans and a leather jacket, with her purse and a special bag slung over her shoulder. He pulled up riding a large, sleek-looking motorcycle, mostly black, with a silver and red blaze outlining the bike's gas tank.

So that's why his text told me what to wear.

She could scratch "control freak" off her list of concerns.

He took a backpack off his shoulders, reached in, and pulled out a helmet, handing it to her before tossing the backpack onto the white garden bench. His leather jacket and black helmet looked good on him. He lifted the faceplate. "I hope you're not afraid of motorcycles."

"Not in the least, but I've never been on one."

"It's simple. You wear your helmet, sit behind me, and hang on to my waist."

The way his ponytail stuck out from underneath his helmet looked cute. He probably wore a helmet in case there was an accident—hard to explain healing from severe brain trauma.

"Where are we going?" she asked.

"My winery. I have to test the recent wine production. We will be alone and can talk in private."

"No one is going with us?" She slipped on her helmet. Gaea had told her the Rule of Two had been passed by the council during her convalescence—but so far, it applied only to vampires.

"We don't need an escort for the winery. The Rule of Two doesn't apply as long as we are within Sierra Escondida's boundaries."

She started to pick up the empty backpack he'd left on the garden bench.

"Leave it," he said. "I'll get it when we return."

She swung her leg over the bike's seat and sat behind him, wrapping her arms around his firm waist as instructed. She dialed her aura back to a wisp of charm, which was easier to do when she felt at ease. She didn't want to make him suspicious again by flooding him with good feelings, and she didn't want to be overwhelmed by its reciprocal effects, either. He pushed the ignition button and put the motorcycle into gear. Once on the road, he asked how she was doing.

"I like it. It's like flying."

"Do you want to go faster?"

"Yes, faster," she shouted over the noise of the engine.

He kicked it up a notch. The rows of twisted grapevines zoomed past her in the darkness, ghostly pale shoots sprouting from woody trunks. She leaned into him, her inner thighs squeezing his tight butt—for support, of course.

She wanted to rub her cheek against his back the way a cat does, but the helmet stopped her. She was happy, happy to be free from her room at Gaea's, happy to be in his presence, even happy to be snuggled up against him.

He slowed down at the gate, waved at the guards, and then sped up again after passing the Hill's wall. She held on tighter as he accelerated, pressing against his muscular back, losing herself in the rush of speed and the motorcycle's vibrations.

He turned onto the back streets of the business district, the buildings dark and closed for the night. He swerved into the winery's driveway and circled the parking lot to the back. By the time he stopped the bike, a giddy excitement spun through her.

What's happening to me? I'm supposed to seduce him, not the other way around. She stepped off the bike a little too fast and stumbled.

He caught her by the arm and smiled knowingly at her. "Are you all right?" he asked.

"I guess I misjudged the distance to the ground," she lied, mortified he may have sensed her arousal.

He gently released her and swung off the bike in one graceful, powerful motion. Soft floodlights illuminated the empty lot. She removed her helmet and placed it on the seat next to his. Taking a comb from her back pocket, she ran it through her wavy hair. When he did the same thing, she smiled at him.

"I like your hair long," she said. "It looks good on you, especially when you wear it loose."

His eyes sparkled, like he was pleased by her comment. "I hope you don't mind if I wear it back for our winetasting," he said, retying it.

She looked away, self-conscious under his intense gaze. His hand touched her back, guiding her toward a trellis-covered walkway, grapevines twined around the open slats. The walkway led to a large, plain stucco building at the back of the winery. She waited while Henry unlocked the door.

"After you," he said with a sweep of his hand.

Inside the winery, she rubbed her arms against the chilliness, feeling it in spite of her leather jacket. Was it artificial refrigeration or the design of the building? Either way, the concrete walls held the cold in well, and she morphed the layer below her skin, thickening it to increase her resistance to the cool air. He'd never notice the change.

He led her through the wine production rooms and down a flight of stairs into an even colder basement. "I'm here tonight to check how the wines are aging," he said. "During the day, the assistant winemaker supervises our employees."

"When we first met, you said you were the winemaker. I didn't realize you meant it literally."

"I've been making wines for over a hundred years." He pointed to an archway leading to a large room, filled with rows of casks. "Our Cabernet production from the past two years, aging in toasted oak."

She followed him into a lab-like room adjacent to the casks—the stainless steel surfaces gave it a sterile look, with test equipment filling one corner. Holding up her bag, she asked, "I brought samples of clone blood. Would you like to try some first?"

"Afterwards. I never drink blood before tasting wine. It might throw off my sense of smell. Does it need refrigeration?"

"No."

"Then leave it here while we test the barrels."

She placed the bag and her purse on the counter. Cabinets above the counter held wineglasses, and he took out a tray of thirty and set them on a cart. He added a clipboard with a printed chart. A lower shelf on the cart held a plastic bin, the type used for washing dishes. He rolled the cart to the first set of oak casks and, after removing a large plug from the top of the cask, took a glass tube and lowered it into the wine.

"We use the wine thief to steal wine from the center of the barrel," he said.

It looked like a long pipette, the kind you might use in any research lab. He placed his thumb over the exposed opening at the top of the tube and withdrew the wine thief. Purple liquid filled it. Positioning the tapered end over a wineglass, he removed his thumb—about an inch of wine flowed into the glass, and he placed the empty wine thief into a tall canister filled with clear water. He swirled the wineglass, held it up to the light, sniffed it, and then brought it to his lips.

She raised one eyebrow. She'd never seen Leopold drink anything but blood and, occasionally, water. Before she could say, "You can drink—" he spat out the wine into a canister sitting on the cart. He repeated the process twice more, made notes on the clipboard, and plugged the cask.

"This wine is much too young for you to taste," he said. "When I find one almost ready for bottling, I'll ask your opinion."

"Fine with me."

He laid the wineglass in the plastic tub and tested the next cask. She watched in silence while he worked his way through the first group, anxious for him to finish so he could try the blood samples she'd brought. After rolling the cart over to another set of casks, he changed pages on the clipboard.

"These are much further along in the aging process," he said, putting wine into a glass from the first cask. He swirled, looked, and sniffed. "Yes, this one is worthy of your attention." He handed her the glass.

She looked straight down into the glass as Leopold had taught her, tilting it to see the color at the edge, and then held it to the light—not murky, a good sign. She swirled it and the legs formed, running down the inside of the glass—a riper wine. She swirled again, placed her nose over the opening, and took a slight sniff of the aroma. No flaws, none detectable by scent. She then took a small sip.

"I'm impressed by your technique," he said. "Do you like it?"

"I do. There's a hint of fruit, like blackberries. And vanilla. It tastes like blackberries and vanilla."

"Right on both accounts. I may have to hire you as a taster."

She smiled and looked away. Something had changed since he kissed her almost a week ago. Now, his flirting felt real. She placed the empty glass in the tub, the same way he had, and walked with him to the next cask.

"Have you heard anything from Tig?" she asked.

"Nothing new. She sent Jayden out of town to interview men who knew the shooters, but it didn't lead anywhere yet."

"Are you taking precautions? Whoever tried to shoot you may try again."

He cocked his head to one side. "You care if something happens to me?"

"I, ah, I—"

He held up his hand. "Don't worry, I'm being careful."

He continued to test the casks, making notes and occasionally giving her one to try. She took a sip from each. What did his palate discern that hers didn't? Of the ones he gave her, they all tasted the same.

"I think..." he said, holding up another glass to the light. "I think you're going about it wrong—your hunt for a mate."

She almost dropped her wineglass. "No one said I was hunting for a vampire mate," she said testily.

"Really?" he asked, a slight smirk forming.

She tightened her grip on the glass. Yeah, she may have kissed him. And pressing up against him on the bike, hell, just being around him, stirred something in her. But she was *not* going to seduce him to buy his silence, no matter what Ari thought.

"There's a rumor going around I'm shopping for a mate," she said, shaking her head. "But it's not true."

"Ultimately you will if you decide to stay with us. You cannot live on the Hill—"

"Unless mated. Yes, I understand, but under special circumstances, the Council can give permission—"

"You cannot build a relationship on a lie."

"A lie?"

"You are pretending to be mortal. You are not. At some point you will reveal your true nature to the one you select. This will create a sense of betrayal. He was deceived. He may wonder in what other ways you have deceived him. This is not good for trust."

"You sound like you speak from experience."

"I assume Karen told you what caused my breakup with Erin."

"She managed to mention it without sounding too pissed off."

He held out his hand, and she released her empty wineglass to him. "We should continue with the testing."

He wheeled the cart to another barrel. After a few more tastings, he said, "I'm sorry Erin felt she had to leave. I handled the situation poorly."

"Why wouldn't you tell her who bit you?"

"I see Karen has spoken of it." He lowered his eyes. "I didn't want others to know about Anne-Louise's demand for tribute."

Cerissa tried hard not to laugh. "That's an old-fashioned word for it."

He looked up at her again, his brow furrowed. "That's what it's called. A maker may demand blood from the vampires they sire."

"Which leads to sex?"

Henry looked almost angry. "I did not sleep with Anne-Louise while I was with Erin."

"Karen certainly thinks you slept with whoever left their mark on you."

"Erin's friends told her a neck bite had to involve sex—she believed them, not me." He looked down at the wine cask again, and the anger on his face drained away, replaced with a look of shame. "She had every right to. I wasn't honest with her. She assumed the worst, and I couldn't dissuade her."

"Why did she see the bite at all? Vampires heal fast."

"The bite of another vampire doesn't heal quickly. It takes the blood of another vampire to heal it." Henry filled a glass using the wine thief and swirled the small amount of ruby-red liquid before sniffing it. "A friend was supposed to leave me a vial of his blood after Anne-Louise's visit, so I could return to Erin with no trace of the bite, but my friend forgot."

"Oh."

"Karen kept harping loudly, insisting I'd been unfaithful. She didn't help matters with Erin."

He shouldn't blame Karen for a problem he created. Rather than disagree, Cerissa asked, "Why does Anne-Louise demand tribute?"

"To maintain the connection between us, the bond. She has refused to let me go."

"But—"

"Forget everything you think you know about vampires. There are some dirty little secrets among our kind, secrets not freely shared, not even with envoys." He wheeled the cart to the next set of casks and unplugged the bung. "It is believed taking the blood of our progeny postpones a vampire's descent into senility."

"You mean it keeps the aging process from suddenly catching up with you?"

"That is the conventional wisdom." He paused to taste the wine and make notes. Shaking his head, he didn't give her the glass, and instead poured it out into the spittoon. "Once a maker releases her progeny, stops taking blood for a year or two, she ceases having power to compel them to return to her. But if she continues to demand blood, as Anne-Louise has, she may keep those she sires bound to her."

"I thought the treaty required makers to release their, ah, progeny, after twenty years."

"You are correct for those who were turned after the treaty was signed. The rest of us were grandfathered under the old rules."

A chill rippled down her spine. He would never be free of his maker.

"But why?" she asked.

"For the same reason your people are concerned. The treaty strictly regulates the creation of new vampires. If drinking the blood of their progeny does prolong a vampire's life, freeing their progeny would deprive them of the benefits, and they would not be allowed to sire new vampires to replace their source. Like any treaty, a compromise was struck to gain greater support for it."

Okay, it made sense on a rational level. Still, she felt sorry for him. "So Anne-Louise has forced you to remain her lover?"

"Even those who were grandfathered have rights under the treaty. I refuse to be her lover when I am in a relationship with a mortal. If she tried to force the issue it would be rape, and she knows the penalty for that."

Cerissa didn't want to ask what the penalty was. With vampires, it could be anything. "Why didn't you tell Erin?"

"And have Erin tell Karen, who would have repeated it all over the Hill? Only a few know the truth."

"You let Erin leave rather than be embarrassed in front of your friends?"

The stern look on his face told her not to push for an answer. His reputation as a founder would be tarnished if others learned he was under his maker's thumb. But why did he need their respect so desperately? He'd gone to a lot of trouble to hide the truth.

"I'm sorry," she said, touching his arm. He'd let her see the "him" behind the founder mask he wore. It took more courage than she had. For all she'd revealed about her Lux origins, she hadn't told him any personal secrets about herself. "Your maker holds on too tightly, and my mother never held on at all."

"I don't understand."

"My *amma* abandoned me when I was three."

He touched her shoulder gently, a look of empathy in his eyes. "What happened?"

She looked away. She couldn't look at him and tell the story. "I still don't know if it was the politics of the time or if she just grew bored living like a human." She raised her hands in resignation. "The East India Company had a stranglehold on Surat. My *pita*'s family was struggling to keep their textile business afloat, to keep food on the table. They couldn't compete with British factories. Everyone in the family was working long hours, doing whatever they could to turn things around."

She snapped her fingers. "And just like that, *Amma* left. No goodbye, no explanation. I lived with my *pita* until he died, and then the Protectors brought me to the Enclave. Even then, my *amma* ignored me—she has my whole life. It taught me not to rely on others at a young age." She shrugged. "I guess that's a good thing."

Henry shook his head in disbelief. How could anyone abandon a small child? He reached out and gently gripped her chin, turning her face so he could see her eyes again.

"Do not belittle your loss," he said softly. "A child should not have to learn such a lesson."

He wrapped his arms around her, and her warm scent enveloped him. He mentally shook himself; he was supposed to be comforting her, not getting turned on. He stroked her back and tried to focus on her words.

"I shouldn't complain," she said. "My *amma* was part of the first generation who tried to live with our human parent. You see, many Lux view humans as lesser than themselves. The Protectors had a theory—raising Lux children among humans would make us more empathetic with them. It wasn't easy for *Amma*, either—no electricity, no indoor plumbing, no computers, and stuck in the kitchen with the other women."

He heard her heart speed up, and the sour smell of anxiety rose from her. His own heart felt heavy in return. He wanted to comfort her, but how?

"I was born during the Great Cyclone of 1782," she continued. "Hurricane-force winds toppled home after home, debris and rain crashed down, the Tapi river flooded over, all while my *amma* was in labor—we were lucky our home still stood the next day. My *pita*'s family never let me forget it. They said I was born of Kali, the goddess of destruction. After everything that happened, I'm surprised *Amma* stayed as long as she did."

He released her so he could look into her eyes. She was smart and courageous, and deserved better. "It still doesn't justify how your mother treated you," he said.

"Well, I'll do better when my time comes."

"Your time?" he repeated. He'd forgotten—at some point, she'd have to bear children by a mortal.

"In a hundred years, I'll move into my fertile stage."

He watched her face closely. "Would you consider raising your child among vampires?"

"Huh?"

"You're building your lab here. You want to live here. In a hundred years—"

"A lot can happen. I'll figure it out when I get there."

Maybe she was right. He'd rarely had a relationship last longer than a few years. And there was always artificial insemination if they stayed together. He froze. What was he thinking? One kiss and he was worried about what they'd do a hundred years from now. He turned away and motioned at the casks. "That was the last one."

He wheeled the cart back into the lab, and she followed. "My employees will take care of this tomorrow," he said, dropping his notes into an "in" basket on the counter.

He walked to the other side of the wine lab, where a table with bottles stood. "The wines are tested here. Once opened, they cannot be sold, but we usually have one or two recorked with an inert gas added to preserve it, and set aside for guests."

He poured her a glass of wine and handed it to her. "This is one of our reserve blended wines," he said. "What do you think?"

She swirled the glass. He could smell the aroma it released from where he stood. She held the glass up to the light and then took a sip. "Excellent. The flavor is superb, and so smooth for a red."

"I am quite proud of this vintage. We've had good sales from it."

"It's your blend?" she asked, and took another sip.

"Yes. I'm told I have a good nose for wines. It's apparently true, as mortals are willing to a pay a high price for ours."

"To know your work is appreciated must be satisfying."

"I am glad to produce a beverage that makes them happy. After all, they produce a beverage that makes me happy," he said, smiling at her.

"Speaking of that beverage..." She returned her wineglass to the counter and opened the bag she'd brought.

He watched her take out three glass containers. Each container held a ruby-red fluid. He picked up one jar, the glass warm to the touch.

"These samples are from three different clones," she said.

"How do you keep them from spoiling without refrigeration?"

"I use a special method to fill the jars." She opened the cabinet where wineglasses were stored and took out three. "Just like winetasting," she said, pouring the samples into three separate glasses. "Go ahead, try one."

He picked up the first glass, and studied the color. *Dark wine*—an appropriate euphemism. A quick sniff and his nose told him *fresh blood*. He took a sip. This was the real thing, much better than stale banked blood, which always left a sour aftertaste from the added chemicals and preservatives.

He polished off the first sample. "What keeps it from clotting?" he asked.

Her face lit up—she looked pleased by his question. "I filter out the clotting factor, so I don't have to add a chemical to keep it from clotting. Does it change the taste?"

"Absolutely. For the better."

He picked up the second one. It smelled just as fresh. He held the ruby-colored liquid to the light. Then he sipped it, lingering over the flavor. Something was slightly different. He couldn't put his finger on it, but it was richer. He tried explaining it to her, but was frustrated. He could describe all the various notes of a wine, but he had developed no language for discussing the taste of blood. After stumbling over his answer, he asked, "How much blood can you take from a clone?"

"They're engineered for two pints of harvest per day. If I go beyond two pints, I'll have to introduce extra iron, which might change the flavor too much."

He studied the color of the last sample, then sipped it—a magnificent nectar of the gods. He rolled it in his mouth to savor it longer, and felt a sudden rush of desire when he swallowed. To hide his arousal, he turned toward the counter.

"The last sample had the highest concentration of red blood cells," she explained. "I used a process called apheresis to draw a higher number of red blood cells from the clones, returning some of the plasma and other blood components back to their bodies. We're still limited to taking two pints a day, but with apheresis, the higher draw doesn't harm them. What you're tasting is the different ratios of red blood cells to plasma."

He studied the empty glass for a moment before rinsing it out in a nearby sink. Out of the corner of his eye, he saw her remove a computer tablet from her purse and jot something down. He bent to rinse his mouth with water, then dried his lips with one of the paper towels from the nearby dispenser, gripping the counter with his other hand. He kept himself anchored there for a moment. He couldn't give in to what he felt for her. *No, it is just the blood. It is just the—*

Without warning, he stood in front of her, wrapping his arms around her. Like a dry twig, his last bit of resistance had snapped. The blur of his movement seemed to catch her off guard, and she dropped the tablet on the counter.

He wanted to make it gentle, but the blood drove him. Pressing his hand against the back of her head, he crushed her lips to his. Her lips parted and he thrust his tongue into her, exploring her mouth deeply, her tongue meeting his with equal passion.

When his lips left hers, he could hear her breathing hard, feel her heart pounding against his chest, and smell the salty-sweet scent of her arousal. He held her close and said softly by her ear, "The blood has that effect."

"Effect?" she asked.

"It excites the passion."

Her body stiffened against his. "Oh. I see."

He closed his eyes, drinking in her alluring scent. He wasn't being honest with her. Yes, the blood had spiked his passion, but it didn't propel him to kiss her.

The story of her childhood, the sadness that at times seemed to palpably roll off her, the sense of her being alone in the world—she needed someone to love her as only he could. There was so much more he had to learn about her, but she had lit the wick of his long-banished passion. He wanted *her*.

She rested her face against his shoulder, his arms holding her close. Each breath she took brought in the fresh scent of his spicy cologne. Part of her wanted to stay wrapped in his arms forever, where she felt protected and understood.

He pulled back, and she let him. She looked up into his eyes—such intense, dark eyes, framed by ebony eyebrows. She felt compelled again to touch his lips with hers.

When his lips parted, she gave an inaudible sigh, letting her own lips open. His tongue sought out hers, more gently this time, as if the passion spent on the first kiss allowed him to regain control, and she once again tasted blood mingled with the scent of cloves. She followed the rhythm he set, the silky feel of his tongue making her insides turn to molten silver.

She surrendered to the feelings, melting against him, until Ari's words, "seduce him or stake him," echoed in her mind and she abruptly broke from the kiss.

"I need air," she said, and ran up the stairs to the door leading outside.

She hadn't meant to use her aura to seduce him. She had dialed it back on the bike. *Hell, I shut it down completely when he started the winery tour.*

So maybe the blood samples had sparked his kiss...or could it be something more?

She stood near the motorcycle, her back to the door, her head woozy. The scent of his cologne stayed with her, the dry, spicy smell now entwined in her mind with the sensations his lips and tongue created.

She heard him lock the winery door behind her, followed by the light clink of jars. He had brought her bag with him.

"Cerissa," he said, his footsteps drawing near.

She turned to him. "I'm sorry. I liked the kiss, I did. But I—I just felt overwhelmed."

"It's all right," he said, putting the bag and her purse on the ground. His arms went around her, and he held her lightly. "We can take this slowly, whatever is comfortable for you."

"Thank you," she said, her cheek resting against his chest. Smelling his cologne again caused several tingles to spark within her. She looked up at him. His deep browns pulled her in once again.

"The next formal dance is in one week," he said. "Would you like to go with me?"

She smiled shyly at him. "I would like that very much." Then it occurred to her. What she'd said to Ari. She couldn't go to the dance with him, not under their rules. "Ah, what about the Covenant? I mean, we can't date within the walls."

He gave a lopsided grin. "I'll clear it with the mayor. It would be boorish for him to refuse, to force you to attend the dance unescorted."

"Then I gratefully accept," she said, stepping back to curtsey.

"Very good," he replied, bowing to her. When he rose, he said, "I have to be out of town for a few nights. I trust nothing will happen while I'm gone?"

She stepped in close again and flattened her palms against his chest. "Henry, please don't worry. The Lux aren't a threat. They aren't going to invade while you're gone."

"It's not that. I don't want you to leave—I've decided to support your project. I want you to build it here in Sierra Escondida."

CHAPTER 35

Cerissa stood at the center of a vacant property on the public side of the Hill's wall. A good location—only twenty minutes north of the main gate, it bordered the freeway, providing easy and fast access.

The late afternoon sun sat above the western mountains. She rotated slowly to see the views in each direction. The mountains behind Henry's house were visible to the southwest of where she stood. The northwest mountain range, forming the other leg of the Hill's valley, tapered off before the wall. A few commercial buildings interrupted her view in both directions—her office would be on the fifth floor, so it didn't matter.

She turned again. Beyond the I-5 freeway, Mordida sprawled along the entire east side of the freeway, with the international airport fifty miles to the southeast. Empty lots lining the Mordida side offered perfect locations to build new housing and amenities for the scientists she would hire.

Sixty acres was a bit small for the type of research campus she wanted to create, but it would have to do. It was the largest available undeveloped parcel in Sierra Escondida. There were a couple of smaller empty parcels adjacent to it. Maybe she could buy all of them before construction began—if she kept the project secret from the other property owners, it might keep the price down.

Only problem is, I don't have enough money to buy any of it, not without new investors.

She trekked back to where the real estate agent waited by their cars. She took her time, carefully picking her path to avoid tripping over a rock or the low scrub brush dotting the uneven, dried dirt, baked hard by the sun.

The story Henry had told her last night about Anne-Louise—she couldn't quit thinking about it. He knew what it meant to hide. He knew what it meant to be trapped, to be under someone else's control. And he knew what it meant to have secrets, secrets you could never share.

I've always had to hide. Why didn't I realize others did as well?

The sadness in him lay just below the surface, mirroring her own pain. She wanted to wrap her arms around him and take away his sadness, just as he had for her when she told him about her *amma*.

All his talk about her "search" for a mate—what was he hinting at? He wanted her to build the lab in Sierra Escondida. Did it mean he wanted her for his mate, or was it something else—keep your friends close, and your enemies closer?

The way he kissed me, he didn't feel like an enemy.

No, he trusted her enough to tell her about Anne-Louise, to place his reputation in her hands. They weren't enemies.

Could he really want me for his mate?

She stopped thinking about it when she reached the cars. She said goodbye to the real estate agent and returned to her room at Gaea's as the sun began to set. She collapsed onto her bed and stared at the ceiling. How was she going to get the money to buy the parcel? Last night, Gaea huffed and puffed about the doctor releasing her from bedrest, and refused to let her meet any potential investors.

She reached over, picked up the remote, and turned on the television. She flicked through the menu and then clicked it off. Nothing she wanted to watch. She rolled off the bed and began pacing, running her fingers through her hair. Maybe if she meditated...

She folded herself down onto the floor, cross-legged in the lotus position, the soles of her feet facing the ceiling, and aligned her chakras until her back was a straight line. Her *pita* had instilled in her the Hindu practice of meditation when she was a child, teaching her to be more aware of her body and mind.

Taking a deep breath in, she focused on the exhale, followed by another inhale. Once centered, the problem became clear. She had all the telltale signs—impatience, irritability, lack of focus, fatigue. Too long spent in human form.

Time to fix that oversight.

She rose from the floor, slipped on her shoes, and quietly snuck along the hall, down the back stairs, skulking out the door leading to Gaea's vineyard. She didn't want anyone to see her leave—especially Blanche. Just beyond the vineyard lay a series of switchback trails, leading to a mountain plateau. The plateau offered a private place to morph into another form. She didn't bring a flashlight—she could adjust her eyes to see in the dark.

Her feet knew the way, allowing her mind to focus on Henry. The second time he kissed her, she'd run away, feeling guilty—she had no intent to seduce him to buy his silence, but her feelings of guilt were overcome by those gorgeous eyes, the color of dark bourbon and just as intoxicating. She brought her fingers to her lips, imagining the cool softness of his lips on hers and the scent of cedar and clove clinging lightly to him. Whose power to charm was winning, hers or his?

She jumped when the phone in her pocket rang, and she looked around. She was far enough up the trail that no one at Gaea's house could have heard it.

"Hi, Cerissa, how's the arm?" Zeke asked when she answered.

"It's better, thanks." She got back into the rhythm of her hike and asked, "How's your trip to South America?"

"Just about wrapped up. I'm going to be back in town soon."

"Oh?"

"Yeah, in less than a week. I'd like to take you out again when I do."

Her lungs tightened. *Why does that sound like another date?* But she needed to learn more about where he had gone and whether he was connected to the vampire dominance movement.

"Why don't you call me when you return? I'd love to hear about your work and how your trip to South America went," she suggested.

"Yeah, sure, when I get back."

She pressed the "end" button and composed an email to Ari rather than phoning. No telling what he was up to at this hour. She asked him to run a deeper background check on Zeke, focusing on government records. She added a request to investigate Rolf too—even if Henry didn't suspect his friend, it wouldn't hurt to look into Rolf's history.

Ari was a whiz at getting deep dirt on people, provided it was stored electronically—he could hack any computer system. His email reply came back so quickly that she almost fumbled the phone: "Anything for you, cupcake. I'll run Henry too, just in case you need some ammunition. So, are you sleeping with him yet? Stake or sex, which will it be?"

"Thx," she typed back, ignoring his last remarks. She slid the phone into her back pocket and finished hiking up the dark mountain to the first plateau. *The perfect place.* She slipped behind a tree, shed her clothes, and morphed, basking in the relief brought on by changing species. The built-up tension fell away like molting feathers, and she loped up the trail to the mountain plateau. She could resume work on Leopold's project in the morning.

Sitting in her office at the police station, Tig uploaded the interview video to her desktop computer. Body-worn cameras were standard issue for police officers on the Hill, and Jayden had put his to good use when he interviewed the guards. The inconspicuous camera was designed to record arrests, a defense against excessive-force complaints. Taken from Jayden's perspective, where he sat at a cheap laminated table, she could see a small interview room at the prison. The video started when the door opened and the first guard walked into view.

"You Captain Johnson?" The guard extended his hand. Jayden's arm came into view to shake hands.

She glanced down at the paperwork. This was Norman Tyler. One of the three guards who regularly worked the cell block where the perps were incarcerated.

"Thanks for taking the time to speak with me," Jayden said in the video. Norman set a cup of coffee in front of him on the gray metal table. "And thanks for the coffee—it's been a long day."

Gray table, gray walls, gray chairs—if you weren't depressed before walking in, you certainly would be afterward. Even Norman's white skin looked a little gray in the video.

"I don't know what I can tell you that ain't in the files," Norman said, slowly lowering his large body into the standard-issue institutional chair.

The camera caught Jayden's hands opening the file. "It says here Luzzari, Giordano, and Moretti were all on the same cell block."

"That's right." Norman slumped forward slightly, leaning against the table for support. He looked like one of those bears in a zoo video, waiting for a treat to be thrown his way.

Jayden turned the files so Norman could see the photos. "Luzzari and Giordano were released before Moretti. Did they know each other?"

"I'm sure those guys spent time talking. No law against that in here."

"How about visitors? Anyone from the outside visit them?"

"Hell, I didn't pay attention to their visitors. Whatever's in the file."

Jayden moved the file back to his side of the table. "Two of them had visits from their families. But not Giordano." He thumbed the page to turn it. "They had different lawyers. The file doesn't say who picked them up when they were released."

"No shit? Let me see." Norman picked up a file and flipped to the end. "That's strange. The exit report is missing. The guard who processed them out—he's supposed to fill it in."

Jayden quickly thumbed to the end of the other two files. "No exit report in these either. Does it happen a lot? That the form goes missing?"

"Nah, that's why I said it's strange—even stranger with all three missing."

"Who's responsible for filing the form?"

"Records clerk. We drop all the forms into a basket at the end of our shift; the clerk puts 'em into the jacket. At least, he used to. Now he just scans 'em into the computer and shreds the form we wrote. We're supposed to get computers so we can enter 'em ourselves, but budget cutbacks, ya know?"

The interview video ended shortly after Norman's explanation. Jayden had followed up with the records clerk, but no one could locate the exit reports. Tig leaned back in her chair and crossed her arms. Nothing much there, aside from the missing reports, but paperwork got lost all the time. *Hmm.* Should she send Jayden back to investigate the guards? She clicked on the next video. She'd decide once she viewed all three.

CHAPTER 36

Henry hurried to his office at the winery. Paperwork sat on his office desk, paperwork he had to complete before his trip to San Francisco. A major distributor of fine wines had asked for the meeting. They were considering his Cabernet for their roster—a big coup if he could land it.

The timing was less than ideal. He didn't want to leave Cerissa, even for a few nights. His passion for her had kept growing, his attempts to stop it as futile as brakes on black ice. The taste of her when they kissed was an appetizer leaving him wanting more. If he had it his way, she'd end up in his bed, where he could taste every inch...

No time for fantasies now. He flipped on the light in the office he shared with Rolf and settled in behind his desk to tackle the stack of papers his secretary had left for him. He looked up when Rolf entered the room. After an exchange of "good evenings," he lowered his head to look at his paperwork again.

He heard Rolf's chair squeak. "You came here alone with her last night? When did you become so *verrückt*?"

He threw down his pen. "Crazy? I'm crazy?" he said, tapping his chest with his fist.

"Yes, crazy. You and Yacov both. You're dating Leopold's envoy and Yacov wants to give mortals voting rights. What's happening with the both of you?"

"*You* could have told me about the mayor's committee. Instead, I had to hear about it from Tig."

"I didn't think they were serious. You're Yacov's friend—you talk some sense into him."

"It's too late for me to stop it. We'll have to hope Yacov and Father Matt can appease them." He picked up the next document in the stack of papers on his desk and waved it at Rolf. "Look, I have a lot of work to do. I don't have time to argue with you."

When Rolf didn't reply, Henry rested his forehead against his hand, his elbow braced against his own desk, blocking Rolf from his field of vision. The document he'd picked up was the immunity agreement, prepared by the town attorney. Tig had called a couple of times already, pushing for his bookie's name, but the agreement was far from satisfactory—an offer of limited immunity. He was convinced the shooting had nothing to do with his bookie, so he decided to hold out for a full immunity deal. He picked up his pen and attacked the document, striking out unacceptable provisions.

Rolf's chair squeaked again, dragging Henry's attention away from the editing process. He kept his eyes focused on the document, trying to ignore Rolf.

"We're not done yet," Rolf said as if no time had passed. "The night Cerissa was shot, what did she tell you that's made you so stupid?"

"She didn't tell me anything."

"I know when you're lying."

Henry lifted his hand slightly, peering up so he could see Rolf without raising his head. Why had he ever agreed to share office space with Rolf? He should have added another wing to the winery instead.

"She was in no shape to discuss anything," Henry finally replied.

"So what is this?" Rolf slapped his desk. "Guilt? You're taking her to the dance because the bullet was meant for you?"

The dance. Rolf knows about the dance already. Henry had spoken with the mayor about it last night after dropping Cerissa off at Gaea's. The mayor seemed agreeable to waiving the rule. Obviously, the mayor spared no time in telling Rolf about the request.

He dropped his hand from his forehead. Hiding behind it wasn't working. He swiveled his chair and looked directly at Rolf. "As I recall, you're the one who insisted I meet her. You wanted me to keep a close eye on her."

"I wanted you to use the eyes in your head," Rolf said, pointing at his own blue eyes, "not the little one between your legs."

Henry narrowed his eyes. "*Madre de Dios,* you should have considered that before you prodded me into spending time with her."

"I also prodded you to send her to a hospital. Did you listen to me then? No. So why are you suddenly infatuated with her?"

"She's pretty and I like her," he replied. "Those reasons have usually been good enough for either of us."

"She's Leopold's pawn. He's using her to get information from you."

"I'm sure Leopold is anxiously awaiting her reports on my hobbies and interests."

"You know what I mean. The lab is just a sham to hide her real reason for being here."

"She sounds quite sincere about her task for Leopold. She merely wants the community to support Leopold's project before buying land for it."

"Bullshit. Something about her isn't right. It's as if everyone on the Hill has fallen under her spell. Are you sure she's mortal?"

His stomach contorted. Was Rolf taking a stab in the dark, or had he overheard something he shouldn't have? Standing up, he replied, "If you'll excuse me, Rolf, I have no time for this nonsense. I have real work to do."

He strode to the testing lab. If he stayed and argued with Rolf, it would only give more credence to Rolf's suspicions. Maybe Rolf would take the hint and leave him alone.

Instead, footsteps followed him. "Is she human?" Rolf demanded.

¡Mierda! He stood at the lab counter, keeping his back to Rolf, his face hidden. "You were there. She bled human blood—you could smell it."

"All I can smell *now* is crap."

Henry let out an exasperated breath. His assistant had left a bottle of wine on the counter for him to test. He focused on the wine bottle's label, trying to remain calm. "She's human. If you don't believe me, ask Dr. Clarke."

"I spoke with the doctor. He thought there was something strange about her. She seemed too strong, too coherent. Her agreement not to go to the hospital fueled his suspicions."

"You make too much out of nothing." He took a wineglass out of the cupboard, avoiding eye contact with Rolf. *Why won't Rolf leave it alone?* He uncorked the bottle and examined the cork closely. "She's a doctor. She knew panicking would only make it worse, and she kept her head about her—an attractive feature for a mate."

"A mate? You aren't seriously considering taking her blood?"

Henry placed the cork on the counter and picked up the bottle. "She has a certain appeal. I'm exploring my options," he said, and sniffed the bottle's opening.

"Just fuck her and get it over with. We both know you can't control your jealousy—you have no business taking any woman for your mate."

He stared at the opening of the wine bottle, his vision a red blur. "Rolf, you're pushing the bounds of our friendship."

"I call it as I see it. Or have you forgotten what you did when Nathaniel poached—"

"Do not say it," he shot back, his hands clenching the wine bottle.

"Put that down and talk with me, damn it."

Henry caught the movement out of the corner of his eye. Rolf reached for the wine bottle and yanked. *How dare he?* Henry held tightly to the bottle's neck, his eyes now focused on Rolf's.

"Release it," Henry demanded.

Rolf didn't. Instead, he pulled on the bottle again.

Hot anger flooded through Henry at Rolf's impudence. He twisted the bottle to break Rolf's hold and instead fractured the thick green glass, leaving him holding the neck, while Rolf grasped the bottom. The cool liquid hit his legs—his tan pants were now drenched in red wine.

"You should not have done that." He drew his lip back and bared his fangs, rotating the neck of the bottle in his hand, using it like a sword, the jagged edge facing Rolf. He brought one foot forward *en garde*. "This conversation is over. Leave."

"Not until I talk some sense into you," Rolf said through his fangs, jabbing the broken bottle bottom toward him.

"I have no desire to draw first blood on you, but I will if you don't leave." Henry circled the air again with the neck's jagged edge. "You have no right to question who I date. I said nothing when you started dating Karen."

"You were already with Erin."

"I would be still, if you had done what you promised and left me a vial of your blood. Instead you rushed off to San Diego."

Rolf froze. "How long are you going to hold it over my head? I told you—Karen forgot to leave it in your mailbox."

"Do you know how I felt, looking for it and finding nothing? Knowing Erin would see Anne-Louise's mark without your blood to heal it. I returned home, hoping Erin would still be asleep for the night, only to find her waiting up for me. Do you have any idea what that moment was like?"

"You can't keep blaming me—you could've told Erin the truth."

"Truth? What do you know of truth, with the secrets you keep?"

"I'm not the only one with secrets. Have you been truthful with Cerissa? Does she know what you really are?"

"She knows all she needs to know." He held his ground, his half of the bottle's jagged end still pointed at Rolf. "You ask *me* to be honest, but have you told Karen the truth, the real reason you rush off to San Diego?"

"Do not go there—"

"Admit the truth, Rolf. You are—" Before he could finish, Rolf lunged at him, aiming the broken bottle bottom at his chest. He dodged and, blocking Rolf's arm with his, slid the edge of his wrist along Rolf's arm, deflecting the sharp glass away from them both. He hooked Rolf's ankle with his foot while grabbing Rolf's shoulder, and forced his junior partner to his knees, the moves automatic from years of practice with Yacov. The bottle half Rolf had held went skittering across the floor.

Pivoting, he swung behind Rolf, poised to drive the jagged glass into Rolf's back, but a sudden wave of empathy stopped him. The younger vampire was no match for him—he'd tweaked Rolf's pride. It was the only reason Rolf attacked.

Henry took a deep breath. He stepped back and strode to the far corner of the room, dropping the bottle neck into an industrial-sized trash can. The crash of breaking glass resonated in the room.

"You're right," Henry finally said. "This is not about Erin."

Rolf pushed to his feet and picked up the pieces of the bottle's bottom half, placing them on the workroom counter. "Then why take up with Leopold's envoy? There must be hundreds of women you could date."

Henry shrugged. "She is the first woman I have been interested in for a long time."

"Are you *in love* with Cerissa?" Rolf asked incredulously.

"It's a distinct possibility."

"You do have a self-destructive streak, Henry. She's dating Zeke."

"That's not true," he snapped.

"Zeke phoned me. He's due back in a few nights and told me he plans on taking her out again."

Henry hesitated, frowning. "I don't believe you."

"You only pick women who bring out the worst in you."

"Do not continue—"

"Even if Cerissa dumps Zeke, she's still Leopold's envoy. Not smart."

"She will not always be Leopold's envoy. If she does find a mate here, I suspect she'll withdraw as Leopold's envoy, to the run the lab full-time."

"You don't know women, do you?" Rolf scoffed. "She will be nothing but trouble for you."

"Thank you for your concern, but I'll be fine," Henry replied with a slight nod. "Now I have to get another bottle out of storage and think up an excuse to explain the broken one."

Henry left the workroom to go into the storage vault. He glanced over his shoulder at the door. Rolf didn't follow him. *Good.*

He took another bottle from the wine rack and stared at the label without reading it. Why was Cerissa still seeing Zeke if she had accepted Henry's invitation to the dance? Perhaps she hadn't understood its significance. He tightly gripped the wine bottle and closed his eyes.

Memories of the duel with Nathaniel flitted across the back of his closed eyelids, threatening to drag him down into his own personal hell. He fought to suppress images he didn't want to recall. When he heard the sound of breaking glass, he opened his eyes in time to see the shattered bottle slice into his fingers. The pain didn't register in his brain. What did register was what he saw: falling in large droplets from his hands, blood and wine darkened the white tile floor beneath him, reminding him of the stain on his soul he could never erase.

CHAPTER 37

Cerissa walked down a beige hallway of a corporate apartment building, the type business people used for extended stays. *As if I don't have enough going on. Why is Leopold suddenly in Mordida?* His summons had arrived one hour ago, demanding she meet him here.

"Come in, my dear girl, come in," Leopold said when he opened the door.

His intense, dark eyes were like Henry's, except they looked more severe against his pale white skin, and something about his thin, angular mustache looked asymmetrical, like one side was slightly longer than the other.

She followed him into the sterile apartment, the living room's décor bland in a stylish sort of way, the kitchen a mere alcove, visible through the opening at the serving bar. A door opened to a bedroom, with big picture windows facing Sierra Escondida's mountains.

"Where do you sleep?" she asked.

"Under the bed. Now please have a seat."

He gestured impatiently to the sofa, and she sat down, crossing one leg over the other, tucking her black skirt around her legs and unbuttoning her suit coat so it hung more gracefully, revealing the soft white blouse she wore. "When did you arrive?" she asked.

"A few days ago, enough time to look at the properties you're considering." He pulled a chair from the dinette and positioned it across from her, then handed her a large envelope.

"What's this?"

"The dossiers you requested—everything we have on all Hill vampires, not just the politically influential. As you requested, I included

214

current visitors, like Blanche. I even included information on Hill mortals, though you don't need their background to do your job."

"Thank you. This will be a big help."

"So tell me, have you made any progress signing up investors on the Hill?"

"I've provided prospectuses to Zeke Cannon, Henry Bautista, and Gaea Greenleaf, but no one else seems interested in investing yet."

"You've been here almost three weeks and that's all you've done?" He ran his index fingers along each side of his mustache, a habit he had when upset.

"Don't forget I was shot," she replied. "Since then, Gaea has refused to let me meet other potential investors."

"Yes, yes, I know. Well, forget about Henry. I don't want to be in business with him again."

Huh? They'd been in business together before? Henry hadn't said anything about a prior business. "Look, he's in favor of the project—"

"What part of 'no' don't you understand?" A dark look crossed his face. "Henry can stay on the outside and watch me get rich."

"But he would make a good partner in our project. I mean, he's a founder. With his backing—"

"Never. I'll move the lab to another community before I let him be involved."

Another community? *Oh, no, that won't work, not now.* She had to build the lab here; it was what Henry wanted. "But the delay," she said. "You wanted us online by next year."

"I do. With your lab, we'll have a reason to reopen negotiations on the treaty. Henry and his cronies forced us to agree—no new vampires." He made a fist and shook it. "I finally had a solid community, a safe community, one in which I could sire new vampires, but he denied me that."

Oh shit. Why didn't I figure this out before? What he'd lost in life, he wanted in death. His wife had died in childbirth when he was still mortal, the baby stillborn, and he had translated this deep loss into a desire to make new vampires.

"I warned Henry—the treaty was only a temporary fix," he continued, this time pointing a finger in her direction. "You, my dear, are the permanent fix. The blood supply you produce will allow us to take this yoke off our necks and expand our numbers."

Her stomach churned. The Protectors would have a fit. "Now, Leopold, when we first spoke, I told you the supply would be limited, just enough to replace bagged blood."

"Initially. With time, you'll expand production. I have every confidence you'll figure it out. The sooner we get started, the sooner we can expand. So yes, speed is important, but I'll take a little delay to keep Henry out."

"What do I tell him?"

"That's not my problem." He stood and motioned for her to follow him to the door. "I'm going to be here a few nights longer. Next time we meet, I want a better progress report."

She drove straight back to Gaea's. Leopold's idea of creating new vampires wasn't going to sit well with the Protectors, but it wasn't the immediate problem. Unless—could Leopold be part of the vampire dominance movement? Leopold had struck her as nonpolitical, particularly after his experience with Count Gustaferro. He wanted nothing to do with mortal politics, but turning mortals into one big cattle ranch wasn't the same thing. Still, if he was part of the vampire dominance movement, why would he invest in producing clone blood?

With the next break in traffic, she signaled and pulled over to the curb. She sent a text to Ari, asking him to monitor Leopold's communications, and explaining why. Finished, she resumed driving and considered her more immediate problem: how to woo Hill investors. When she arrived home, she found Gaea in the parlor off the main hallway, talking with Blanche.

"I'm sorry to interrupt," Cerissa said, standing in the doorway, the dossier packet tucked tightly under her arm.

Gaea smiled graciously. "Not at all. Do come in. Blanche and I were sharing the latest gossip."

"I just had a quick question. How do I reserve a room at the country club?"

"Why would you want to do that?" Gaea asked, looking puzzled.

"To hold a meeting and invite the community. It's time I explain the project to a broader audience and solicit potential investors."

"My dear, you must understand. Now is not the time."

Blanche looked smug. "Give her the real goods, Gaea. No one's gonna invest in her project."

"Now, Blanche, there's no need to be mean," Gaea said.

"You're not doin' her no favors pretending. No one on the Hill wants her here."

"Is that true?" Cerissa asked.

Gaea gave her a weak smile, sympathy in her hazel eyes. "You must understand, it takes time for the community to accept an outsider."

"But I'm Leopold's envoy. Under the treaty—"

"Fuck the treaty," Blanche spat. "Bunch of stupid old fellas wrote it."

Gaea shot Blanche an unmistakable warning glance. Turning back to Cerissa, she said, "Be patient. Give them time."

"Don't make no never mind," Blanche sneered. "Ya might as well pack up and shuffle off. They all know Leopold is using ya to spy on us. He's behind the shootings."

"That's not true."

"It's what the mayor believes."

How did that happen? Had Rolf convinced the mayor? "Gaea, tell her it's not true."

"Enough, you two. Cerissa, the mayor is just being cautious. He's letting you go to the dance, but he doesn't think the community is ready to invest in your project just yet."

Blanche turned her nose up. "He doesn't trust ya."

"Blanche, I said enough. Cerissa, come with me." Blanche stood as well, and Gaea held up her hand. "You stay here," she ordered.

Gaea slipped an arm around Cerissa's shoulders and walked with her into the hallway.

First Leopold, and now this—Leopold probably wanted their project on the Hill to lord it over Henry because of the treaty. Without that motivation, would Leopold pull the plug? This was her first mission as a Watcher for the Protectors. What would they do if she failed? Certainly nothing so drastic as taking her wings...would they?

"Cerissa," Gaea said, getting her attention.

"I have to find some way to prove we're serious."

"Be patient, dear."

"I can't afford to be patient."

She said goodnight to Gaea and walked upstairs to her room. She had to find a way to convince them. Something, anything, to show them the project was the real. With Henry out of town, she couldn't turn to him for help.

She opened the door to her room, and almost screamed.

A man stepped out of the shadows near her window.

CHAPTER 38

"Hey, Ciss, how's it hanging?"

"Ari!" she screeched in a whisper, clutching the packet of Leopold's dossiers close to her thudding heart. She held her breath and looked behind her. No one in the hallway—Gaea hadn't followed her upstairs. She sucked in air and pressed her fingers against the bedroom door, quietly closing it. "Don't ever do that again," she said in an angry whisper.

At six foot four, Ari towered over her. He crossed his arms. "Do you want to know what I found out or not?"

She clenched her jaw and gave him the evil eye. "Keep your voice down. Gaea will hear you."

"Okay," he said, lowering his voice, but not by much. He grabbed one of the slipper chairs, turned it around, and straddled it, his chin propped on its back, his large frame dwarfing the little chair.

She wouldn't let his silliness lighten her mood. "You have results on Leopold already?"

He laughed. "I'm good, but not that good. I've been monitoring his emails and phone calls for *years*. I'll use what you learned and search the data to see what I can find."

"If it's not Leopold, what's so important you just popped in?"

"Well, good news and bad news."

Damn. The last thing she wanted to hear. "Do I have to ask?"

"Let's start with the good news. Even though Zeke does work for the government, they have no clue vampires exist."

"You're sure?"

"Look, Ciss, we have contacts so deep into all the secret agencies—of all the countries—that they can't hide anything from us. It's time you started paying attention to the playbook. We keep close tabs on what humans know about the supernatural—including us, remember?"

"We're not supernatural, and I'm not arguing it with you."

"Keep telling yourself that, kid, keep telling yourself that," he said, smirking at her. "Anyway, those agencies don't know vampires exist; they don't know we exist. So all is well on that score—Zeke hasn't sold out his people."

"That's a relief."

"Now here's the bad news. Zeke *is* working for the government—black ops, special assassination work. They use him a few times a year, mostly in Central and South America, to get rid of people they view as troublesome. He's a reliable operative, as far as they're concerned. He always gets his target, and is in and out without getting caught."

She collapsed onto the other slipper chair. "Damn. Double damn."

"You're so cute when you swear."

She leaned back in the chair, using her arm to cover her eyes and block out the light. This was worse than any news she could have imagined. "Just get on with it," she said.

"One thing does concern them. They think he's a psychopath, since he always slits the victim's throat and drains their blood. He leaves them dangling by their feet or leaning over a bathtub, and he takes the blood with him. They don't know he's drinking it—they just think he's got this obsession, and they like it, because of the terror factor."

She lowered her arm and looked over at her cousin. "Do they know where he lives?"

"Nope. He picks up his instructions in Los Angeles, at various prearranged drop locations. They've tried tracking him and can't, but as long as he delivers what they want, they keep paying him."

Thank God. If the government figured out Zeke lived on the Hill, it wouldn't be long before they took a closer look into what the Hill hid.

"How do they get in touch with Zeke?"

"They wire $10,000 into his bank account. When he sees the transaction hit, he goes to Los Angeles to pick up his next set of instructions. They pay him the rest when he's done."

"Wow. I felt something was off, but not this off."

"Too bad, too. The guy's stinking rich, though he doesn't spend any of it. I hacked his account. He sends his earnings to a bank account in a country that refuses to share information with the good ole U.S., and then he funnels it to different stockbrokers around the world. He's set up his own investment firm, with one client—him. That's how he hides it. He believes in buying and holding stocks for the long term."

"Why is he gone for so long if he's just there to kill one person?"

"Good question, Ciss. From what I could piece together, he does his own investigation. If he doesn't think the scumbag deserves killing, he passes on the assignment. His government handlers are quite irritated, it shows in the file, but there's nothing they can do to force him to kill someone. They need him more than he needs them."

"At least he's not killing innocent people," she said, letting out a little sigh.

"Yeah, but he's a hired killer. You can't have him as an investor in the lab. You're going to withdraw your offer to him, right?"

She ran her hands through her thick hair, pushing it back behind her ears. She needed Zeke as an investor. Maybe the Protectors would understand. Maybe she could make them understand.

"Ciss, are you listening? A Watcher can't be involved with someone like him. You know the rules."

"Just give me some time to figure it out. He has money, and I need investors or this thing is going to fall apart."

He tapped his watch. "Five minutes. That's all the time you need to consider it. You can't have an investor who's a cold-blooded killer. Not even one who kills bad guys."

"Yeah, but I need to get investors from somewhere."

"Why don't I just transfer a couple million to your account?" he asked, taking out his phone and swiping the screen. "The Protectors will never miss it."

"Can't. Leopold believes I'm a poor but honest researcher. If I suddenly showed up with a lot of money…"

He looked up from his phone. "Okay, then I'll set up a shell corporation to fund it."

"Still won't work—Leopold won't trust outside money. He holds veto power and he only wants investors from the treaty communities. We need Zeke's money."

"Too bad, toots. You got to cull Zeke from the herd."

"I said I'd think about it."

"You do that, so long as you decide the right way. I've got to report it."

"Why?" she asked, her stomach churning, a thread of fear forming. "It's not what the Protectors are looking for—why give them ammunition to hate vampires?"

"Kiddo, if you're going to lose your objectivity, maybe you are the wrong Watcher for this assignment. Our job is to watch and report. The Protectors decide."

"But we're already keeping things from them."

"That's to save your skin. We can't hide every bad fact."

"But—"

"A group of vampires is conspiring against humanity. Zeke might be part of the conspiracy. You've got to get back on track and do your job."

He was right. As much as she hated it, they had had to report Zeke's contract work. "Okay." She sighed. "Do what you must."

"Now, do you want the news on Henry?"

"Ah, is there anything to tell?" she asked, crossing her fingers.

Ari laughed. "He seems to be an altar boy in comparison to Zeke. He travels on business frequently, but he doesn't work for the government and he doesn't work for any mafia-type group. I didn't see anything in his business contacts to explain why someone wants him dead. He does gamble regularly—mostly sporting events. He has a girlfriend in New York, though."

"You mean Anne-Louise?"

"That is the name I got."

"She's his maker. Anything else?"

"Nope. That's it for Henry. Want to hear about Rolf?"

"Don't tell me—he's a serial killer."

"Not unless he's really good at disposing of the bodies."

"What do you mean?"

"Every few weeks or so, he flies his jet to San Diego. When he does, all email and text messages stop for at least one night he's there. He must leave his phone on the plane, because the tower pings show him at the airport for the night, which makes no sense. He doesn't get a rental car. He probably takes a taxi and pays cash."

"I can't believe Karen lets him get away with disappearing off the grid. Could he have a lover? Or is he visiting his maker?"

"I tracked down his maker; she's still in Europe. From what I found out, she never liked him. She turned him for political reasons during World War II."

"You're sure there's nothing to tie him to the shootings? Tig said the shooters had been in a prison in San Diego."

"Look, unless Rolf uses the grid, I don't have any way to trace him. He may have visited the prison where the shooters came from—or stayed a hundred miles from it."

"Would you keep tracking him? See if any patterns develop?"

"Sure, Ciss, it costs me nothing. If I see something amiss, we can plant a tag on him and see where he really goes."

She stood up. She had things to do. "Thanks, Ari."

"No worries, kid, glad to help. Before I go, can you answer my question?"

"What question?"

"What's it like to sleep with a vampire?"

Cerissa crossed her arms. No way was she discussing her love life with Ari. "You're horrible."

"I try to be," he said. "Does that mean you finally have?"

"No, I mean, it's none of your business."

"Come on, Ciss. What's it like to sleep with the undead? I've tried kink, but nothing that kinky. Necrophilia. Might be worth a try."

Cerissa took in a deep breath and let it out slowly. "Even if I had a lover, I wouldn't share personal information with you."

"Now, now, Ciss, no reason to be defensive. From the way Henry kissed you—"

"Those damn lenses," she whispered in a low growl.

Ari raised his eyebrows in a good imitation of Groucho Marx. "You keep kissing him like that—I guarantee *he'll* bed *you*."

"I'm not having this conversation."

"But Ciss—"

"Here." She stood and tossed him the packet she held. "Do something useful—scan these into the system. Leopold finally gave me dossiers on all the vampires and their mortal mates. I need access pronto. If anything concerns you, drill down on it."

"All right, cupcake, but next time I want to hear all about Henry." He popped open the crystal of his watch, touched its face, and vanished out of sight.

She plopped back onto the slipper chair. Zeke was an assassin? She had a hard time believing it, although she'd had her doubts since he first called her "little lady." Only Ari could get away with calling her nicknames; he'd done it since they were kids.

Ari had just disappeared when her phone rang. Zeke. She took the call. He'd returned from South America and wanted to see her. She told him she wasn't available and had to focus on Leopold's project. She clicked off the call.

What to do? She began pacing back and forth, wearing a path in

Gaea's brocade carpet. Ari was right—she couldn't let Zeke invest in the project. If he got caught, the bad publicity would be devastating, and that was just the practical side. Morally, the Protectors would never allow it.

And Leopold—he was being unreasonable. He wouldn't let Henry invest, and now Zeke had to be scratched off the list. She had no other leads. Not to mention Gaea's news—the community didn't want her here. She picked up a pillow and threw it across the room. It bounced against the closet's mirrored door, rattling it, and landed on the floor. *Screw the Protectors. Maybe I should just leave.*

A small pain started in the center of her chest and her throat tightened. The same pain she felt when her *amma* abandoned her. Why did leaving the Hill dredge up those old feelings? She stopped pacing and stood there, her eyes opening wider, the realization hitting her.

She didn't want to leave Henry. Her feelings for him weren't just a by-product of her aura, or a reaction to Ari's "stake him or seduce him" suggestion.

Her feelings for him were real.

She took a deep breath and shook her body, like a wet cat trying to get dry. Why wouldn't her dread let go? Somehow she had to find a way to stay here, to convince the Hill her project was real. Until she did, her shot at having something more with Henry was nil.

But how? Who could she turn to for help? Well, throwing things didn't help. She picked up the pillow and slid open the closet door. Another problem—she didn't have anything to wear to the dance. *I bet Karen doesn't have the same problem. Karen would know—*

That's it! Karen may be the answer. She picked up her cell phone and began composing the text message.

CHAPTER 39

"I can't believe you haven't bought your dress yet," Karen said. She was behind the wheel of her Audi, driving them through Mordida. A hair band held her auburn hair away from her face. "Gaea should have suggested it weeks ago."

A large pickup truck made a left-hand turn in front of her car. Karen slammed on the brakes. "Asshole," she yelled, leaning on the horn. "Probably has a short dick."

Cerissa wrapped her hand so tightly around the grab handle that it was in danger of being dismembered. *Maybe I should use a little aura on Karen, just enough to calm down her driving.*

Once they were through the intersection, Karen acted like nothing had happened. "Things getting serious between you and Henry?" she asked.

"Serious?" Cerissa repeated.

"If you're going to the dance with him, sounds like you're getting serious." The driver ahead of them braked for the next yellow light. Karen pounded the horn, stopping within inches of the black bumper.

"Fucking idiot!" Karen yelled, making rude gestures at the car in front of her.

She does that again, I swear I'll get out at the next signal. I don't need answers this badly.

Turning back to her, Karen asked, "Is it serious?"

"Ah, it's all happening kind of fast," Cerissa said. "There's so much I don't know about Henry, except for the fact I can't stop thinking about him."

Karen laughed. "Look, when your potential mate has lived almost two hundred years, it can take a while to really know him, and the hormones get ahead of our heads sometimes. But Henry's not more complicated than any other male."

"I'm beginning to think they're all complicated."

"Yeah, but they'll never admit it." The light turned green and Karen floored the accelerator again. "You know, Henry might be a good match for you. You're reserved—he likes that in a woman."

"Maybe."

"So I take it you two haven't—"

Why was everyone so interested in her sex life? "I don't want to rush into anything, and neither does he."

Karen laughed. "Not like me. I tend to jump feet first. Sometimes it works, sometimes it doesn't, but I have fun along the way."

"Karen—"

"Look. Deep down, Henry's a good guy. He won't take you for granted or make you feel used. If you're willing to accept he's been unfaithful in the past, I hear he's dynamite in bed."

Eww. How much of her sex life had Erin confided to Karen? Cerissa didn't want to know.

"What about Zeke?" Karen asked. "Zeke told Rolf you're his girlfriend."

"He what? How could he? I told him—"

"Everyone on the Hill knows he made a play for you at the casino and then you went with him to the square dance. *And* you had a private goodbye with him before he took off on business. You can see how he might have the wrong idea."

"I told him I wasn't interested, that we couldn't date, that we're only friends. Not once, but twice. Told him. With words. What is wrong with him?"

"Yeah, sometimes guys can be thickheaded. Maybe third time's the charm?"

She sighed. "All right, I'll tell him a third time, but this better be the last."

"Good," Karen said with a laugh, parking the car. "I hope you won't mind if I do some shopping, too. I have my dress for the dance, but I can always use something new."

Four hours later, Cerissa had spent all the money she'd won at the blackjack table. She had a gown for the dance, along with some social clothes Karen ordered her to buy. Karen had a good eye for color and style—not surprising, given her marketing background.

"Knowing Henry as I do," Karen said, leading the way back to the car, "we'll stay away from basic slut for now. But you do need a strapless bra for your dress."

"Ah, I don't have one. Should we go back inside after we drop these off?" Cerissa carried the full-length bag containing her dresses, while Karen juggled the other packages. "If you don't have time, I can come back tomorrow."

"I know just the place to get your bra. And don't worry about the time. I told Rolf I wouldn't be home when he woke. Shopping has to take priority sometimes."

At the car, Cerissa carefully hung her dress on the backseat hook, spreading it out over the seat. Now unencumbered, she followed Karen to a lingerie store called "Everything Sexy." Karen made it to the display of bras first and held up an ivory strapless number. "This will look lovely with your skin tones, and it's designed for your dress style."

Karen handed it to her and went back to browsing.

Cerissa started looking through the racks next to Karen and picked out a bustier. "You mentioned Rolf wasn't expecting you home tonight. Rolf travels on business, doesn't he?"

"Both he and Henry travel. Henry tends to take the San Francisco trips."

"And Rolf?"

"We have some of our big distributors in San Diego. He'll go down there a few times a month to wine and dine them."

"Do you go with him?"

"Sometimes, but most of the time he goes alone." Karen raised her eyes from the display rack. "You don't have to ask; I can see it in your face. How come I trust Rolf? Well, I just do. I've seen his expense vouchers, the receipts for the trips, and he's offered to take me, but with all the marketing work I do for the winery, it's too much—I can't work both day and night, you know?"

"Sure," Cerissa said, flipping through the rack of bras in front of her. "You've seen his receipts—what part of San Diego? I mean, does he stay close to the San Diego community's headquarters?"

Karen gave her a *why do you want to know* look. Thinking fast, Cerissa added, "I might have to travel there on business. It would help to know which restaurants are good."

"Most of his receipts are from the La Jolla area—a lot of gourmet restaurants there. It's closer to our distributor's office than downtown. He gets permission from the San Diego community to visit their territory, but he doesn't go to their headquarters. He doesn't have much time."

Hmm. According to her lenses, La Jolla was about a half-hour's drive north of the San Diego community's downtown location. *Maybe Ari could work with that information. At least it's a start.*

Karen held up a bra, one with a front clasp between the bra cups. "No back clasp to show through. You'll want one for the stretch top you bought."

Cerissa slid the hanger's hook over her arm and began wishing they had a shopping cart. The sound of her phone's trill got her attention, and she had to juggle things around, temporarily placing the collection of lingerie on a nearby rack, leaving her free to reach into her purse.

Henry's text read: "Tomorrow 8p horseback riding? Idea to discuss with you."

"Yes. Looking forward to it," she texted.

"Meet at the corral," he wrote back. "Bring your own dinner, I'll bring wine."

"See you then. I'll bring something for you too."

She returned her phone to her purse. Karen was still on the other side of a round rack, eyeing a vivid blue bra. "Karen, I have something I want to ask. Have you heard any rumors about my project with Leopold?"

"Only the ones Blanche is spreading."

"What?"

Karen looked up from the blue bra. "You didn't know? Blanche has been telling everyone your project isn't real, that it's all a front so you can spy on us for Leopold. Look, Rolf and Frédéric said the same thing, but from what I hear, it's Blanche who's been driving the train on this one." Karen lowered her voice. "Vs—they're kind of paranoid."

Cerissa stepped closer so they could talk quietly. "What should I do?"

"You need to discredit the bitch. Start a rumor about her."

"I couldn't. It wouldn't be right to lie."

"She did it to you."

"Just because she plays dirty doesn't mean I should," she said with a sigh. Some things were just not right to do. "There must be another way."

"Well, you could show them the project's real."

"I've been racking my brain, trying to figure out how. We need money first—that's why I'm looking for investors. We have seed money; it'll take more than what we have to build the lab."

"Chicken and the egg problem."

"Huh?"

"You can't build the lab without money, and you can't get investors from the Hill without proof the project is real."

"True," Cerissa agreed. "Real estate is expensive. You need a guarantor or a track record to get a loan. Our project doesn't have either. Leopold refuses to sign as guarantor; his latest identity is too new, he doesn't feel it's well enough established to get the kind of financing we need, and he doesn't want to transfer money to his new identity and have it taxed."

Karen wrapped an arm around her shoulder and gave her a hug. "You'll come up with something, I'm sure you will. Just think outside the box, you know?"

"Thanks."

Karen handed her some more bras to try on, and pointed toward the rear of the store. "Dressing rooms are through there."

Cerissa scooped up the rest of her selections and walked through the curtain of red beads to the row of small white cubicles. After latching the plywood door behind her, she dropped the lingerie on the bench.

She tried on the bra and panty set first, twisting and turning in front of the mirror. *Karen's right, the color looks nice against my skin. But will Henry like it?* She sat down on the little bench, holding her head in her hands. Of course he'd like it, but that wasn't the problem. For all of Ari's teasing, he had hit too close to the truth. If she kept kissing Henry the way she had at the winery, they'd end up in bed.

She took off the bra. In the mirror, she saw her tightly crinkled nipples. Just thinking about Henry had excited her.

What would it be like to have his hands cup my breasts, his fingers touch my nipples?

She shook her head at her reflection and tried on the next bra. Thinking about Henry would only distract her. She had to get the community to trust her. She had to find investors for the lab. She had to figure out who was behind the vampire dominance movement.

Maybe she should cancel her date with Henry. They could go horseback riding another time. She picked up her phone and opened Henry's last text message, her thumb hovering over the keypad. She didn't want to cancel, but she'd learned a long time ago what she wanted didn't matter. Her mission had to come first.

CHAPTER 40

SIERRA ESCONDIDA POLICE DEPARTMENT—THE NEXT NIGHT

Tig stared at the screen of the computer in her police office. She gave up trying to write a polite email to Yacov. The potential suspect list—people who might hold a grudge against him—had yet to appear on her desk. When Henry called earlier, asking her to increase patrols on the wall tonight, he'd told her Yacov had taken over preparing his list too.

She had already sent two reminders to Yacov, asking for his list. Really, how long could he take to write it? And Henry—she couldn't believe he sent back the immunity agreement unsigned, demanding all sorts of changes.

She didn't understand those two. They were known to bet at poker on worse odds. The case was growing cold and everyone was losing interest in it. She didn't want to wait until the next attempt on the Hill succeeded. Sure, that would motivate the survivor—if there was one—but she wasn't losing anyone on her watch.

Her only other lead was the prison. She didn't like coincidences, the missing exit forms. If the person who picked up the prisoners was connected to the attacks, one of the guards may have been bribed to lose the forms.

Speculation, but it would explain why all three forms were missing.

Jayden's written report was on her desk, which meant he was back on the Hill. Two days ago, he'd driven to San Diego to investigate the guards.

A sticky note on top read: "Video is on your computer desktop."

She picked up the report and skimmed through it first. Two of the guards were dead ends. Their background information—deeds, vehicle registration reports, criminal history, work history in the prison system—didn't hint at any abnormal spending habits. Both were married and lived in the suburbs near the prison. Jayden had followed each on their days off. According to his report, they had done pretty predictable things: home improvement projects, grocery shopping, and golf. At night, no sign of any vampire coming or going, and both wives had gone out during the day, so they could rule out their spouses.

Information on the third guard, Norman Tyler, had been more interesting.

Jayden had tailed Norman to an apartment in Vista, a little far from the prison, but near enough to commute if you didn't mind spending two hours of your life on the freeway each day. She double-clicked the video player icon and started the surveillance video Jayden left for her, two video files: a handheld camera, along with his body camera.

She synced them up and started playing the videos side by side— grainy night videos, headlights flaring whenever a car drove past. She fast-forwarded to Norman's arrival at the Vista apartment, an old-fashioned two-story building, with each apartment on the second floor facing a suspended balcony. The videos were shot at slightly different angles, so she had a pretty good view of the entire scene.

When Norman got out of his car, a person emerged from the shadows created by a large elephant ear palm. The person's face was hidden from view by an oversized hoodie. After a brief hug, Norman escorted Hoodie up the stairs into his apartment on the second floor. No clue if the hooded person was a vampire—Hoodie could have been a thin, short male or an average height, small-breasted female.

Damn it! If Tig had gone with Jayden, she would have been able to identify Hoodie. She had an eidetic memory when it came to smells. She knew the unique scent of each vampire she'd ever met. And even if she hadn't met Hoodie before, she would have been able to tell if Hoodie was vampire.

Movement on the video caught her attention. The door to Norman's second-floor apartment opened, and he walked out alone. The cameras captured Norman climbing down the formed concrete stairs, the wrought-iron rail bending when the big man leaned on it with each step. At ground level, instead of walking toward his car, Norman headed straight for Jayden.

Jayden's car started and the video from the handheld camera jerked as he pulled away from the curb. Norman darted in front of him, moving fast for a large man, his hands in the air. His white skin flared on camera, Jayden's headlights illuminating him.

"I just want to talk," Norman yelled through the windshield when Jayden's car stopped inches from him.

"Keep your hands visible," Jayden yelled back. The handheld camera jerked again as he tabbed down the driver's-side window.

Norman kept his hands out and stepped closer. "Why are you following me?"

"Who's in your apartment?" Jayden shot back.

"Not so fast. Tell me what this is about."

"You know what this is about."

"The three dead prisoners?"

"The only connection between all three is the guards."

"You think I'm involved? You're nuts. They can't pay me enough. Do you have any idea how large my pension will be if I stay another ten years? I'm not going to risk my pension for a stupid bribe. They can't offer me enough—I'll get eighty K a year for life if I make it to fifty-five."

"Then you won't mind telling me who's in your apartment?"

"A friend."

"Your friend got a name?"

"Look, Johnson—that's your name, right? Captain Johnson?"

"That's right."

"Well, Johnson, I'm not telling you anything else. We're done here. Quit following me or I'll report you to the local police. You're out of your jurisdiction."

"Go ahead. I'll be glad to tell your superiors what we suspect."

"If you know what's good for you, you'll leave before the Vista police get here and you have to explain yourself."

"Go ahead and call them."

"You sure you want to do that? In this neighborhood, well, you kind of stick out," Norman snapped.

"Why won't you tell me who's in your apartment?"

Good. Jayden didn't take the racist bait.

"Go to hell," Norman replied. He flipped off Jayden and stomped up the stairs.

The video ended there. With his surveillance blown, there wasn't much for him to do in San Diego. Tig tapped her fingers on her desk. What next? More surveillance of Norman? Maybe she should send Zeke or Liza to follow the guard at night.

She looked up from her desk when she heard the door to her office open. Jayden barged in and plopped down on her couch. She picked up his report and waved it in the air. "How did you let this happen?" she demanded. "Now Norman knows he's a suspect."

"I can't figure out how he spotted me. If Hoodie was a vampire, maybe he or she saw me in the dark."

"Were you using your phone? He could have spotted the light."

"Hey, I know procedure. I was watching for Norman, not playing with my phone."

"Then how did he spot you? You must have done something wrong."

Jayden stood up and stuck out his chin. "I've had four hours' sleep. If you want to play the blame game, I'm outta here."

She took a deep breath. Working for Phat hadn't prepared her for working with her own mate. Phat had demanded perfection. The two words he forbade her to speak were "I'm sorry" when she screwed up.

"Captain," she said.

He stood there, anger in his eyes. "What, *chief?*"

"Sit down," she replied.

He didn't move.

"Please," she added, a little more gently. She wasn't saying she was sorry.

Slowly, he lowered himself back onto the couch. *Good.*

"So, Hoodie never came out?" she asked.

He ran a hand over the top of his shaved head. "I stayed until sunrise." He leaned his head back against the couch. Fatigue lines showed around his eyes. "Hoodie either slept in the apartment or crab-walked down the back wall and sneaked out the alley."

"Then we need to send a vampire team to follow the guard."

"Yeah, that makes the most sense. They can do things I can't."

"And you can do things they can't. I appreciate the day work you did on all three guards."

He gave a quick nod. Okay, they were back on even ground—time to step past this interpersonal shit. She flipped to the end of his report, where a still photo of Hoodie was stapled. "From the video, Hoodie looked short and thin. Lots of vampires turned before the 1900s could fit Hoodie's description. Bad nutrition and illness kept heights short."

Jayden nodded. "I can think of a dozen vampires on the Hill alone who could be Hoodie. At least we know it's not the mayor," he said with a straight face.

She let out a snort. Yeah, the mayor's paunch disqualified him—he could *never* be Hoodie.

Jayden smiled back at her. "I've got to get some sleep," he said, standing up.

"Okay, I'll see you tomorrow at dusk," she said. A little more damage control couldn't hurt, so she added, "I'll meet you at your room."

He leaned over her desk and pressed his lips to hers. "Deal. I'll see you then."

He started to leave and turned around abruptly. "Ah, I almost forgot. Did you leave this for me? It was on my desk." He dug into his back pocket and handed her a folded 911 report. "A mountain lion was in the hills just south of Gaea's house."

"No, I hadn't seen this yet. Who reported it?" she asked, unfolding it.

"Yeah, I get where you're going—all were reports from residents who sensed its presence. No one saw it in person."

"As long as it stays up in the mountains, it's not much of a threat." She could go hunting for it. If she darted it, she could relocate it on the other side of the mountain—it might convince the cat to stay away. It couldn't be a vampire; there was no recorded case of a vampire transforming into anything other than a wolf or a bat.

"Please put out a warning," she said, "just to alert everyone to be cautious. We don't want it taking out some mortal who goes hiking on the mountain."

"Will do." He looked up for a second, like he was considering something. "One other thing. Did you move stuff around on Maggie's desk? It's been all messed up."

"How can you tell?"

"Hey, I know it's not as neat as she kept it, but I was starting to have a system. I sort of knew the contents of each pile before I left for San Diego. Now it's all scattered."

"It wasn't me. Maybe Zeke was looking for something. While you were gone, there was a small burglary in the commercial district. Zeke helped with the investigation. I'll ask him."

Her phone rang. Jayden waved goodbye and left.

"Mayor?" she said when she answered.

"Good evening, Tig. I hate to impose, but I need you to deliver two warning letters. I don't have anyone else I trust to do it."

She rolled her eyes. "Could one of my officers do it?"

"I'd prefer you do it. Budget constraints, you know. We spent enough overtime on Jayden's San Diego investigation. Stop by my office and I'll give you the letters."

Cheap bastard. He could have used one of his administrative assistants to do it. It didn't require a police officer. She had enough on her plate. How was she supposed to solve the case if they kept pulling her six ways from Sunday?

"Who are the letters for?" she asked.

"Henry and Cerissa."

Now it made sense. A touchy situation, so he wanted someone with enough *gravitas*, and it couldn't be Rolf. "I'll do it," she said. "I shouldn't have any problem finding them."

CHAPTER 41

Cerissa ignored the darkening road in front of her as she drove to meet Henry at the corral. Three nights had passed since she saw him at the winery, and her resolve to cancel their date had died when she re-read his text message. Maybe the idea he wanted to discuss was a solution to her investor problem.

I can't pass that up, can I?

She parked the car and walked to the split-rail fence, stopping to watch him. He lifted the saddle onto Candy's back, handling it like it was made of paper rather than heavy leather. His ponytail was neatly tied back, his tight jeans tucked into his riding boots, his muscular butt looking sexy as he worked.

But this is a business meeting, not a date. At least, that was what she'd say if anyone asked. She couldn't risk violating the Covenant.

So this was business, just business.

Yeah, right.

Anticipation buzzed straight through her from crown to root, her breath catching in her throat, her skin tingling, her body ready for him. The same way she'd responded when she first saw his magnetic eyes at the dance, except this time, her heart fluttered as well.

"Are you going to stand there watching me all evening?" he asked lightheartedly.

She opened the gate and walked over to him. His hands were busy tightening the saddle strap. He kissed her before buckling it, and then offered her Candy's reins.

"You look lovely," he said.

"Thanks," she replied, glancing down. She'd worn a white shirt with her jeans, a small animal-print scarf tied at her neck. She felt self-conscious under his gaze, and to cover up her awkwardness, she handed him two small sacks. He slid them into one of the nylon saddlebags, and then placed a wine bottle wrapped in a picnic blanket in the other padded bag.

Candy took a step closer, nudging her for attention. She reached out to pet the horse and felt her balance waver. The sound of gunfire rang in her ears. She closed her eyes, clutching Candy's bridle.

It's all in my head.

Henry gripped her arm, steading her. "Are you all right?" he asked.

"I'll be fine."

"A flashback?"

"I'm sorry. Just give me a moment."

"I should have anticipated this."

She still held tight to Candy's bridle. The horse nuzzled closer, allowing Cerissa to lean her face against Candy's soft cheek. "Are you sure it's safe?" she asked. "I'm more concerned with your wellbeing—"

"I spoke with Tig. She promised to increase the patrols along the wall. But if you aren't comfortable, we can go riding another time."

"I'll be fine." She buried her nose in Candy's mane, the clean smell of horse musk grounding her in the present. She stroked the horse's white blaze and, after giving her neck a final pat, let go and swung up into the saddle. Henry released her arm after she was firmly in the saddle, and joined her, riding a gelding. The floodlights bordering Rolf's property lit the trail.

The gelding paced Candy, keeping the two horses side by side. "Have you had any further luck wooing investors while I was gone?" he asked.

"Not so far. I have to prove to the community the project is real."

"How would you do that?"

"I could provide samples of clone blood—would that convince them?"

He pursed his lips for a moment. "You would need to prove it didn't come from a regular mortal. Could you bring a clone to show them?"

"Not yet—I have to develop a life-support system using human technology. I'm sure I can do it, but it will take time. With all the rumors floating around saying the project isn't real, I need to do something."

"I see. Let me consider it. Even if I told others the blood was produced from clones, they might say I was biased."

She smiled slightly. "Would they have good reason to say that?"

"Indeed they would," he said, smiling back at her, "which brings me to why I wanted to talk with you. As I told you at the winery, I want your lab built here in Sierra Escondida. I'm willing to invest in your project to make it happen."

She froze in the saddle. *Shit. How can I tell him no? I can't tell him what Leopold said. I don't want to hurt him, not after he's been so supportive.*

"Ah," she said, "I don't think Leopold would like me mixing business with pleasure."

Henry glanced over at her and wrinkled his brow. *What a strange evasion. She's been so desperate to get investors; why turn me down now?*

"Are you having second thoughts about the project?" he asked.

"No, not at all. It's just—"

"Leopold."

She looked crestfallen. "He won't let you invest. I think it has something to do with the treaty..."

"It's not only the treaty." *The old curmudgeon still carries a grudge over the restaurant.* He reached over and patted her leg. "Don't let it trouble you."

They rode in silence for a while, Cerissa looking pensive. "I meant it," he said. "Don't worry about Leopold. I'm not offended."

"It's not that. Ah, I wanted to tell you something, so you didn't hear it from someone else. Zeke asked to see me when he returned."

"I already heard," he said, dropping all expression from his face. His grip tightened on the reins, and he felt the abyss beckon to him.

"You did?"

"Rolf mentioned it."

"I should have known he would," she said, rolling her eyes. "I just wanted to be open with you about it. I've made it clear to Zeke before that I wasn't interested in dating him, but judging by his persistence, I'm not sure he really heard me. So I've made a decision. I'm not going to see him anymore, not even on business."

He relaxed his grip on the horse's reins, his dark thoughts retreating. "I'm glad to hear that."

"I'm glad you're glad," she said, and looked away. "Ah, is there any possibility Zeke hired the shooter?"

"Zeke?" He allowed his surprise to register in his voice.

"Zeke left town so quickly after I was shot."

"He goes to South America for his work—he doesn't always have advance notice. Tig is well familiar with it."

"Do you know what he does there?"

He dropped his face into a mask again. It was not for him to reveal Zeke's secrets. "Zeke is no threat to anyone on the Hill."

He clicked on an LED flashlight to light the entrance to a connector trail. From the dirt road, he guided his horse onto the narrower path leading to a park-like area, and her horse followed.

Floodlights threw circles of light around picnic benches and a baseball diamond. He avoided those, wanting a little more privacy.

"How does this look?" he asked, using the flashlight to indicate a secluded, grassy area surrounded by large oak trees.

"Lovely."

They dismounted, and he unfastened a saddlebag, handing it to her. She slid out a plastic food container from the bag. "Treats for the horses," she said.

"Let me take the bits out first." He swapped out their bridles for halters to make it easier for them to chew.

While he hung three electric camp lanterns from the trees, she fed the horses carrots and apple quarters. He admired the way she treated them with respect—a light stroke of their fur, an offer of food. Very thoughtful of her to bring enough for both horses.

"Is there any reason Zeke might want you dead?" she asked.

He stopped cold, holding the third lamp in midair. Hadn't they finished their conversation about Zeke? Why did she want to know more?

"We are on good terms," he replied, and finished fastening the lamp to a tree branch.

She didn't look persuaded. "How can you be sure?"

"I did a favor for him many years ago, for which he has remained grateful throughout the years."

Okay, so he was cutting the truth with a sharp knife. He hadn't killed

Nathaniel as a favor to Zeke, even though the death of Zeke's maker set the cowboy free.

"Maybe he's tired of being grateful," she said.

"I have no reason to suspect his gratitude has turned to bitterness." He wished she would leave it alone. He didn't want to be reminded of what happened, let alone speak of it. "Perhaps you don't remember—Zeke was closer to the shooter. He could have been shot instead of you. If Zeke was behind it, he wouldn't have been in the line of fire."

Henry reached for her hand, bringing her fingers to his lips. She smelled of fresh apple. He softly kissed her folded fingers, and then said, "You won't be seeing him, so there's nothing further to discuss."

"Actually, there is." She looked away, her eyes carrying a certain shyness. "Are you dating anyone else?"

He liked the sound of her question—much better than talking about Zeke.

"I have dated others since Erin, but no one has held my interest—until now," he said, and kissed her fingers again.

"Really? You don't have a new girlfriend lined up?"

"Perhaps I'm looking at her."

A rosy color flooded her cheeks. He took her reaction as a good sign. Before he could say anything else, Candy nudged at their linked fingers. "I think someone is impatient," he said to the horse, releasing Cerissa's hand.

Cerissa took out the last apple quarter and offered it to Candy in the flat of her hand.

Rolf is wrong—Cerissa will be mine. She looked so beautiful under the starlight. *If she knew what I did to Zeke's maker, would she still want to be my mate?* No, it was better not to think of the past. It only led to sins he'd fought so hard to forget.

Cerissa stroked Candy's forehead one more time while the horse snuffled the plastic bowl to make sure everything was gone. Satisfied, Candy seemed content to munch on grass, and Cerissa snapped the lid on the bowl. She stepped over to the picnic blanket Henry had spread out, took off her boots, and lolled back.

Henry's eyes followed her while she stretched. The way he looked at her—so intense, yet not threatening.

Is that what real desire looks like?

Whatever it was, she liked it.

"Wine?" he asked, joining her on the blanket. He uncorked the bottle and poured her a glass. She reached into her saddlebag and pulled out the same warming sack she'd brought to the winery. Instead of a glass jar, inside was a shiny blue pouch, like those used for children's juice drinks.

She accepted the glass of wine he held out to her and offered him the blue pouch. He rolled the pouch in his hand and sniffed it. His eyes asked the question.

"The corner is serrated; just tear it off. You can pour the blood into your own wineglass. Some pouches come with a drinking straw or a spout on top. If you have a preference—"

"I cannot imagine drinking it from a child's straw."

She smiled. He was always so proper and dignified. Next time she'd give him one with a straw, just to be silly. After pouring the blood into a wineglass, he sniffed the glass before tasting his drink. She watched his fangs extend. She hadn't noticed his fangs when he tried the first samples. Had he hidden them from her before? He seemed relaxed now and willing to let her see who he was.

He took another sip. "This is excellent, but it's different from the others."

"I'm trying a ratio between normal blood and the second strongest sample," she replied, retrieving her sandwich from the same bag and unwrapping it. "Something less overpowering, but still satisfying."

"Indeed. You have hit the mark with this one. Still, you may want to produce the stronger one, as its effect might be useful."

"So the stronger one might be like Viagra for vampires?"

"Something like that. This one doesn't have as strong an effect, so you are safe, for now."

She smiled, but lowered her eyes to avoid his intense gaze. He looked so good, stretched out on the picnic blanket, propped up on his elbow, savoring his beverage of choice. She swallowed the last bite of her sandwich and stuffed the trash into the saddlebag.

The scent of his cologne drifted her way on the light evening breeze, exciting a pleasant stir in her middle. Except for the horses, they were all alone, not another soul in sight. Would he be dessert? She palmed a breath mint she'd hidden in her pocket and discreetly slipped it into her mouth.

He poured her more wine and set the bottle aside, leaving nothing between them but her glass. He lifted his own glass, saluted her with it, and drained the last of the blood. "Thank you for bringing it." He set his glass aside and added the empty blue pouch to the saddlebag. "I'm impressed by the quality and freshness. Did you harvest the blood this afternoon?"

"I packaged it yesterday, so it's at least a day old." She took a sip of wine, and almost choked. Breath mints and Cabernet were not a good mix.

He reached for her wineglass. "May I?"

She handed it to him, and he took a small drink, but he swallowed it instead of spitting it out as he had at the winery. Now it was her turn to raise her eyebrows.

"A small amount causes no harm," he said. "The alcohol mixes with the blood I drank. It is somewhat like feeding on a human who has been drinking."

"If you fed on someone who was drunk, would you get drunk?"

"It would have an effect."

He handed the wineglass back to her. She took another sip, ignoring the strange taste of wine and mint, and set the glass aside. Rolling onto her back, she stretched out on the blanket and looked up at the stars. Cicadas filled the silence with their high-pitched buzzing.

What would he do next? She took a deep breath. *The real question is— what do I want him to do?*

Henry watched her. Slowly, he moved closer. The warm musk wafting off her and the sound of her rapidly beating heart weakened his resolve to take things slowly. She turned toward him and smiled her golden smile. He took it as an invitation, and kissed her.

Her warm lips opened, her soft tongue tentatively seeking his. He reached for the first button of her shirt without breaking from their kiss. Her breathing quickened when his hand moved to the next button, followed by the next, until her shirt was completely undone. He slid his hand underneath the open shirt, moving the fabric aside until he'd revealed her bra, and eased back to look at her.

"You are so beautiful," he said, his heart speeding up.

He leaned back in to slowly trail light kisses along one side of her neck, stopping to untie the scarf she wore. It was like unwrapping a beautiful gift, to see her jugular naked in the moonlight. She relaxed against him with each kiss he laid along her now bare neck.

Caressing her neck, he allowed his fingers to move down her throat to her breast, focusing on the soft skin beneath his fingertips. He watched for the slightest indication she wasn't enjoying it, for any sign she wanted him to stop. When he saw none, he moved his hand over the lacy fabric of her bra until his hand enfolded her roundness. He had no need for Viagra—her soft breast beneath his hand was enough to make him grow hard. He moved his hand to the other breast, learning by touch the territory along the way.

His fingers brushed across something smooth and plastic between her bra cups. He paused to explore it, discovering she was wearing a bra with a front clasp, which sent another pulse of excitement through him. To have chosen the bra for its ease of entry—she must want him to touch her.

"May I?" he whispered close to her ear, fingering the clasp.

Her fingers replaced his, and she popped open the clasp. He nipped at her earlobe and ran his hand under one cup, his palm passing over her nipple. He felt her shiver, the soft bump growing firm with his touch.

He rose to kiss her lips, allowing himself the pleasure of touching her breast and massaging her nipple while his tongue explored her mouth. After a few moments, he slid his hand to the other breast. He gave the second nipple as much attention as the first, gently pinching and rolling the hard tip between his fingers.

His skin became alive with a rushing, excited sensation traveling the length of his body, and an aching desire to explore more of her. He ran his hand across the firm muscles and soft skin of her stomach, until his fingertips reached the top of her jeans. Following the edge of the rough fabric, he found the button, only to feel her slightly stiffen when he touched it.

Not yet. He wrapped his arms around her and rolled onto his back suddenly, taking her with him, so she was on top of him. He helped her to sit up, straddling him, her bottom now firmly pressed against his hardness.

He moved the bra and shirt away so he could look at her breasts.

Exquisite. Dark brown nipples on soft, rounded mounds, her nipples in tight buds—all he wanted to do was wrap his lips around them. He rose up on his elbows, ready to kiss those beautiful breasts, and she blushed a deep shade of cinnamon brown. He froze.

"I'm sorry, Cerissa. I—"

She pressed two fingers against his lips. "It's all right. I, ah, I liked what you were doing. I just felt, well, exposed, the way you were looking at me."

She removed her fingers from his lips.

"Perhaps we should stop for now," he said, "before I get carried away."

She neither agreed nor disagreed, but she did roll off to lie down next to him, her head on his shoulder. She wrapped one leg around his and remained silent except for the sound of her soft breath.

"Tell me what you're thinking." Her body tensed up again. "What is it?" He stroked her hair. "Please tell me."

She remained silent for a few more moments. "I'm afraid," she whispered.

"Of me?"

"No, no, not you. Never you."

"Then what?"

Another pause. He waited for her.

"I'm afraid of what I'm feeling."

He suppressed his desire to reassure her. Over the decades he'd learned to keep his mouth shut when someone uttered a heartfelt truth.

But when she remained silent, he held her closer and said, "Tell me more."

"I—I have something to confess."

He waited.

"When I told you about the Alatus Lux, well, my Lux supervisor suggested I bed you to buy your silence."

This is just a ploy to her? A wave of betrayal engulfed him, a dizzying feeling of falling, like being in a plane that was spinning out of control toward the ground, his eyes narrowing, his thoughts coming in a rapid rush of words.

Her and her damn aura—how dare she deceive me—and after I kept her secret from my community—

"But I didn't," she said, sitting up suddenly and clutching her shirt closed, her eyes meeting his. "I told him I wouldn't. It wasn't fair to you, not after you promised to trust me. So I didn't set out to seduce you, I just opted to stay close, so you wouldn't change your mind about keeping my secret. But then I found myself looking forward to seeing you, and thinking about you when we were apart, and being so happy when I was in your presence again."

She looked away. "I started feeling, ah, guilty when you kissed me, but also looking forward to being kissed by you again."

So she hadn't betrayed him. Then what was scaring her? He pushed himself out of his mental muck and reached for her, inviting her back into his arms. She lay back down and nestled her head on his shoulder again.

"Everything has always been easy for me," she continued. "Taking human form and learning to be one. It's what our people do. Up until now, the hardest thing I've done is to use technology from this era in my experiments. Humans are so behind us in science. That's what led to my cloning project."

"Why do your feelings frighten you?"

Her grip on him tightened. "It's one thing to grow up learning how people act in public. I can mimic their public behavior. But what they do in private, how do I know when the time is right, or if..." she said, and hesitated. "Or if I'm any good at it?"

He kissed the top of her head.

"I'm not supposed to remind you I'm different," she said. Her fingertips kept brushing against his chest, the light touch making him hard again. "What are you thinking?"

"I think I should take this slower. I'm feeling..." Should he tell her? He didn't want to rush her, to have her run away. "I, I want to make love to you. Whether it's here or we go back to my house, I want you."

"And I want you too." Her voice was so soft that he wasn't sure she'd spoken. It was only her hot exhale against his neck that reassured him he hadn't imagined it.

He took a deep breath. "But we will wait. I want you to be sure you are ready for a relationship with me."

She sat up, her blouse falling open again, her eyes focused on him. "I already know I want to be with you. I don't know how I do, but I know."

"If you still feel the same way after the dance, just say yes, and I will take you back to my house."

She smiled that golden smile. "You have a deal."

Cerissa refastened her bra, not bothering to button her shirt for now, and lay back down to snuggle closer to Henry, a sense of calm blanketing her. Being honest with him was the right decision. He still accepted her. She kissed his shoulder and wrapped her arm across his chest, squeezing tightly.

The sound of rapid hoofbeats broke the silence. A galloping horse was headed their way. Could it be another shooter? She clutched her blouse closed and looked around for the source—they were out in the open, so she had no way to protect Henry here. Should she flash them to someplace safe? He shot to his feet and grabbed her arm, pulling her up with him. Off balance, she couldn't tap her watch.

The chief of police rode up, reining her horse to a stop.

"Cerissa Patel," Tig said, swinging off her horse. "I have a letter for you from the mayor. You have one week to prove your project is real or your diplomatic privileges will be withdrawn." Tig held out an envelope.

"This could have waited until we returned," Henry said, his voice low and angry.

"Sorry, mayor's orders. He wanted me to deliver it now."

"How dare he?" Henry said.

Cerissa accepted the letter and slit the seal with her finger. She walked the letter over to one of the hanging camp lanterns. She'd made the mistake of seeing something a mortal couldn't before. No reason to make the same mistake again just because her hands were shaking. She felt Henry's hand on her shoulder as he read along with her.

There was more to the letter than Tig's short explanation. She had to prove to the mayor her project was genuine if she wanted to attend the dance. And if she didn't provide sufficient proof within one week, they'd revoke her diplomatic privileges and send her back to New York.

Tig held up a second letter. "This one is for Henry."

He reached for the letter and ripped it open impatiently. Cerissa read the single sentence along with him: "Your request to take Dr. Patel to the dance is provisionally granted subject to Dr. Patel proving her project is legitimate."

CHAPTER 42

Tig watched Henry and Cerissa read the second letter. Why did she feel sympathy for them? The envoy seemed like a good match for Henry. Cerissa brought out his protectiveness, something she hadn't seen with other women Henry had dated. And Cerissa was smart—Henry needed someone who would challenge him, who wouldn't be intimidated by his sharp mind.

Cerissa looked up from the letter. "Why?"

"Political pressure," Tig replied, feeling irritated with the mayor for using her as a messenger. She might as well put the blame squarely in his court. "There's a rumor on the Hill you're spying for Leopold. Bring the mayor proof your project is real, and you may attend the dance."

Cerissa's eyes widened with disbelief. "The dance is only two nights away. How am I supposed to satisfy him by then? I gave him our prospectus. Why isn't that enough proof? It satisfied the Securities and Exchange Commission."

"Anyone can create pretty paper. He wants more solid evidence."

Cerissa helped Henry ready the horses, and she rode beside him back to the corral. In the silence, anger seemed to roll off him.

"I'll fix this," she told him. "Trust me, I'll find a way."

"I do trust you. It's the mayor I don't trust."

At the corral, Henry walked her to her car. "Do you want me to go with you?" he asked.

"Thanks, but I've got a lot of work to do." She glanced at the dashboard clock—almost eleven. "If I need help, I'll text you."

Once on the road, she phoned Gaea and explained what had happened and why she wouldn't be home tonight.

"I'm sorry," Gaea said. "I told Winston not to do it."

"Thanks, Gaea, I appreciate your support, but I need to do something fast to turn this around. Ah, could I use your living room to give a presentation to the community tomorrow night? Until I explain the project, no one is going to invest."

"Winston didn't want any meetings just yet..." Gaea said, and then she gave one of her little sniffs, the kind that meant her mind was made up. "But I think he needs a lesson. He still hasn't learned to listen to me."

Gaea paused again. Cerissa could almost see Gaea tapping at her chin in thought.

"I have an idea," Gaea said. "Would you like me to invite some of my friends? I'm sure you have enough to do tonight without worrying about the guest list. I'll take care of the invitations."

"Oh, thank you, Gaea. Yes, that would help immensely," Cerissa said. "May Henry invite some of his friends?"

"I think we can manage to accommodate them. I'll have Dylan start moving furniture out of the living room."

By the time the call ended, she was parked at Leopold's apartment in Mordida. She texted Henry about the meeting at Gaea's house. He wrote back right away. He wouldn't attend since Leopold didn't want him as an investor, but he knew everyone on the Hill and promised to coordinate invitations with Gaea.

Now, she had to do her part: provide proof the project was real. But how?

Henry left the corral shortly after Cerissa and drove straight to the town hall. Winston was where he expected to find him, sitting behind his office desk.

"Now, Henry, you must understand," the mayor began.

"I understand nothing. Dr. Patel is Leopold's envoy. Your actions violated the treaty—you will bring war down on us."

The mayor *harrumphed.* "The town attorney looked into it. We have no obligation to host an envoy for longer than a few weeks, at least, not without something more substantial than what she is selling. There's been too much concern because of the attacks."

"Public opinion should not sway you from doing what is right."

"We're a democracy, Founder. You should know that as well as anyone."

"Then perhaps instead of Rolf, you will be facing me at the next election."

The mayor's eyebrows shot up. "Now, now, there's no reason to do anything drastic. If Dr. Patel and Leopold come up with proof the project is legitimate, well then, I'll reconsider it."

"The dance is in two nights and I intend to have Cerissa on my arm." Henry scowled at the mayor. "For the sake of your political career, you had better accept whatever proof she provides."

Cerissa knocked on Leopold's door. When he opened it, he looked surprised. "Cerissa, dear girl, what are you doing here?"

"We have work to do. They think our project is fake. If you want the lab built here, we have to act quickly."

He held the door only partway open, blocking her from entering. "I see," he said. "Why don't you come back at midnight?"

She put her hand on the door, pushing a little. "Why can't I come in now?"

"I'm about to have dinner."

"So?"

"My dinner is not coming from a bag."

"Oh," she said, followed by "Oh!" when she finally understood what he was saying. "But Leopold, live feeding—"

"Is nothing for you to worry about. The Hill will never know if I have some local Mordida strange."

"But if we don't fix this by tomorrow, I can't attend the next dance." From the look on his face, Leopold didn't care. "I'll miss a perfect networking opportunity," she added quickly. "And I'm on probation—they're going to kick me out if I don't have proof in a week. That's the mayor's order." She showed him the letter.

He snorted. "The *mayor's* order? We'll see about that." He glanced down at his watch. "Give me half an hour, just long enough to feed and get rid of her."

"Leo, who is it?" a woman asked from inside the apartment.

"Just my niece," he said, hooking his head to the right, indicating the direction of the building exit. "She won't be staying."

He raised his thumb and pinky to his ear and mouth, pantomiming a phone call, and whispered, "Thirty minutes. We'll fix this."

Cerissa left Leopold's apartment and drove over to a nearby coffee shop. The restaurant's name was advertised in big orange lights, the interior mocked up to look like a fifties diner. She was quickly seated by a window—the place was almost empty at this hour. The tabletop's pattern looked like old-fashioned linoleum, edged with shiny chrome. She ordered a slice of blackberry pie and tea to justify her use of the booth.

The mayor is an asshole kept circling through her mind. She wanted to drop a handful of silver coins down his pants and give a new meaning to "that itching, burning sensation."

She placed a pad of paper between her knife and fork and pushed the tableware out of the way, leaving her computer tablet on the bench seat next to her purse. The blank page felt overwhelming. Where to start? A mix of anger and panic tightened her chest.

She glanced up when the waitress delivered her order. Oozing out of the blackberry pie, the filling looked more like glop than berries. She took one bite and pushed it away.

Karen had told her to think outside the box. She started with a clean page and wrote "20 hours" at the top—if she was going to walk into the dance on Henry's arm, she had to come up with a way to convince the mayor by tomorrow night—the night before the dance. Then she wrote "proof" in the center of the pad and drew a tight little box around the word. Symbolically, everything else would be written outside the box.

She wrote "blood" and circled it. She wasn't ready to bring a clone to the Hill, so she started to cross "blood" out, but stopped herself. This kind of brainstorming required her to let the ideas flow—she could eliminate rejects later.

She then wrote "tangible proof" on the page. Not specific enough. She needed something to wow them, something flashy. "Morph," she wrote. Morphing would be tangible proof she wasn't human, but it proved nothing about the project, and the results could be unpredictable, not to mention the Protectors would give breech birth to a cow if she did.

The most tangible thing she could visualize was a rock. What would a rock prove? Throw it through the mayor's window, maybe? It would be emotionally satisfying, but not proof. She wrote it down anyway. Rock. Dirt. Real estate. Nothing new there—she'd been shopping for weeks and nothing had changed—she didn't have enough money to buy the parcel she needed. She wrote it down anyway and circled it, not that it did any good, as buying wasn't an option. Wait—"option." She wrote it down, but needed something more, a concept she knew existed but couldn't remember.

She powered up her tablet and searched for Sierra Escondida's website, starting on the town's homepage. *Nothing.* She clicked through a few links. There it was, on the planning department webpage. She opened the PDF and quickly skimmed through it. *This just might work.* She sat back and smiled.

SIERRA ESCONDIDA PLANNING DEPARTMENT—THE NEXT AFTERNOON

Cerissa yawned, something she didn't do too often. Five hours of sleep usually sufficed, but she had no time for sleep, not if she was going to get this done in time. Signs of an impending sunset were visible through a nearby window in the Sierra Escondida planning department annex, which was located in the business district. Daytime businesses needed access to the planning department, and by placing it in the business district, the town kept unknowing mortals off the Hill.

She stood at the service counter, waiting while the planner went through the application checklist for a second time. Bored, she glanced around. The large room was painted a bland institutional beige. Modular gray cubicles carved out desk space for the land-use planners who worked for the town. Stand-up signs littered the counter and provided instructions for filling out applications.

Last night, Leopold had been good to his word, joining her at the restaurant and agreeing to her plan. Now, all she had to do was wrap up here, and make it back to Gaea's before her presentation to potential investors tonight.

"Have you prepared a preliminary environmental assessment?" the planner asked.

"We only obtained the option to buy this morning." She handed him a copy of the purchase option agreement. "We plan on completing a full Environmental Impact Report on the project."

"An EIR?" he asked. "Why not try for a mitigated neg dec?"

Neg dec was shorthand for a "negative declaration," a review process under California's environmental law taking less time to complete. "We understand an EIR can take longer. We want the certainty you get with an EIR. They're less easy to challenge."

"All right then," the planner replied, taking a rubber stamp off the counter, changing the date, and pounding it onto the application. He then stamped the extra copy she'd brought with her. The planner handed her back her stamped copy.

"Thank you," she said, hugging the paperwork to her chest like a prize.

"Just remember, we have thirty days to determine whether the application is complete. If it isn't, you'll have to provide additional information before we can process it."

She was fine with his answer. Thirty days was better than zero. She left the planning department building and drove straight to the mayor's office.

Since rising, Henry had tried multiple times to call Cerissa. Each time it went to voicemail. When his phone rang and her name appeared, he quickly answered the call.

"All is well," were her first words once he had the phone to his ear. "I'm on my way back to Gaea's for the presentation. The mayor seems mollified. I'm off probation."

"How did you accomplish it so quickly?"

"I contacted the real estate agent and told her I would double her commission if she could get us a signed sales option by noon. The vacant land had been on the market so long that the owners were more than anxious to do it. With the option to buy locked in, we don't need a loan right away, so Leopold didn't have to sign as a guarantor and we have more time to raise money from investors."

"And the land option satisfied the mayor?"

"I took it one step further. I contacted a local company in Mordida, one specializing in large-scale land-use projects. I offered them a similar bonus to get the zoning applications completed today, at least enough to pass the initial plan-check phase. Spent all the capital Leopold invested and maxed out my credit cards, but I don't care—it worked. The mayor gave me a thirty-day pass to remain on the Hill while the plan-check process is completed."

He took a deep breath, relief flooding through him. "I wish I could attend your presentation."

"I know you'll be there in spirit."

"I'll see you tomorrow night," he said, wishing he could see her tonight. "I'll pick you up at eight for the dance."

"I'm looking forward to it." He could almost hear the smile in her voice. "I'll wait for you at Gaea's."

Email To: Mayor Winston Mason
CC: Marcus Collings, Town Attorney
From: Vice Mayor Rolf Müller
Subject: Leopold's Envoy

Mayor:

I am appalled to learn you gave Leopold's envoy permission to attend the dance. I demand you place a motion on the next town council agenda to reject Leopold's biotech project. We must remove his envoy from the community once and for all.

The Covenant forbids unmated humans on the Hill. No loyalty bond seals her lips. Her presence here is a threat to the security of Sierra Escondida. We cannot allow this to continue. It must end now.

Very truly yours,
Vice Mayor Rolf Müller

Email to: Vice Mayor Rolf Müller
CC: Marcus Collings, Town Attorney
From: Mayor Winston Mason
Subject: Re: Leopold's Envoy

Rolf:

Leopold's envoy has applied for approval of a development project. We can't agendize it yet; the project has to go through all those preliminary legal stages, which are overseen by the town attorney. I cannot legally put it before the council until those steps are complete. As far as ejecting Dr. Patel goes, now that we have proof of Leopold's intent, I don't view her presence as the threat you do. If you insist the council discuss this issue, I'll place it on an upcoming agenda, but it will not be the next meeting—that agenda is already full and I don't see it as the crisis you do.

Warmest regards,
Winston

"You can't send that," Tig said, looking over the mayor's shoulder at the iPad he was typing on.

"My message to Rolf wasn't meant for your eyes."

"If it wasn't, why are you writing it in such a public place?" Tig looked around Jose's Cantina to see who else was there. She wouldn't find Jose—he was no longer among the living. After his death, the founders kept the Cantina open, a casual place to gather, play a hand of poker, or just gossip. Jayden was so exhausted that he'd fallen asleep early, so Tig had pulled on a pair of jeans and a t-shirt and headed over to Jose's. She craved more company. Even the mayor would do, so she took a seat next to him.

The mayor tapped "send" on his email to Rolf. "That should put Rolf over the edge," he said. "Elections are a good eighteen months away, but it doesn't hurt to start early."

An unsettling thought—she was used to working with the current mayor, even if he could be difficult at times. But Rolf? If he became mayor, how long would she stay chief of police? "You think Rolf will run?" she asked.

"I've conducted some informal polling. Rolf's name keeps coming up. He's probably started an exploratory campaign. I suspect Frédéric is working with him."

"What does Rolf have to campaign about? You do a decent enough job running this place."

The mayor scowled at her. She'd made the mistake of being blunt. "You've done a good job, Winston," she quickly added. He was certainly better than the alternative. "You want to tell me what Rolf would do differently?"

"Leopold's envoy, for one. Polling shows sixty percent of Hill vampires accept Cerissa's presence on the Hill."

"Then why did you have me deliver a warning letter?"

"Because the other forty percent can't be ignored. Henry was right, but for the wrong reason. I couldn't risk letting her stay in light of Rolf's concerns, because too much was at stake if Rolf was right." He scratched at his bald pate. "The girl has proven she's serious about the project. Now I'm only doing what the treaty requires. Besides, from what I can tell, half of those who didn't want her here are already part of Rolf's base. The rest sway with the wind, and with proof the project's real, spot polling shows they're fine with her staying—for now."

She quickly did the math. That meant eighty percent now supported the mayor's decision to let Cerissa remain. "So you can afford to ignore Rolf's base."

"Exactly."

She sat back in her chair, her conversation with the mayor sparking an idea. Until she came to the Hill, she'd never voted in an election. When she was mortal, Masaai women had no say in how things were run, and working for Phat, she had no interest. Jayden had only been on the Hill a year, but she could already see the look in his eyes. He'd voted his entire adult life—being shut out made him feel like an outsider. Maybe it was time to nudge things in a new direction.

"There's something else to consider," she said.

252

"What's that?" the mayor asked.

"After the way Rolf put his foot in his mouth over the Rule of Two, if mortals were allowed to vote, you'd have an even larger percentage backing you against him."

His gray eyes lit up. "You may be on to something, chief. You just may be."

CHAPTER 43

GAEA'S HOUSE—LATER THAT NIGHT

Cerissa walked to the front of Gaea's living room, stopping by the large marble fireplace. The mantel was higher than she was tall, carved with an intricate grapevine pattern, the fruit full and ripe. Dylan had placed an easel in front of it for her. She carried a collection of foam-core boards the architectural firm provided and leaned them against the fireplace, placing the first one on the easel.

She preferred using a PowerPoint presentation, but she'd had no time to prepare one. After leaving the mayor's office, she'd barely had enough time to shower and change into a business suit.

Metal folding chairs in two rows looked out of place in Gaea's elegant living room. The attendees filled the chairs—eleven resident vampires and a smattering of mortal mates. Not bad on such short notice. Some of the mortals came without their vampires. Blanche was in the back row, frowning at her.

"Thank you all for coming." Cerissa flipped the paper cover from the first board on the display easel, revealing a large, colorful rendering of the research lab's exterior, designed in a pleasing Mediterranean style. "Today, we took the first step to bring the Biologics Research Lab to Sierra Escondida." She replaced the color rendering with a new board, an aerial photo of the lot—a photo the architect provided. "We now have an option to buy this parcel. We are seeking investors to take the next step—complete the land purchase and construct the lab."

The next board was a layout of the lab's five stories.

A hand shot up in the audience, a pretty pale blonde woman, one of the five founders. Henry had certainly delivered. "What will the lab produce?" Abigale asked, holding up the colorful booklet Cerissa had handed out to each attendee. "Your literature speaks of biological medicines. Is that all?"

The moment of truth—Leopold had finally given the go-ahead, so she could tell them the lab's real purpose.

"We've perfected a method to clone embryonic stem cells," she replied. "Using that technology, we will be able to produce medicines, products like leather and, ultimately, blood for the treaty communities."

A murmur ran through the small audience. Abigale's delicate hand rose again. "How do you plan on cloning human cells without mortal authorities shutting you down?"

"Good question," Cerissa said. "All of our research is legal. Using advanced gene surgery, we have created an organic machine to produce human blood." She'd talked it over with Leopold and decided to avoid the phrase "human clone" for now. Creating genetically modified clones didn't violate existing laws, but the concept came with too much emotional baggage. "Some of what we do won't be eligible for federal grants because those funds can't be used for research on new lines of stem cells—that's why we need private investors."

A male in the back raised his hand—Marcus Collings, the town attorney who was also a founder. "Will this blood be better than banked blood?"

Thank you, Henry. He had clearly primed the pump with these questions. "The blood we produce will be fresher than banked blood and, because of our storage mechanisms, won't require preservatives or anti-clotting agents. We have every expectation it will be superior in taste."

She fielded another dozen questions, using words to persuade them; she refused to use her aura to influence investors. Not only wouldn't it be fair, but buyer's remorse could set in once her influence wore off.

When the questions died off, she said, "We will email the full prospectus and investor forms to anyone who is interested in investing. Please sign up at the table by the door. And if you have any questions, I'm happy to meet with you one on one."

Once the last guest was out the door, she hugged Gaea. "Thank you. I couldn't have done it without you."

"Oh, go on with you," Gaea said, returning the hug. "But you should have told me sooner what your lab would produce. It would have piqued the community's interest. I mean, this could be a huge change for us."

"You're right, of course," Cerissa said. The same thing she had told Leopold months ago—but she had to present a united front. "We were concerned the community would grow impatient. It'll be years before we're up and running."

Gaea smiled at her. "When you live as long as we have, you learn to be patient."

Blanche walked over and flashed her fangs in a sneer. "Just because you gave a speech doesn't mean they believe you."

"Now you behave yourself," Gaea said to Blanche.

Cerissa ignored Blanche's nastiness. It didn't matter if Blanche was so insecure that she thought the only way to win was by lying. Cerissa had more important things on her mind now. Six of the vampires and two mortals had provided email addresses. Between the land option and tonight's presentation, she'd nailed it.

She said goodnight and trudged upstairs to her room, the fatigue finally catching up with her. *Just a few more steps.* She dropped her purse near the closet door and plopped onto the bed. Lying face down, she hugged her pillow and sank into the soft mattress, closing her eyes. A few moments later, she rolled over and stared at the pathetic crystal chandelier above her. Sleep wouldn't come. She wished she could go see Henry instead. He trusted her and believed in her, and his faith made her feel something she'd never felt before.

And now they can't kick me off the Hill. The mayor had given her one week to provide proof, and she'd done it in thirty-six hours. *Both Leopold and the Protectors will be happy.*

Then the realization hit her so strongly that she suddenly sat up. She hadn't done it for either of them. For the first time in her life, she'd really done something just for herself—so she could go to the dance with Henry.

Wow. Well, now I'm wide-awake. She got up, took out her contact lenses, and, using her phone, emailed prospectuses to those who had signed up. When Gaea called her to the front door, she guessed her visitor might be Henry, too eager to see her to wait for the dance. She ran down the stairs. Her stomach clutched when she saw who it was.

"Hi, Zeke," she said. "I wasn't expecting you."

"You've been a bit unavailable lately," he replied, taking off his hat and holding it in front of him. "Heard you had a little gathering here tonight. Thought I'd stop by to see how it went."

Gaea frowned and looked from Zeke to Cerissa, concern written on her face. "Cerissa, if you would like to talk to Zeke in the parlor, I'll be nearby."

"Thank you," Cerissa said, leading Zeke to the small parlor off the entryway.

Damn. This is what I get for procrastinating. I should have taken Karen's advice and called him before this, made sure he understood. She offered him a chair and took the tapestry one opposite him.

"I've missed you," he said.

"Zeke—"

"I brought you this." He pulled a small jewelry box from his shirt pocket and opened it: a lovely string of pearls, with a moonstone pendant. If she accepted it, the moonstone would mark her as his. He didn't want to date—he wanted to go straight to being mated.

She shook her head. "I can't accept it."

"But I want you to." He reached for her hand and put the box in it. "I want you to wear it so you can go to the dance with me."

"I'm sorry, but I'm already going with Henry." She placed the jewelry box on the antique table nearest Zeke.

Zeke's eyes narrowed, a dark look crossing his face. "So it's true? I heard the rumor—I just couldn't believe ya'd do that to me."

She sat up straight. *You owe him nothing.*

"Zeke. *Enough.* I told you from the start I wasn't interested. How many times do I have to repeat myself?"

"But I thought—"

"At least I was honest with you."

A guilty look replaced his dark one. "What do ya mean?"

She needed to woman up and finish this. "You lied to me about your work for the government. I know what you do, the trail of bodies you leave."

"Henry told you."

"He didn't," she said. How much to reveal? "I have other sources. I'm an envoy, remember? I can't be associated with someone who does what you do. I'm sorry."

"I don't believe you."

"I don't give a damn whether you do." She stood up. "You should leave."

He stood up too, but he didn't leave. He grabbed her and pulled her to him. "No one does this to Zeke Cannon."

She pulled away from him, and he grabbed both of her wrists. Forcing one wrist to his lips, he kissed her skin, sending an unpleasant shiver down her back. His fangs flashed as he opened his mouth to bite.

"What's the penalty for biting another vampire's human *against her will?*" she asked before he could strike.

He stopped and glanced up from her wrist. "Henry hasn't had your blood yet."

Henry? She was Leopold's envoy; that was what she meant. Would Henry's rights be greater than Leopold's under these circumstances? Exhausted, she couldn't remember which violation brought the greater penalty—she had removed her lenses and couldn't look it up. But if Zeke thought she meant Henry, she'd play along, because clearly the vampire-centric rules didn't view her consent as important. *Grrr.*

"Can you be absolutely sure Henry hasn't bitten me?" She looked him straight in the eyes as she said it. "I say I'm his. So what's the penalty if you bite me by force?"

Zeke looked uncertain for a moment. Then he pushed her away hard enough that she fell back onto the chair.

"Who needs you," he spat. He grabbed the jewelry box and stormed out, slamming the front door.

She exhaled. If she had used her aura to defuse the situation, it would only cause him to cling tighter.

Gaea appeared at the parlor door. "Did Zeke leave?"

"Yes, and he won't be back. Please don't consider him a welcome visitor to me any longer."

"Wise decision, dear. If you want to join us, we're about to watch a movie."

"Thank you, Gaea, but I need sleep. I'll see you tomorrow night."

CHAPTER 44

The card game at Jose's Cantina wrapped up around three in the morning. Henry strode out of the cantina feeling jubilant. Everything was falling into place. He had permission to take Cerissa to the dance. She might even accept his invitation afterward. Winning at cards hadn't hurt either, and the town attorney finally revised the immunity agreement, adding the provisions he wanted. All reasons to feel good again.

He drove the short distance to his house, turning onto the long driveway where it switch-backed up the front half of his property. Native oak trees grew on the slope bordering his land to the left, with rows of grapevines on his right, covering the lower hill. The vines led up to his home.

He rounded one of the sharp curves and slammed his foot on the brake. A large boulder sat in the narrow driveway. Even without his car's headlights illuminating the rock, he couldn't have missed it, since it stood as tall as the Viper's hood. He sat there for a moment staring at it.

"Not again," he groused. The slope to his left had been a source of rocks and boulders rolling onto his driveway for some time now. The last contractor who had fixed the retaining wall had shored up the slope sufficiently. Why were boulders once again littering his driveway? He couldn't swerve to his right because of the deep irrigation ditch, and the steep slope on his left blocked his way on that side. The rock had managed to come to a rest in a short, level area where the driveway curved.

He set the parking brake and walked to where the driveway flattened out, the headlights casting long shadows of him against the slope. The boulder had left a gouge on the slope when it rolled down, smaller rock and dirt trailing after it onto the driveway. He would clean it up later. The boulder was the main problem right now.

He picked up the rock and heaved it to the side of the driveway, beyond the irrigation ditch, and watched it roll down the slope to the bottom. It was then he heard it: the faint rustle of a vampire moving quickly. He whipped around and found himself facing Zeke, who held a silver knife.

Adrenaline snaked through him, his vision narrowing on the silver blade. One cut would leave necrotic tissue behind, returning his flesh to its dead state. Enough cuts and he would become withered and helpless, easy to stake.

"I thought we might have a little palaver," Zeke said, rotating the knife's point. Moonlight glinted off its highly polished edge. "Put your hands up where I can see 'em."

"I have no quarrel with you," Henry replied calmly, raising his hands, palms open, keeping them in front of him rather than over his head.

"That's a matter of opinion," Zeke shot back. "You stole from me."

"I did not."

"Cerissa was mine."

"Not according to her." Henry moved his focus from the silver knife to Zeke's shoulders. *Watch the shoulders.*

"I asked her out first. That makes her mine." Zeke took a step closer to him. "And you told her what I do in South America."

"I did not. She asked, but I didn't tell her."

"It had to be you—you're the only one who had anything to gain." Zeke waved the knife again. "You've poached my human, and you'll pay the penalty, the same penalty my maker paid."

"There is no penalty to pay because I've done nothing wrong."

Henry gauged the distance between them. He couldn't keep backing up—the irrigation ditch was behind him, and he refused to run.

"She claims she's yours now," Zeke growled. "She told me so tonight."

"I have not taken her blood."

"Why would she lie to me?"

"In your heart you know the answer." He kept his eyes focused on Zeke's shoulders, watching for the slightest movement. "You can still walk away from this. I am not one of your mortal victims—you'll find it much harder to beat me."

"That's where you're wrong. I know your weakness, your weakness for whores."

Henry clenched his hands into fists. "Heed my warning and leave."

"What, you don't like the truth? Cerissa's no different than any other whore you've had."

A white-hot flash of rage shot through him. He charged at Zeke, one hand locking around his knife arm. Zeke's free hand grabbed his other wrist. A standoff. Henry shifted his weight, trying for leverage to throw Zeke, but the cowboy was gripping his wrist too tightly.

He rocked back on one foot and threw his weight forward. It broke Zeke's grip, but Zeke lunged at him. Henry felt the hot slash of silver as he pulled away. Blood bloomed on his shirt.

Zeke jumped back out of reach, glancing at the bloody slash, a hard smile forming on his face.

"I grow tired of this nonsense," Henry spat out. Pain radiated through his side. He had to get his anger under control. "Either make your move or leave."

Zeke's shoulder dipped to drive the knife forward. Henry saw the move telegraphed before the thrust finished, and slid aside, grabbing Zeke's outstretched arm. Using Zeke's momentum, he pulled the cowboy off balance and pushed Zeke's wrist toward the ground. With his free hand, he punched Zeke in the face three times fast. Zeke staggered backward with each blow. The crunch of his nose breaking told Henry when to stop.

The pain in his side became distant, replaced by a sense of satisfaction. Grabbing Zeke's wrist with both hands, he twisted it in opposite directions, a quick back-and-forth motion that snapped the bone. The knife dropped and he caught it by its leather handle. Zeke grabbed for his broken wrist and stumbled backward, stopped by the steep slope.

Now Henry held the knife pointed at Zeke. With Zeke disarmed, all he had to do was drive the knife through Zeke's heart and his problem would disappear. No witnesses, not like when he killed Nathaniel. No one need know. He felt a warm flush of exhilaration, envisioning the moment of the kill and the power it came with—

And the guilt that would follow. The voice in his head whispered to him: *You won't be able to hide it from Cerissa—she will hate you when she finds out.*

"Shut up," Henry growled.

"I didn't say nothin'," Zeke said over the back of his hand, which was now pressed against his bleeding nose.

Henry stared at Zeke, the temptation to kill still strong. If he did, the face haunting his dreams wouldn't be Nathaniel's—it would be Zeke's.

But if he didn't kill him, would Zeke return for another try? Killing the cowboy would prevent another attack, but would Cerissa understand? Her opinion mattered more than his safety.

"Leave," Henry ordered, "or I'll call Tig and have you banned for this."

Zeke backed away, moving rapidly up the slope into the woods beyond. Henry collapsed into the driver's seat. The pain in his side returned, increasing with each movement. He backed down the driveway and drove to Yacov's house. If he asked Rolf for help, he'd only hear "I told you so."

He lightly knocked at Yacov's back door, the one leading to Yacov's home office. Shayna would be asleep, and he didn't want to wake her. Yacov looked surprised when he opened the door. He motioned for Henry to enter and then quietly closed a connecting door between the office and his house. A single torchiere lamp lit the cluttered office, the amber lamp shade giving the room a warm glow.

"What happened?" Yacov asked softly, his eyes fixed on Henry's bloody shirt.

Henry laid the silver knife on Yacov's desk and told him about Zeke's ambush. Lifting his shirt, he showed Yacov the blackened slash in his side, the skin puckered around it like a clam's lips. The muscles around the slash contracted painfully as he moved.

Yacov opened a vein in his wrist to drizzle blood over the black-edged skin. "Well, my friend, what do you want to do about Zeke?"

A good question. A very good question. "Nothing," Henry finally said. "Bringing this before the town council will only put the spotlight on Cerissa."

"Are you sure? This could be linked to the other attacks."

"Zeke's ambush was poorly planned. Whoever is responsible for the other attacks hides behind humans."

"Still—"

"I will not make this a council matter. Zeke will remind them of what I did to Nathaniel. I don't want Nathaniel's death stirred up over this. Not with Cerissa here."

Yacov touched his shoulder. "Nathaniel's death was more than a century ago. You've changed, Henry, and the community has changed."

"No," Henry said, shaking his head. He couldn't take that risk.

Yacov gave him a look saying he didn't approve.

Henry shook his head again. He wouldn't budge on this.

"All right, here's what we'll do." Yacov picked up a plastic jeweler's bag and slid it over the knife. "I'll send you an email confirming what you've told me, and I'll keep the knife. If there's ever a question raised, I'll have a record of our conversation, and the evidence."

"Thank you, Yacov," Henry said, tucking his torn shirt back into his pants. "That should work."

"So, my friend, are you still taking Cerissa to the dance?"

"Absolutely. To do anything else is to admit guilt."

"That's not the only reason," Yacov said with a knowing grin.

They'd been friends too long to lie to each other. Yacov could always see right through him. "She told him she is mine now. I intend to find out if it's true."

"Then you've called Leopold?"

"Leopold?"

"Both you and Zeke have overlooked something. By treaty, no one may take her blood until Leopold releases her."

¡Mierda! The treaty—how had he forgotten it? "I'll text Leopold now and call him when I rise."

Yacov gave him a hearty pat on the back. "I just hope he lets you buy out her contract, because the last thing you want again is trouble with Leopold. The very last thing."

CHAPTER 45

GAEA'S HOUSE—THE NEXT NIGHT

Cerissa slipped into her high heels and glanced at the clock. Henry would arrive any minute to pick her up for the dance. A knock sounded on her bedroom door. *Is he here already?* She opened it to find Gaea standing there, holding a small bottle.

"Oh, don't you look lovely," Gaea said. "I brought you some

perfumed lotion—just a little dab of it on your hands and throat."

Cerissa sniffed the bottle's pump. Chanel No. 5 was a classic perfume from the early 1900s. "This won't be too strong?" she asked.

"Not at all, the lotion isn't as strong as the perfume." Gaea squirted a dab on Cerissa's hands, and then placed a small dot of it on her throat.

"You're sure?" Cerissa asked, rubbing in the perfumed lotion. "I thought—"

"He wears cologne. His sensitive nose can handle a little perfume. Now don't wrinkle your brow like that; you don't have to figure it out. Tonight you have other things to figure out."

A warmth rose to her cheeks at being reminded of Henry's invitation. She had warned Gaea not to worry if she didn't return after the dance.

"Lovely, just lovely." One of Gaea's fingers roosted underneath Cerissa's chin, guiding her head left, then right, while Gaea closely scrutinized her makeup. "Now, I want you to wait up here for him. Don't stand by the door. It makes you look too eager."

"But I am eager to see him." She followed Gaea into the hallway.

"Trust me. Stay here and use the stairs to make your entrance. And move slowly."

She laughed. "In this dress, I don't think I could move fast if I wanted to."

The dress Karen had picked out was a beautiful shade of silky indigo, nicely complementing her nutmeg skin tone, and it hugged her in all the right places, with a slit up the back at her feet so she could walk, just not easily. Between the tight skirt and high-heeled shoes, she felt constrained. Why did men like their women so off balance and restricted? So they couldn't run away? *Ha.* If anything, she wanted to run *to* Henry, not away from him.

The doorbell chimed. Instantly, her stomach quivered and she lurched toward the staircase. Gaea laid a hand on her shoulder, stopping her. "Wait here until I call your name."

"All right, Gaea, whatever you say. Just go open the door, please."

Gaea smiled at her and walked down the staircase. The muffled sound of the front door opening was followed by Henry's voice, asking for her. She peeked around the corner. Gaea appeared at the base of the stairs.

"Cerissa, Henry's here," Gaea called up to her.

She rounded the corner of the hall and stopped at the top of the stairs. Henry was standing in the entryway wearing a classic tuxedo with his silky black hair tied back, the crisp white tuxedo shirt accenting his deep caramel skin. Her heart skipped a beat and she began the slow walk down the staircase.

Henry stood transfixed. Cerissa looked like an enticing goddess. She wore her hair high up on her head, with tendrils trailing down her neck. The evening gown showed off her remarkable figure, and her dangling diamond earrings pointed right to her tasty neck, tempting him.

Not that he needed any coaxing.

When she made it to the last stair, he reached out for her. "You look beautiful," he said, bending to kiss her hand, catching the light scent of perfume.

"Thank you, Henry."

"You two make such a lovely couple," Gaea cooed. "Don't wait for me. I'll be along shortly with Dylan. He returned home late, so he's just now getting ready. We'll see you two at the dance."

Henry escorted Cerissa to the Viper and held open the door. "Your magic chariot awaits."

"Thank you, Henry." She stood by the car door and turned to him. "And thank you for your support last night. Abigale and Marcus asked good questions. I suspect you had something to do with it."

He gave an exaggerated bow, sweeping his hand as if tipping a nonexistent hat, and looked up at her, grinning as mischievously as he could. "Certainly you don't think I planted shills to help you?"

In reply, she smiled that brilliant smile of hers. A wave of regret followed in the wake of her smile. He hadn't received Leopold's permission yet. Leopold's email said he wasn't available to talk tonight, but made his terms clear—if Henry wanted to take her blood, he would have to pay the contract price. He had no idea how much—or what—that price would be.

During the drive, Cerissa held his hand whenever he didn't need to shift gears, her stomach doing more fluttery flip-flops. She was happy to be with him again, yet the closer they got to the country club, the more she dreaded it, dreaded seeing the vampires who didn't want her here. Last night she'd been determined to go to the dance. She'd proven the project was real, and they had no reason to fight her presence now.

Then why did she want to be anywhere with Henry but here?

He parked and opened the door for her. Offering his hand, he pulled her into an embrace and gently kissed her. "I would not want to smear your lipstick," he said when the kiss ended. "At least, not yet."

She smiled and looked away. He sounded so confident and looked so handsome. "Henry, I..." she began, struggling for the right words.

"What is it, Cerissa?" he asked, raising her hand to his lips.

"Would you mind if we left the dance early?"

"You are that eager?"

Her cheeks flooded with warmth, and she buried her face against his chest. *He thinks I'm asking to go back to his place.*

"I mean... I meant..." she stammered. "I'm not exactly the most loved person at the moment...I thought we could make a quick appearance and then go into town...."

He stepped back, gently releasing her. "Not without an escort." She looked up at him, and he smiled crookedly. "Cerissa. There are those who fear anything outside our norm. When they come to know you as I have, they will accept you."

She took a deep breath and slowly let it out. He was right. She needed him to be. "Okay, let's do this."

The dance was already underway. She entered the country club with her arm in the crook of his, and they walked down the elegant carpeted hallway and through the large double doors into the main ballroom. *Talk about déjà vu—three weeks ago I arrived with Zeke guiding me through this room.*

The band was already on stage, the room decorated as a nightclub. Small tables covered with white tablecloths faced the dance floor. An arrangement of candles in cut-glass holders, the jars filled with black sand, sat in the center of each table, with a wreath of flowers surrounding the candles. Streamers and balloons in purple and silver added to the festive motif.

Heads turned in her direction as they made their way through the partygoers. Some looked curious, but others seemed angry.

"Henry, they're watching us," she whispered.

He put an arm around her shoulders, pulling her protectively closer. "They watch because I have the most beautiful woman in the room on my arm."

That's not the reason. They stare because they want me gone. Well, too bad. I'm not going anywhere.

She straightened her spine, trying to project confidence as they walked to the table Karen and Rolf were at. Henry held out a chair for her.

"You look spectacular," Karen said.

"Thanks." Cerissa accepted the chair Henry offered, placing her small beaded purse on the table next to Karen's. "You look beautiful too. Forest green is a great color on you."

Karen's long dress was made of soft velvet and had a gathered waist with a low-cut V-neckline. "I'm so glad you made it," Karen replied. "When I heard the mayor wasn't going to let you attend the dance, I couldn't believe it."

"Fortunately, we were able to clear up our little misunderstanding quickly." Leopold had decided to refer to it as a "misunderstanding" rather than charge the mayor with a blatant violation of the treaty. She owed the mayor a little payback. *If not silver coins down his shorts, maybe I could sneak some silver powder into his sock drawer. Wouldn't be hard to do.* The hotfoot treatment would serve him right.

"Cerissa," Henry said, getting her attention. "May I get you something to drink?"

"Sure, Cabernet would be fine, thank you."

"And Karen, may I bring anything back for you?"

"I'm good, Henry." Karen still had half a glass of wine in front of her.

Rolf had been talking to Frédéric, who was sitting on the other side of him. When Henry left, Rolf turned to her. "You've been seeing a lot of Henry."

"I enjoy being with him," she replied, trying to sound friendly.

"He will not be fooled forever."

She sent a wisp of her aura toward him. "Rolf, there's nothing—"

"The shootings just happen to coincide with your arrival?" He snorted, his eyes narrowing.

"There are such things as coincidences. Can't we start over?"

His scowl deepened. "Not when I think you're a threat to the very fabric of our society."

"Rolf, I'm not a threat to your community, and I'm not a threat to your relationship with Henry, either."

He banged his fist on the table. "I will find out what your real motives are."

Karen shushed him. "Rolf, that's enough," she said, glancing around as heads turned to look in their direction. "This is a party. Behave yourself."

Rolf glowered at Karen, his lips tightly pressed together, before his cold eyes moved in Cerissa's direction again.

"Fucking new blood," he spat. He pushed back his chair and stomped off. Frédéric, who'd been watching the exchange, raised his eyebrows and took off after Rolf.

Damn it. My charm hasn't worked on Rolf before—why should tonight be different? Some people seemed immune to her aura. She wished Rolf wasn't one of them. "I'm sorry to create a problem between you and Rolf," she told Karen.

"Don't worry about it. He'll have forgotten in five minutes, or the next time he's horny, whichever comes first." Karen gave a light snicker. "He growls, but he's really quite tame."

"I don't think Rolf would appreciate your characterization," Henry said.

Cerissa whipped around in her chair to see him behind her. Why did he have to walk up at that exact moment? She accepted the wineglass he handed her and took a big gulp.

Karen's eyes gave him a warning look. "Just stay out of it," she said. "Rolf was being a jerk and I was telling Cerissa why she shouldn't take him seriously."

"All the same, you should show Rolf the respect he deserves."

"And he should show Cerissa some respect."

"What did Rolf say to Cerissa?"

Cerissa couldn't let her friend carry the burden alone. "Rolf was being insulting, but it doesn't matter. I ignored him and he went away in a huff."

"I'm sorry, Cerissa," Henry said, sitting down next to her and taking her hand in his. "Rolf can get fixated on something and lose track of his manners."

"Just what I was saying," Karen said, standing up. "I'm going to find him—it's been long enough to let him stew." She glided off in the direction Rolf and Frédéric went.

Cerissa took a sip of her wine. "Henry, why don't we dance? I'd like to get back into the mood of the party."

A slow ballad was playing. Henry led her onto the dance floor and she went into his arms. The touch of his fingers on her shoulder, the gentle way he cupped her hand in his, relaxed her, reminding her of their evening in the park, and his offer. She looked up into his eyes, and his deep, dark browns looked back at her. The dark brown slowly receded until the pupils of his eyes were almost circles of solid black.

Is he thinking what I'm thinking?

The band switched to a more upbeat song, and Henry moved them into a modified swing. He was an excellent dancer with a strong lead. With his pitch-black hair neatly tied back, his ponytail swung slightly with each turn. The tuxedo showed off his broad, muscular shoulders and trim waist. Butterflies flitted about in her stomach, her body humming at the thought of touching him more intimately.

She felt drawn to him in a way she couldn't explain to herself. Not just her desire to feel him naked against her, but something more, something softer, which caused her heart to feel infinitely fragile.

CHAPTER 46

Tig noted the arrival of Henry and Cerissa. Now, all the founders were at the dance. She positioned herself near the back of the room and watched for trouble. Jayden stood by her side. Things had been a little tense between them since she had criticized him for his blown surveillance. While they got dressed for the dance, he'd suggested they spend time enjoying the party together—a good sign he'd forgiven her.

Still, she was never truly off duty. Even wearing an evening gown, she had to remain alert for trouble and scanned the crowd. She caught sight of Yacov walking toward her, Shayna at his side.

"Good evening, my friend," Yacov said, when he made it past the last table to where she stood. "You're looking charming tonight. Are you and Jayden enjoying the party?"

Jayden slipped his hand around Tig's. "We're going to. She's promised to dance a few dances with me before the night is out."

"Yes, later," Tig replied, "after I'm sure all is secure."

Yacov smiled at her. "You can't be on duty all the time. You should relax and have fun."

"I'll relax when our community returns to normal."

"I understand, I understand. When you have time, I'd like to hear the results from your investigation of the prison guards."

"Now, Yacov," Shayna cut in, "just as you said, she's here to have fun, not work. No reason to ask her about the case now."

Tig shook her head. "It's no problem, Shayna. We've been watching the prison guards. I'll tell you if we get any promising leads, but it would help if you gave me your list of suspects." She'd put off sending the third email reminder, unable to phrase her message politely. "Henry told me you had taken over the task."

"You mean I haven't given those to you yet?" Yacov asked, tugging at his beard. "I emailed those lists to you a week ago. I swore I did."

"It's fine. Just email them to Jayden when you get home tonight."

"Of course, my friend, of course. And Shayna is right. I should not have brought it up. To atone for it, I suggest we make our way to the dance floor. Will you join us?"

Cerissa focused on her feet without looking at them, trying to keep up with Henry. He was a master of the mambo. When the song ended, he slipped an arm around her waist, leading her off the dance floor. She wanted to fan herself, and not just from the heat of exertion. The sheer sexiness pouring off him as they danced had lit her fire.

"Karen and Rolf have returned," he said. "I want to make sure all is well."

From the look on Rolf's face, his mood had lightened. Perhaps he was going to behave himself in front of Henry. Karen acted like nothing had happened. Cerissa sipped on her wine, glad for the refreshing liquid. Henry and Rolf began discussing winery business. It left her with a few moments to catch her breath and look around.

The mayor and his crowd were at one table, and Frédéric was now sitting with them. Gaea and Dylan were on the dance floor. *Good, they made it.* She glanced over to where Blanche was sitting with seven other vampires—probably the "singles" table. No sign of Seaton, Gaea's problem child.

"May I have this dance, miss?" she heard Zeke ask from behind her, his voice flat and cold.

What the hell? She swung around in her chair. His eyes seemed to focus past her on Henry.

She had no idea how to respond. Human rules said the polite thing was to accept, dance one dance, and return to the person who'd brought her. After how rude he'd been to her last night, she wanted nothing to do with him, but she had no idea what vampire rules were. She was at the party as Leopold's envoy, not as Henry's mate—at least, not yet. Did that mean she had to dance with anyone who asked?

Tig spotted the trouble and strode off the dance floor, moving in their direction. She had to stop Zeke before Henry reacted. If violence erupted, the council would be pissed—and not just with those two. They would blame her for not preventing it. She tried to move past the mortal mates who stood in her way, but someone grab her arm. She spun around, ready to act, only to see Yacov.

"Wait and watch," he said. "Nothing will happen. Trust Henry."

"I can't take that risk, Founder." Tig pulled free and began moving again.

Cerissa glanced around the table. Rolf's face was frozen. Karen shrugged her uncertainty. She couldn't see Henry; her back was to him because she'd turned to face Zeke. The way Zeke hovered over her, she felt trapped. Surely he wouldn't attack her at a public event? She quickly stood and backed away, ready to defend herself if necessary, slewing her eyes toward Henry. He didn't look happy—his fangs were out, his eyes almost solid black. In spite of how he looked, he silently inclined his head as if to say, *Go ahead.*

She took a deep breath and relaxed her posture. *Okay then. I guess I go.* She nodded to Zeke and headed toward the dance floor.

Tig stopped in her tracks. It appeared Yacov was right. The crowd opened up to let Cerissa and Zeke through, and they began to dance. Henry and Rolf stayed behind.

"Come sit with Shayna and me," Yacov whispered in her ear. "We're going to take a break from dancing. Bring Jayden and sit with us. Our table is close to Henry's. If something happens, you'll be near, but for now, just watch and let them work it out."

She nodded to Yacov, accepting the invitation, and signaled to Jayden. He came over to join them. She walked to Yacov's table, but her eyes remained glued on Henry and Rolf, who were watching the dance floor like living statues. Karen fled the table for the bar, reminding Tig of a doe who didn't want to get stuck between two angry bucks.

She looked back to the dance floor. She still needed to have a talk with Zeke. He was a police officer and should know better than to breach the peace this way—after all, she held her officers to a higher standard than the rest of the Hill, and he knew it. If she had anything to say about it, he'd pay a sizeable penalty for this disturbance.

Henry watched Cerissa slide into Zeke's arms, and his jealousy felt like a hand squeezing his heart. The abyss didn't take long before it began taunting him. *She'll never be faithful,* it whispered. *She'll never be satisfied with one mate. She will live too long to stay with you for a lifetime. You will have to kill again to protect what's yours.* He stood at the edge of his reason, the dirt under his mental feet giving way.

"That should never have happened," Rolf said. "I told you Cerissa's presence would undermine the Covenant."

"Enough. I do not have any claim on her. Yet," Henry replied, his voice frayed, betraying his true feelings. "I may not like it, but Zeke was within his rights."

"He wasn't. There are no rights here because there are no rules to cover this. Mortals who are not blood-mated to a vampire are forbidden at these dances. We decided it a long time ago."

"You mean, *I* decided it a long time ago. You weren't part of the community when the decision was made."

"Zeke should never have approached her this way," Rolf said, slashing the air with his hand. "Never. You're entitled to call him out, just as you did with Nathaniel."

"No, Rolf. Until she is mine, I have no authority to challenge him over this."

"Then he makes you look like the fool you are."

He narrowed his eyes. "I suggest we change the topic. I would not want to strain our friendship any further over this."

"Fine," Rolf spat out.

Henry scrubbed a hand across his face. *This is my fault. If I had called*

Leopold a week ago, the matter would be resolved by now. Yacov's confidence in him, his friend's belief he'd changed, was the only thing stopping him from breaking off a chair leg and driving it through Zeke's heart.

"Henry?" He turned at the sultry voice. Blanche stood behind him, wearing a slinky beaded gown, her eyes darkly accented with glittery bronze makeup, her eyebrows drawn on in thin lines. "Since Cerissa went off with Zeke, would ya like to dance with me?"

"No thank you."

Her fingers trailed down the sleeve of his tuxedo coat. "Come on. Let's have ourselves a little fun. Make your girlfriend jealous."

The idea had momentary appeal. It would teach Cerissa a lesson. She should never have accepted Zeke's invitation. But Yacov wouldn't approve. "You are kind to offer," he finally said. "But I must decline."

"I still hope you're considering my proposal."

"You'll have my answer tomorrow."

She brushed his cheek with a French manicured fingernail. "Only if the answer is yes."

Cerissa refused to make eye contact with Zeke. He said nothing while they danced, but by the rough way he turned her, he was angry. That was fine with her. She was pretty pissed off too.

She sensed something strange against her back. When they went through another turn, she saw his wrist was bandaged with some kind of brace. Vampires usually healed during their daytime sleep—if he had it wrapped, he must have broken a bone, which could take a few days to heal. Something looked wrong with his nose, too, but she didn't try to figure it out.

Zeke brought her close to his chest for a moment. She immediately stepped back, fighting against his grip, regretting her decision to accept the dance. But she had to...didn't she?

A quick glance at Henry and Rolf told her she'd made the wrong choice. *Damn. Whatever the consequences, I should've told Zeke to get lost.* Without a rule or order to guide her, she never did the right thing.

Then she saw Blanche walk up to Henry, touching his face in an all-too-intimate way. She wanted to pluck each of those fake fingernails off Blanche's hand. Irritated with herself, she couldn't keep quiet any longer.

"Why did you ask me to dance?" she asked Zeke.

"Because it should be me sitting next to you, not Henry."

"I'm sorry you feel that way."

"You said you were here on business. Were you lying to me?"

"I didn't plan on falling for Henry, it just happened," she said, looking away. "I never meant to hurt you."

He pushed her through another turn. When she was near him again, he said, "You can't love Henry. Not him. Not if you value your own skin."

"You're just saying that because you're bitter."

"Ya don't know what you're getting yourself into, missy. That Henry, he's a hard case."

She furrowed her brow, puzzled by the term.

"I mean, he's a violent man. You'd be safer with me as your mate than him."

"Zeke—"

"I'm giving you the real deal. I was there. I saw what he's capable of."

"Enough. I don't want to hear it."

"Can't say I didn't warn you."

When the song ended, she abruptly walked away, leaving Zeke standing on the dance floor. *That should send a message.* His comments about Henry were the words of a hurt and jealous man. She hurried past the first few tables, and the partygoers stared as she marched by. *If some residents don't like my presence here, what must they think now?*

All she wanted to do was return to Henry's side. She hadn't expected the reception she got when she did. Antarctica would have been warmer. She turned off her lenses with a few blinks, grabbed her wineglass, and suggested they step outside for some air. She needed privacy for this discussion.

The area surrounding the country club was one large cultivated garden, featuring night-blooming flowers, the scent of jasmine perfuming the night air. One path led to an outdoor amphitheater.

She walked along the path, Henry following her in silence. She selected an isolated park bench, sat down, and placed her wineglass on the ground. Henry stood in front of her, his expression still frozen. She took his hand and pulled him down to sit next to her. The look on his face threatened to shut her out.

"Zeke did that to make us miserable," she said. "It looks like he succeeded."

"Why did you accept?"

"I didn't know whether I was even allowed to say no. You nodded, so I accepted."

"Had I suggested you decline, he would have challenged me, a duel to the death."

She stared at him, aghast. "A duel? You must be joking."

"I am not. He attacked me last night; we fought." He rubbed his side. "Are you all right?"

He dropped his hand to his lap. "I'm fine."

"Why did Zeke attack you?"

He shrugged. "Because of you. He thought I trespassed on his property."

"I'm no one's property."

"You told him you were mine. He asked you to dance to test whether it was true. To see how I would react."

Her eyes widened as the chain of events fell into place. She'd refused Zeke's gift, and Zeke had taken it out on Henry. Leopold had warned her—vampires could be territorial. How had she failed to anticipate Zeke's reaction? She should have warned Henry after Zeke left.

"I'm sorry," she said.

He couldn't look at her. Not with jealousy still seething through him and the risk of violence so close to the surface of his skin. He clasped his hands tightly together, keeping his eyes focused on the ground between his feet. Pushing her away was the last thing he wanted, but he had to know the truth.

"You still didn't answer my question," he said. "Why did you accept?"

"I told you—because it seemed like what I should do."

"It was not because you wanted to dance with him?"

"Are you joking? I resented his request."

"Then who were you looking for?" He'd seen her looking around the room before Zeke walked up. Was she looking for him? He couldn't get the possibility out of his head.

"I wasn't looking for anyone in particular."

"Then why?"

"You were talking business and I was slightly bored by it." She reached over and took his chin in her hand, turning his face. "Not once did I think of Zeke," she added.

He pulled his chin from her grasp and looked down at his hands again. "Cerissa, this is an unusual situation. I am sorry if I've offended you. I didn't understand why you accepted. It's so far outside my experience I could only think of one reason."

Her hand wrapped around his. "Perhaps you need to trust me."

"I do trust you," he said, raising her hand to his lips. He'd trusted Sarah too, and then Nathaniel lured her away...

"Henry, what is it?"

Trust. If he trusted her, he had to tell her the truth, before she heard it from Zeke or someone else. He sighed and returned her hand to her lap. If she was going to reject him for it, better now than later—it would likely destroy her trust in him, but she needed to hear it from him.

He turned to face her. "Not many people on the Hill know this, but in 1889, I killed Zeke's maker in a duel over a woman. Zeke thought I deserved the same for stealing you from him."

A moment of dizziness engulfed her. So that was what Zeke was alluding to on the dance floor.

She didn't like it, but did it change anything?

Cerissa took a breath. It had happened a long time ago, in a century operating under different rules. And even though Zeke attacked Henry, he hadn't killed Zeke.

"You're both alive," she finally said.

"I—I value your opinion too much to revert to the old ways. I sent Zeke on his way with a broken wrist and a bloody nose."

Why did that make her feel better? "I'm glad you're okay."

"Cerissa, if, knowing about my past, you don't want to be with me, I'll take you back to Gaea's."

He'd been honest with her and he hadn't killed Zeke. She didn't know what she would have done if he'd killed Zeke in a fight over her. *We'll just keep this a tight little secret from the Protectors.* They weren't as forgiving of those who killed. With her lenses turned off, even Ari would never know. She softly touched Henry's forehead with her fingers.

"It's not for me to judge you," she said.

His brow remained wrinkled, small stress lines around his eyes. *Doesn't he believe me? Or is there something more?* With his confession, the weight should have lifted from his shoulders. Why did he still look so worried?

He stood up and drew her into his arms, the tension around his eyes finally easing. He leaned toward her to offer a kiss. Instead of accepting the kiss, she nestled her head on his shoulder. There was one more thing they needed to settle. "What did Blanche want?" she asked.

"Business. She wants me to invest in her idea for a winery."

"Really? Then why did she have her hands all over you? You said you didn't have any other girlfriends."

He stepped back to look at her, furrowing his brow. "Are you jealous?"

She couldn't look him in the eyes. Of course she was jealous. The way Blanche touched him…

"Do I have any reason to be jealous?" she asked.

"Of course not. Women like Blanche, they didn't have much power in the era they were born. They learned to use their sexuality to get what they needed. I don't blame her for it—she's a product of her times."

She kept her eyes averted. "You're awfully understanding."

"You do sound jealous."

"She's been nothing but mean to me. I don't want you going into business with her."

"Have no fear of that," he said. She glanced up at him, and a slight grin formed on his face before he continued. "Tell me, how is her behavior any different from your attempt to seduce me?"

He wasn't fighting fair. She pushed away from him and turned, giving him her back. "It wasn't *my* idea to seduce you. Blame that one on Ari."

His hands wrapped around her waist, pulling her back until her shoulders were pressed against his firm chest. His lips gently touched her neck, sending a pleasant shiver down her spine. She softened against him, and he turned her around to face him again.

"I'm glad you did seduce me," he said softly. The distant music from the band filled the silence. "May I have this dance?"

With his arms around her, she swayed to the music, her cheek resting against his shoulder again, breathing in the scent of his cologne. Should they leave now and go to his place? No, she needed to make one more appearance at the dance. She didn't want to give the rumor mill any false hope. After the song ended, she took his hand and walked by his side back to the country club. They were almost at the table when she stopped him and started to turn around. "I left my wineglass in the garden."

He caught her before she could leave. "No matter. Let me get you another."

He continued to escort her back to the table. Once she was seated, he bent over to kiss her. She smiled to herself. Now why didn't it bother her one bit when *he* acted possessive? The implication wasn't lost on Rolf, either—the look of shock on his face was worth it. He got up to follow Henry.

As soon as Henry and Rolf were gone, Karen scooted her chair closer to Cerissa and asked, "Is everything all right?"

"It is now. Much ado about nothing."

"Isn't that the truth? Rolf has been ranting and raving about the Covenant this, the Covenant that." Karen smiled a big grin, making the corners of her eyes crinkle. "You're shaking things up. It's good for them."

"I don't mean to. I guess I'm so outside their norm, their rules don't cover me."

Karen leaned in close and whispered, "They're so afraid of their vampire nature that they don't trust themselves to behave without a rule to cover every situation."

Funny, the same could be said for her. Was it just a matter of trial and error, discovering how to live without the Protectors' constant supervision? Maybe mistakes were to be expected. Just like in the lab—postulate a theory and experiment to find the answer.

"Hello…Cerissa," Karen said, waving her hand in front of her.

"Sorry, I zoned out. Everything's okay between Henry and me now."

"Are you going home with him tonight?"

"Karen!" Cerissa felt a warm flush of embarrassment.

"I'm assuming he's asked you already. If he hasn't, he's a fool."

"No offense, but that's between him and me."

"No worries," Karen said, and polished off her drink. "But I want to hear all about it when you do."

Henry returned with wine for Cerissa, and Rolf followed with another glass. Karen accepted it, and then leaned toward him, flashing a fair amount of cleavage in the process. "Rolf," Karen said seductively, "aren't you going to ask me to dance?"

Rolf's eyes brightened as they traveled from Karen's breasts to her face, a slight leer forming. "Of course, *Fraulein,*" he said, gently bringing her hand to his cheek and kissing her palm. "Would you do me the honor?"

Karen took his offered arm. Once on the dance floor, Karen winked at her over Rolf's shoulder.

"So what were you two talking about?" Henry asked.

"That there has been entirely too much talking and not enough dancing."

"Then allow me to remedy the problem," Henry said, standing.

A slow love ballad played. They moved together like one being. She enjoyed having his arm around her waist, feeling him turn her this way and then that. He didn't say anything, but she caught him watching her intently when he led her through a turn. She flowed up against him, her breasts brushing against his chest.

Was she really ready for this? Her body teeter-tottered between shimmering excitement and pit-of-the-stomach fear. He pressed her closer, until her hips moved against his in beat to the music, and the shimmering excitement won out.

His eyes locked on hers and turned solid black before he whirled her through a breathtaking spin. Centered in his arms again, the answer seemed clear. She wanted to possess and be possessed by him. She raised her lips to his ear.

"Yes," she whispered.

"You are sure?"

"If the invitation is still open...."

"It is."

"Then yes, Henry, I'm sure."

CHAPTER 47

Cerissa waited while Henry opened the doors to his drawing room. The familiar river-stone fireplace, white plaster walls, solid wood, and leather furniture—it felt like home. She took the seat he offered—a large leather chair identical to his—and laid her fingers in the grooves created by the claw-shaped arm rest to still them. Her palms had started sweating, her hands shaking, as soon as she stepped into the room.

What if he doesn't like me in bed? What do I do then?

She glanced up at him. He looked so good—she wanted to feel his hands on her, take him into her, taste him.

Then why am I so nervous? Because for the first time this matters to me?

He smiled gently at her. "Would you like some wine?" he asked.

"That would be nice, thank you." A bottle had been left open to breathe on the sidebar. He poured and handed her the glass. She used both hands to take it so he wouldn't see them tremble and took a sip. "This is the same vintage you gave me the night we toured the winery," she said.

"Very good. I wondered if you would recognize it." Then his expression grew serious. He knelt in front of her and kissed her softly. Her pulse raced and her heart pounded like a lopsided centrifuge.

He sat back on his heels. He seemed to be searching for something, the way he looked into her eyes.

"Are you nervous?" he asked.

"Is it that obvious?" She looked down into the wineglass. *Hell, he can probably smell it on me.* She took a deep, calming breath and raised her head to look into his eyes.

He brushed her face with his fingers. "If I told you there was no reason to be nervous, it wouldn't make a difference, would it?"

She gave him a small smile. "Probably not. I want to be with you, but...."

"If you prefer, we can just sit and talk. You can enjoy your wine and then I can take you back to Gaea's. You do not have to do anything you aren't ready to do."

"I'm ready, it's just, well..." She took a sip of her wine.

"Hmm," he said. "It's a warm night. Let's go outside and walk. Come," he said, standing and holding out his hand. "Bring your glass." She followed him out the French doors, which led to the pool patio. "I have been enjoying the spring nights to stargaze. My telescope is set up in the gazebo. Would you like to see?"

"Sure."

At the edge of the gazebo, he had a high-quality telescope pointed at the night sky. He took off his tuxedo jacket, laid it across one of the lounge chairs, and leaned over to look through the eyepiece, adjusting the scope.

"I have it aimed at Mars right now," he said, offering the scope to her.

She placed her wineglass on the nearby table and gazed through the scope. The red planet came into view. When his cell phone trilled, she glanced over at him.

"I'm sorry," he said, taking it from his pocket to look at the caller ID.

"You're expecting a call?"

He slid his finger across the screen, sending it to voicemail. "Business does not stop just because I have a date with a beautiful woman."

Leaning back over the telescope, she peered through its eyepiece again. A vast, flat area dominated the view, the reddish-orange mass resembling Asia. He gently touched her back, running his fingers enticingly down her spine to its base. *If his fingers feel this good, what will it be like having him inside me?* She took a deep breath. If she kept thinking about it, she would never do it.

She straightened up and turned, bringing her lips to his, flowing up against his chest, her hips pressing forward until she felt him grow hard against her. He wrapped his arms around her and crushed her to him, his tongue entwining with hers. The electricity from his kiss flowed straight through her center, making her wet with desire.

He stepped back from her. "If you keep kissing me like that, I won't be able to restrain myself."

"I was hoping you wouldn't restrain yourself," she said softly.

She didn't need to tell him twice—every inch of him hungered for her. He swept her up into his arms and carried her into the guesthouse, kissing her as he walked, past the couch to the king-sized bed, and set her on her feet. Feeling for her zipper, he quickly had her out of her dress.

His breath caught at the sight of her, a euphoric feeling of lightheadedness overtaking him as blood rushed to his groin, tightening everything. She had looked so beautiful in her gown, but now, standing before him in a bra and thong, she was stunning. The mound of her breasts above her bra, the slight curve of her waist, the small brown mole on her stomach, the soft, dark area between her thighs—he wanted to devour them all at once.

She tugged on the ends of his tie and the bow came apart, the fabric sliding from around his neck. She dropped it on the nightstand and soon he was shirtless. Rather than wait for her to do it, he quickly undid his belt and fly, and stepped out of his pants while she pulled back the covers of the bed and slid onto the sheets, beckoning him to follow.

He lowered the lights, doffed his underwear, and slid into bed, keeping his hips back so he wouldn't ram into her. He felt hard as marble, the flow of blood to his *pene* like liquid fire. He edged closer to her. The musky aroma of lust wafted off her—a good sign, one that aroused him even further.

He brought his lips to hers, sensed her nervousness, and pulled back to stroke her cheek. The slight taste of her fear on his lips made her all the more alluring. He wanted to plunge into her and prove to her she pleased him just by being her. But the mix of fear and excitement in her eyes told him to move slowly. He wanted her to relax, to enjoy being in bed with him. Her pleasure mattered most to him.

She reached out and traced the base of his throat with her fingertips, gliding toward his crucifix. He'd forgotten to take it off. Slipping the chain over his head, he took it from her fingers and kissed it before laying it on the nightstand.

"Why did you take it off?"

He rose up on his elbow to look at her. "Because the only thing I want to tickle your skin is mine," he replied, stroking her lips with his thumb.

She smiled and reached her hands behind his head, untying the leather string holding back his ponytail. The fine strands settled on his shoulders. She wove her fingers in and pulled him closer, her lips already parted and waiting for him. He took full advantage of it, his tongue caressing hers with rugged need.

The touch of her fingertips tortured him; the silky feel as she swept them down his chest, brushing tentatively along his stomach muscles, and then going lower until she wrapped her whole hand around him. She squeezed gently, flaming his desire. He pulled her to him and kissed the contour of her beautiful neck, sorely tempted to sink his fangs into her soft, fragrant skin, but he couldn't. *Not yet.*

Starting at the base of her ear, he planted little kisses down her neck, onto her shoulder, and over the mound of one breast. The bra had to go. He slid his arms around her, unfastening the hooks to free her. He flung the bra at a nearby chair but didn't wait to see if it landed. Her beautiful breasts had his full attention. Her nipples were crinkled tightly, the brown tips hard. He pressed up against her breasts, sending currents spiking through him. She slid her hands around his waist, pressing her hips to him, forcing his erection against her warm, slick center. Placing gentle kisses all over her face and neck, he slowly worked his way lower to kiss her breasts. The salty taste of her skin felt good on his lips.

When he licked a nipple, she gave a sharp intake of breath. "Don't stop," she said softly.

He gave a light chuckle—he had no intention of stopping. He ran his fingers along her body while he continued to caress her nipples with his lips, stopping when he touched the side straps of her thong. Gently lifting her, he pulled the thong down, taking it completely off her, his lips never leaving her breast.

Her hand wrapped around his stiffness again, rubbing and gently squeezing, building the pleasure in him, his heart pumping harder with each squeeze.

He gently raked each nipple with his teeth, but he was careful to keep his fangs sheathed. She sighed when his lips left her breast to travel lower, but with her hand gripping him, he'd have to be a pretzel to reach between her legs with his lips.

Instead, he lightly touched her between her legs with his fingers. She was wet with excitement. He ran his thumb around her clitoris, gently sliding a long finger inside her center, curling it to stroke her in two places at once. The moan she let out told him he'd hit both spots. He continued to stroke her, slowly increasing the pace, watching her eyelids flutter, her face take on a rapturous look—she had never looked more beautiful. He licked a nipple, and she moaned again.

She released him and slid her hands under his arms, urging him to roll on top of her. He wanted to bring her to climax first, but she tugged at his arms again. He gave her breast one last lick and looked into her eyes. "Cerissa?"

"Yes, Henry, yes," she replied, her voice liquid. "I want you in me."

He positioned himself between her legs, lowering his hips to enter her slowly, carefully. She let out a little gasp, and he caught it with his lips, kissing her deeply. Her hands glided along his back until she lightly squeezed his butt. Her touch and the feel of her tight sheath wrapped around him almost pushed him over the edge. *Not yet.*

Extending his arms, he supported himself on the palms of his hands and looked at her. The sight of her below him filled him with warmth, his chest expanding with an emotion he had not felt for a hundred years. She had slipped into his heart just as surely as he had entered her body.

"You are so beautiful, *mi amor*," he said, before bringing his lips to hers. Slowly he raised his hips, pulling out and then slowly pushing in. Her hips rose against his, her fingers squeezing his butt, urging him faster. He pushed up on his hands to look at her again.

Her neck lay enticingly before him. He wasn't free to take her blood yet, and he bit his lip, resisting the urge to bite her. Closing his eyes didn't help either. Her scent intoxicated him. He lowered himself to kiss her—keeping his mouth busy helped. When she broke from the kiss, she wrapped her arms around him and brought his face down against her shoulder.

Ah, the agony of desire.

He could imagine the feel of his fangs piercing her neck, her warm, tangy taste filling him up. Silently, he recited the batting averages of the Bugles, his favorite baseball team. When the distraction didn't work, he raised himself up again and focused on the feelings enjoyed by the lower half of his body, creating a different problem. When he could no longer hold out for her, he came, the spasms of pleasure rocketing through him.

He continued to hold her, propped on his forearms, his cheek resting on her chest, his back rounded, trying to stay in her as long as he could. When the fullness of his passion subsided, he gently rolled off her and pulled her onto her side to face him. He kissed her softly on the lips and continued to run his fingers across her back and sides. She did the same, touching his chest with her fingertips, tracing the outline of his pecs. She looked serious, so intense.

If he hadn't already known, he was now certain: he was lost for good. Not only had she cracked his heart, she owned his soul. There was nothing he could do to fight it.

He slid his hand along her stomach toward her legs. He wanted to taste her, to lick her and watch pleasure shoot through her too. He rose. She stopped him before he reached his destination.

She hadn't spoken a word, but he understood her message. He would wait, for now, and respect her choice. He hugged her close to him, holding her head against his shoulder. Being close to her neck no longer bothered him. The overpowering relaxation brought on by a different release lessened his desire to feed.

"I hope you enjoyed yourself," he said, finally breaking the silence.

Her heartbeat sped up, and he smelled a whiff of fear. He didn't push for an answer. He didn't want to embarrass her. He'd had enough experience to know not all women orgasmed the first time—that was why he always left time for a second round. Or did it have to do with her being Lux? *Better not to ask just yet.*

He kissed the top of her head. "Would you like something to drink?"

"I am thirsty," she replied.

So was he.

"I'm not sure what we have in the refrigerator. I try to keep it stocked, but I have to admit I hadn't planned on being out here tonight."

She looked up at him and smiled her golden smile, reassuring him. "Whatever you have will be fine," she said.

"Wait here. I will be right back."

Cerissa watched him walk away, enjoying the sight of his tight butt and other large, manly parts swaying between his legs as he disappeared into another room. She stretched against the soft sheets. Her nerves had gotten the better of her. *What do I know about the art of love?* She closed her eyes. *A few bad affairs didn't teach me how to be a real woman in bed.*

She inhaled deeply, the lingering scent of cloves and other spice from his cologne caused her to tingle anew, the desire between her legs begging for satisfaction. His touch, the way he filled her up—her muscles clamped down on emptiness. If only she had the courage to let him do what he'd suggested. But what if he tried and she didn't come?

I need to get out of my own head or this will never work.

She opened her eyes at the sound of his footsteps. He carried a guest robe. She had a brief view of his front before he cinched his own robe shut, blocking a spectacular sight, one causing more sparks to course through her. She liked seeing him naked—his muscular chest, covered in curly black hair, a narrow line of fine hair running down his stomach to point at his other endowments. He offered her a robe before turning away.

She rolled out of bed and slipped on her robe. When Henry had carried her in here, she had tunnel vision, focusing just on him. She looked around the room for the first time. A television and couch created a sitting area, with a king-size bed in the middle of the room and a small kitchenette at the far end, separated from the rest by a granite counter. She sat down on a stool at the counter and watched him.

He took a bottle of water out of the refrigerator and put a glass next to it. Then he opened one of the cupboards and shook his head. He seemed uncertain over what to do next.

"If you're hungry, we'll need to return to the main house." He tried one more cupboard and shrugged.

She cocked her head. His usual self-confidence had vanished. He seemed, well, nervous. At least she wasn't the only one experiencing that emotion. Or was it something else? He hadn't tried to bite her. *Does he have misgivings because of Zeke?* Well, she wasn't going to raise it if he didn't.

"Water is fine for now," she replied, pouring it into the glass.

"Bring your drink and come join me on the couch."

The couch was deep. He bent one knee, leaning it against the back cushion, leaving room for her between his legs. She cuddled up to him, her back resting on his chest, her legs stretched out, holding the glass of water in one hand. His strong arms wrapped gently around her, and he kissed the back of her neck, sending a pleasant tingle across her skin. Being held by him was pure joy.

"Tell me something about your life you haven't told me yet," she said.

He paused before answering her question. It dawned on her how frequently he paused before speaking. She took another sip of water from the glass she held and placed it on the coffee table.

"Looking at the stars," he finally said, speaking softly near her ear, "reminds me of my first trip to California. I was twenty and my father chose me to claim our land grant, instead of my older brothers. He decided I would start a ranch here and export goods back to Veracruz, even Spain. The journey took many months over land, and I was homesick at first—I missed my mother. She was a good woman, and we were very close while I was growing up."

"Why did your father choose you to go?"

Another pause. "Because I reminded him of my mother's father."

"He didn't like your grandfather?"

"My *abuelito* was half Totonac. The Totonacas lived along the Gulf of Mexico before the Spanish conquistadors arrived."

Bingo! She had guessed he wasn't part Aztec or Mayan.

"My grandfather's mother, Antonia, worked for his father Jose. It was not uncommon for the surviving Totonac people to take on the Spanish names of their conquerors. Antonia cooked for the ranch." He paused again, longer this time. "Jose had no sons by his wife."

"Your great-grandfather was married to someone else?" she asked, unable to keep the surprise from her voice.

"He had an affair with Antonia. That is probably the politest term for it. She would not have had much choice if my great-grandfather wanted her. When Antonia gave birth to a son, arrangements were made and the child—my grandfather—was presented as his wife's child."

"Like the biblical Hagar and Sarah, but with a twist."

"Indeed. The priest who made the baptismal record was bribed to write *español* rather than *mestizo* by his name."

She didn't recognize the term *"mestizo,"* and couldn't look it up. She had removed her contact lenses before leaving the dance. "Spanish rather than…?"

"Mestizo means mixed race—European with indigenous people."

"The priests kept track of race?"

"Until it was made illegal, yes. My father married my mother knowing she was a quarter Totonac."

"If he resented her parentage, why did he marry her?"

"The answer to any question beginning with 'why' is 'money.'"

"Your grandfather's family had money?"

"And my father's family did not. My darker skin, my wide Totonac nose and distinctive profile, these reminded my father constantly he had married a *mestizo.*"

"I love your face!"

She tried to turn around to look at him. His arms held her in place, stopping her. "But my father did not. So he sent me away."

She thought back to their winery visit. To protect his image in the community, he'd kept Anne-Louise's hold over him secret. No wonder he craved the respect afforded a founder. His father never gave him the respect all little boys desired.

"I'm sorry," she said.

"Don't be." He kissed the back of her neck lightly. "It led me to this moment, which I would not exchange for anything."

Looking at the stars also reminded him of something else: she was not of this world. He'd never seen her real appearance. Could she make love in her Lux body? Aside from her blue, six-fingered hand, she hadn't volunteered to show him more. In some ways she was like the rabbits he'd raised as a child. If he moved slowly and let the rabbits come to him, he could pet their soft fur, even coax one into his arms. Move too fast and the rabbits would bolt to the back of the cage.

His curiosity could wait.

"What do you think of when you look at the stars?" he asked instead.

Still holding her in his arms, he felt her fingertip run lightly over his wrist. "Freedom," she replied, sounding wistful.

"Freedom?"

She turned to look at him, and this time he let her. She bent her knees, sitting back on her heels, looking so perfectly nymph-like. "The stars are like a map, pointing the way. I wish I had the freedom to follow them, to go wherever I want, to do what I want, without anyone telling me where to go or what to do. I look up at the stars and fall into them." She glanced down at her lap and looked like she was praying. "As a young child, I was taught I have a purpose to fulfill. Being Lux doesn't leave much room for free choice."

He tilted her chin back up so he could see her eyes. "What about what you want?"

"My wants don't matter to the Protectors."

"Do you always do what they tell you to do?"

"I guess I do."

"Why?"

"It's the price for being Lux—for earning their love and approval."

"You shouldn't have to earn anyone's love," he replied, looking at her intently. He cradled her face between his hands and brought her close to him. "Love should be freely given."

She closed her eyes and felt his lips on hers—a soft, gentle kiss; a physical benediction. When he released her, the way he looked at her—there was love in his eyes. She took a deep breath and laid her cheek against his chest, turning her body so she was pressed against him. She let him hold her, accepting from him what she'd always wanted from her family.

Within a few moments, she felt something hard pushing against her side.

"I'm sorry, Cerissa," Henry said, a smile in his voice. "You have that effect on me."

She sat back and chuckled. "I'm glad I do."

She stood and led him back to bed. She untied his bathrobe, taking a moment to enjoy the sight of him naked, to see his bare skin respond when she caressed him.

He kissed her neck, sending a pleasant shiver all the way to her toes as she slipped out of her own robe. Would he bite this time? His lips continued their journey to her breast. Pleasure coursed through her when his long tongue captured her nipple. She pulled him into bed and, lying on her side, slid forward, raising her leg over his hip and taking him into her.

She held still, bathing in the feeling of him filling her, of the current flowing from her nipples to her root chakra as he continued to suckle her. She began moving against his shaft, angling her hips to rub his full length against her cleft. Pleasure built within her, but she wanted more and, in one motion, rolled him on his back until she was looking down at him, his hair spread out wildly on the pillow.

His eyes turned solid black, followed by a slight curving of his lips. *Okay, he doesn't mind if I take control.* He reached for her nipples, pinching and rolling them hard, at the edge where pain and pleasure became one.

She moved her hips, seeking more friction against him, like an itch just out of range of being scratched. She changed the angle of her hips and found what she was looking for, riding up and down on him, producing wet slaps of her cleft against his skin, which he met motion for motion. The suction pulled on her exquisitely, drawing her closer to the edge. She lowered her lips to his again, hungrily devouring his tongue, her hips cocked to find the same spot over and over again, just a little more, just a little more, just a little more—

He gripped her hips and plunged deeper into her.

The pleasure exploded through her, the feelings washing over her in wave after wave of blinding release. Soon he bucked under her, and she opened her eyes to watch his turn solid black again as he came, his penis spasming within her. She rode him through his orgasm until his hands on her hips told her when to stop.

When he finished, she snuggled in closer. His body wasn't as warm as hers, but it still felt good to press her hot skin against his. His fingers stroked her hair and his lips caressed the top of her head. She rose to look at him.

His eyes held such an intense acceptance of her—it cut her to the core. She felt like her heart had been split wide open and he had burrowed inside her.

She buried her face against his chest. Her feelings caught in the back of her throat, tightening with two hundred years of suppressed pain. No one had ever shown her love without demanding her obedience. Tears flooded her eyes, and she choked back a sob. He had touched a place deep within her—a place of longing that had known only pain. She wanted to weep, to cry for all the empty years she'd spent not feeling loved. She hid her face against his chest, hoping he mistook her tears for sweat. If he asked, she wouldn't be able to explain why she cried.

She finally closed her eyes, her tears drying. She grew drowsy with the comfort of being held. She must have fallen asleep, because he woke her with a kiss on the crown of her head. She still lay on top of him, her cheek against his shoulder.

She sat up, straddling him, and yawned.

He reached up with his thumb to stroke something from her cheek. "How are you feeling?"

"Wonderful," she said, smiling.

His eyes were so serious. She liked his serious look. Hell, she liked all his looks. A peaceful tranquility filled her, spiced with an edge of excitement. Was this what love felt like? She reached out and touched his face, stroking his cheek.

He smiled back at her. "I hate to say this, but I should get you back to Gaea's at a reasonable hour."

She glanced at the clock on the bedstand. How could he consider four in the morning reasonable? She slid off him to sit cross-legged. He looked so wildly handsome after their lovemaking.

"Gaea will want to know you arrived home safely," he added. "She won't forgive me if I get you home with no time for her to question you about our night together."

She smiled at his observation, running her fingers through his curly chest hair, twirling a lock around her index finger. She didn't want to leave.

"And if you're to get back into your pretty ball gown, we should shower first. Come," he said, sliding out of bed and offering her his hand, "the bathroom is through here."

Oh well, there's always tomorrow night. She stopped at the mirror while he started the water. The mirror revealed what she had already deduced: her black eyeliner had smeared when she cried, and now had a crosswise streak where he'd run his thumb across it.

She looked like a hideous circus clown, one with evil intent on its mind.

"In the medicine cabinet," he said before disappearing under the spray of water.

She opened it and found a cream she could use as makeup remover. A tissue moistened with the lotion did a quick job of cleaning away the black smudge. She was lucky he hadn't broken into laughter when he saw her. At least he didn't ask her to explain.

Her makeup wasn't the only thing wrecked by their lovemaking. Her updo was half down. She pulled out the remaining bobby pins and ran her fingers through it. That didn't help. She wrapped her hair in a knot to keep it from getting wet and found a hair band in a drawer. As she put her hair up, he began lathering his body with soap, his hair held away from the water by a large white hair clamp. She bit her lip to keep from laughing at the silly way it looked.

He motioned for her to join him in the shower, making room for her. She pulled open the glass door and stepped under the spray, and then backed away quickly from the scalding water.

Yikes. Didn't he know how to operate the cold handle?

"Is it too hot for you?"

"Ah, I can adjust myself to it."

"I can make it cooler." He reached for the faucet.

"No need. It's easy enough for me to morph a bit to accommodate the heat. I'm comfortable in it now."

She stepped under the spray, and he scrunched his eyebrows at her. Did the idea of her morphing disturb him?

"Henry, is everything all right?"

He kissed her. "Everything is fine. Now turn around so I can wash your back."

She obliged him. "But I'll wash the front, or we'll be here until sunrise."

After drying off, she went in search of her underwear. The thong lay on the floor next to the bed, and the bra hung from a chair arm. She got into them and slipped on the dress, then tried to figure out what to do with her hair. She could morph it into an updo again, but perfectly coiffed hair might seem odd to Gaea. And what about Henry's look in the shower? He seemed uneasy over her morphing comment.

Sighing, she ran a brush through the stiff waves. The results were less than satisfactory. *Oh well. Sometimes pretending to be mortal stinks.*

He was dressed in no time, right down to the perfect bow of his tuxedo tie. By looking at him, you'd never know they'd been in bed. The same couldn't be said for her. She stepped into her high-heeled shoes, and he escorted her back to the house, picking up his tuxedo jacket from the gazebo along the way.

It was close to five in the morning when they arrived at Gaea's front porch. She stood facing him. "It's been a lovely evening, Henry. Thank you. For everything."

"It is I who should thank you. I had the honor of having the most beautiful woman at the dance on my arm."

She leaned in for an unhurried goodnight kiss. The front door opened behind her and she froze with her lips pressed to his.

"So there you two are," Gaea exclaimed. "I wondered when you would return her home, *Señor* Bautista."

"Safe and sound," Henry replied, with a half-grin, "*and* at a decent hour."

"Decent my ass," Gaea said, her fists firmly planted on her broad hips. "Well, do you want to come in or are you just going to dump her at the door and run off."

"If that's an invitation, Gaea, I would be happy to come in, but I must leave in fifteen minutes. I'll need time to make it home before sunrise."

Seated comfortably in Gaea's parlor, Cerissa listened while Henry and Gaea gossiped about who attended—and who didn't attend—the dance. She suppressed a yawn and settled back into the tapestry chair, feeling like she was glowing. She reached out and took Henry's hand. Without taking a beat in his conversation with Gaea, he raised her hand to his lips.

"I don't want to leave," he said, "but I should be going."

She squeezed his hand. "I'll see you tonight?" she asked. A small ache grew in her chest—she wanted to spend the day with him, impossible as it was.

"Of course," he said. "Yacov and I have tickets for the Mordida Bugles."

"Bugles? A concert?"

"Baseball game. And I ordered an extra ticket for you. We have an early moonrise. I can pick you up ten minutes after sunset. We should arrive at the game a little after it starts."

"Sounds fun. I would love to—"

"Have you forgotten?" Gaea interrupted her. "I was going to hold another open house tomorrow night. You asked to meet more potential investors."

Henry spoke before she could. "You can postpone the meeting. Cerissa is mine now."

"That isn't quite true," Gaea said, "and you know it. If I'm not mistaken, and I rarely am in this, I don't detect the scent of fresh blood in the room."

"Gaea, that's enough," Cerissa said, feeling her face grow hot.

"Until he has taken your blood, he has no claim on you. He cannot keep others away from you. The choice remains entirely with you, Cerissa."

Henry glowered at Gaea. "A mere formality."

"Just because you wrote the Covenant doesn't mean you can ignore it when it suits your fancy."

"Gaea, please stop," Cerissa said. What must Henry think? She didn't want him to feel pressured. "There is no need to argue about this. Henry and I will go to the game, and I can meet with investors the following night."

"Are you sure about this?" Gaea asked, concern in her voice. "Perhaps we should talk further after Henry has left before you make your decision."

"That won't be necessary," Henry said. "Cerissa has made her mind known. We should respect it."

"Only because it serves your purposes, *Señor* Bautista." Gaea waggled a finger at him. "Don't act like you've staked your claim when you have yet to invest your fangs in it."

Cerissa stood up—the conversation had become much too embarrassing. "It's time for me to walk Henry to the door and say goodnight. Gaea, I will see you later."

Henry stood and bowed formally to Gaea.

Outside by his car, Henry said, "Cerissa, I—"

She stopped him with a kiss. Too quickly, his lips left hers. She gazed into his eyes. "I'm looking forward to tonight," she said.

"As am I." He raised one eyebrow. "After all, I owe you a few more orgasms."

She buried her face against his chest, a warm flush crawling up her neck.

"As I said before," he whispered in her ear, "we can move slowly, whatever you are comfortable doing, but I do intend to see to you pleasured."

She felt his lips on her cheek before he backed up and bowed to her.

He drove off and turned onto the main road. She sat down on the garden bench, the white metal seat a pattern of grapevines, and pressed her fingers against them. His headlights soon faded in the distance until she could no longer see them. The early morning air cooled the heat of her embarrassment. Would she ever truly be comfortable in bed with him? The confidence in his voice—he was certain he could please her with his tongue. Maybe she should let him try.

She took a deep breath and slowly let it out. The garden smelled fragrant with the night-blooming jasmine and the earthy scent of the nearby vineyard. The sun's edge slowly peeked out over the eastern mountains on the other side of California's central valley.

A wistful sadness momentarily overcame her.

I will never be able to share this with him.

Then she pictured Henry naked, and a smile grew on her face. There were so many other wonderful things she could share with him. She couldn't wait for nightfall.

CHAPTER 48

Cerissa slept until almost four in the afternoon. After a quick shower, she pulled on a pair of jeans and a stretch top. Her phone buzzed while she was getting ready.

A text message from Henry: "I'll buy you dinner at the stadium."

Sweet of him, but she couldn't begin the night on an empty stomach. She needed fuel to maintain human form. She went downstairs and grabbed a sandwich. Finished, she returned her clean dish to the cupboard and heard the utility room door open behind her. Blanche and Seaton emerged.

"This is goodbye," Blanche said, sounding cranky. She held up a crumpled letter. "Gaea must have left this by my bed. The old bat didn't have the guts to tell me after the dance. The stupid board turned down my residency application. I have to leave tonight. Not that I really wanted to stay in this vampire prison."

Good. Blanche got what she deserved. "I'm sorry you didn't make it," Cerissa said, trying to be a gracious winner, "but I don't see how you can call the Hill a prison."

Blanche stepped through the kitchen, dodging the late afternoon sunlight coming through the kitchen window to pull the blinds shut. "Living in isolation from the real world—what would you call it? A rich ghetto? Just because those assholes have money doesn't make it any less a prison." She took a couple of blood bags out of the refrigerator and held them up. "I mean, look at this crap we drink."

"But if they had accepted you, you'd have gladly lived here."

"Hey, it's not like I don't got options. I'm fixin' to go to San Diego next."

"Good luck with that," Cerissa said, and resumed walking to the door. Time to get ready—sunset wasn't far away.

A hand latched on to her shoulder. "Just wait a minute. Goin' somewhere?" Blanche asked.

Cerissa turned around. "I have a date with Henry. We're going to the baseball game in Mordida. Now if you'll excuse me…"

"This won't take long." Blanche sat down at the kitchen table and motioned for Cerissa to join her. "No hard feelings, okay? We're gonna see each other around, so why doncha let bygones be bygones."

Cerissa remained standing, crossing her arms. "Blanche, you spread lies about me. Why should I ever forgive you?"

"Because it's just business. You can't take business personally. My maker taught me that long ago, when he cut me loose. If you carry a grudge, it'll eat you right up. Better to forgive and forget."

"You'd like that, wouldn't you? But I'm not giving your conscience a free pass. No way." She turned again to leave.

Blanche grabbed her arm, pivoting her around and holding her fast. Cerissa rolled her eyes. *Not this again.* Her lenses had alerted her, but Blanche latched on before she could escape. *I should rip off her arm and beat her with it. Then she might show me some respect.*

But that wasn't an option, either—any attempt to fight back would give away she wasn't mortal.

"Look," Blanche said, smirking and showing some fang. "Let me make it up to you. If you decide you want to become one of us, see me. You're smart. I bet you'd make a good vampire, and until I join a treaty community, I can turn anyone I want."

"Let go of me," Cerissa demanded.

Blanche glanced guiltily in Seaton's direction. "Oh, sure," she said, licking her lips and taking a step back. "Ya know, someday things will change. When that day comes, you'll want to be on the side of the winners. Come see me and I'll help you out—I owe it to you after what I put you through."

"I'll keep that in mind," Cerissa replied, and left the kitchen, walking fast.

Wow, that was bold. Cerissa ran up the stairs to her room. Had Blanche really meant what she said? Or was she just blowing off steam? Either way, it didn't matter. This couldn't wait. She needed to tell Ari—right *now.*

As soon as the sun set, Henry was out the door and driving toward Gaea's house. When his cell phone rang, the caller's name displayed on his dashboard and he tapped the steering wheel's "accept" button. "Leopold—thank you for calling," he said.

"Do I understand this right? You want to buy out Cerissa's contract?"

"I would like to make her my mate."

"And what makes you think I have any interest in letting you take her blood?"

"I thought for a fair price—"

"You talk of fair. Were you fair when you sold *Enrique's* against my wishes? Were you fair when you forced me to sign a draconian treaty?"

"The others agreed—"

"And now our situation is reversed," Leopold interrupted, sounding triumphant. "What do I want? The amount I would have made on *Enrique's* if we had kept the restaurant going another twenty years—what it would be worth in today's dollars, that is."

Henry pulled over to the side of the road. The phone call had his whole attention now.

"Any amount you name will be purely speculative. Tastes change. The restaurant may have sold at a loss by then."

"The owners who bought it from you sold the restaurant at a healthy profit twenty years later. So I know the amount to the penny—$1.2 million in present-day dollars."

"That's a lot to pay for an envoy's contract."

"But it's my price. I have a lot invested in her. You want the girl, you'll pay it."

He gripped the steering wheel tightly. Last night had chased away any lingering doubt—he had to have Cerissa as his own, even if it meant paying a ridiculous sum to a petty man.

"All right, you have a deal," he said. "I'll start the wire instructions tonight—you should have the money before sunrise."

"You *are* in a hurry. I should've asked for more."

"You're getting more than a fair price. Send me a confirming email with your bank account number. I'll have Marcus draw up the formal agreement."

"I don't care about a written agreement," Leopold scoffed. "As soon as I have the money, you can have her blood, but not a minute before." The clicks of a keyboard sounded from Leopold's end. "I've sent you the routing number for the wire transfer."

Henry stared at his phone, waiting for the email to come through. "There is one more thing," he said. "I will tell Cerissa. Please don't speak to her about it."

After last night's conversation with Gaea, he feared Cerissa might take offense, but he had no choice—he couldn't ignore the treaty.

"Going to lie to her?" Leopold asked.

"I am merely going to tell her I have your blessing to proceed."

"That's up to you, Henry, but let me warn you, based on what I know about Cerissa..."

"What?"

"Don't ever lie to her." Leopold laughed, a deep guffaw of secret knowledge.

Henry clicked off the call and tapped his phone to open Leopold's email. After copying the wire transfer information, he opened the app for his Swiss bank account, and pasted in the routing and account numbers. A few more taps completed the transaction. In about three hours his bank would open and the transfer would be completed—the time zone difference was one of the many reasons he used a Swiss bank.

By the time he and Cerissa returned from the game tonight, the deal would be done. He could take her back to his house and make love to her without holding back.

He raised an eyebrow when the phone rang again. He wasn't expecting Yacov's call. He put the Viper in gear and pulled away from the curb. "Are you at the gate already?" Henry asked. "I have your ticket. I'll be there soon—a small business matter delayed me."

"I'm sorry, my friend. I can't make it tonight. Shayna twisted her ankle today during theater rehearsals and can barely walk. I would feel terrible leaving her alone."

"Another time," Henry replied, as graciously as he could. "Tell Shayna I hope she recovers quickly."

Henry punched the button to disconnect the call and clenched his jaw. What to do now? Rolf was entertaining wine distributors in the stadium's luxury box owned by their winery. Rolf had taken Frédéric as his second. The last thing Henry wanted was to be in the crowded skybox with them, knowing how they felt about Cerissa. Besides, he wanted to focus on Cerissa and not have to glad-hand his way through the room.

If he started calling friends now, he might find someone who could use Yacov's ticket to satisfy the Rule of Two. He pulled over to the curb again and started working his way through his contact list.

Cerissa closed her bedroom door and phoned Ari—if he was back in Miami, it wouldn't be too late to call him.

"This had better be good," Ari said when he answered.

"I don't care if I'm interrupting your love life. I need you to run a report on Blanche."

"Just because she's spreading rumors about you doesn't mean—"

"She just threatened to turn me vampire."

"So what?"

"It doesn't make sense. Blanche has less than five years to acquire her buy-in money, and even for some of the less expensive communities, I don't see her having enough capital to pay the buy-in for two vampires."

"Can you get to the point?"

"I told you the point. Under the treaty, she has to pay the buy-in for any vampire she makes during the grace period. The rule is intended to keep unaffiliated vampires from over-breeding."

Ari scoffed. "I repeat, so what? She made an idle threat because she lost out to you."

"Look, you told me to get back on track and do my job. I'm doing it. You asked me to spy on them and report back anything suspicious, anything that could lead to the vampires who are a threat to humans. What if Blanche's threat means she's part of that group?"

"You think—"

"Blanche feels free to turn mortals into vampires because she thinks the current power structure is about to crumble. It's the way she said it— '*someday things will change*.'"

"Okay, okay, I'll look into her background more closely."

"Thanks, Ari. I have to run—call me later." She grabbed her purse and ran downstairs. Henry should be here by now.

Tig's office door at the police station stood open. She'd just arrived and planned on working her way through a stack of paperwork, a stack that threatened to topple over onto the floor. Jayden rushed in and stopped in front of her desk, looking agitated. "You're not going to believe this," he said.

"What's happened?"

"Remember the guard, Norman Tyler?"

"Yes, yes," she said. "We should send Liza and Zeke to San Diego, to track down Hoodie. They can leave tomorrow night."

"Too late. The guard's dead."

"Fuck! How?"

"Throat slashed with a knife."

"Where did they find the body?"

"In a ditch off the main road, near the prison—he was only dead a few hours. No idea how he got there. His car wasn't found."

"Any markings a vampire did it?"

"From the ME's report, most of the blood is accounted for."

"Do you have the time of death?"

Jayden handed her the preliminary autopsy report. "Between four and six this morning," he said, "based on a liver temp of eighty-seven degrees. Probably closer to five a.m.—he got off work at four thirty and the body was discovered around ten."

"Fuck! We can't rule out a vampire." She felt like putting her fist through the wall, but the paperwork to have the wall repaired would just add insult to injury.

"Take a closer look," he said, handing her a photo. "Look familiar?"

She studied the photo of the dead guard. The red slash across his throat looked like a second smile. Jayden walked over to a special file cabinet in her office and unlocked it. Only the two of them had keys. He pulled out a file and held up the photo of a different dead man—one of Zeke's kills.

She threw the guard's photo down on the desk and snatched the one he held. "Damn. If Zeke left the dance before eleven and took a private jet to San Diego, he could have made it in time. There's a small airport near the prison—easy to get there before dawn. Have you checked with the guard gate?"

"They weren't much help. New guy said he'd have to check with whoever had last night's duty. They're supposed to call me with a list of who left the Hill last night and didn't return." Jayden picked up the photo of Zeke's victim from her desk and returned it to the file cabinet. "Zeke could be behind the attempts on Yacov and Henry."

She shook her head. Her evaluation of Zeke couldn't be that wrong. "He has no motive. Cerissa arrived after the first shooting, and Henry didn't hook up with her until after she was shot." Tig picked up the photo of the dead guard and looked at it again. "Someone who's familiar with Zeke's out-of-town work could have killed the guard to set up Zeke."

"Lots of people on the Hill know what he does," Jayden replied. "But not many have the details we do."

She squinted at the photo of the dead guard, trying to see something small. "Do you have any close-up views of the slash?"

He shuffled through the photos. "Here you go. What are you seeing?"

"That," she said, pointing to some scar tissue on the guard's neck, below the slash. "Repeated bite marks."

"Are you sure? Those could just be skin abnormalities."

"White skin does hide scarring better. Use the loupe, you'll see it," she said, taking the device from the drawer of her desk and handing it to him.

He held the jeweler's loupe over the photo. "Damn. Those do look like bite marks. So Hoodie *was* a vampire."

"Possibly. He definitely had close contact with a vampire, an asshole who didn't bother to heal the bite marks." Most Hill residents swapped vials of blood, healing their bites with another vampire's blood to prevent repeated scarring. "It confirms what I've suspected all along—a vampire is behind this."

Jayden pointed at the bite marks in the photo. "How did I miss this when I interviewed him?"

"Don't beat yourself up. Norman's shirt collar would have hidden it," she said. She'd learned the hard way—needlessly criticizing him wouldn't improve his performance, or their relationship.

"But he didn't seem nervous," Jayden said. "He was relaxed and open, no sign he was trying to cover up anything." He threw the photo back on the desk. "I keep thinking about how Norman looked when I first met him. Gray and clammy. I'd chalked it up to the heat in the interview room, but it could have been caused by overfeeding."

She'd seen the same thing when she viewed the video. *Damn.* If she had been there, she would have smelled whether his blood was weakened from overfeeding.

"Even when he confronted me," Jayden continued, "he didn't seem afraid, more like he was angry."

"If he's the connection to the vampire behind this, they probably mesmerized him to forget. There was no way for you to spot his lies if he didn't know he was lying." She tossed the photos back on the desk. "But I don't think Zeke was Hoodie. Hoodie looked much shorter and skinnier than Zeke."

"So what?" Jayden asked, straightening the photos so they were side by side. "More than one vampire may be involved. Zeke could have killed Norman."

"I'm not buying it," she said. "Do the San Diego police have any suspects?"

"I don't have the full police report. I called the ME this afternoon and she sent me the photos along with her prelim. I'm waiting for the detective on the case to return my phone call." Then his face lit up. "Hey, did you ever get Yacov's suspect list? He promised to send it last night. We need it now more than ever."

She frowned. "I thought he sent it to you."

"Nothing in my email."

"Shit. The reminder better come from me. I'll send it later tonight. I've got something else to do first." She snatched up the photos and headed for the door.

"Where are you going?"

She stopped at the door. "I have a deputy to interview. And he better not have left the Hill."

The station's front door buzzer sounded. She signaled Jayden to stay seated. He wasn't on duty, and she wanted to see who it was, since she wasn't expecting anyone.

"Mayor," she said, surprised to see Winston easing the door shut. "Is something wrong?"

"Unfortunately, it is. We must do something fast. If we don't, we'll have a mob action on our hands."

CHAPTER 49

Henry slammed the car door shut. No one was available to satisfy the Rule of Two—at least, no one he was willing to ask, and he refused to join Rolf and Frédéric in the skybox. He'd even called Gaea—she was meeting with her financial advisor tonight, seeking advice about investing in Cerissa's project. He didn't want to delay Gaea's investment, so he didn't press her.

Anger flew through his body, like a thousand buzzing bees. Taking a deep breath, he strode to Gaea's front door.

As soon as Cerissa opened the door, her golden smile sliced right through him. He took her in his arms, and her warm lips eagerly sought his. Being with her drained the anger from him, and it wasn't her ability to charm. What he felt for her made his anger flow away like water down a storm drain.

"I hope you had a good day," he said, when the kiss ended.

"I missed you," she replied, hugging him tightly, her hips pressed tight against his.

Hmm, maybe we could skip the game and go back to my house? He mentally shook his head. He had promised her a night at the game and dinner out. He would find some way to fulfill his promise.

He turned at the sound of a car pulling into Gaea's driveway—Tig's police cruiser. What was the chief doing here?

"Cerissa Patel," Tig said as she walked up. "Your diplomatic privileges have been revoked. You're to come with me."

"Absolutely not." Henry placed himself between Cerissa and the chief. "She has done nothing wrong."

"Step aside, Founder. You have no right to interfere."

Henry didn't move. "I have every right to interfere. She's mine."

Tig stepped in close to him and sniffed the air. Henry ground his teeth, the bee's buzzing in his veins again. *If the chief doesn't step back—*

"She isn't yours," Tig said. "You haven't taken her blood yet. You aren't marked by the scent of her blood."

Cerissa moved around him. "But I satisfied the mayor's conditions. He retracted the warning letter. I don't understand what this is about."

"You violated the Covenant by going to Henry's house last night. You had permission to be at the dance, but not his house, since you're not his mate. I'm to escort you off the Hill. Pack your bags. We leave now."

Henry couldn't believe what he'd heard. They were going to enforce that obscure rule now? More than a few mates had been brought to the Hill *before* the bite, to make sure they wanted to stay. More importantly, how had the mayor found out? Only Henry, Cerissa, and Gaea knew he had yet to take Cerissa's blood.

From behind him, he heard Gaea *huff*. "This is the mayor's order?" she demanded.

"Yes, ma'am," Tig replied.

"I'm going to whip his pompous ass for this. I told Winston to give Henry a few more nights." Gaea put a hand on Cerissa's arm. "I'm sorry, dear. I shouldn't have gossiped. I never thought Winston would do something this stupid."

Henry clenched his fists. He couldn't let the mayor force Cerissa to leave. In three hours, the wire transfer would go through and he'd be free to make her his mate.

"Can you give us the night to work this out?" he asked the chief. "By sunrise, I'm sure the situation will be rectified."

He could feel Cerissa's blush from a foot away. He looked at her and she turned away, clearly embarrassed. Was he presuming too much?

"I'm sorry," Tig replied. "I don't have any leeway here. I'm just doing my job."

"Then I'll go with her," Henry said.

"Sorry, Founder," Tig said, motioning for him to move out of the way. "Rule of Two. You can't go into Mordida alone."

Cerissa took his hand, her blush fading. "I'll get a hotel room in town. I'll call you once I'm settled in and you can get Yacov to go with you."

Tig shook her head. "No hotel room. You're not permitted to stay within our jurisdiction."

"I can't get a flight out now." Cerissa held up her arm, pointing to her watch. "It's too late. What do you expect me to do, drive all night? That's ridiculous."

Tig seemed to consider it. "You can get a hotel for one night. By tomorrow, you must be on an airplane back to New York, by order of the mayor."

"Not if I have anything to say about it," Henry said, his voice a low growl in his throat. He was going to have words with the mayor—maybe more than words.

Cerissa took out her phone and searched for something, tapping through a few menus. Looking up at him, she said, "Okay, I've reserved a room at Mordida Inn. I'll call Leopold and he can work this out through diplomatic channels. Please? Let him handle it."

She was asking him to stay out of the political fray. She squeezed his hand and let go. Tig escorted her into Gaea's house, and Gaea followed them. Blanche came out when the others left.

"I'm real sorry they're kicking your girlfriend off the Hill," Blanche said. "Hey, I hear you have tickets for the baseball game. I could go with you. Whatcha say? A night out before I leave for good?"

"I'd rather go alone," Henry mumbled as he shot a disgusted glance at her. He ran down the porch steps and got into his car. He'd had enough. All the rules under which he lived felt like a silver noose at his throat. Because of those rules, he was paying Leopold an outrageous sum for Cerissa's contract, and now they were banning her from the Hill.

Damn the Rule of Two. He changed gears as he sped toward the Mordida Inn. *No one will ever find out.*

Tig helped load Cerissa's luggage into the envoy's rental car and then got into her police cruiser. Henry's car was gone. *Strange.* Had he gone to see the mayor? She checked her phone. No missed calls.

The mayor should never have allowed Cerissa to attend the dance. Sure, the town attorney said the rule didn't apply to an envoy, and the treaty trumped the Covenant. But the residents' sensibilities were sorely challenged by that technical violation. And then everyone saw her leave the dance with Henry. The mayor couldn't ignore the implications—not after having it confirmed by Gaea's phone call. He had to act before the rumors got out of control.

She followed Cerissa's car to make sure the envoy left as instructed. Halfway through the business district, she flashed her cruiser's blue and red lights. Cerissa got the message and pulled over.

"Don't say anything, just listen," Tig said, once Cerissa's window was down. "The mayor didn't want to do this."

"Then what am I doing out here?"

"There are still some who think you're spying for Leopold. They're using your relationship with Henry as an excuse to put pressure on the mayor."

"If Henry takes my blood, then I can return?"

She considered it for a moment. Cerissa had passed her security check. There wasn't anything else stopping her return. "It shouldn't be a problem."

The envoy said goodnight and drove off in the direction of Mordida. Tig walked back to her cruiser, taking a deep breath and letting it out. For some reason, every time she was around Leopold's envoy, she felt the desire to protect her—the same protectiveness she had once felt for her younger co-wives. What an odd way to feel about this stranger.

"What are you doing here?" Cerissa demanded when she found Henry standing by the hotel elevator.

"I'm here to help," he said, taking the suitcase handle from her and following her into the elevator.

Yeah, she could guess what his idea of help was. He hadn't taken her blood when they made love last night. That was his choice. Now he was being coerced into it and she refused to go along. How had he put it? Love should be freely given.

She held her tongue until the door to her room shut.

"I don't need your help," she announced. Anger had stripped away her fear of making a mistake in the private realm. She took a soda out of the hotel refrigerator and plopped down on the couch.

He placed her bag on the luggage stand and stood there looking confused. "You're mad at me? This is the mayor's fault, not mine."

"Really? Then why didn't you take my blood last night?" She popped the can's top—loudly—and took a sip from her soda.

He shifted his weight from one foot to the other and looked away. After a moment, he turned back to her. "I didn't think you were ready for that commitment."

She slammed the can down on the coffee table and stood to face him. "Why didn't you ask me? Or are you not ready?"

His dark eyes flashed anger, turning solid black. "Shall I show you I am ready?"

"Yes."

"You really have no fear of what I am, do you?"

She crossed her arms. "You won't change the topic that easily."

"Cerissa, once I take your blood, you cannot date others until I release you. Until I decide. Not you. I didn't want to make the decision for you."

"Bullshit!" she exclaimed, not keeping her voice down. She didn't care if the tourists in the room next door heard her.

"Cerissa!"

"If you truly want a relationship with me, it has to be as equals—you can't own me."

Yeah, she'd had enough of that with the Protectors. They'd controlled her life from birth, without a concern for what she wanted. He had to understand she wasn't going to take the same treatment from her boyfriend. No, she was not.

"I didn't mean I would own you," he replied. "It is our way. I—"

"Your way. I can't live as a second-class citizen. If this relationship is going to work, that has to change."

"But the Covenant—"

"I don't give a damn about the Covenant. What needs to change is how *you* treat me. *Now.*" She took a step closer to him and jammed her finger into his chest, his muscle harder than she remembered it from last night. "Your Covenant is only a step better than those behind the vampire dominance movement."

"The what?"

She turned away and covered her face with her hand. *Oh shit. I really do need to get out of the spy business and back into the research lab.*

"Ah," she began, turning to face him again. "There are rumors some vampires want to turn mortals into their slaves, keep them in herds—in other words, no more mates."

He shook his head. "Those rumors have been floating around for years. It won't work—the idea never gains any traction. We love our mates too much to turn them into slaves."

"Not according to your Covenant." She poked his hard chest one more time. "You act like you're superior to the rest of us, but in truth, your rules are archaic, a throwback to a patriarchal era."

"I—" he began, but then abruptly stopped. "That's just what Shayna said."

"Shayna?"

"My friend's wife."

She took his hand in hers. This was too important to leave it unsettled, and not just because she wanted back on the Hill. "If you're truly ready for the next step, it will be by our rules, not theirs."

"Very well. Our rules. Then here is our first rule: I will save the taking of your blood for when I have you in my bed."

She stepped back. "Procrastinating again? I'm not allowed anywhere near your bed on the Hill."

He glanced at the hotel bed, and then at his watch.

Why was he concerned about the time?

"I have a proposal," he said, a mischievous grin growing on his face. "Let's go to the baseball game. I promised you a fun evening—I don't want you to think I'm only interested in sex."

She smiled. She couldn't help it. She ran her finger along his jaw line. "You'd rather go to a ballgame than make love?"

"It's not either/or," he said, catching her finger and kissing it. "I plan on having both."

She wrapped her arms around his neck and kissed him. Then she remembered—she'd worn her lenses because they were going to a public event. Oh well—Ari could edit it for her. She didn't give a damn if Ari saw the video. She blinked and turned off the recorder, leaving her lenses set to monitor and warn her in case of any danger.

CHAPTER 50

Cerissa waited while Henry opened the car door for her. She had assumed another vampire was waiting in the lobby to give them privacy, someone who would satisfy the Rule of Two. When she learned he had no one with him, her gut tightened with concern. How could they attend the game without an escort?

"Please get in," he said. "It'll be fine."

She slid into the Viper, and, after closing her door, he took something out the trunk of the car. She couldn't see what he was doing. Then he got in behind the wheel. He now wore a black blazer over his button-down shirt.

"What will the council do if they catch you?" she asked.

He waved his hand. "This is my first offense. A fine, nothing more."

"But aren't you making it worse by attending the baseball game? We don't have to go. I can eat dinner at the hotel."

"I promised to take you to the baseball game, and I intend to keep my promise."

She eased back into her seat and looked out the car's window as they gained speed on the main boulevard. He had more experience breaking rules than she did. Shouldn't she trust his judgment?

The stadium sat halfway between the Hill and Mordida's international airport, less than a mile from her hotel. Five minutes later, Henry turned the car down the lane reserved for VIP parking. It was a short walk to the reserved seat entrance. The security guy looked in her purse, and then raised the metal detector wand to run it across her body, asking her to turn around. She now faced Henry, who winked at her and then looked past her shoulder. The wand dropped back to the guard's side, and they passed through without any further searches.

Why had Henry avoided the metal detector? The wand wouldn't reveal he was a vampire. She shrugged to herself. Maybe the detection device was made with silver parts.

Their seats were in the premium club section right behind home plate. Once they settled in, Henry glanced up at the luxury boxes above their heads, and she followed his gaze, not sure what he was looking for.

She pushed her hair behind her ears, feeling the frizzies start to form in the damp night air. The crowd fell silent when the batter stepped up to the plate, the field awash in artificial light. The scoreboard read 0-0, bottom of the second inning. Minutes later, the crack of the bat sent the ball into the stands—a home run for the Bugles.

Henry cheered like a kid. His face lit up, his fist pumping the air. He was enjoying himself, sharing something special with her. She tried to follow the action, to cheer and clap whenever he did, but watching him was more interesting than watching the game. He seemed suddenly younger, not like the serious Henry she saw on the Hill. When he booed the referee, she giggled. *Jeez, when did I become so girly?*

Henry focused his eyes on the game, but Cerissa's accusations niggled at him. Was protecting mortals nothing more than a smoke screen for treating them as property? Father Matt had compared the Covenant to Jim Crow laws. Was he right? After all, a benevolent dictatorship was still a dictatorship.

He scratched at the back of his head. The Covenant was designed to protect mortals. Vampires couldn't be trusted not to harm mortals, not without strict rules. He couldn't see a way around it. Not if they were going to keep the Hill safe.

Yet tonight, he'd rebelled against those rules. An uneasy feeling rooted in his gut. How did he get trapped between securing the safety of his community and feeling like a prisoner inside his own walls?

Cerissa squeezed his hand and he squeezed back, but he kept his vision focused on the field. He didn't want his eyes revealing his thoughts.

And what about my deal with Leopold? How will Cerissa react when she learns about it? His stomach lurched. She couldn't learn he'd paid $1.2 million for her. If she found out he treated her like chattel, she'd never become his mate. He had to tell her something—maybe he could tell part of the truth. But what about Leopold's warning? *Don't ever lie to her.*

No, he had to be honest with her. He couldn't build their relationship on a lie. Once they were back at the hotel, he'd tell her everything.

It was the bottom of the fourth inning. Cerissa's stomach rumbled—an unfortunate side effect of pretending to be mortal. She hoped Henry hadn't noticed.

He looked over at her. "Would you like to order food from the server?" he asked. "I promised you dinner. Our seats include food service, or I can escort you to the concession stands."

So he had heard her stomach rumble. At least she could count on him to be gracious about such things. "I'd like to stretch my legs, if you don't mind missing part of the game."

"The Forty Miners are up next. I can miss that."

She smirked. Henry took his team loyalty seriously. She climbed the steep stairs, glad to be out of the hard folding chair. Henry walked behind her. "I'd like to try a hot dog," she said over her shoulder. "They're the traditional food of baseball. I looked it up."

"Yes, hot dogs and peanuts." He caught up with her and wrapped his hand around hers. They walked side by side across the sparsely occupied concourse in the direction of the nearest booth offering food.

"Then I'd like to try both," she said. They passed a few people carrying other food choices. Garlic was one of the only foods she couldn't eat when around vampires. She missed it. "But I'll skip the garlic fries— this time," she added with a grin.

"Indeed," he said, a little menace in the humorless look he gave her.

Teasing him was such fun. She leaned her head against his shoulder, enjoying their closeness as they walked across the breezeway to the food stands.

"Stop right there," a man ordered.

Henry whirled around, shoving her behind him. Cerissa peeked over his shoulder to see two vampires, one man and one woman, armed with handguns.

"What do you want?" Henry asked, producing a gun of his own.

"You," the man said. He had a military-style buzz haircut. Buzz motioned with the end of his gun. "Come with us and Leopold's envoy can stay here, unharmed."

"Don't," Cerissa whispered. "It's a trap." She pressed up against his back and felt the hard outline of another gun under his blazer.

"Perhaps it's a trap, perhaps not," the female vampire with bright red hair said. Cerissa's eyes tracked her. Red slowly circled in on Henry's left. "But if you don't go with us, she's dead right now."

No choice. Cerissa blinked her eyes. In the speed it took to think "how," her lenses gave her what she needed: the muscle memory to handle a gun. With vampire-like speed, she grabbed the gun out of his back holster, chambered a round, and aimed the Glock at Red. The U-shaped sight made it easy to find her target.

Red froze.

"I do believe the odds have improved," Henry said with a chuckle. "She's an expert shot."

A bold bluff. A Watcher is forbidden from killing, but he doesn't know that. Red's gun was pointed directly at her. *Stalemate. Now what?*

The sound of a gun slide being pulled back almost caused her to jump. To the side, Rolf, Jayden, and Tig were spread out—a large enough arc that they had clear shots at Red and Buzz, without Henry or her being in their path of fire.

Tig pointed a large pistol at Buzz. "Freeze," she ordered.

"We're not leaving unless Henry is with us," Buzz said.

"Then you're not leaving," Tig replied.

A slight movement—Red's gun swung to point at Henry. *Fuck the rules. I can't lose him.* Cerissa squeezed the trigger on the Glock.

Red's gun went flying.

A rapid fire of other guns followed. Henry's body crashed into her, forcing them both to the ground. Her gun arm was trapped across her body, his weight pinning her down.

"Henry!" she screamed, struggling to get free.

"All clear," Tig shouted.

Cerissa finally pushed out from under him. "Henry!" she yelled, shaking his arm. "Talk to me."

Buzz was on the ground, a growing red splotch on his t-shirt. She ran her hands over the hole in Henry's button-down shirt, looking for blood.

"I'm okay," Henry said, glancing at his chest. "But they ruined my favorite shirt."

She wasn't taking his word. She pulled at the buttons on his shirt and found something hard underneath the fabric.

"Stop." His hand grasped her wrist and he sat up. "There is nothing you need do. I'm wearing an old-fashioned heart shield—leather bonded to steel. I never leave the Hill without it."

She watched as he dug his fingers into the hole and plucked out the squashed bullet. A whiff of burning flesh and he quickly dropped the bullet into Tig's gloved hand. He shook his fingers the way a mortal did after touching something hot.

Tig examined the bullet. "Silver. Small caliber, low velocity. I bet it'll match the bullets the other shooters used."

Still kneeling, Cerissa threw her arms around Henry, hugging him tightly.

"Are you okay?" he asked her.

Her ears still rang from the gunfire, and the acrid smell of gunpowder caused her to rub her nose. Too much to process too quickly—Buzz and Red were on the ground, not moving, but mortals walked around them like an invisible force field kept them out. She gawked—she'd never seen the vampire ability to cast mass hypnosis demonstrated before.

"Cerissa, are you okay?" he repeated.

"I'll be fine," she finally said. "You're okay—that's all that matters."

He patted her back and let her go, standing up. He offered her a hand. "Is everyone else all right?" he asked.

"We're good," Tig replied. "Jayden, please photograph and print those two before they mummify."

No bystanders were hurt. Not even a stray bullet in the breezeway wall. Cerissa took a good look at Red. Her own bullet had gone through Red's gun wrist, but someone else put a bullet through Red's heart. Henry stooped over to pick up a casing from his Beretta.

"Good shooting, Henry," Jayden said, as he leaned over the body. "Clean through the heart."

Tig snorted in disgust. "I would prefer having one alive." She picked up Red's arm, examining the wound in her wrist. "Good shot for a civilian, Cerissa. A vampire couldn't have done better. When I saw your bullet hit her arm, I aimed for her heart."

"Um, er," Cerissa stammered. She couldn't let Tig suspect the truth. "Ah, I'm not that good. I was aiming for her chest too."

Tig raised a skeptical eyebrow. "Henry, we'll need your help to carry the bodies out."

Cerissa wrapped her arms around herself, the gun still gripped in her hand. She felt cold, a little shaky, but relieved. She hadn't killed Red. Would the Protectors have understood killing in self-defense of another? Not likely.

Jayden squatted near Red's body and pressed the dead vampire's fingers against a small device. A short time later it *dinged*. "They aren't in V-Trak."

"I'll send their photos around the listserv," Tig said. "We'll see if any security chiefs recognize them."

Cerissa took a deep breath and let it out. Still holding the Glock at her side, she followed the group as they carried two dead vampires to the parking lot, leaving a trail of gray dust on the black asphalt. Where had these two assassins come from? Their fingernails had no ridges. They were both young vampires—very young. Was their maker waiting outside to help them?

She didn't care whether the Protectors would understand or not. She wasn't letting go of her gun until she knew Henry was back on the Hill and safe.

CHAPTER 51

Henry stepped up into the back of the police van, hunched over, carrying the redhead's legs. Rolf had the shoulders, and together, they eased her into a body bag. Tig and Jayden slid the male into a black bag.

Henry hurried out of the van to be at Cerissa's side. She looked a little shell-shocked, her arms wrapped around herself, the gun still in her hand.

"I'm sorry this happened," he said, wrapping his arms around her again.

She returned the hug, her gun pressed flat against his back. "It's not your fault."

"Yes, it is. I should never have brought you here without a proper escort. After the previous attacks, I should have known better."

A hand gripped his arm, pulling him away from Cerissa before she could respond.

"Step back," Rolf demanded. "She's not your mate."

He let go of Cerissa only because he didn't want to drag her with him. But Rolf's impudence wouldn't remain unpunished. Henry spun around and slammed Rolf against the police van.

"Funny way to thank me for saving your life," Rolf said with a snarl.

Tig slid her arm between them, pushing at his chest. "Okay, guys, break it up."

Henry took a step back, raising his hands. He didn't want to make things worse by resisting the chief. "What do you mean you saved my life?"

Rolf brushed his hands over his shirt, smoothing out the wrinkles where Henry had grabbed him. "You bought your tickets through our corporate account," Rolf replied. "When two of the three were scanned in, the account notified me. I left the skybox to find out who was using them.

I didn't expect it to be you. When I saw you without an escort, I called Tig."

Rolf could have come to Henry, warned him to leave. Instead, he'd betrayed him by phoning the chief. "You're not much of a friend," Henry said with disgust.

Rolf flipped his straight blonde hair to the side, brushing it out of his eyes. "Shit, Henry. I'm on the council. I had no choice. I couldn't look the other way. Frédéric would know."

"Pitiful excuses," Henry retorted.

"This is not the place for this conversation," Tig said. "Henry, you need to return to the Hill with us."

"I drove Cerissa here—her car is at the hotel. I'll take her back there first." He had to take her blood now, before he appeared in front of the council, and he preferred the privacy of her hotel room to the front seat of his car.

Tig reached for her handcuffs. "I should put you under arrest and take you back in the van."

"We can't leave Cerissa in the parking lot. She doesn't know how to drive the Viper," he insisted, hoping Cerissa wouldn't disagree. He placed his hand over his heart. "I give you my word of honor: I'll return to the Hill."

Tig frowned. "All right, you can drive your car back to town hall. Bring her with you—she witnessed what happened. Gaea can take her to get her stuff later." Tig climbed into the van. "And keep your fangs off her. The council's been called into session—no tampering with the witness. They may want to question her about tonight's events, and they'll want her mind clear of your influence."

Henry led the way back to his car. No telling what the council would do, but he could guess. He glanced at his watch. Leopold hadn't received the money yet. *And I can't take her blood now even if he had the money.*

The money. Guilt settled onto on his shoulders. Why hadn't he told her the truth when he had the chance? He didn't know how he was going to explain it to her now.

Cerissa's hands shook when she handed Henry the Glock—the aftermath of adrenaline. She rubbed her nose again, trying to remove the acrid smell lodged there. Her stomach woke up the minute she got into Henry's car, grumbling over the acid bath washing through it. She took an energy bar out of her purse and gobbled it down, expecting Henry to start the car.

Instead, he sat in the driver's seat, his face unreadable.

"Cerissa, there is something I should tell you," he said.

What now? Her stomach rolled in spite of the food.

"I was—I was not fully honest with you. I held off making you my mate until I was sure you were ready, but there was another reason I waited." He bowed his head, speaking toward the car's stick shift. "I had to get Leopold's consent first, since you are his envoy. I now have it."

She reached for his hands, entwining his fingers in hers. "You didn't need Leopold's consent. My contract has a twenty-four-hour notice clause before letting someone take my blood." Now it was her turn to look away. "I, ah, I gave him notice the night I received the warning letter. You could have taken my blood when we were in bed together...if you had asked."

He raised his head. A range of emotions played across his face, until his eyes narrowed.

"Are you mad at me for giving Leopold notice?" she asked.

"I'm..." He stopped.

Why was he upset? She hadn't mentioned it before because she didn't want him to feel pressured. "Henry?" she asked, squeezing his hands between hers.

"I'm not mad at you."

"Then who are you mad at?"

Her lenses detected the microscopic changes. The slight glance of his eyes up and to his right, the tensing of the muscles around his mouth—he was about to lie.

"Tell me the truth," she demanded. "The whole truth."

Henry turned away, chagrin written all over his face. "I contacted Leopold to get his permission to take your blood. Just before we left tonight, I paid him for it."

"How much?"

"The amount is unimportant. What is important is the principle. He misled me."

"Leopold is my business partner. *How much?*"

"One-point-two million."

"That son of a bitch!" she exclaimed. She sat there, staring at him. *Unbelievable.* She raked her fingers through her hair. "I'm going to throttle Leopold."

"Please don't—"

"I'll make him give the money back."

He turned to face her again. "I can fight my own battles."

"Your battle? *Your* battle?" Now it was Henry she wanted to throttle. "Why didn't you discuss it with me first?"

"It's not our way. You are his envoy. Under the treaty—"

"I'm nothing but property to be bought and bartered—"

"Never. But envoys have special status under the treaty, the penalties severe for any vampire who feeds on an envoy. It cannot be otherwise if they are to travel safely among us."

"All right, I get it. You were playing by your rules. But in the future—"

"In the future we will play by our rules. I'll discuss a decision with you first. I promise." His eyes once again communicated his embarrassment. "This has been an expensive lesson to learn."

She tried not to smirk. Really. She tried. "All right, I'll wait for you to work it out with Leopold. But if he doesn't return the money, I want to talk to him."

"Agreed."

Then it hit her. This whole misunderstanding could have been avoided if she'd just pulled up her big-girl panties and told him he could have her blood last night. *Damn.* She'd used the rules to get Zeke to back off when he threatened to bite her. How could she now fault Henry for following them?

"Ah," she began, "I'm sorry I didn't tell you last night. When you didn't bite, I was—I was too afraid to say anything."

He smiled and brushed her cheek with his hand. "*No te preocupes, no es nada, mi amor.*"

"Thanks. But what do we do now?" Tig had been clear. Cerissa couldn't let him take her blood now, not until after she testified.

"We throw ourselves on the mercy of the council," he said.

"Are they known for being merciful?"

His eyes took on a faraway look. He put the car in gear and backed out of the parking space. "Not really."

CHAPTER 52

Cerissa worried for the entire ride. *Just a fine, right? Nothing more, he said.* Tig had arrived at the town hall complex ahead of them and was waiting for Henry, opening his car door before Cerissa could even unbuckle her seatbelt. She hurried to follow them.

"Wait a minute, little lady," Zeke said, grabbing her arm. Her momentum spun them around.

"Cut the 'little lady' crap," she said in mid-spin.

When they stopped, Zeke stood there looking surprised. "Okay, I reckon I can do that." He let go of her. "But you can't go in there."

"Why not?"

"Vampires only." He was dressed more formally than she'd seen him before—white shirt, gray sports jacket, and a double-string tie made of brilliant blue silk.

"But it's a town council meeting. They can't exclude the public."

Zeke laughed at her. "The last district attorney who tried to investigate us for breaking that law didn't get too far. Dude couldn't remember his own name by the time he left."

She was getting real tired of this whole vampire superiority complex. "But Tig wanted me as a witness."

"That's another reason to stay out here." He took a cigar out of his coat pocket, clipped one end, and lit it. "They'll call you when they're ready for you."

"I just want to know what's happening to Henry."

He laughed again. "You don't need to go in, I can tell you that. The council doesn't cotton much to having the rules ignored. So they'll probably make an example of him," he said, gesturing with his cigar to emphasize his point. "But we're not savages—all very civilized around here. My guess is they'll fine him. But to a vampire with as much money as he has, a fine won't mean much. I don't know what else they might throw in."

Not good. When she had skimmed the Covenant, she hadn't focused on the penalties. Her throat tightened. How could she protect Henry out here? She needed to be in the council chambers, to tell his side of things.

"You're sure I can't go in?"

"Absolutely sure."

She slumped down onto a nearby bench and let out a weak sigh.

He placed a foot on the bench and leaned near her, his cigar wedged in the corner of his mouth, one fang keeping it in place. "I'm sorry 'bout what happened last night at the dance."

"Zeke, you need to understand, I'm Henry's mate now."

He sniffed the air. "That's just a mite strange."

"Strange?"

"You fibbed to me the other night. He hasn't bitten you yet, has he?"

She crossed her arms. "It's none of your business."

"Well, it's like this, missy. Until he does, you're like an unbranded filly in the corral. Any cowboy could still claim you."

"No—they—can't," she said, biting out each word.

"Whatever you say, missy, but a cowboy can't help wonder why Henry hasn't put his mark on you."

"It's none of your business." If Zeke didn't shut his mouth, she was going to put *her* mark on *him*. And it wasn't a mark he'd enjoy. "Please just leave me—"

The doors to the council chamber flew open, slamming against the stucco wall. Henry strode out, his eyes cold with anger, and they flashed in her direction. He ran to her, his fangs extended, and pushed Zeke away from the bench where she sat.

"Stay away from her," Henry yelled.

She stood up, grabbing his arm. "Henry, no!"

Tig wedged herself between the two men, her stun gun drawn. "Henry, back up," the chief ordered.

Henry didn't move. Another vampire was soon at Henry's side. Cerissa's lenses identified him as Yacov. "My friend," he said, pulling at Henry's arm, "this is not helping your case. Come, I will drive home with you."

"Cerissa, stay back." Henry swept his other arm behind him, his fingers finding her, pulling her behind him.

She pursed her lips and narrowed her eyes. This whole possessive thing was getting old, fast. "Henry, I—"

Before she could finish, Zeke flicked his cigar stub at Henry's feet, the umber-colored cylinder barely missing his shoe. Henry exploded into motion, lunging at Zeke.

"No you don't," Tig said, shoving a stun gun against Henry's side. With a flash of blue light, Henry dropped to his knees.

"No," Cerissa shouted, reaching out to Henry.

Yacov blocked her path as he scooped Henry up off the sidewalk. "I'll get him home," Yacov said in her direction. "Gaea will give you a lift to her place."

She stood rigid with anger, watching Yacov lead an unsteady Henry to the Viper. She didn't want to wait for Gaea, but she didn't want to make things worse by following them.

Tig grabbed Zeke. "You're coming with me."

"What did I do?" Zeke asked. "It was Henry. You saw it. He came after me."

"Yeah, you're as pure as the driven snow." Tig frog-marched him in direction of the police station.

"Cerissa," Henry called out as Yacov shoved him into the passenger seat. Yacov closed the passenger door, waving her off.

She'd taken a step toward the Viper in spite of Yacov's instructions when she heard Gaea say from behind her, "My word, child, why are you here?"

Cerissa turned. "Tig's orders. She thought I might be needed as a witness. Zeke wouldn't let me go in."

"We'll talk when we get back to my house." Gaea reached out to take Cerissa's hand. When she didn't move, Gaea's eyes flicked toward the onlookers. "Don't draw attention to yourself. Come with me. Now."

Cerissa ignored the other vampires who had gathered around. Gaea didn't look happy. Well, Cerissa wasn't either. But standing here wasn't getting her questions answered. She glanced over as the Viper pulled out of the parking lot.

"Let's go," she said, and sighed in resignation.

Tig called out for Jayden as she pushed Zeke inside the police station ahead of her. Jayden met her at the conference room, where she parked Zeke. "Wait here for me. I have to talk with the mayor first."

"But chief—" Zeke began, starting to stand up.

"Stay there. Jayden, keep an eye on him, okay?"

Jayden's hand traveled to his belt, where his stun gun was strapped. "Will do."

Tig found the mayor in his office. She closed the door behind her—they needed to talk in private.

He started ranting as soon as she was inside. "I had a promising date with a local beauty in Mordida tonight. Had to it cut short because one of our founders thought he was above the law." He slammed his briefcase down on the credenza behind his desk. "Whatever you want can wait until tomorrow night."

She knew better than to rush him when he was in this kind of mood. She avoided the uncomfortable guest chair and sat back on his leather couch, waiting for him to wind down. She needed to discuss the next step now that Henry was under house arrest. From the look on the mayor's face, the knock at his office door didn't make him any happier.

"Who is it?" he yelled.

The door banged open. Rolf entered without so much as an "excuse me" and slammed the door shut behind him. "It's your fault this happened."

"You think this was something more than Henry thinking with his dick?" The mayor turned his back on Rolf and started shoving papers into his briefcase. Tig continued to watch the exchange from the couch, suspecting Rolf hadn't noticed her presence.

"Going to the game was probably Cerissa's idea," Rolf yelled. "To put him in a vulnerable position. Henry could have been killed—what if that was her goal all along?"

The mayor turned his back to Rolf and rolled his eyes in Tig's direction. "If that were true, Cerissa could have killed him and blamed someone else long before now. She didn't." The mayor snapped his briefcase shut and swung back around to face Rolf. "I don't see tonight as her doing. This was all Henry."

"He would never have gone alone but for her."

The mayor *harrumphed*. "It was your idea to ban Cerissa from the Hill. How'd you think he'd react? He's probably as sick of all the restrictions we live under as I am. If you had your way, any mortal kept on the Hill would be in chains. I've had enough." He stood up. "I'm going home."

Rolf placed his hands on the mayor's desk and leaned toward him. "The council should have taken a stronger stand, *mayor*. We didn't do enough to stop Henry's foolishness."

"Your problem is you listen too closely to the gadflies during public comment. Idiots. Bring back the whipping post, they say. Make an example of him, they say. They just want free entertainment at Henry's expense. Because they're bored. Frankly, Rolf," the mayor said, pointing his finger in Rolf's face, "if it's anyone's fault, it's yours."

"Bah. Cerissa is the problem."

"You're supposed to be Henry's friend. You should be watching his back better—helping him, not working against him."

"Don't make this about me. As soon as I found out, I phoned Tig."

"My point exactly. If you were really his friend, you would have invited him up to the skybox instead of tattling to Tig. He would have been safe with you long before those goons showed up."

Tig had to agree. Now that she'd pieced all the parts together, Rolf didn't need to call her. Had that been Rolf's plan? Have her arrive, just a little too late to do anything about the attack?

Rolf straightened up, pushing out his chest like a self-righteous prig. "I did what the Covenant required."

"Take that stick out of your ass, Rolf." The mayor shook his head. "Henry took you under his wing when he first brought you here. This is a fine way to repay him."

"Be careful, Winston," Rolf said, his lip curled in a sneer. "Be very careful."

"Don't be an idiot. If you want to help Henry, be his friend. He's apparently enamored of the girl." The mayor grabbed his briefcase. "Be more supportive and he might confide in you."

He walked past Rolf and dodged out the back door of his office, slamming it behind him.

Tig stood up. The sound of her movement caused Rolf to spin in her direction. He glared at her before striding out the same door Winston had. *Wonderful.* She was in the wrong place at the wrong time. He'd probably find some way to get back at her for witnessing his tantrum. She shrugged to herself. *Nothing to be done about it now.* She stretched and walked the short distance back to the police station.

CHAPTER 53

Cerissa trod heavily along the stone path through Gaea's garden. The scent of night-blooming jasmine turned sour in her nose, the smell cloying. She tore a daisy from its stem as she walked by. Its white petals were folded in for the night, and she began plucking them, ripping each fragile petal one by one from its green receptacle.

Gaea clucked her way over to take a seat on the white garden bench. A look of sympathy in her eyes, Gaea patted the spot on the bench next to her. "Quit pacing. He won't be by tonight."

Still holding the petal-less daisy, Cerissa sat down next to Gaea. "How do you know?"

"Because the council has ordered him to stay away from you."

"They what?"

"He's under house arrest. He can't leave his house and you can't visit him—no direct contact, no phone calls, no emails, no text messages. You're a witness to what happened. They don't want you two conspiring to change your stories about it. Understand? The council was furious with the chief for letting him drive you back alone."

Cerissa threw the dismembered flower onto the ground. "I'm Leopold's envoy," she said, starting to stand up. "The council can't stop me from seeing him on Leopold's behalf."

Gaea pulled her back down. "Now, dear, it's only temporary. It's just for two weeks until they hold the real hearing."

"Oh."

"But they could make it a permanent order if he defies them."

Cerissa focused on the dark vineyard beyond Gaea's flower garden. "It doesn't matter what they do. They can't keep us apart."

"He could have ensured that last night. He didn't."

"There's a reason for that, Gaea, and it's between Henry and me." She wasn't about to tell Gaea the reason. No matter how much she liked Gaea, she could no longer trust her not to gossip.

"Cerissa, listen. You must be careful." Gaea patted her back, a gentle flutter of taps, like burping a baby. "Some of the council members blame you. The only reason you're still here is because the council wants you to testify at Henry's hearing. In two weeks, when they decide Henry's penalty, they'll decide whether to send you back to New York."

"If Henry and I become blood mates, they couldn't vote me off the Hill, could they?"

"It would make it harder for them to do so. But a lot has happened. Take the time to be certain Henry is the one you want."

"I—"

A *thump* came from Gaea's front porch, and Cerissa turned to see who it was. She hadn't heard the front door open. Blanche dragged two suitcases behind her, the wheels bouncing down the stone steps.

"I heard about the ban," Blanche said, stopping by the bench. "Surprised they let you back in, but they'll eventually send your ass down the road just like they did to me."

"Time for you to leave," Gaea said, standing up. "Here, let me help."

Gaea took Blanche's upper arm and twisted her in the direction of the driveway, where Blanche's Fiat was parked.

"Ow!" Blanche yelled. "You're ripping my arm out!" She dropped one bag, her arm flopping at her side. To Cerissa's trained eye, it looked like a dislocated shoulder.

Gaea grabbed the bag before the handle hit the ground, and gave a disdainful sniff. "I'm sorry, dear. But you need to learn when to keep your mouth shut."

Cerissa smiled for the first time since Henry was arrested. Not nice, but being nice didn't protect her from bullies. Which reminded her— Blanche may be more than a bully. She took out her phone and texted Ari, letting him know that Blanche was on her way to San Diego, so he could start tracking her.

Finished, she walked to the house with Gaea. "We'll need to go back to the hotel later to get my car and luggage," she told Gaea. "I'm going to my room for now."

"Of course," Gaea said, opening the door. "But no sneaking out to see him. The council is serious. You wouldn't want to get Henry in deeper trouble."

Tig strode into the police station's conference room. Now that Henry's little adventure was wrapped up, talking with Zeke moved to the top of her list.

Before she could sit down, Zeke asked, "Does this have something to do with Henry?" He flicked one end of his double-string tie with his thumb as he spoke. "'Cause if it does, it's Cerissa's fault. She misled me."

Tig laid a file folder on the table. "We'll talk about Cerissa in a moment. There's something else we need to discuss first."

"Somethin' else?"

He kept flicking the tip of the tie back and forth. It was his tell—hell, anyone on the Hill who'd played poker with him knew about it. They had the advantage whenever he wore one of his string ties to a game.

She slapped open the file folder. The photo of the dead guard stared back at Zeke. "Is this your work?"

Zeke picked up the photo. "No, ma'am. I understand why you're asking, but no, I didn't do this."

She kept her eyes on his. "What time did you leave the dance last night?"

"Well, after I danced with Cerissa, I didn't feel too much like hanging out there. So me and some of the guys put together a poker game over at Jose's."

"Who was with you?"

"Well, let me see. The mayor sat in on a few hands."

"What time did the game wrap up?"

"I quit when I was ahead. It had to be around three or so. I went home and checked on my herd, watched a little television, and by then it was dawn."

Not enough time for him to get to San Diego and kill the guard. She seriously doubted he would use the mayor as an alibi unless it was true. Winston would never lie for him.

Zeke started to stand up. "If that's all, chief, I'll mosey on home."

Tig motioned for him to remain seated. "How did you break your wrist?"

"Oh, this?" He held up his arm and wiggled his fingers. A stretch bandage supported it. He lowered his hand and began fiddling with his tie again. "Stupid horse I was shoeing kicked back and snapped the damn thing. Doc put a brace on it the other night, but it'll be right as rain in a few days."

He was lying about something, but she didn't see any use in pushing the issue. "One more thing. Last night, you shouldn't have asked Cerissa to dance. You're a police officer—you should know better than to risk a breach of the peace."

"It was Henry who breached the peace by stealin' Cerissa away from me." He kept flicking his tie.

"You'd had her blood?"

"Ah, not yet. But I would've." He sounded like a petulant child.

Tig leaned forward and gave Zeke what she hoped was a penetrating look. "I don't want to see you anywhere near Cerissa again." Zeke didn't respond. "Do you hear me? She's clearly chosen Henry—let it go. We don't need a problem with Leopold."

Zeke stayed silent, a sullen look on his face. She reached across and grabbed him by his tie, pulling him halfway across the table. She was tired of watching him flick the damn thing. "You won't like the outcome if you force a showdown in front of the council."

"Yes, ma'am," he said, still sounding sulky.

She continued to hold him inches from her. "You better cut the attitude. Not every community will let you moonlight. You want to keep feeding your habit, you'll toe the line."

"Ma'am?" He sounded less sure of himself. "I don't reckon I follow your drift."

She released him, giving him a firm push back into his chair. "I know about the supply you bring back from South America, the blood of your victims."

"I—"

"Don't bother to deny it. It's an open secret you have a taste for adrenaline-spiked blood. I ignore it because your activities happen far outside my jurisdiction, but I can tell you this. Not everyone is as understanding as I am. So leave Cerissa alone, if you don't want to see yourself booted off the Hill and dealing with a community that *isn't* as understanding."

She dismissed Zeke. The buzz of the station's door alarm told her he was gone, and she walked down the hall to her office. Jayden was stretched out on her couch, working on his iPad. He sat up when she walked in.

"So what happened at the council meeting?" he asked.

"About what you'd expect." She eased into her desk chair. "Henry called the mayor a fuck-up—all couched in formal language, of course.

The mayor almost flew off the dais, ready to bang the gavel on Henry's head. The rest of the council was just as bad. At one point Rolf called Cerissa a whore, and Henry almost threw the lectern at him."

"I wish I could have seen that," Jayden said. "So what stopped him?"

"Yacov. The town attorney is smart—he got Yacov to represent Henry at the hearing. It was all set up—Henry didn't have time to do anything. He couldn't get a postponement." She stretched and picked up the pen on her desk, twirling it between her long fingers. "The council couldn't let this fester. They had to come down hard on Henry, and fast, or they'd lose control of the community."

"Well, while you were at the hearing, I was doing real police work. I spoke with the detective, the one investigating the guard's death. He's invited me to drive down tomorrow and join them."

"Well done."

"And here," he said, plopping two cell phones on her desk. "No wallets, but each of the assailants had a burner phone. This one was password protected." He tapped the blue-cased phone. "The other isn't. I've finished going through it—looks like they wiped it clean before coming after Henry. We could get a warrant for the phone company, see if anything is in the cloud, but that'll take some time to process."

"I'll see if the Mordida crime lab can help us bust the password on the other one," she said, closing her eyes and leaning back. "I have to wonder whether it was Rolf who hired them."

"Why would Rolf do that? He's the one who called you."

"The same thing I said when Cerissa was shot. Rolf's best alibi was to be there and make sure the shooter was dead. By calling me, he appears to protect Henry while giving those two a head start." She felt tired, unusual as it was.

"Why don't we go home?" Jayden asked. "You could use some relaxation." There was a hint of suggestion in his voice.

She looked at the two burner phones on her desk and tossed down the pen she'd been playing with. Jayden was right. Whether she took the phones to the Mordida crime lab now or an hour from now made no difference. The night crew handled emergencies only. Something like this would be left for the day shift.

She stood, and he started to lead the way out. She reached for his hand, bringing his palm to her lips. Her fangs extended as she smiled at him. In one fast movement, she kicked the door to her office closed and pulled him into her arms.

"Tig, not here," he said, losing his smile. "We should go back to the house."

"If you don't tell anyone, I won't," she said with a playful grin. "Henry isn't the only one on the Hill who can misbehave."

She kissed the silken skin of his neck and began unbuttoning his uniform shirt, feeling him relax. Once she had him undressed, she pushed him down onto the office couch. She liked the sight of him naked, and pictured in her mind what she'd do next. A bit messy, but she could always have the upholstery steam-cleaned later.

CHAPTER 54

THE NEXT MORNING

Cerissa sat at the little table in her room, staring at her business plan, getting nowhere. She ran her fingers through her hair. *What am I going to do now?* Two weeks until Henry's hearing and the thirty-day clock was ticking on her land use application. Here she was, stuck at Gaea's house, banned from meeting with investors. She couldn't move forward with her project and she didn't know what the future held.

Last night, Leopold ordered her to stay put and wait it out. He was almost gleeful when she told him Henry was in trouble. It took all the willpower she could muster, but she honored Henry's wishes and said nothing to Leopold about the money he extorted from Henry.

But two weeks? How could she wait two weeks to see Henry? Her heart hung heavy in her chest, her mind skittering like a coin tossed onto a ceramic plate.

The doorbell rang. Dylan had left for classes, so she hurried downstairs and opened the door. A delivery guy stood on Gaea's porch bearing an arrangement of red orchids. She signed the clipboard and accepted the delivery. Only one person could have sent those orchids. After placing the vase on the nearest hallway table, she opened the small card.

My dearest Cerissa, the card began. *Please accept these as a token of my sincerest apologies for putting you at risk last night. It was poor judgment on my part. After I resolve this matter with the council, I hope we may resume where we left off. Your humble servant, Henry.*

She sank down onto the nearest chair and read the card a second time. How could she answer his message? Gaea had said she couldn't visit him. Electronic contact was also forbidden—they were probably monitoring his phone and email.

How to respond? Then it occurred to her. She took the flowers with her so Gaea wouldn't see them, and drove into town, parking her car in a lot at the local shopping mall. It wouldn't be noticed there while she was gone. She flashed to the Enclave.

"Hi, chief, I'm driving home," Jayden said, his voice projected from the speakerphone on Tig's home office desk. She could hear road noise in the background. "But I'm dead on my feet. I may grab a hotel room halfway there."

Tig understood. Caffeine could only do so much. After they had made love last night, Jayden slept four hours and then drove to San Diego. He'd been there all day, investigating the guard's death. She'd been stuck here, dead to the world. She ground her teeth and flipped the switch on her home computer. The hard drive began whirring.

"What did you learn?" she asked.

"Not much. His family knew the guard was dating someone new, had been for about six months, but they had no idea who."

"What about his apartment in Vista?"

"He lived alone. Nothing in the apartment gave us any clue as to Hoodie's identity. Whoever killed the guard got there before us."

"Things out of order?" she asked.

"Just the opposite. It was all clean and neat—too clean and neat. It just didn't feel right. Normal people leave a little mess, a little clutter."

"What about fingerprints?"

"There were five partial sets found at the apartment besides his. Three sets have been traced to family members and a friend, but the other fingerprints don't belong to anyone who's admitted to being in the apartment, and the thumbprints aren't in the DMV database either."

Tig stayed silent for a moment. Many vampires, even those living on the grid, avoided the DMV. The DMV thumb-printed drivers, making it harder to be "official"—the thumbprint would be in the system, and when they changed identities, the old one would match up with the thumbprint of the new identity. Recent improvements in fake fingerprint overlays made this less of a problem, but if they used an overlay, their real thumbprints wouldn't be in DMV records either.

"Were you able to get a copy of the unidentified fingerprints?" she finally asked.

"We're on the same wavelength. Check the file transfer directory. I uploaded them."

"Good job," she said, a warm burst of hope straightening her spine. *About time we caught a break.* She clicked the computer icon for the portal and selected the file, then started the comparison program. "Okay, V-Trak is running. Any corrupt DNA in the apartment?"

"A ton. The lab tech had a hell of a time getting his equipment to work right. Sample after sample came back corrupted."

That could only mean one thing—vampire DNA. Similar to mortal DNA, but because some sequences were bizarrely altered, the lab machines reported the sample as unreadable or corrupt.

"What about the crime scene?" she asked.

"Hang on," he said. "Have to change lanes."

She waited, tapping her fingers on the desk. The computer still hadn't finished its comparison of the fingerprints.

"Okay, I'm back," he said. "The guard's body was dumped about a mile from the prison. No fingerprints, other than the guard's, but whoever did this left behind the knife."

"The killer must think the knife can't be traced."

"Probably, or they were interrupted and got careless. What about on your end?" he asked. "Have you been able to identify the two dead vampires?"

She let out a frustrated sigh. "I've run them through all the fingerprint databases I have access to. No wants or warrants, nothing."

"But the DMV should have their human thumbprint. They were young enough."

"I know, but they're not showing up." She didn't state the obvious—the bodies may have mummified faster than Jayden could print them, altering the fingerprints. And the ones lifted from the phones were smeared partials. "When I dropped off the phone at the lab, the tech said there's a backdoor bug they may be able to exploit. It could take them a day or two to run it down and crack the password."

"What about the security listserv? Anyone recognize the photos?"

She ran her fingers through her hair, pulling at the short, tight curls. "Nothing yet. But we should give them time—it was almost sunrise when I sent out the alert."

Her computer dinged, a sign the search was finished. She switched back to V-Trak and then slammed her hand on the desk. "Damn. No fingerprint match for the guard's apartment. We're back to square one."

Henry peered into the refrigerator to see what he had in stock. Regrettably, the clone blood Cerissa had given him was now gone. He took out the oldest bag of donor blood—best to use it up first, before it got really weak.

After heating it up, he cut off the bag's corner with scissors and poured the red fluid into a tall metal coffee cup, rolling the cup between his hands, the heat warming his cold fingers.

He took a couple of sips. The chill he felt upon rising began to fade, but the blood didn't make him feel any better. The trip to the baseball game had been a fiasco. ¡Estúpido! What was he thinking? He should never have taken her to such a public place without an escort. He wrapped both hands around the warm mug and took a long, deep drink.

The touchscreen sitting on his kitchen counter controlled his downstairs stereo system. He pressed the soft key, selecting his favorite jazz music. The trumpet's mournful wail, the notes cutting through his heart, deepened his longing for Cerissa.

Using the same touchscreen, he brought up the program for his vineyard and checked the remote sensor to see how much fluid flowed in each plant's veins. He made a tiny adjustment to the irrigation system. At least his vines were doing well, even if he wasn't.

He swiped the screen again to look at his email. Nothing from Cerissa, but then, Gaea would have warned her. He stared at the message list. She had every right to be angry with him. She had been right and he had been wrong—they should have had an escort with them.

He gave up and went outside to get his mail and newspapers. He'd started to go back in when he spotted a cardboard box on the front porch. The box was labeled with his name, but didn't bear any postage. With all the recent attacks, he wasn't taking any chances when it came to strange packages. He sniffed it to make sure there was no explosive residue. It smelled faintly of Cerissa, so he took the package inside to his drawing room.

Large and rectangular, the box was maybe five inches deep. He placed the newspapers and mail on an end table. The music played in the background, and after taking another sip of blood, he put down the tall mug and popped the sealed ends off the cardboard box. He pulled out a large framed print: a stunning glossy color photo of the planet Mars, the iron-ore surface a deep reddish orange, the polar ice caps a soft white.

He had never seen this photo before, even though he had perused most of the photos available on the internet. This photo was different, the resolution so crisp the thousands of craters seemed to explode from the planet's surface, the colors vivid and intense, reminding him of flowing lava.

The corner of the matte was signed "Cerissa." On the back, an inscription dated today: "To Henry—Looking forward to many evenings stargazing together. C."

He placed the framed photo on a chair and sat down in his chair opposite it. He stared at Mars and sipped his blood. Thirteen nights seemed very far away.

The doorbell rang and his heart quickened. Could it be Cerissa? He wanted desperately to see her, but not at the risk of being banned from his own community.

When he reached the front door, he turned on the security camera and looked at the small monitor on the entryway wall. Tig stood on his front porch, holding her chief's cap in her hand. His shoulders drooped, the disappointment running off his fingertips like water. He opened the door.

"Good evening, Founder," she said. "My apologies for the intrusion, but the mayor asked me to stop by and see you."

"Then this isn't a social visit."

"No. May I come in?"

Henry stepped aside and, with a sweeping gesture, answered her.

"Are you alone?" she asked, her eyes pointed in the direction of the upstairs landing.

"I am abiding by the council's ruling, if that's what you're asking."

"Do you mind if I look around?"

"Yes, I do. But I suspect I have no choice in the matter."

"The town attorney didn't want to issue a warrant. No reason to have a warrant on your record, unless you insist."

"How thoughtful," he replied, letting the sarcasm show in his tone.

Tig strode through the entryway and into the drawing room. He followed her. "When was Cerissa last here?" she asked.

"The night of the dance."

Tig visibly sniffed the air and walked further into Henry's drawing room. "Her scent is here, but it's faint."

"I am not a liar."

"Henry, don't make this any more awkward than it already is." She walked to the far end of the drawing room and stuck her head into the adjoining library and music room.

He burned with anger over the intrusion. *An insult.* The mayor had no business sending Tig here. Then he remembered the photo, and his hot anger turned to icy fear. He quickly removed the photo from the chair.

"Please sit down, Tig." He started to turn the photo around to hide Cerissa's signature on the matte, and then remembered the note on the back. Tig would see today's date, so instead he propped it on the floor against the wall, photo forward, placing the box in front of it.

"Wait a moment." She followed him to where he stood by the photo. She moved the box away and kneeled down. "That's an amazing photograph. Mars, right?"

"Yes. It arrived today."

She looked closer. "Cerissa's name is on the matte."

"I'm sure she ordered it before the unfortunate incident at the stadium. The night of the dance I showed her Mars through my telescope."

She stood up. "You bring a lovely woman to your home and you spend the night looking at a planet? I'm learning new things about you, Founder," she said, slapping him on the shoulder.

He was in no mood to be teased. "Do what you came here for and leave."

"Lighten up, Henry. I don't care if Cerissa sent you the photo yesterday or today, or if you have her hidden away upstairs. This whole thing is politics, and you know it. I told the mayor I'd stop by and check on you. I have. I can report back that you haven't violated the council's ruling. Okay? You started to ask me to sit down. Was there something you wanted to discuss?"

The list. He'd almost forgotten the list. He returned to the fireplace mantel and picked up an envelope he'd left there. "The list you requested—people who may hold a grudge against both Yacov and me," he said, handing it to her.

She opened the envelope and slid out the single page it contained. "I wish I'd had this weeks ago."

"Yacov swore he emailed it to you long before the dance, and again afterward—and he wasn't wrong. You can see the date, and his email address is at the top of the printout."

"I never received it." She scanned the list. "Why three groups of names?"

"The first group—both Yacov and I voted against granting them permission to turn their mate vampire. The second is a list of those who wanted to move to the Hill and were denied."

"Why is Blanche on your list?" she asked.

He picked up his tall mug, considering his answer. "Do you mind if I drink while we talk? I could warm some for you."

She waved her hand. "Go ahead. I'm fine. Why Blanche?"

"I wrote in her name because the homeowners' board just voted to deny her residency." He took a long sip from his mug. "But at the time of the attacks, her application was still pending. She had no motive to attack either Yacov or myself."

"And the third group?"

"Those we ordered staked when Yacov and I were still on the council. The death penalty is not often meted out, but when it is, surviving makers or offspring may try to seek retribution."

"What about your bookie?" she asked. "Is his name on here?"

Not a question he wanted to answer, but the town attorney had finally provided an acceptable immunity agreement, so he no longer had any excuse to delay. Too bad he hadn't signed the agreement *before* the Bugles ballgame. He could have used it to get out of his house arrest. Problem was, he hadn't revealed anything to Tig yet, and the town attorney had been clear on the point.

"So?" she asked, looking at him expectantly.

"My bookie's name is Petar Petrov. We had a small problem with him, but we settled it."

"We?"

"Yacov and I. I had placed a bet for us through one of his mortal companions. She wrote down the wrong amount."

"How much?"

"She wrote fifty thousand apiece when it should have been five thousand. When we lost, Petar tried to collect the erroneous amount."

"What happened?"

"We settled it—we split the difference."

"You each paid twenty-five thousand instead of fifty thousand?"

"Exactly. Nothing worth killing over."

CHAPTER 55

THE NEXT NIGHT

Cerissa stood on the mountain plateau behind Gaea's house, looking at the valley spread out below. A series of rarely used trails ran across the mountain range, all leading to this private place, a place where she could change form when she needed to.

Like a creepy itch, staying human too long irritated her.

She had to clear her mind. A carefully worded message had been taped to her bedroom window, asking her to meet Henry here at four in the morning. She understood what he hinted at—he was coming to take her blood.

She took a deep breath, trying to release the tight pain building in her chest. Her heart longed for nothing more than to become Henry's mate.

But too many things didn't make sense. How could he get free tonight? Wasn't someone guarding him, making sure he didn't leave? That was why she hadn't used Lux technology to flash to him inside his house.

And why did he just happen to pick this location for their rendezvous? She regularly hiked up here, but she had never mentioned her habit to him.

She undressed and morphed into her native form. As a precaution, she set up electronic wards around the area to extend the reach of her contact lenses. The clearing was bordered by pine trees, and the brush became denser beyond the trees. If anyone entered the area, the wards would alert her.

Stretching her wings to their fullest, she walked to the edge of the plateau to look at the valley again. Lights dotted the landscape, the vineyards creating dark patches of shadow against the low foothills.

Her contact lenses blinked a red warning. Someone had entered the airspace above her. The soft flap of wings followed by the crunch of feet landing on pine needles—she was no longer alone.

"Hello, Ari," she said, drawing her wings back in. She had asked him to meet her here, an hour before Henry's planned rendezvous. She needed advice, badly. *Yeah, I must need it* very *badly if I'm asking him for advice on my love life.* She remained facing the Hill's valley.

"Ciss, what the hell do you think you're doing?"

"Standing on a mountain."

"I saw the video of you and Henry at the hotel room," he said. "You can't let him take your blood."

She remained facing the Hill's valley. "Why not?"

"You can't become bonded to Henry. Not until the Protectors decide what to do with the vampire communities."

She spun around to face him. "What are you talking about?"

"Ah, your assignment had special rules. You can't let a vampire bite you."

"Why? Nothing happened when I fed Leopold."

"You fed him by cutting yourself with a knife. You've never had fangs pierce your skin. From what we've figured out, fangs contain some sort of venom that's involved in the transformation to vampire. The Protectors don't know what effect it will have on you."

Her eyes got wider. "Wait a minute. You're the one who told me to seduce Henry. What did you think would happen? With vampires, sex and blood kind of go together."

"I, ah...I read your orders last night."

"You hadn't read my orders *before* this?"

"Hey, I have a lot on my plate right now. You aren't the only Watcher I'm running."

"You're too busy screwing *Ducky* to read my orders."

"Kid, you could've read them too."

"I did, but you're the one who told me to seduce him. You!" She pointed at him and fluffed out her wings. "I thought you got revised orders—how was I to know?"

"Look, the Protectors aren't sure they'll let the vampire communities survive, not if they're a threat to humanity—"

"Wait a minute. Nothing in my assignment said anything about destroying the vampire communities."

"They didn't want you to know. They thought you'd be able to do your job better if you didn't."

"What about the non-interference rule? Huh?" She raised both hands. "The least amount of interference possible—destroying all vampires sure isn't the least amount."

He looked at her like a doctor about to give bad news. "The non-interference rule only applies to humans."

Oh shit. Her stomach clenched and bile crawled up her throat, her mouth turning sour. Why hadn't she thought of that before? The Lux didn't need vampires in order to survive—they only needed humans.

"Look, Ciss, the Protectors haven't decided anything yet, but they don't want you in too deep if they have to pull the plug. You're upset, I understand—"

"But you don't understand. I can't let them hurt Henry or Leopold or Gaea or Liza or Karen or Tig or even that pompous mayor. None of them deserve to die for being what they are—or for loving who they love." She ruffled her feathers as the words fell rapidly from her mouth. "No—no, I won't let the Protectors do anything to my community."

"Your community? Just because you slept with Henry doesn't make you one of them."

True. Except the feeling ran deeper than that, and not just to her root chakra; the feeling ran straight to her heart chakra.

"Are you listening to me?" Ari demanded. "You need to take a step back."

"It's a little late for that."

"Kid, I'm sorry, but you can't get in deeper."

She turned her back on him, looking out over the Hill's valley again. A tree branch creaked—or was it the sound of her heart breaking?

"I...I won't stop seeing Henry," she finally said.

"Of course you'll stop."

She flittered the tips of her wings and turned to face Ari.

"I love him."

Ari shook his head. "Pathetic. First vampire you screw, you think it's true love."

"But I do love him."

"Kid, you need to ease up on the stabilization fluid. You're staying in human form too long. You're starting to sound like one." He raised the back of his ivory-colored wings and fanned them out, signaling his impatience. "For now, stop everything with Henry until we fix this with the Protectors."

"We can't 'fix' it with them—if you tell them now, they'll take my wings." She clutched her wings around her, her eyes wide open as it all sank in. "This is so much worse—why did you ever convince me to seduce him? Why did I listen? The Protectors are going to kill me."

"I'll do what I can to convince them otherwise, kid."

"No, you won't."

"Now, Ciss—"

She released her wings, spreading them out. If she wanted freedom to choose her own path, she had to make her own decisions, even at the risk of being wrong. "You'll keep this a tight secret until I decide what to do. The Protectors will know nothing—they can't, not yet."

"Kid, I can't keep editing your vids."

She pointed a finger at him. "You'd better, not unless you want them taking your wings, too."

"What are you talking about?"

"If my wings are on the chopping block, you'll be there right next to me. You screwed up my orders, not to mention your cover-up. You've been lying to them. What will they do when I tell them?"

"That's blackmail!" he shouted.

"You bet it is."

A sly grin formed on his pale blue face, a look of respect. "We're going to make a great team, kid."

"We don't have a choice now. Once I'm established on the Hill, maybe then we can find a way to convince the Protectors vampires aren't a threat, and get their blessing."

"I never did like following orders anyway," he said with a shrug. He reached for the watch on his blue arm, tapping it twice. "I'll see you later."

"Wait—what did you find out about Blanche?" She'd almost forgotten about her mission. Henry's house arrest had blocked everything else from her mind. She had to get back on track to protect her community from the vampire dominance movement.

"Still searching," he said. "I'm having trouble getting a handle on her, aside from the stuff Leopold gave you. She lost most of her money when the derivatives market crashed. But I'm not seeing anything in her electronic records that's suspicious. She's sort of a wanderer. Nothing stands out."

"Did she make it to San Diego?"

"Last I checked. Her cell phone signal pinged there last night."

"Keep working it."

"You got it, kiddo."

Once he blinked out of sight, she took a deep breath and let it out. She may have convinced Ari, but whatever leniency she expected from the Protectors would vanish if she let Henry take her blood. She fluttered the tips of her wings again. Could she persuade the Protectors to change their minds? Surely Henry would understand a small delay while she worked things out. And the town council—how would they react if she let Henry have her blood now? It might be better if they waited the two weeks until the council decided Henry's punishment.

Her chest constricted. It felt like someone had wrapped a tight metal band around her and was slowly twisting it tighter. She didn't want any delay. She imagined losing him, and her chest tightened even more, tears welling in her eyes.

She'd been crazy to think she could follow orders and still have her freedom. Freedom—a private code word she used for a much more heretical concept: free will.

She held up her hand to the stars, spreading her six fingers to filter their light, finding Mars and the North Star in the spaces in between. The Protectors claimed no member of the Lux had free will. About that they were wrong, she was sure of it.

But they had been right about one thing. Raising her with her human parent had changed her.

Pita. She'd briefly known her father's love. He had believed in the cycle of lives, of death and rebirth, of the journey to self-perfection and self-knowledge as a way to end the cycles. But she remembered foremost his belief in free will. *We have control over our lives and our choices can change the cycles.*

The truth showed through as brightly as the stars arrayed between her splayed fingers—the cycles had to change. She could no longer be a slave to her people, trading her obedience for their approval. Funny, how revealing herself to Henry had first caused her to acknowledge her human side. Well, it was time to claim the human part of her birthright and determine her own path in life. Her choices wouldn't be perfect, but they would be hers.

Her breath caught in her throat. Was that why her *amma* left? The Protectors had ordered *Amma* to live with *Pita* and raise her child among humans. *I wasn't her choice.* She closed her eyes as the truth sank in.

Love has to be freely given.

She closed her fingers, blocking out the starlight. She couldn't live without Henry's light, his love. If he was willing to take the risk, he could have her blood. The Protectors be damned.

The red flash of her lenses, followed by a distant crunch of someone walking through dry brush, alerted her. More footsteps? Too early to be Henry, and no flutter of wings, so Ari hadn't returned. She stretched her wings and, in one short hop, perched in one of the pine trees. She pulled her wings in tight around her. In the distance, a figure dressed in a black hoodie stopped on a higher ridge, a rifle slung over its shoulder, a backpack in the other hand.

She sniffed the air, but the person was too far away to smell. The figure crouched down behind a rocky outcropping—a vantage point from which both trail entrances to the plateau could be observed.

She let her lenses zoom in and adjust on the person's face. Shock slid through her. No, it couldn't be. What was *that* vampire doing up here?

CHAPTER 56

Tig looked incredulously at the screen of her cell phone. She wanted to throw the device across the office. "Winston, I don't have time to check on Henry again. We're on the honor system here, since no one wants to pay to house him in our jail."

They always hired a jailer, someone to feed the prisoner and oversee visiting hours. She and Jayden didn't have time for that nonsense.

"Rolf keeps bugging me." The mayor sounded irritated too. "He believes Henry is going to sneak out and visit Cerissa. He's turned into a complete idiot lately."

"I checked on Henry last night. He understands the deal. Look, I've got evidence to process from the stadium shooting and a dead guard in San

Diego. Jayden just got back—I need to debrief him. I don't have time to play nursemaid to a founder."

"Just see what you can do."

She slammed down the phone on her desk and looked up when Jayden tapped at her door. She nodded for him to enter, and slid her phone into her shirt pocket so she wouldn't forget it.

"I looked up Petar Petrov in V-Trak," she told him. "Henry's bookie isn't part of the treaty communities, so no fingerprints on file. Yacov confirmed Petar is still taking their bets. That makes it unlikely he would try to kill or kidnap them."

He stretched and relaxed back on the couch. "Are you going to interview him?"

"Yacov agreed to give me Petar's phone number, but he said it was a waste of time. According to Yacov, the way Henry bets on baseball, Petar will make triple the amount he wrote off before the season is over."

"Yeah, the home team hasn't had a winning streak lately," Jayden said, scratching at the back of his shaved head. "Got anything else?"

When did she start reporting to him? She clenched her jaw—first the mayor, now Jayden. "Zeke's alibi checked out. He didn't kill the guard."

"But we may find out who did," he said, looking smug.

She was in no mood to play guessing games. "Spit it out."

"The crime lab called while you were on the phone. They cracked the shooter's phone and emailed us a transcript. I waited to open it—figured you'd want to see it first."

About time he recognized I'm in charge. She opened the email program and clicked on the lab's email. "Hope this helps," the email read. A PDF was attached.

Jayden got up and walked behind her; she felt him reading over her shoulder. She opened the attachment to reveal a series of text messages from the night Henry and Cerissa were attacked at the stadium. She didn't recognize the phone numbers, and quickly typed a search into V-Trak. Nothing.

Her mind worked furiously to put the pieces together—as she'd suspected, someone on the Hill was the pivot point, someone in a position to know when Yacov and Henry might be vulnerable. Yet the fingerprints in the guard's apartment didn't match anyone on the Hill. She stared at the three messages again.

The first read: "Watch the Hill gate. He may be leaving without an escort. Follow and kill him."

Forty minutes later, the reply: "He's with the envoy."

And within minutes: "He's the priority. Kill them both if necessary."

The time stamp on the first message read 7:32 p.m.—a few minutes after her arrival at Gaea's to escort Cerissa off the Hill, and a good two hours before Rolf called Tig for assistance. It couldn't be Rolf—it had to be someone at Gaea's house, someone who knew Henry was leaving the Hill.

Then it dawned on her. She'd left Henry and Blanche alone on the porch when she went inside to get Cerissa's luggage.

"I was right—there are no coincidences." She darted out of her office to her clerk's desk. She heard Jayden follow her. "When did we get the portable fingerprint scanner?" she asked him.

"Ah, shortly before Yacov was shot." From the look on his face, the light bulb had gone off for him, too. "I fingerprinted Blanche and Seaton the old-fashioned way."

"Did Maggie compare their fingerprint cards to what was on file already?"

"I don't know. Maggie slipped and fell the night I fingerprinted them. I found their fingerprint cards on her desk and locked them away with the other sensitive papers." He pointed toward the file cabinet behind Maggie's desk, and then pulled a keychain out of his pocket, dangling it from his fingertips before tossing it to her.

She caught the chain and inserted the key, popping open the file cabinet's lock. She rummaged through the unfiled paperwork and pulled out two fingerprint cards. She slapped the first one onto the flatbed scanner behind Maggie's desk. "Just what the council gets for being cheap," she said. "They should have paid to have someone replace Maggie while she's on medical leave."

The white light traveled the edge of the scanner cover—when it stopped, she opened the cover and repeated the process with the second card. After opening V-Trak on Maggie's computer, she imported the fingerprints for Blanche and Seaton, typing in the date they were taken, and then started the program to compare the new card to Blanche's existing set in V-Trak. Jayden waited quietly, perched on the desk next to her.

"Bingo," he said, when "NO MATCH" appeared on the screen, right next to Blanche's fingerprints.

Tig shook her head, and started the program to run a comparison of Blanche's real fingerprints to the fingerprints found in the guard's apartment. "Blanche probably had a fake set entered into V-Trak years ago."

"But wouldn't one of the other communities have discovered that by now?" Jayden asked.

"Few security heads will demand a new print card like I do. If the photo matches what they have in V-Trak, they don't question it. I got burned a few years ago. Since then, I require a full print card for all new vampires on the Hill, including guests."

Jayden frowned. "I bet Blanche was the one who messed with Maggie's desk, trying to steal the real fingerprint card. Zeke told me he hadn't touched anything."

"The sidewalk Maggie tripped on was slick with oil," she said. "Blanche may have poured oil on the sidewalk to make it slick so Maggie would slip. That would have delayed the comparison of Blanche's fingerprints."

"No way to prove it, but you're probably right." He looked puzzled for a moment, and picked up the paperwork that had been attached to the fingerprint card, studying something on it. He ran back to her office, and then returned. "The phone number texting their orders—it's not Blanche's number."

"Maybe she had a burner phone too. If her prints match the guard's apartment, we'll have enough evidence to justify searching her belongings for it."

The computer program's hourglass stopped spinning, replaced with the word "MATCH."

She exhaled sharply. "Blanche was in the guard's apartment. She was probably Hoodie—she fits the body type. I need to warn Gaea."

"Blanche isn't at Gaea's anymore. She left the night after the dance."

"Where was she headed?"

"Got it right here," he said, searching through the clerk's desk. He pulled out the departure guest form. "She wrote 'San Diego community.'"

Tig checked the time on her cell phone—a little after three in the morning. "Too late to fly there tonight." If she left now, she'd be lucky to get to downtown San Diego by six in the morning. Not enough time to put Blanche under arrest and find a safe place to sleep during the day. "I'll call the head of security for San Diego and get him to put Blanche in chains."

"What about Seaton?" Jayden asked.

"Just to be safe, let me check." She ran Seaton's scanned prints against what was in V-Trak. They matched. "Gaea told me her idiot lodger plays video games all night. Call her anyway and give her a heads-up, just in case, while I call San Diego."

Her cell phone buzzed. She looked at the caller ID—the 911 switchboard was transferring a call. She clicked the phone's accept button. "Yes?"

"I've got Rolf Müller on the line, report of a mountain lion on the low ridge."

"Did he see it?"

"Yes, ma'am. It ran off into the brush headed in the direction of Henry's place. He's asking whether he should get his rifle and follow it."

"Tell him to put his guns away. I'm on my way." She couldn't let him shoot a specially protected species. If the animal was GPS-tagged, state officials would descend on them, looking for it. She couldn't afford the distraction now—not with everything else going on.

She slapped the phone into her pocket and sprinted to the armory cabinet. She wished Rolf had seen a wolf instead—if it was one of the usual suspects, one of the vampires who liked to run the hills, she'd have an easier time resolving the matter. Instead, she was dealing with a real wild animal.

She grabbed an air rifle from the cabinet, took a tray of darts loaded with a heavy animal tranquilizer from a nearby refrigerator, and headed for the door. Jayden followed her outside.

"Mountain lion spotted over by Henry's place," she told him.

Damn. Why did everything have to happen at once? Given the bad blood between Zeke and Henry, she didn't want to send Zeke to Henry's house. She couldn't call Liza either—the councilwoman was out of town, and Rolf couldn't be trusted not to go all big-game hunter and kill it. *If I don't take care of this now, everyone will have their rifle out, it'll be a free-for-all out there, and some poor mortal will get hurt.*

"You want company?" Jayden asked.

"No, I can handle this." She climbed into the police van. "You call Gaea, warn her. I'll take care of Blanche and the lion."

She drove in the direction of Henry's house and phoned her counterpart in San Diego. He told her Blanche hadn't shown up yet, but if she arrived, he promised to take her into custody.

She called Jayden and warned him—Blanche was still on the loose. "Put out an APB to the treaty communities, and send a reverse-911 message to all Hill residents, warning them, then double the guard at the gate. I want the wall patrolled, too; call Rolf and Zeke, and have them organize it. No way is Blanche getting back in."

Once Jayden hung up, she told the van's voice-controlled phone, "Dial Henry."

"Good evening, Tig," Henry answered.

At least his tone was cordial this time. "I'm on my way over to your house. Rolf spotted a mountain lion on the ridge. It may be making its way in your direction."

"I have no intention of going outdoors, since I'm still under house arrest."

"I didn't want to surprise you. I'm going to park in your driveway and hike up the dirt road on your property, try to dart it before it hurts someone."

"Very well. Then I wish you a good hunt."

She heard the click—he didn't wait for her to respond. Her skin was thick enough that it didn't bother her, but she had meant to brief him on Blanche. It probably didn't matter. In a few minutes, he'd see the reverse-911 alert as a text message, telling him Blanche was behind the attacks.

But too much about it didn't make sense. Why was the guard killed? To silence him, or had someone else killed him as revenge for being Blanche's tool? She thought again of Yacov. How long had he stayed at the dance? She couldn't recall when he left.

She shook her head. It was unthinkable. Yacov was an honorable man—he wouldn't have killed the guard. No, the guard must have been killed to silence him, to hide Blanche's involvement. Even if Blanche altered his memory, the gaps would be evident to anyone who knew the truth and questioned him.

Still, it bothered Tig. She couldn't believe the young vampire was working alone, Blanche wasn't experienced enough to pull this off. Sure, Blanche was desperate to get into a community, and she needed money, but how did killing Yacov and Henry accomplish that? The founders voted five-zip to reject her application for residency—eliminating two votes did nothing for her.

Phat's demand for perfection had taught her to dig deeper, to not accept surface answers. One missed detail could wreck a plan or cost a life. So what was she missing?

"Probably a lot," she mumbled to herself. Hill residents worked too hard to keep their secrets from her. If she had all the facts they hid, she just might be able to piece it together.

She slowed the police van when she turned up Henry's driveway. She'd done everything she could to keep her community safe. A good run chasing the mountain lion would give her a chance to clear her head and try to make sense of Blanche's senseless act.

Henry angrily tossed his cell phone onto the kitchen table. He strode into the drawing room, threw open the drapes, and turned on the outside floodlights. The pool area was now brightly lit. The light should discourage the wayward cat from coming near his home. He didn't object to the *pumas* who populated his mountainside; they'd lived in the area long before he was born. But he resented this one.

With tonight's mail, another unstamped delivery arrived. This time, it was a single-page letter, and it looked like Cerissa had used a standard laser printer:

Dear Henry,
Meet me at the plateau on the mountain behind Gaea's house, where the trail behind her vineyard ends, at 4 a.m. tonight. Gaea usually watches television around that time, so I should be able to slip out without her seeing me. We have something we must do.

His heart quickened when he read it the first time. Unsigned, but it had to be from Cerissa. He'd sniffed the stationery and caught her scent.

She was right. He had to take her blood before the next council meeting. The mayor had forwarded an email to him with the message: "Thought you should know." Below the mayor's comment was an email from Rolf, blaming Cerissa for what happened and demanding they throw her off the Hill.

They couldn't ban her once Henry had her blood. It was a risk worth taking. Besides, the council wouldn't have to know right away. This was just a precaution, in case things went sideways at the next hearing.

He shook his head. Now he had to wait for Tig to leave. He stood there staring at the pool house. He had opened his heart to Cerissa—both in bed and out—and then screwed it up by taking her to the ballgame without an escort.

A movement caught his eye. The cat was running across the lawn, its long, loping stride taking it in the direction of the pool house. Should he get his rifle? No, with Tig out there somewhere, he didn't want to risk even a temporary injury to the chief.

He watched the large blonde *puma* slink through the shadows, along the bushes by the pool house, then through the gazebo. It hesitated. To come closer to the house, the cat had to pass across the brightly lit patio. His eyebrows shot up when he saw the cat's next move. It ran around the pool and up onto his back steps. Swishing its black-tipped tail this way, then that, it came close to the windowpanes of his French doors. He could see the black outline of its coral-colored nose pressed up against the glass, its golden luminescent eyes peering in at him.

Who knew what the cat was thinking? At the sound of Tig's van pulling into his driveway, the *puma* took off at a run. He considered returning to the kitchen to retrieve his phone and call Tig. He should tell her the direction it went, but something stopped him. For some inexplicable reason, he found himself rooting for the cat.

CHAPTER 57

The drawing room's mantel clock chimed the hour, telling Henry what his body already sensed: another impending dawn. He closed the book he was reading, opened the small drawer in the end table, and placed the book in it. His phone still sat in the kitchen, his email unread. He should really check it before going to sleep. Reluctantly, he stood up from his comfortable chair.

The doorbell rang; his email would have to wait. The last time he had looked, Tig's van sat parked in his driveway, effectively trapping him at home. At least she'd had fun tonight. He would have, too, if it hadn't been for that damn cat. He hoped Cerissa wasn't angry with him. She had to know it wouldn't be easy to meet.

The doorbell rang again. Tig must be impatient. Then again, it was close to dawn, so her impatience was understandable.

Moving soundlessly, his slippers gliding across the entryway's burnt-orange tile, he cinched up his bathrobe belt. Certainly Tig would forgive his informality. There was no crime in being comfortable in his own home.

As he swung open the door, he said, "How went the hunt—"

A loud bang cut off the rest of his words.

Fire shot through his belly. Pain. Agony. Silver.

Four more shots, each shot causing fire to shoot through a different part of his gut. He dropped to his knees in front of a masked shooter, the barrel of the gun moving in the direction of his heart.

He lunged at the knees in front of him. The shooter fell backward, sprawled on his porch. Henry crawled toward the gun and grabbed for it, but blackness closed around him.

Tig tracked the mountain lion to the ridge above Henry's vineyard before following it to the foothills behind Gaea's place, and then she lost it. With any luck it would keep going to a higher elevation and back into the wilderness. She sat down cross-legged on one of the large rocks and focused on the remaining question: what motive did Blanche have for killing Yacov or Henry?

The young vampire had nothing personal to gain by their deaths. And Yacov and Henry's list—none of Blanche's relatives were on it; no one on the list was connected to her. Then again, she could be working for someone else.

Hmm. Were the attacks politically motivated? An act of terror? An act of war?

A faint first glow of morning appeared in the east, easier to see at this elevation. *Time to get going.* She stood up, dusting off her pants. If she jogged down the trail past Gaea's house, she would make it home in time, but there was one problem—she'd left her police van at Henry's house. Should she return to get it?

She shook her head. Not enough time. She looked at the trail leading past Gaea's, and took it. No harm in leaving the van behind. Jayden could pick it up after sunrise.

Henry opened his eyes to see a gun pointed at his heart. "If you want something done right," a woman said, "do it yourself."

She removed her mask and took out a phone.

"Blanche," Henry croaked.

"It won't be long. Just need to prove it was me." Using her phone's camera, she fired off a few photos of him lying on the Spanish pavers covering his porch, and then turned around to take a selfie standing over him.

"There, sent." She smiled at him, the same stupid, coy smile she'd used on him before. "What, didn't ya want to see your girlfriend?" she asked, leaning over him. "I never took you for a chicken. But when you didn't show up—"

"You wrote the note?" Henry asked, his voice raspy.

"I even stole a piece of Cerissa's underwear from her laundry basket before I left Gaea's. Rubbed it on the page—betcha it fooled even the great Henry Bautista."

He convulsed and doubled over on his side. He panted a few breaths to control the pain. "Why?" he gasped.

"Don't think by keeping me talking, Tig'll show up to rescue you. She's on the other side of the mountain by now, chasing some stupid mountain lion." Blanche stuffed the mask and phone into her back pocket. "But the answer to your question is simple: revenge."

Then he caught a sound, the rustle of leaves in the oak grove by his garage. Someone was there. Why hadn't Blanche heard it?

"Revenge?" Henry asked with great effort.

She laughed. "Don't you get it? With your death, the wars will start again."

He started coughing, tasting his own blood on his lips. "Wars?"

"Yeah, wars." She pulled a piece of paper from her pocket and shoved it into his bathrobe pocket. "Thanks to this email, everyone will believe New York is behind this. The shooters I hired were supposed to carry the same email from Leopold, but the stupid idiots couldn't even get that right."

"Leopold ordered my death?"

She spat on the ground. "You are dumb, aren't ya? Leopold isn't involved. I spoofed his email address, but everyone will think he ordered you killed. That email will make sure of it. I was gonna kill Cerissa too, make it look like she tried to kill you on his orders, but this will have to do."

"Who—"

"Listen up. I'm never going hungry again. Not this girl. And I'm not going to work my ass off pretending to be mortal, playing by the rules you and the others like you forced on the rest of us. Hypocrites. You know what Leopold said to me when I came to him for a loan to try and dig myself out after losing everything to those stupid derivatives? He offered to give me a *job*. A *job*! Fucking asshole. Well, now he won't be laughing."

"But he offered to help...." Henry stopped, the pain tearing through him.

"Work? You think that's help? You made your fortunes stealing from mortals, but no, we can't. So tell me, how many humans did you kill to get rich before the treaty was signed?"

"I didn't kill anyone for money."

A twig snapped in the oak grove. She didn't seem to notice it. Who was there?

"Yeah, right," she said. "Well, fuck you and your treaty. We're going to shred the damn thing and replace it with something better."

"We?"

"I'm going to be one of the Brethren, one of the ones served by mankind."

Brethren. Not a name he knew, but something clicked, something Cerissa said. The vampire dominance movement—was it real?

Blanche pointed her gun in the direction of the town hall. "What you built—you had the right idea. You just didn't go far enough, you and the others like you, a bunch of weak, tame bloodsuckers. We were always meant to be in charge, not just inside your walls, but out there." She swung her arm around to point at Mordida. "You might as well bring a cow into your house and give ole Bossy her own room. Mortals should be our prey, not our partners."

The woods were silent again. Who was in the oak grove and why didn't they do something?

"Will you allow me a final prayer?" he whispered, doing the only thing his fuzzy brain could think of to stall for time. With great effort, his hand moved to the chain at his neck. He pulled it out and displayed the crucifix.

"Go ahead," she said. "But make it quick, unless you'd rather roast to death when the sun's rays hit you."

He wrapped his hand around the cross and closed his eyes. He began David's Psalm, the one about shepherds and not fearing death. He no longer feared death.

By the fourth verse, the Psalm on his lips became blurry, his brain struggling against the effects of the silver, the pain in his gut cutting the words from his mind. He heard the rustle of movement again, followed by a low growl. A gun fired. Blanche's scream told him all he needed to know. Someone had come to his rescue. Perhaps too late to save his life, but at least Blanche would die, too. He took a breath, just to know what it felt like one last time, and commended his soul to God.

"Henry, wake up, please, wake up."

Cerissa's voice. What was Cerissa doing here? *If Tig catches her here, the council will cast her out for good. I can't let—*

The searing pain reached his brain, stopping all thought, waking him to the present. His eyes blinked open, and he focused on the wrought-iron chandelier above him. No memory of being moved to his foyer. Cerissa knelt next to him, naked, her bare arms streaked with blood. *My blood.*

He turned his head. Blanche lay on the tiles nearby. Bloody drag marks led from the open door to Blanche's body.

"Please, Henry," Cerissa said, her voice finally making sense. "What should I do? I removed the bullets. Will that be enough? They don't teach this kind of thing in medical school. What do you need?"

Henry lifted his head—his bathrobe was open and someone had played tic-tac-toe with a knife on his stomach. The incisions, made where each bullet entered, still burbled blood, coating his skin. A thin, sharp kitchen knife, one he used to gut fish, lay next to him on the floor. His silk boxer shorts, the ones with the pink flamingos, were coated dark red. He'd never intended for Cerissa to see them. *Oh well, too late now.*

Her bloodstained fingers held up a silver bullet. "I took out all five slugs. I counted the shells just to be sure." She placed the bullet on the floor next to Blanche. "What do I do now? Will your skin close on its own, or do I need to stitch the holes?"

At first the words wouldn't come out. She must have sensed what he needed, and looked at her own wrist. She hesitated—her front teeth bit into her lower lip and her face struggled with some unspoken emotion. Why didn't she want to give him her blood? Whatever caused her uncertainty, he knew she'd come to a decision when her green eyes met his again. She wiped off the knife on his bathrobe and opened a vein in her wrist, holding it over his lips.

Not exactly the way he'd planned to take her blood, but right now he couldn't be picky. He sucked deeply, gratefully, feeling the metallic tang wet his voice.

"Call Yacov," he whispered against her wrist. "I need his blood."

"Rolf is closer."

"Rolf is too young. Yacov's blood is stronger; it will heal silver necrosis. Bring me my cell phone…kitchen table…I should make the call." He pushed her wrist aside, and Cerissa sprinted toward the kitchen.

He looked over at Blanche. The teeth of a large animal had ripped out Blanche's throat, the claws splitting her body open from neck to belly. Blanche's still-beating heart had been scooped out, and lay on the tile floor next to her. The sinewy organ gasped with each pump like a waterless goldfish. The jagged edge of the aorta's floppy tube jiggled with the effort. Until someone put a stake through it, Blanche wouldn't die her final death.

Cerissa rounded the corner at a run and skidded on the slick blood, dropping to her knees next to him again. She handed him the phone.

The call to Yacov didn't take fifteen seconds.

"He's on his way," Henry said. He held out the phone for her to take, but it slipped from his fingers. She caught it.

"Where is Tig?" he asked, assuming she had been the one who butterflied Blanche's chest.

"She's not here."

"She left?" He continued to stare at the damage done to Blanche's body.

"No," Cerissa said, hesitating. "Tig's up on the mountain."

Then who attacked Blanche? And what brought Cerissa here in time to perform surgery? He couldn't figure it out.

"Why are you here?" he asked weakly.

"I received a letter from you."

"It wasn't from me," he said. Pain shot through him, and he held his breath until it passed. "Blanche sent it. I got one, too."

"I knew something wasn't right." She used a finger to hook her hair behind one ear, leaving a smear of blood on her jaw in the process. "I was on the mountain, waiting for you, when Blanche arrived with a rifle. After an hour, she left, hiking in this direction. That's why I followed her. When she took the trail to your house, I came down the dirt road by Rolf's vineyard so she wouldn't see me."

"You hiked that distance? I don't see how…." His throat dried up again. Reaching for her arm, he reopened the wound with his tongue and drank the precious liquid again until his voice returned. He didn't understand what had happened—the mountain range was ten miles of steep trails and rough terrain. Cerissa couldn't have hiked that far.

"Explain," he finally whispered.

"Tig is tenacious. I couldn't hang around to warn you. She kept following me, so I led her near Blanche's hiding spot, but Tig didn't sense her presence."

"Tig was consumed by the hunt—it blocks out all other scents."

"Tell me about it. I finally gave her the slip and flew down here. I wish I'd gotten here sooner."

"Flew? You flew?" He took a few more pulls on her wrist.

"Then I had to change back to being a cougar—I couldn't attack her in my native form."

His eyes widened as he understood what Cerissa was telling him. He released her wrist. "You were the *puma*? You said you aren't a werewolf—"

"No, Henry, I'm not a were-anything. I'm your guardian angel." She smiled down at him. "Third time I've saved your life now."

"Do not joke. Tell me the truth."

"I am."

The sky, visible through the open doorway, turned lighter—no time to discuss it now. "You should leave before Yacov arrives," he said.

"Not until I know you're all right."

"You have done all you can. Yacov—his blood—he is old. It will cure my wounds."

"What if the silver had gone through your heart?"

"We would not be having this conversation." He glanced over at Blanche, whose disembodied heart still pulsed. Why hadn't Cerissa rendered the death blow?

Cerissa bit her lip again. "I should stay until he arrives."

"No. I can explain this somehow, but not if you're here. The ban, it complicates things." Why had she dragged Blanche in here? Now the tiles would have to be scrubbed clean. "We will not turn the body over to Tig. Yacov will accept my white lie, but Tig would not. So you must be gone, and Yacov will destroy Blanche's heart."

He closed his eyes. His head spun, his focus fading. Had she said she flew here? Or had he imagined that part? Nothing made any sense. It didn't matter. Her blood was inside him—she was his now. The council couldn't take her away.

"I love you," she said, squeezing his hand tightly. "Henry? Open your eyes." She patted his cheek, her voice rising. "Are you okay? Henry? Please don't die. Please."

His lids slowly fluttered, until he was looking into her beautiful eyes again. "Don't fear, *mi amor*. I will live forever."

"You'd better."

That brought a weak smile to his lips. He reached up to touch her face. "In two weeks we will be together, and no one will be able to separate us."

"You better believe it," she said. "I didn't save you to lose you."

He raised her wrist to his lips and kissed the red wound, tasting her blood on his lips one more time. He released his grip, and she held up her wrist so he could see. The cut began to fade, the skin smoothing out, the blood disappearing.

She smiled at him, her sunny smile that meant everything to him.

The sound of a car turning from the road to climb his driveway—she couldn't be here when Yacov arrived.

"Go. Now," he commanded with all the authority he could muster. "And leave the door open for Yacov."

She leaned over him and kissed his forehead. A sense of peace washed over him, warming him to his core.

"Be well," she said.

He watched her walk away. Still naked, she paused at the door and looked back at him. Then she was gone. Long white wings trailed to the ground behind her as she strode off.

Wings? *No, not possible.* She'd called herself his guardian angel— *No, my mind must be playing tricks on me.*

He tried to sit up so he could see her again, bracing himself on his elbow. If he did die, he wanted the last thing he saw to be her.

There she was, walking across his lawn. Gracing her shoulders were beautiful, long white wings, just like the angels wore, the angels painted by the Renaissance masters. She raised them, took another step, and was gone.

He lay back down on the cold tile floor, satisfied over seeing Cerissa one last time. Or would sunrise be the last thing he saw? He watched the sherbet-pink glow begin over the garage buildings. He had missed seeing the sun.

The lingering tranquility brought on by her kiss began to fade. Perhaps Yacov wouldn't make it in time and the sun's rays would reach him here on the floor, ending it all. There were many reasons he deserved to die. If he just let go, he would fall into the dark abyss for all eternity.

But what will happen to Cerissa?

Cerissa. His heart expanded and gave a slow *ka-thub*. He loved her; he couldn't lose her now. His mind took a step away from the edge, away from the darkness, away from oblivion, and he whispered a short prayer of gratitude.

After all, with Cerissa in his life, his final walk through the valley of death could wait.

CHAPTER 58

Cerissa didn't go far. She had to make sure Henry was all right. Perched in one of the large oak trees by Henry's garage, she watched Yacov arrive and enter, pulling the door closed behind him, shutting out the impending dawn. A few quick flaps of her wings and she stood on Henry's porch, her ear pressed against the heavy wooden door.

"What happened?" Yacov asked.

"Blanche shot me. Silver. I need your blood."

"Of course, my friend."

Silence fell. Yacov must be feeding him. She ran her thumb over the place in her wrist where Henry had taken her blood. She brought her wrist to her mouth, kissing the spot his lips had wrapped around. Sure, she'd used the knife instead of letting him bite her. What if fang venom sent her into a deep sleep or made her ill? She couldn't take that risk, not with his life on the line.

There would be plenty of time later to experiment. They were blood mates now. No one could change that—not even her people.

But her immediate concern was Henry's recovery. Would he really be all right? Yacov was the only person with him. The house wasn't monitored, or someone working for Tig would have arrived by now. If Henry followed his usual pattern, he'd sleep in the basement. She had stayed in cougar form to follow Blanche. While she was sans clothes, her wristwatch had stayed on during her trek across the mountain. She glanced at it. Another twelve minutes before the sun fully rose. There was time.

Henry took another deep pull, feeling grateful for his close friendship with Yacov. A sizzling-cold energy zapped through him, his skin tightening as the wounds closed and the pain in his abdomen muted.

"Are the bullets still in you?" Yacov asked.

Henry didn't stop gulping the savory fluid. His fingers swept the cold floor on which he lay, encountering the sticky pool of his own blood. He pointed to where the bullets lay on the floor next to a knife.

Yacov nodded. "Perhaps you should stop now. I don't need any more offspring."

His friend was right. He couldn't risk going through the turn again and ending up a weak fledgling. He released Yacov's arm. "Thank you," he said. "The sun is almost up. You should sleep here."

"Have you called Tig?"

He had no intention of reporting this to the chief. "I cannot."

"But it was self-defense." Yacov looked uncertain, and his eyes slid toward the knife on the floor. "Wasn't it?"

"Cerissa was here. Tig cannot know."

"Aha," Yacov said. "I thought I smelled the scent of another person."

"Tig knows Cerissa's scent."

Yacov's face bore a look of gentle reprimand that Henry knew all too well. "My friend, you must do the right thing and report this. Cerissa's presence is a small matter, one that Tig will overlook."

Henry didn't think Tig would forgive him that easily, but that wasn't the real reason. "I do not want Tig seeing the body."

"You shouldn't be ashamed," Yacov replied, patting Henry's shoulder. "The beast comes out when we're threatened. I know all too well."

Henry shook his head. Yacov may think he was the one who ripped out Blanche's heart, but Tig wouldn't be as easy to fool. She'd test the fur on the body, find no corrupt vampire DNA, and want to know why. He couldn't explain it—hell, he didn't understand it himself.

"Tig cannot see this," he said, shaking his head.

"Hmm." Yacov leaned over Blanche's body, looking more closely at the teeth marks. "You don't want anyone knowing that you can still transform into a wolf?"

"Er—"

"Trust me. We can fix this." Yacov reopened the wound in his wrist and started to pour his blood onto Blanche's throat and chest.

"Put the heart back in first."

"Wouldn't it be better if we just staked it?"

"If we're going to tell Tig, she will want to question Blanche."

Yacov looked thoughtful. "You could be right." He spread the ribcage, picked up the heart, and dropped it in, then pushed the ribs into place. Blood from his wrist hit the shredded skin, causing it to knit together. The claw marks and other signs of an animal attack were soon erased. "There. Satisfied?"

He nodded his agreement. Tig might still find animal hair on the body, but it wouldn't be her focus with the wounds gone. He rolled to his knees and, with some difficulty, stood and adjusted the belt of his bathrobe. He reached for the foyer cabinet, opening the door to retrieve a cable made of silver from among the weapons he kept there. The silver cable was covered in plastic so it wouldn't hurt his hands. He tried to lift it, but just as quickly dropped it, falling to his knees again, still too weak to handle the deadly metal, even wrapped.

Yacov retrieved the silver cable and bound Blanche in it. Once she was tied tight, he picked her up. "Do you have a refrigerator we can toss her in? Can't leave her out here all day."

"The game room." He slowly stood. His head spun a bit, and his feet were unsteady beneath him, but he managed to lead Yacov to the spare refrigerator. Yacov removed the empty trays, folded up Blanche, and stuffed her in, dialing the thermostat cold enough to preserve fresh meat.

"Yacov," Henry said, feeling the tug of dawn pull at him. He leaned up against the wall, and Yacov slipped an arm under his, helping him downstairs into the basement when the sharp pain in his side returned. Each slow step reminded him he owed Cerissa his life.

When they reached the corridor carved from the granite bedrock underneath his house, Henry slipped a key ring out of his bathrobe pocket, fumbling for the one that would open an empty crypt. Yacov caught the keys before they fell from his hand.

"I'll call Tig before I sleep," Yacov said, patting his back reassuringly. "It will all work out."

Henry pointed to the right key, and Yacov slid it into the lock of the guest door. "Good sleep, my friend," he said, handing Henry the ring of keys before disappearing inside.

After a couple of tries, Henry managed to open the door to his own crypt. Once inside, he threw the deadbolt and leaned with his head on the closed steel door. He couldn't let Tig find out what Cerissa was; he had to come up with a believable story, a story to protect his beloved from Tig's inquisitive mind. But how could he explain the unexplainable? He had to find a way. *He must.*

The cold metal door provided no answer. His eyelids became heavy, and he pushed away from the door, wishing he had time to change out of his blood-soaked bathrobe.

"Henry, are you okay?"

His eyes opened wide. "Cerissa?"

She stood there in human form, naked and smiling at him. *My beloved.*

"Flash technology," she said, pointing to her wristwatch before rushing to put her arms around him. She'd zeroed in on his precise location by tracking her own blood, which now flowed through his veins. "I had to know you were all right."

He leaned against her. "Keep your voice down. Yacov is across the hall."

She supported him as he stumbled over to a small cot. "Is that what you sleep on?" she asked. "We'll need a king-size bed at least." She took a quick glance around the small crypt. "Well, maybe a queen-size bed."

He sat down heavily on the cot. "You will not be sleeping here."

"Why not?"

"A well-fed tiger is not a threat. A hungry tiger—"

"You're no threat to me."

"You cannot be here when I wake. You will leave before then."

It was so cute, the way he gave orders—like she was *ever* blindly following anyone's orders again. She untied the leather string that held his long black hair. He lay back onto the cot, folding his hands across his chest.

She moved his hands aside and opened his bathrobe. "Let me check your wounds."

The damage was already healing. She ran her fingers across his taut stomach muscles, tracing the pink lines where she'd removed the bullets, to the edge of his silk boxers…

"Enough," he said, stopping her hand. "I need to sleep."

He wrapped his hand around her head and pulled her close for a soft kiss. Her core warmed with anticipation, but now wasn't the time.

She rolled onto her side, her head on his shoulder, and cuddled in close. His arms wrapped around her.

"Promise me you'll leave before dusk," he said groggily.

She took a deep breath and let it out. "Yes, Henry, I will."

She'd humor him this time. Besides, she didn't want to run into Yacov.

It was then she noticed it. He'd become very still, frozen, really, as he fell into the deep sleep of the dead. Something fiercely protective swirled within her at his vulnerability. When he awoke, she'd be gone, as promised, but soon, she intended to never leave his side again. No matter who commanded otherwise.

"I love you," she whispered in his sleeping ear.

She liked the feel of those words on her lips.

CHAPTER 59

Dawn was minutes away. Tig jogged up to her house, still carrying the unfired dart gun. What was Jayden doing outside? Dressed only in pajama bottoms, he had the phone pressed to his ear. Someone must have woken him up.

He ended the call and said, "You were right. Blanche was behind the attack on Henry."

"What happened?" She walked past him into the house. She didn't have much time.

"They caught Blanche," he said.

"San Diego?"

"No, that was Yacov on the phone. Blanche shot Henry—"

She whirled around to face him. "She what?"

Jayden held up his palms. "He's okay, don't worry. Yacov stopped Blanche in time, and now she's locked inside Henry's spare refrigerator."

"How did Blanche get back in?"

He ran a hand across his head. "Yacov didn't know. I'll check with the gate guards, see what happened."

Her eyelids began to droop. Not much time left—she had to get to her sleep room before the sun rose. She turned to climb the stairs to the second floor. Jayden followed her.

"Why didn't Yacov call me?"

"Your cell phone went to voicemail. He got routed to me through the switchboard."

I was probably in a dead zone. Shit.

"By the time you wake up," he added, "I'll have a better idea what happened."

She stopped at the door to her sleep room and threw it open. "I should have posted guards on Henry and Yacov."

"Yeah, like the council would have agreed to that expense. Don't blame yourself."

He gripped her shoulder, the type of touch intended to comfort. Instead, it just upped her own anger at herself. She dropped the dart gun in the corner, the butt of the gun making a loud *thump*.

"Follow up on whatever you find out," she said. "And write up a staff report. Ask the council to approve security cameras along the walls. They like paying for toys—well, now's the time. The proposals are all on my desk."

"You got it."

At least she could depend on him while she lay helpless during the day. Thank the ancestors for that. She stretched out on her bed, not bothering to change clothes.

And sat up just as suddenly. "Do you think Blanche came in through the mountains?"

"It's possible…"

"We'll need security cameras along the mountain trails, too."

"I'll add it to the staff report."

She lay back down. "And look through that damn paperwork on Blanche. I want to know everything about her, starting with every community she's visited since she went broke."

"I got it, Tig." He stayed standing at the door. "You still think Blanche was working for someone else?"

"Blanche had the imagination of a mouse tick. I'll know more after I talk with Henry and Yacov, but I'd bet my badge she was." Tig closed her eyes, the impending dawn dragging her down. "Oh, and send someone to pick up the police van at Henry's. I left it parked there."

The sound of Jayden's footsteps was followed by his warm lips on hers. Too soon, his lips left hers.

"You can't be perfect all the time, Tig," he whispered. "Let go and let me help."

"But this is what happens when I'm not perfect," she said. Just what Phat had said each time she screwed up.

"No one died. You're doing everything you can. We'll figure this out together."

His words eased a little of her self-blame. He was more than her mate—he was her partner, someone she could trust and rely upon. She fought the lethargy and ran her fingers along the muscular bulge of his bicep, the spark of arousal mixing with longing.

His lips touched hers again, and then she heard his key turning, locking her in for the day. He was right. She had carried Phat around in her head for too long. She couldn't be perfect all the time. She'd heard it before—what was the new saying?

Progress, not perfection.

And once she had Blanche in her hands, there would definitely be progress.

Author's Comments
and Upcoming Events

Thank you for taking the time to read *Dark Wine at Midnight*. I hope you enjoyed it.

Book 2 in the Hill Vampire series, *Dark Wine at Sunrise*, is slated for publication this coming winter. *Sunrise* will pick up with Tig's attempt to get the truth out of Blanche, while Henry and Cerissa fight to overcome the obstacles standing in the way of their romance. But it gets more complicated for all of them when a serial killer starts taking victims in a neighboring city. Is it a vampire addicted to adrenaline-spiked blood, or is there something deeper and darker at work?

Want to be among the first to know *Sunrise's* release date, and receive special announcements, exclusive excerpts, and other FREE fun stuff? Join Jenna Barwin's VIP Readers and receive Jenna Barwin's Newsletter by subscribing online at: https://jennabarwin.com/jenna-barwins-newsletter/

And if you enjoyed *Dark Wine at Midnight*, please consider telling your friends or posting a short review on your favorite online retailer or review site. Word of mouth and reviews are an author's best friend and much appreciated.

Although this book has been through many rounds of editing, it's always possible for errors to slip through in the publishing business. If you find errors, or have any comments about the book you want to share with me personally, please contact me at: https://jennabarwin.com/contact.

You can also find me at:
Facebook: https://www.facebook.com/jennabarwin/
Twitter: @JennaBarwin https://twitter.com/JennaBarwin
Instagram: JennaBarwin https://www.instagram.com/jennabarwin/

ACKNOWLEDGEMENTS AND DEDICATIONS

To my husband Eric—thank you for your support and all you do to make my life as a writer easier.

To my early beta readers—Kay, Marie, Patty and Luanne—thank you for putting up with my learning curve, and for your gentle suggestions and re-directions.

To my editing team—it takes a team to polish a story and ready it for readers. Katrina, Katie, Arran, and Trenda—you all were fantastic! Any errors in grammar, clarity or plot are mine, not theirs. Their full names and/or business names are:

• Katrina Diaz
• Katie McCoach, KM Editorial
• Arran McNicol
• It's Your Story Content Editing

And my book cover designer, Momir Borocki, did an outstanding job on the cover design.

There are many other wonderful people who have helped me improve my writing, and also helped me tackle the business of being a writer. The generosity of other writers, who have freely shared their expertise, is greatly appreciated. Thank you everyone, for your support and help!

Printed in Poland
by Amazon Fulfillment
Poland Sp. z o.o., Wrocław